DUNDEE TOWNSHIP PUBLIC LIBRARY DISTRICT
3 1783 00010 498
P9-CAG-338

A Perfect Peace

OTHER BOOKS BY AMOS OZ

In the Land of Israel

Where the Jackals Howl and Other Stories

Soumchi

The Hill of Evil Counsel

Unto Death

Touch the Water, Touch the Wind

Elsewhere, Perhaps

My Michael

A Perfect Peace

Amos Oz
Translated by Hillel Halkin

A Helen and Kurt Wolff Book
Harcourt Brace Jovanovich, Publishers
San Diego New York London

HBJ

Library of Congress Cataloging in Publication Data
Oz, Amos.
A perfect peace.
"A Helen and Kurt Wolff book."
Translation of: Menuḥah nekhonah.
I. Title.
PJ5054.09M413 1985 892.4'36
84-25171
ISBN 0-15-171696-X

Designed by Lucy Albanese
Printed in the United States of America
First Edition
A B C D E

Part 1

Winter

1

One day a man may just pick up and walk out. What he leaves behind stays behind. What's left behind has nothing to stare at but his back. In the winter of 1965 Yonatan Lifshitz decided to leave his wife and the kibbutz on which he had been born and raised. He had finally made up his mind to run away and start a new life.

All through his childhood and adolescence, and for all his years in the army, he had been hemmed in by a tight little circle of men and women who had been interfering every step of the way. He had begun to feel they were keeping him from something and that he mustn't let them do it any more. Often, when they sat around talking in their usual way of some "positive development" or "negative phenomenon," he could barely grasp what the words meant. Sometimes when he stood by himself at a window toward the close of day to watch the birds fly off into the twilight, he calmly accepted the certainty that these birds will all die in the end. Should an announcer on the evening news speak of "grave indications," he would whisper to himself, So what? If, while taking an afternoon ramble by the burned-out cypress trees at the far end of the kibbutz, he should run into someone who asked what he was doing there, he would say, as if loath to reply, "Oh, I'm just walking around." Yet a moment later he would ask himself, "What *am* I doing here?"

A splendid fellow, they said of him on the kibbutz. If only he weren't such an introvert. But that's the way he is, they said. A sensitive soul.

Now, at twenty-six, of a reserved, or was it pensive, demeanor, he found himself longing to be alone at last, entirely alone, to find for himself what it was all about. There were times he felt his whole life passing by in a clamorous, smoke-filled room where a tedious argument about some bizarre matter dragged endlessly on. He neither knew what this argument was about nor wished to take part in it. The only thing he wanted was to pick up and walk out, to go someplace else, a place where he was waited for—and would not be waited for forever. Benya Trotsky—whom Yonatan had never seen, not even in a photograph—had run away from the kibbutz and from the country in 1939, six weeks before Yonatan was born. He was a raving theoretician, a fiery student from Kharkov who had chosen to become a conscientious laborer in a stone quarry in the Upper Galilee. Then he lived for a while in our kibbutz, where, against his principles, he fell in love with Hava, Yonatan's mother; he loved her in the most honored Russian fashion—with tears, oaths, and feverish confessions. It was too late, for Hava was already pregnant by Yolek, and had moved into his cabin at the far end of the settlement.

One evening, at the end of that winter, after endless complications, letters, threatened suicides, hysterical cries behind the hayloft, group discussions, efforts to find a reasonable solution—after a nervous breakdown and a discreet medical treatment—it came this Trotsky's turn to stand guard duty. Armed with the kibbutz's antique revolver, he had faithfully watched over us until the break of dawn, when, stricken by ultimate despair, he lay in wait for her in the bushes by the laundry room. Leaping out he fired at her at close range. Then, with the piercing howl of a shot dog, he ran blindly to the cowshed, where he fired twice at Yolek, who was finishing the night milking, and once at Stakhanov, our only bull. With startled kibbutzniks, roused from their beds by the shots, now hot on his heels, the wretched man dived behind a pile of manure and aimed the last bullet into his own brain.

All those shots had missed their targets, and not a single drop of blood had been shed, yet the lovesick youth fled the kibbutz, and even the country. He ended up a hotel tycoon in Miami Beach, a holiday resort in East America. Once he sent us a large donation for the construction of a music room. At another time he wrote us a letter in a strange Hebrew. In this he aspired, or threatened, or simply volunteered, to be Yonatan Lifshitz's real father.

On the bookshelf in his parents' home, hidden among the pages of an old Hebrew novel, Yonatan had once found a biblical-sounding love poem on a yellowing sheet of paper, apparently composed by this same Benyamin Trotsky. The lover in the poem though was called Eleazar of Maresha and his beloved Azuva daughter of Shilhi. It was entitled "But Their Hearts Were Not True." At the bottom of the page a few words were penciled in a round, untroubled handwriting. But Yonatan could not decipher those words because the letters were Cyrillic.

Never in all the years had his parents so much as mentioned the B. T. affair in his presence. Except once, during a fierce quarrel, Yolek had said to Hava in Polish, *"Twój komediant,"* and she had hissed at him:

"Ty zboju. Ty morderco." ("You crook. You murderer.")

The whole thing was incredible, the old-timers on the kibbutz sometimes recalled. From a range of just two or three feet, that joker, he managed to miss a bull!

Yonatan was trying to imagine some different place, a place suitable for him, some way of working and resting just as he pleased, away from ever being encircled again.

His plan was to go far away, as far as he could get, to a place as different as it could be from the kibbutz, from the youth camps, from desert bivouacs, from the long lines of hitchhiking soldiers at road junctions blasted by hot dry winds and the stench of thistles, sweat, dust, and dried urine. Perhaps a strange, truly big city, with a river, with bridges, and towers, and tunnels, and fountains with monstrous gargoyles spouting water—fountains nightly fingered by a rare, electric light, where a lonely woman might be standing, her face turned to the light of the water and her back to a square paved with cobblestones. A faraway place where anything is possible—love, danger, arcane encounters, sudden conquests.

He fancied himself stalking with the light tread of a young jungle-cat the carpeted corridors of a cold, tall building, pushing past doormen into elevators whose ceilings glowed with round eyes, carried along in a stream of strangers, all intent on their own affairs, each utterly alone, his own face as inscrutable as theirs.

And so he had the idea of going overseas to study while working at some odd job, as a night watchman, say, or an attendant, or even a courier such as he had seen advertised for in a brief notice in the *Help Wanted* column of the newspaper. Not that he had the vaguest notion of what a courier might do, but something told him nonetheless, that's for you, friend. He imagined himself at the controls of the latest machines, before instrument panels and blinking lights, surrounded by determined men and cunning women. By himself at last, in a rented room high up in a skyscraper in some foreign city—no doubt in America; no doubt in the Middle West of the movies, where he would spend his nights preparing for entrance exams, acquiring a profession that would set him out on the high road to life itself. And then on to the place where he was waited for, and would not be waited for forever.

At the end of that autumn Yonatan got up the courage to hint of his plans to his father.

Though it was Yolek, in his capacity as secretary of the kibbutz, who initiated the conversation. Early one evening he cornered his son at the foot of the stone stairs leading up to the recreation hall and urged him to take over the management of the tractor shed.

Yolek spoke in a low, secretive voice. A moist breeze blew over them. The evening light was clouded, the light between one rain and the next. A sodden bench was covered with wet walnut leaves. Wet walnut leaves had already buried a broken sprinkler and a pile of burlap sacks. Yolek was a broadly built man. From the shoulders down he was drawn in rough, straight lines, like a heavy packing crate, but his gray unhealthy face, with its scattered pouches of wasted skin, looked more like an aging philanderer's than a principled old socialist's. Whereas Yonatan was tall, thin, and slightly distracted-looking. He stubbornly kept his eyes on the bench, the buried sacks, and the broken sprinkler. Suddenly, in a low, rapid voice, he burst into a torrent of speech.

No! Absolutely not! He didn't even want to hear about it. Running the tractor shed was not for him. He had work in the citrus groves and there was still the grapefruit to get in. "When it stops raining, I mean. Today, of course, we couldn't pick, but as soon as it clears we'll start again. And besides, the tractor shed—what do I have to do with tractors?"

"That's something totally new," said Yolek. "Nowadays no one wants to work in the tractor shed. Mazel tov. Some years ago we had fierce battles around here because everybody wanted to be nothing less than a mechanic, and now suddenly working with nuts and bolts is beneath all of you. Scyths! Huns! Tatars! I don't mean *you* personally. I'm talking in general. Look at your young Labor Party hacks. Look at your young littérateurs. Never mind. All I ask is that you take over the shed for as long as it takes to find a permanent solution. And if I ask such a favor from you, I expect you to give me better reasons for refusing than just sobs."

"Look," said Yonatan, "look, I simply don't feel I'm right for it."

"Not right for it!" said Yolek. "You do feel, you don't feel, you're right, you're not right—what is this here, a drama ensemble? Are we a bunch of actors trying to decide who's going to play Boris Godunov here? Tell me, once and for all, will you, what this is all about with you people—the *right* person, the *wrong* person, all this spoiled, capricious nonsense of self-fulfillment, or whatever the hell you call it. What's being the right or wrong person got to do with work, eh?"

"Look, I'm just saying that it's not for me," said Yonatan. "What good does it do to get angry? I'm not made for that kind of work, and that's it. Besides, I'm having second thoughts about my future altogether. And here you are, arguing about young Labor Party politicians while we're both getting soaked. See, it's raining again."

Which wasn't what Yolek heard him say. Or perhaps he heard correctly and preferred to back off. At any rate, he replied: "Right then. Sleep on it and give me a yes or no. No point standing here arguing all night with the rain pouring down on our heads. And speaking of heads, you ought to get a haircut."

One Saturday, when Yonatan's younger brother Amos was home on a short leave from the army, Yonatan snapped at him:

"Why talk so much about next year? You have no way of knowing where you'll be a year from now. And neither do I."

To his wife Rimona he said: "Do you think I need a haircut?"

Rimona took a long look at him. With a diffident, delayed-action smile as though she had been asked a delicate or even dangerous question, she replied: "You look nice with long hair, but if it bothers you, that's different."

"Nonsense," said Yonatan.

It saddened him to have to part with the smells, sounds, and colors he had known since childhood. He loved the fragrance of evening as it slowly descended in the last days of summer over the newly mowed lawn—across which, by the oleander bushes, three mutts would be fighting furiously for the remains of a torn shoe. Some old pioneer in a peaked worker's cap would be standing on the path, reading a newspaper, his lips moving as if in prayer. An elderly woman carrying a blue bucket with vegetables, eggs, and a fresh loaf of bread would pass the old man by without so much as a nod because of some ancient feud. "Yonatan," she would say softly, "look at the daisies at the edge of the lawn. They're so white and clean, just like the snow that fell every winter back in Lupatyn." And the sound of a recorder from the children's house would mingle with the cries of birds, while in the distance to the west, beyond the citrus trees, beyond the setting sun, the engine of a passing freight train would bleat twice.

Yonatan felt sorry for his parents. For the Sabbath eves and the holidays when the men, women, and children, nearly all dressed in their very best, freshly ironed white shirts and blouses, assembled in the recreation hall to sing the old songs. For the tin shed in the citrus groves where he sometimes stole twenty minutes from work to browse in the sports pages. For Rimona. For the sun coming up like a bloodbath at five on a summer morning, behind the rocky hills to the east above the ruins of the abandoned Arab village of Sheikh Dahr. For the Saturday hikes among those hills and ruins—he and Rimona, Rimona and he with Udi and Anat, or sometimes just he alone.

In bed at night, unable to sleep, Yonatan thought that whatever was waiting for him must be wondering where he was and would, if he didn't hurry, move on without him. In the morning, he padded out to the porch barefoot and in his underwear, to put on his work clothes and mud-caked boots, one of which had yawned open a few days before, its laughing mouth full of rusty nails. Over the frozen screams of the birds he heard himself being paged to pick up and go, not to the grapefruit grove, but to some wholly different place, a place that would be the right place because it would be his own. He had better not be late.

Day by day he could feel something fading in him. Was it illness? Sleeplessness? Sometimes, of their own accord, his lips would murmur: Enough. That's it. Finished.

All the beliefs and ideas that they had instilled in him since childhood had shriveled. Rather, they had simply paled away in his heart. If they discussed at a general kibbutz meeting repeated violations of the egalitarian ethic, or the need for collective authority, or even for plain honesty, Yonatan, sitting by himself at the farthest table in the dining room, behind the southernmost column, would sketch naval destroyers on the paper napkins. If the discussion turned into a particularly long one, he would proceed to aircraft carriers, ships he had never seen except in the movies and illustrated magazines. Whenever he read in the paper of the growing threat of war, he would say to Rimona, nonsense, that's all these idiots ever do, and turn to the sports section.

Shortly before the high holidays he resigned from the Youth Committee. Ideas and opinions seemed to fade away. A sadness rose and fell like the wail of a siren, though even when it fell, as it sometimes did at work or during a chess game, he could feel it pierce him like a foreign body in his heart, in his throat, in his chest, in his gut, just as when he was small and did something bad and wasn't caught or punished but still he shook with fear all day long and at night in bed in the dark staying up till all hours—you crazy fool, you, what have you done?

Yonatan longed to get far away from this grief like those rich people in books, in Europe, who fled to snow-covered mountains to escape the summer heat or to the warm south to cheat the winter. Once, when the two of them were unloading sacks of fertilizer from a truck, he said to his friend Udi:

"Hey, Udi, what's the biggest fraud in the world?"

"Those meatballs Fayga cooks for lunch three times a week. Nothing but stale bread with a little meat seasoning."

"No," Yonatan persisted. "I mean really. The most colossal fraud there ever was."

"All right," said Udi unenthusiastically. "I guess it's religion. Or communism. Or both."

"No," said Yonatan. "It's the stories we were told when we were children."

"Stories?" marveled Udi. "What in the world made you think of that?"

"They were the exact opposite of life, that's what they were—got any matches, Udi? Remember that time, that commando raid on the Syrians in Nukeib, how we left a dead Syrian soldier with half his body shot away in a jeep and put his hands on the wheel and stuck a lit cigarette in his mouth and took off? You remember that?"

Udi took his time answering. He dragged a sack off the truck, carefully squared it off to form the base for a new pile. Then, exhaling, scratching himself, he turned around to look at Yonatan, who was leaning against the side of the truck, smoking. Udi laughed.

"What are you doing? Philosophizing on me in broad daylight?"

"Nonsense," said Yonatan. "I was thinking of a dirty little book I once read in English about what the seven dwarfs really did to Snow White while she was sleeping off the poisoned apple. It was all a fraud, Udi. That, and Hansel and Gretel, and Little Red Riding Hood, and The Emperor's New Clothes, and all those sweet stories where everybody lived happily ever after. It was all a fraud."

"Talking about fraud, take my matches out of your pocket

and give them back. Come on, let's unload the rest of this fertilizer before Etan R. comes along. Only thirty more to go. Take a deep breath."

Yonatan took a deep breath and calmed down.

It was almost a surprise how easy the decision was. The obstacles turned out to be minor. Shaving in front of the mirror, he would whisper:

"He just picked up and left."

The preceding summer, several months before Yonatan made up his mind to leave, a sad thing happened to his wife. Not that Yonatan saw it as a cause for his decision. Words like "cause" or "effect" meant nothing to him. Like those bird migrations Rimona loved to watch every autumn and spring, Yonatan saw his leaving as time running out.

Two years before, Rimona had lost a baby. Then, when she became pregnant again, she was delivered at the end of the summer of a stillborn girl. The doctors advised against her trying again, at least for the time being. But Yonatan no longer wanted to try anyway. All he wanted was to pick up and go.

Now, some three months later, she was borrowing books about Africa from the kibbutz library. Every evening she sat by the table lamp, in the soft, warm brown light cast by its straw shade, copying the details of various tribal rites onto little index cards: hunting rites, rain rites, ghost rites, fertility rites. In her placid hand she entered notations of drumbeats in the villages of Namibia, sketches of Kikuyu witchdoctors' masks, descriptions of Zulu ceremonies for the appeasement of dead ancestors, of medical amulets and incantations from the land of Ubangi-Shari. One day she bought herself a new record in Haifa, on the jacket of which a naked black warrior was spearing an antelope. In English letters designed to look like campfires, it advertised *The Magic of Chad.*

Meanwhile, the hay was being baled in the fields and brought into the haylofts. The soil was being turned by heavy plows hitched to caterpillar tractors. The white-and-blue flames of summer gave way to a low, gray light. Autumn came and went. The days grew short and bleary-eyed, and the nights grew ever deeper. Yonatan supervised the orange picking, while his friend Udi took care of shipping the harvest.

One evening Udi proposed that over a cup of coffee the two of them review the bills of lading so they could prepare an interim statement.

"What's the rush? The season has just begun." Yonatan was in no mood to budge.

"If you don't have the patience to do the accounting," Udi suggested, "perhaps I should do it myself."

"All right. Fine."

"Don't worry, Yoni. I'll keep you filled in."

"You don't have to."

"What do you mean I don't have to?"

"Listen, Udi. If you'd like to be the boss around here, be the boss." And he left it at that.

He didn't like words and didn't trust them. And so he prepared for the talk with Rimona slowly, deliberately, seeking to anticipate tears, arguments, pleas, accusations. But the more he thought about it, the fewer justifications he could find. Until he was left with none. Not even one.

He had to give Rimona the bold truth. The bold truth might even be expressed in a single sentence. "I can't give in any more," or perhaps just "I'm late."

But Rimona was sure to ask, "Giving in to whom?" or, "Late for what?" What was he going to say then? She might even burst into tears or gasp, "Yoni, you're out of your mind!" To which he knew he could only mumble, "Sorry," or, "Well, that's that," only to have her turn his parents and the whole kibbutz against him.

Look, Rimona, it's not something that can be said in words. Maybe it's like your *Magic of Chad.* Not the magic of Chad. There's no magic there. Or anywhere. What I mean is, I don't have a choice, and my back's against the wall, as they say. So, I'm going.

Yonatan picked an evening several days off. If she started accusing or pleading, he would simply clam up.

All the while, like a member of an underground on the eve of an uprising, he was careful to go about his usual business. At the crack of dawn, he would be out on the porch in his underwear, climbing into his work clothes, conducting a sleepy battle with the laces of his boots—hating the laughing one—wrapping himself in his shabby old battle jacket and heading for the tractor shed. When it rained, he would cover his head and shoulders with a sack and run cursing all the way to the shed. For a couple of minutes he would do push-ups on the filthy concrete floor before checking the oil, fuel, and water in the old gray Ferguson, and try to get its coughing, reluctant engine to turn over so he could take Udi and their crew of teenage girls out to the groves. Gathered around the tin shed to receive their clippers, the girls had dimly brought to Yonatan's mind some half-forgotten tale of reprobate nuns who had run away from their cloister to consort with a woodsman living in a hut.

Yonatan rarely spoke while working. Once, though, handing the sports section to Udi during a break, he remarked, "All right, if that's what you want: the bills of lading are yours this year, but keep me in the picture all the same."

At the end of the day Yonatan would return home, shower, and dress in warm, clean clothes, light the kerosene heater, and sit down with the paper. By four or four-fifteen the winter light would start to dim, but it was twilight by the time Rimona arrived from the laundry and put coffee and cake on the table. Sometimes he would wash the mugs and plates as soon as they finished their coffee. Occasionally, while changing a burned-out light bulb or fixing a leaky shower tap, he might answer a question she asked or listen wearily as she answered one of his.

One evening, on the radio news, a certain Rabbi Nachtigall talked about religious revival. He used the phrase "a desert wasteland and a wilderness." For the rest of that night, and, indeed, through the next day, Yonatan absentmindedly recited these words as if they were a mantra: The magic of wilderness. The wasteland of Chad. The desert of Chad. The magic of wasteland. Breathe deep, friend, he told himself, and calm down. You've got all the time in the world between now and Wednesday.

Tia, his brownish-gray German shepherd, spent the winter days sprawled on the floor by the heater. No longer young, she seemed to suffer from rheumatism in cold weather. In a couple of places her coat had grown threadbare, like a worn-out rug. Sometimes she would open her eyes abruptly and look at him so tenderly that it made him blink. Then she would sink her teeth into her thigh or into her paws to get rid of some invisible pest, and rise with a shake of her coat, which seemed at least a size too large for her. Her ears flattened, she would cross the room and collapse again by the heater, sighing and shutting one eye, although her tail would go on twitching for a moment before it, too, fell silent. Then her other eye would shut, and she would look for all the world as if she were asleep.

Tia developed sores behind her ears, which soon filled with pus, and the veterinarian, who visited the kibbutz twice a month to check its cows and sheep, had to be consulted. He prescribed a salve and also a white powder that was to be mixed with milk and given her to drink. It was hard to get her to swallow it. He had to postpone it again. From time to time he would go over the words he had prepared for Rimona. But what words? The wasteland of Chad? Picks up and goes?

The winter began to take hold. Yolek came down with the flu and suffered cruel pains in his back. One evening Yonatan dropped by, and Yolek berated him for not visiting more often, for refusing to take over the shed, for the nihilism of Israeli youth in general. Hava interrupted, "You look sad and tired, Yonatan. Maybe you should take a day or two off. Rimona deserves some rest too. Why don't you two go to Haifa? You can sleep at Uncle Pesach's and go to a movie."

"And get a haircut," added Yolek. "Look at you."

Whatever you leave behind will stay behind. All those personal effects that you won't be needing where you're going. As strange as your room will be without you, as strange and empty as the shelves that you made above your bed, as strange and dusty as the chessboard that you carved all last winter from the trunk of an olive tree, as strange as the garden with its iron poles on which you meant to trellis a grape vine and never did. Fear not. Time will pass. The curtains will fade in the assault of the sun. The magazines at the bottom of the bookcase will turn yellow. The crabgrass and the nettles and the weeds that you fought against all these years will again raise their heads in your backyard. Mildew will flower once more around the sink that you fixed. Plaster will peel. The railings on the porch will rust. Rimona will wait for you until she understands that it's senseless to wait any longer. Your parents will stubbornly blame her, each other, you, the times, the latest fads, but they too will finally make their peace. "Mea culpa," your father will exclaim in his Polish Latin. Your pajamas, your battle jacket, your work clothes, your paratrooper boots will be given away to someone your own size. Not to Udi! Maybe to that hired-hand Italian murderer who works in the metal shop. Other personal belongings will be packed in a suitcase and stored in that little closet above the shower. New routines will strike roots. Rimona will be sent to one of those kibbutz courses in applied art and soon be decorating the dining hall for parties and holidays. Your brother Amos will be discharged from the army and marry his girlfriend Rachel. Maybe he'll even make the national swimming team. Fear not. Meanwhile you will get to where you are going and see how different, and right, and fresh it all is. And what if ever on some distant day a memory comes to you of an old familiar whiff or the sound of dogs barking far off or a driving hailstorm at dawn and you suddenly fail to grasp what it is you have done, what madness might have possessed you, what devil lured you from your home to the end of the world?

It was raining hard. Orange picking came to a halt. The cheerful teenage girls were sent to the kitchen and the stockrooms. Udi volunteered to fix the tin roof of the cowshed and the sheep pen that had been blown away by the winds. And Yonatan Lifshitz agreed to take over the shed as his father had asked several weeks earlier. "I want you to know that this isn't a permanent arrangement," he said. "It's just for now."

To which Yolek replied, "Eh? Right! Good. Just get the place into shape, while we catch our breath. Who knows? Maybe you'll find an unknown source of self-fulfillment there. Maybe some day the fashions will change and that kind of work will be it again."

"Just remember," said Yonatan, "I haven't promised you anything."

And so Yonatan began to put in six hours a day in the tractor shed. There wasn't much to do except take routine care of the tractors and make an occasional repair if it was simple enough. Most of the other farm machinery, still and frozen, slumbered away the winter beneath the tin roof that rattled in the wind. The engine oil grew black and viscous. The instrument panels were clouded by vapors. You had to be out of your mind to try to wake these monsters from their sullen hibernation and get them running again. Let them rest in peace. I'm here because of the cold and the rain, he told himself, and not for long either.

At ten o'clock every morning he would slosh his way from the tractor shed to the metal shop to drink a cup of coffee with the lame Bolognesi and have a look at that day's sports section.

Bolognesi was not really an Italian. He was a Tripolitanian hired hand with a dark, stubbly face, a mouth that smelled slightly of arak, and a torn ear that resembled a rotten-ripe pear. A lanky, stooped man in his middle fifties, he lived by himself in a shack, one half of which had once housed a shoemaker, while the other half still served on occasion as a barbershop. Although he had served fifteen years for chopping the head off his brother's fiancée with an ax, the precise details of the affair were not known. Naturally, different and occasionally gruesome versions of it circulated. He wore a permanently pinched look, as if he had just bitten into a piece of spoiled fish that he could neither swallow nor spit out. Whether it was because he had become a pious Jew while in jail, or for some other reason, President Ben-Tsvi had decided to pardon him. In a letter to the kibbutz, the Committee for Reformed Convicts had officially vouched for his character, and so he was taken on as a helper in the metal shop and given his tumbledown, tarpaper half of a shack to live in.

Since settling on the kibbutz, he had taken up in his free time the art of knitting he had learned in prison and made marvelous sweaters for the kibbutz children, and sometimes, for the young ladies, stylish outfits copied from knitwear magazines bought with his own money and studied carefully. He spoke little in his feminine voice and always with extreme caution, as if whatever he said might implicate him or embarrass you. Once, during their coffee break, Yonatan, without looking up from his newspaper, asked, "Say, Bolognesi, why do you keep looking at me like that?"

"Look your shoe," said the Italian with extraordinary delicacy, barely parting his lips. "Your shoe she's open and the water she gets inside. I fix'a your shoe right away?"

"Don't bother," said Yonatan. "Thanks anyway." He went right back to the debate between two sports columnists over the upset in yesterday's League Cup semifinals. Then he turned the page and started to read about a Jewish orthopedist from South America, also a football star, who had come to live in Israel and signed up with a Jerusalem team.

"I no fix'a, you no thank'a," insisted Bolognesi with melancholy logic. "Why you thank'a me like that? Wha' for?"

"For the coffee," said Yonatan.

"You want I should pour'a 'nother?"

"No thanks."

"Look. 'Scuse'a me, what you call'a this? Again you thank'a me for nothing? Wha' for? No fix'a, no thank'a. And no get'a mad neither."

"All right," said Yonatan. "No one's getting mad. But why don't you pipe down, Bolognesi, and let me read my paper in peace?"

And to himself he said: No giving in this time. Tonight. You'll do it tonight. Or, at the very latest, tomorrow night.

That afternoon, when Yonatan returned home, he lit the kerosene heater, washed his hands and face, and sat down to wait for Rimona in one of the twin armchairs, his legs wrapped in a brown woolen blanket against the cold. Spread before him was the morning paper, in which from time to time his eye would pick out some item that struck him with amazement. In one, the President of Syria, Dr. Nur-ad-Din el-Atassi, a former gynecologist, and the Foreign Minister, Dr. Yussuf Zu'ein, a former ophthalmologist, had both spoken before a large, frenzied rally in Palmyra to call for the extermination of the state of Israel, the ophthalmologist swearing in the name of all those gathered not to spare one drop of its blood, since blood alone could expunge its affront to the Arabs and rivers of blood had to be crossed if their own holy road were to lead to the sunrise of justice. In another, an Arab youth, on trial in Haifa for peeping through a window in a Jewish neighborhood at a woman getting undressed, defended himself in fluent Hebrew by citing the precedent of King David and Bathsheba. Judge Nakdimon Zlelichin, the newspaper related, was so tickled by this novel plea that he let the youngster off with a stern rebuke and a warning. In the corner of an inside page was an account of an experiment performed in the Zurich zoo, in the course of which unseasonable light and heat were admitted into the bears' house to test the depth of their hibernation: finally one bear awoke only to go mad.

Lulled by the steady, monotonous drip of the rain in the drainpipe, Yonatan soon dozed off and let the paper drop. It was a light, troubled sleep of groggy reveries that turned into nightmares. Dr. Schillinger from Haifa, the gynecologist with the stammer who had treated Rimona and advised her against trying again, became a cunning Syrian agent. On behalf of the secret service, Yolek urged Udi, Yonatan, and Etan R. to undertake a dangerous journey to some northern land and lay the serpent low in its lair with an ax stroke from behind. Unfortunately, since they were all made of wet absorbent cotton, none of the six bullets in Yonatan's revolver was able to penetrate his target's skin. The man simply grinned with rotten teeth and hissed, *"Ty zboju!"* Yonatan opened his eyes and before him stood Rimona. "It's a quarter after four," she said, "and getting dark. Why don't you sleep a little more while I shower and make us coffee?"

"I wasn't sleeping," he replied, "I was just thinking. Did you know that the dictator of Syria is also a gynecologist?"

"You were sleeping when I came in," said Rimona. "And I woke you. But we'll have coffee soon."

She showered and changed clothes while the water boiled in the electric kettle. Slim, shapely, and clean in a red sweater and blue corduroy pants, she served the coffee and cake. She looked like a shy schoolgirl with her long, light, freshly washed hair, enveloped in a bitter scent of almond soap and shampoo. They sat in the twin armchairs, facing each other, letting the music from the radio fill the silence. After that came music from a record, the throbbing, sensual beat of the African bush.

Even at the best of times Rimona and Yonatan spoke sparingly to each other, and then only when they had to. Quarreling had long since become pointless. Rimona was gathered in her own thoughts, her feet tucked under her, her hands pulled back into the sleeves of her sweater. She looked like a lonely little girl freezing on a park bench in winter.

"When the rain stops, I'll go out for more kerosene. The tank's nearly empty," she offered, breaking the silence.

Yonatan stubbed out his cigarette on the side of a copper ashtray.

"Don't. I'll get it. I have to talk to Shimon anyway."

"Why don't you give me your jacket so I can tighten the buttons while you're out?"

"But you spent a whole evening tightening the buttons just a week ago."

"That was your new jacket. I want to fix the old one, your brown one."

"Do me a favor, Rimona. Leave that old rag alone. It's falling apart. Either throw the goddamn thing out or give it to the Italian. He makes coffee for me every morning and even thanks me for it."

"Yoni, you're not going to give that jacket to anybody. I can fix it, just take it out a bit in the shoulders, and you can still wear it to work to keep you warm."

Yonatan said nothing. He emptied a matchbox onto the table, tried making a simple geometric pattern, swept it away, made another, more complicated pattern, and swept that one away too. He gathered up the matches and returned them neatly to their box. A cracked old, bone-dry, mocking voice rasped within him: That joker, he couldn't even hit the side of a bull from three feet away. "But Their Hearts Were Not True." Yonatan recalled the only possible answer.

"I'll mend it," Rimona persisted. "You can wear it to work."

"Oh, great!" said Yonatan. "It'll be a sensation. I'll show up for work one morning in a sport jacket. Maybe I'll wear a tie too, put a white handkerchief in my breast pocket like a secret agent, cut my hair short as my father has been nagging me to do. Can you hear, Rimona, how strong that wind is!"

"The wind may be strong, but the rain has stopped."

"I'd better go out then. Talk to Shimon. Get the kerosene. And I really ought to sit down with Udi too, and go over the accounts. What's that?"

"Nothing. I didn't say anything, Yoni."

"All right. See you."

"Wait a minute. Don't wear your new jacket. Wear the old one. I'll mend it when you get back."

"Oh, no, you won't, because it'll be soaking wet."

"We said that the rain had stopped, Yoni."

"We said! A lot of good that does. What if we did? By the time I get back, it will be raining again. In fact, there it goes. Just listen to it come down. It's a flood!"

"Don't go out, Yoni. Sit down a while. I'll pour some more coffee. And if you're looking for something to give your Italian, why don't you give him that can of instant we never use? I like to brew us real coffee, good and strong."

"Listen, Rimona. That Italian! You know how he says, I'll pour you a cup? 'I'll pour'a you a cup.' You know how he says, It's raining cats and dogs? 'It's rain'm catch'm dog.' But you're not listening. Why is it that every time I say something to you, you never listen, you never answer, you're never there. Why?"

"Don't get mad, Yoni."

"Now you too. What's the matter with all of you today? Since I got up this morning everyone's been telling me not to get mad when I haven't been mad at all. Suppose I feel like getting mad, then what? I have no right to? Everyone wants to argue with me all day long. You, Udi, that Italian, my father, Etan R. Everyone! It could drive you mad. Every day that crazy Italian wants to fix my boot. Every evening it's you with that rag of a jacket, and every night it's my father with some new job he's cooked up.

Do me a favor, will you? Take a look at this newspaper, at those Syrians my father wants peace and brotherhood with, those Syrians he'd like to take to his bed, look how they talk about us. The only thing they want is to slaughter us all and drink our blood. Hey, you're dreaming again. You're not listening to one word I say."

"I am, Yoni. What's wrong with you? I'm not your father."

"I don't care who you are, I just want you to listen to the rain instead of telling me that it's stopped and sending me out for your kerosene. Do me a favor. Go to the window, you're not blind, are you, and have a good look at what's happening out there."

Rimona and Yonatan continued to sit opposite each other in silence, the darkness deepening all around them. Treetops stirred noisily as though raided by an ax. A frightened lowing of cows could be heard through the shriek of the wind. Yonatan suddenly thought of the abandoned Arab village of Sheikh Dahr. This very night, the downpour might be crumbling the last of its earthen hovels, dust to dust, the ruins of its low stone walls might be surrendering at last, a loose stone toppling down, earthward in the darkness, after twenty years of clinging to its mates. There couldn't be a soul on the hills of Sheikh Dahr on a night like this, not one stray dog, not a single bird. What a perfect hideout for a murderer like Bolognesi or Benyamin Trotsky. Or me. No one there. Only stillness and the dark and winter winds. Only the smashed minaret of the mosque, twisted like the trunk of a felled tree. A nest of killers, they told us in our childhood. A den of bloody bandits. And once it was leveled, they told us we could sleep in peace at night. The minaret from which they sniped right into the kibbutz had been sliced in two halfway up by a direct mortar hit, a hit, so they say, that was aimed by the commander-in-chief of the Jewish forces himself.

Once, when I was a boy, I went by myself to Sheikh Dahr to

look for the buried treasure of gold coins that was supposed to be under the floor of the sheikh's house. I began to pull up the painted green tiles to look beneath them for the secret steps that led to the hiding place. Shaking with fear, because of the owls, the bats, the ghosts lurking there at night to choke you from behind with their thin fingers, I kept on digging but all I found was strange gray dust like the ashes of an ancient fire and a wide rotten board. I pulled it to one side, and beneath were old harnesses, a threshing sled, some bits of an old wooden plow, and still more dust. I dug on until evening came and some ghastly bird screeched. Then I took off. I ran down the hill but made a wrong turn at the fork in the wadi and had to run back through all those crumbling houses and out into those fields full of thorns, past the hoary old olive trees—and I ran and ran till I reached the old quarry. Far-off jackals were howling. Close by I was only a boy and those dead old villagers were thirsty for blood, for a bloodbath like those Syrian doctors, I was out of breath, and all I had to show from Sheikh Dahr in the end was a stitch in my chest and that terrible fear and sadness that keeps eating you, that keeps nibbling and gnawing at your soul to get up right away and go look for some sign of life in the wasteland, that endless rain that keeps falling outside in the dark and won't stop all night long or tomorrow or ever after. That's been my whole life. I don't have any other. The one I have keeps rushing by, and right now I'm being paged to get up and go because who will give me back the time that I've lost and what if I arrive too late?

Yonatan stood up. His hairy hand groped for the light switch. When he found it at last and turned on the light, he blinked for a moment, frightened, or perhaps amazed, by the strange circuit connecting his will, the white switch on the wall, the yellow light on the ceiling. He sat down again and turned toward his wife.

"You're falling asleep."

"I'm embroidering," she replied. "By springtime we'll have a nice new tablecloth."

"Why didn't you turn on the light?"

"I saw that you were thinking and I didn't want to disturb you."

"It's only a quarter to five," said Yonatan, "and we have to turn on the lights. As in Scandinavia. Or in that taiga or tundra we learned about in school. Do you remember the taiga, the tundra, Rimona?"

"Are they in Russia?" asked Rimona carefully.

"Nonsense," said Yonatan. "They go all around the Arctic Circle. In Siberia. In Scandinavia. Even in Canada. Did you read this week that whales are becoming extinct?"

"You told me about it. I didn't bother reading because it's nicer when you tell me."

"Now look at the heater!" said Yonatan angrily. "It's going out already. Rain or no rain, I must get the kerosene before it starts smoking."

Rimona, her back softly curved against her chair, kept her eyes on her embroidery like a diligent schoolgirl at her homework.

"Take the flashlight."

Yonatan picked it up and left in silence. Then he came back, filled the heater tank, and went to wash his hands, but the engine-oil stains around his nails refused to come off.

"You got all wet," said Rimona gently.

"Never mind," said Yonatan. "It's all right. I wore my old brown jacket as you told me to. Don't worry about me so much."

With Tia fast asleep at his feet, he spread the latest issue of *Chessworld* on the table and concentrated so hard trying to solve a difficult problem that he forgot about the cigarette he was holding until an ash fell on its pages. As he relit the cigarette, a wave of tiny tremors ran through Tia's fur from head to tail. Her ears stiffened momentarily, then dropped again. But Rimona kept her peace. So fragile was the silence between them that now and then the tick of the bulky tin alarm clock reached him from the bedroom.

Rimona had narrow hips, small, firm breasts, and long hands and fingers. From the rear, her thin, clean lines made her look like a girl at the onset of puberty, like a well-bred product of a finishing school, one who had been taught to stand erect, never to wriggle her behind, to sit ramrod-straight with her knees kept together, and always to do dutifully just what she was told. On the rare occasions when Rimona lifted her long hair to wear it in a high bun, baring the light nap on her neck, Yonatan would beg her to let it down again, for the nakedness of it was so naked that it shamed him. Nearly always her dark, widely set eyes had a veiled look. So did her lips, which, chill and shaded, reflected an imperturbable calm. Not even when she spoke, not even when she smiled, did it vanish. And, in any event, she smiled infrequently, the smile beginning not on, but around, those lips and spreading slowly, hesitantly to the corners of her eyes. It always made her seem like a little girl who has just been shown something that little girls are not supposed to see.

Yonatan was sure that Rimona was unaffected by most of what she saw and heard. I might as well be living with some expensive painting, he thought angrily, or with a governess training me to be forever content. To banish such thoughts, he would resort to the words "my wife." This is my wife, he would whisper to himself. This is Rimona, my wife. This is my wife, Rimona. But the words "my wife" seemed to belong elsewhere—to families of long standing, to the movies, to houses full of children, bedrooms, kitchens, and maids—not to Rimona, who cared about nothing, unless perhaps tribal amulets from Swaziland, and that only when half-asleep, because at heart all things were the same to her. My wife. She has my old brown jacket on the brain again and now it's wet.

"Listen. Rimona. Maybe enough is enough."

"Yes. I'm almost done. I've taken it out in the shoulders. Would you like to try it on?"

"No way. I've already told you a thousand times that rag should be thrown into the garbage. Or given to that Italian."

"Fine."

"What's fine?"

"Give it to the Italian."

"So why did you spend the whole evening working on it?"

"I was mending it."

"Why the hell did you have to mend it when I kept telling you I'd never wear it?"

"You saw yourself. It was torn in two places."

After the ten o'clock news Yonatan stepped out on the little porch to smoke a last cigarette. By its small, round glow he could see how light, and yet how persistent, the rain was. He liked to feel the cold against his skin and inhale the damp smell of saturated earth. It was too dark to see the ground. He stood there waiting, knowing not for what. He felt sorry for his brother Amos, who might be with his buddies on this awful night setting up an ambush for Arab infiltrators behind the rocks at the mouth of some wadi near the border. He felt sorry, too, for the baby stillborn to Rimona at the end of the summer. No one had ever told them what had been done with her. Yet somewhere out there in that darkness, in the thick mud, lay the little body whose curious stirrings deep in her mother's womb he had felt with the flat of his palm only five months before. Again there came the sound of muffled barking from afar; where, if not from the ruins of Sheikh Dahr? Suddenly he knew what had happened: the end of his cigarette had dropped to the floor. The magic of Chad, he exclaimed, much to his own surprise. He bent down to pick up the flickering butt, cast it into the rain, breathed deeply as its tiny glow was extinguished, murmured okay, okay, and stepped back inside the house.

Rimona locked the door behind him, drew the curtains, and stood between the couch and the bookcase like a mechanical doll whose spring has unwound.

"Is that it?" she asked, then added with a half-smile, "Yes. All right."

To which Yonatan replied, "Yes. That's it. Let's go to bed now."

"Now," she repeated.

He couldn't tell if her response was meant to be a promise, a question, an expression of surprise, or maybe just consent.

"In the end I never talked to Shimon. Never went to see Udi about the accounts either."

"So you didn't," said Rimona, "don't let it bother you. You'll go tomorrow. Maybe tomorrow the weather will clear."

In their double bed, each curled in a separate heavy winter blanket, Rimona by the wall and Yonatan nearer the window, they shut out the pelting of the storm with late music on the radio and spoke in whispers.

"Yoni, on Thursday you have an appointment with the dentist. Don't forget."

"I won't."

"It'll start clearing tomorrow. It's been raining for three straight days now."

"Yes."

"Yoni, listen."

"What?"

"The thunder! And the wind is so strong. The window panes are rattling."

"Yes. But don't worry."

"I'm not worried. I just feel sorry for the birds. Should I turn off the radio?"

"Yes. And go to sleep. It's almost eleven, and I have to be up at six-thirty."

"I'm not worried."

"Go to sleep, Rimona. We're not out in the storm."

"No. We're at home."

"Then try to fall asleep. I'm tired. Good night."

"But I can't fall asleep. You always fall asleep right away, but I don't."

"What's the matter, Rimona."

"I'm worried."

"Then don't be. That's enough. Go to sleep. Good night."

The two of them lay still in the dark with open eyes, not touching. She knew that he wasn't asleep, and he knew that she knew. Outside, low clouds were swept eastward toward the mountains that kept their own peace, massive and congealed, belonging only to themselves, yet to themselves strangers.

2

It took Tia two weeks to recover from her sores. She was again drowsing by the heater. One evening, when she stopped breathing for a moment in her sleep, Yonatan was terrified that she might have slipped away. Once he discovered it was a false alarm, he made up his mind: Tomorrow night.

That same night a young man arrived at the kibbutz. He had walked all the way from the main road, a distance of six kilometers, and entered the village by way of the muddy tractor road that passed the farm buildings. He soon enough encountered the smells of the place—the sour fumes of the poultry run, the stench of the sheepfold, the pungent rot of wet hay, the fetid stink of cow manure and a plugged sewage pipe by the barn, the bubbly ferment of moldy orange peels in the slop pile.

The first person to run across him in the fading twilight was Etan R., who was carrying fodder to the feedstalls in the cowshed. Noticing a thrusting, scrambling movement in the thick bushes behind the fertilizer shed, Etan surmised that another calf had escaped from the cow pen and the thought of it made him hopping mad.

That latch came loose again because Stutchnik forgot to fix it and I didn't wire the gate shut. Only this time, for a change, I'm not going to do a thing about it. No, I'm going to go yank that Stutchnik right out of his Jewish philosophy group in the lecture hall and haul him down here in his best clothes to take care of his own mess. I don't give a damn. It's the second one broken loose this week, and Stutchnik is going to lose his chance to sound off any more about how careless we all are and about how the young ones are going to seed from too much easy living. But hold on, that's not a calf.

The young stranger came plunging out of the bushes face first, followed by shoulders and hands, the latter frantically pushing the wet foliage aside. He was wearing corduroy pants and a short, light-colored jacket, and he appeared to be running straight for Etan R., who was tempted for a second to trip him up and get in the first blow, but the stranger suddenly stopped in his tracks and stood there wet and shivering. He must have come a long way in the rain before getting lost in the underbrush. The water that streamed down his cheeks from his soaking-wet hair made him look pitiful. Over one shoulder hung a skimpy army knapsack; one hand held a large guitar case.

Etan R. eyed the newcomer. He was hardly more than a boy, skinny, with narrow, sharply slanting shoulders, and so unsteady on his feet that a modest push would have been enough to knock him down. Etan's initial apprehensions gave way to a feeling of mild impatience. A large, blond, hairy man, pug-nosed and lantern-jawed, he planted his heavy work boots far apart and stared hard at the newcomer before finally speaking.

"Good evening."

The two words sounded more like a question than a greeting, because Etan still regarded the stranger as very strange indeed.

The young man flashed a quick, overly broad smile that vanished at once, replied good evening in a vaguely foreign accent, and inquired where he might find the head of the kibbutz.

"You mean the secretary of the kibbutz. The secretary is sick," said Etan R. in his imperturbably slow voice.

"Of course," replied the young man, as if the merest child would have known that kibbutz secretaries were prone to ill health. "Of course," he repeated. "I understand quite well and wish him a speedy recovery. But responsibility on the kibbutz, if I'm not mistaken, is collective. There must be a deputy, or someone on temporary duty."

Etan R. nodded his massive head several times. He was sufficiently amused to be on the verge of smiling, but his amusement faded when he caught a better glimpse of the young man's face with its sharp green look bordering equally on gaiety and despair, the eyes nervously blinking. There was, in fact, something tense, frightened, and, at the same time, fawning about his whole demeanor, something almost cunningly submissive. Etan R. refrained from smiling, and said in a harsh military voice, "All right, then. What can I do for you." This time there was not even the hint of a question.

The young man did not reply at once, as if he had instantly grasped that the secret of Etan's superiority lay in delaying one's answer and had decided to play the same game himself. He hesitated, shifting his guitar case from his right hand to his left. Then, with an abruptly decisive movement, he stretched his hand and said:

"Hello there. I'm pleased to meet you. My name is Azariah Gitlin. I'd like to stay here. I mean live here. The only justice left today is on the kibbutz. You won't find it anywhere else. I'd like to live here."

Etan had no choice but to grasp the hand held out to him.

Azariah Gitlin responded at once.

"Look, comrade, I don't want to be misunderstood from the start. I'm definitely not one of those people who come to a kibbutz with all kinds of personal problems and expect to find heaven on earth. But you people still relate to each other. Everywhere else in the world there's nothing but hatred and envy and cruelty. That's why I've come. I want to join you and change my life for the better. And in relating to others, I believe, one relates better to one's own inner self. So I would like, if I may, to speak to whoever is in charge."

A foreign accent. Unable to place it, Etan felt his impatience grow. The spot where they were standing, on a slope on the edge of the settlement, was deserted. Some thirty meters beyond them was the perimeter fence, through whose rusty coils of barbed wire a dim light showed. The concrete path at their feet was covered with a layer of muck. Every step squished and gurgled with a foul, suppurating sound.

Once, Etan R. recalled, Stutchnik had told him about some student living on the kibbutz thirty years ago who had run amuck with a revolver and fired at anyone who came near him.

A wind was blowing. The air was raw. Frost-stricken lawns on the hillside were gradually sinking into darkness. Shade trees mourned their lost leaves. Even the nearest houses seemed to be not near the two men, but far away and far apart. Mist rose from the large puddles of water at the bottom of the hill. A girl laughed somewhere in the distance.

The young man shifted the guitar case back to his right hand. Etan R. bent his head to make out the time on his watch. His work clothes reeked of sweat, sour milk, and manure.

"All right," said Etan. "That's fine."

"It's all right? I can stay? I'm ready to start work tomorrow. Any work. I have all my papers with me, and a letter of recommendation."

"Hold on a minute," said Etan R. "Look. Follow that path until you reach the bakery. There's a sign on the bakery that says bakery. That's how you know it's the bakery. Just past the bakery there's a fork. Bear left along the cypress trees. When you get to the end of them you'll see two houses. Is that clear so far?"

"So far it's fantastic."

"Hold on a minute. Don't run off. I'm not done yet. When you get to the two houses, cut between them. You'll see a long, raised building with four porches. Past it you'll see a second building, also on pilings with four porches. Knock on its next-to-last door. That's Yolek's. Yolek is the secretary. He's your man, the head of the kibbutz you said you were looking for."

"The man you said was critically ill?"

"Ill. I don't know about the critical. One look at you will revive him. You'll get all your questions answered, and he'll tell you what to do. Are you sure you won't get lost?"

"Never!" answered Azariah in a pale fright, as though he had just been asked whether he intended to make off with something valuable. "In the army I was almost sent to a special reconnaissance course. Well, it was a pleasure meeting you. 'The smiling face is hard to erase,' they say. My name is Azariah. Will you allow me to thank you?"

Etan R. shrugged twice on his way to the cowshed. Did that guitar case really hold a guitar? This country, he reminded himself, is full of jerks. A guitar case can be for guitars, and it can be for other things too. It's anyone's guess. He felt a renewed uneasiness, perhaps because the stranger had seemed so ill-at-ease himself.

If that young man's looking for someplace to hide, Etan thought, he couldn't find a better place than a kibbutz. Everything's aboveboard, no questions asked. The only place you can still find a little justice in the world is on the kibbutz. An oddball? Well, we've got a Bolognesi who sits around knitting dresses, why not someone who's looking for justice. No skin off my back.

Just to be on the safe side, though, Etan decided that after he finished the night milking and took his shower, he would inquire about the newcomer. Maybe, he thought, I should have walked him to Yolek's to make sure he wasn't up to something.

By the time Etan had finished distributing the fodder to the feedstalls and was hooking up the rubber tubes of the milking machine, he had forgotten all about the stranger.

The last light had died away. It had grown colder. Carpets of fallen leaves turned black in front yards. Dead leaves, whispered to by the wind, gave off a wet, moldy odor that mingled with the smell of standing water. The lamps along the muddy path shone with a doubtful light, more like some sickly yellow substance than incorporeal waves. In the windows of the houses lights burned too. Looking at them from the outside, you saw only flapping curtains and human silhouettes because the panes had frosted over. You could hear a child shout; you could hear sounds of laughter and of scolding, and sometimes strains of music from a radio. As soon as they escaped through the windows and walls, the gayest of the sounds seemed to have a spell cast over them: once outside in the rain they turned woebegone. And yet in the midst of all this frost and darkness, which was not yet the darkness of night but a grayish, winter-sunset darkness, you could imagine, behind each fogged window, families laughing, straw mats piled high with babies' toys, the smell of bathed children, heaters burning with blue flames, women in woolen bathrobes. There, within, life was flowing truly and unhurriedly such as you have never known it, such as you have longed with all your soul to touch, to be part of, so that you need no longer be the outsider in the dark, but, as if by magic, the neighbor, the friend, the equal and brother of those inside, accepted and loved by all until nothing could stand between you and them.

How, then, to penetrate the smells, the indoors, the chitchat, the rugs and straw mats, the whispers, the tunes, the laughter, the feel of warm wool and the sweet fragrance of coffee and women and cookies and wet hair, the rustle of a newspaper and the rattle of dishes, the crisping of snow-white sheets spread by four hands on a soft wide double bed in a lamplit room, the rain drumming outside on the lowered blinds.

Somewhere along the path, in the rain, he saw three ancient men standing, catching a breath of air, then leaning toward one another as if to share some secret or perhaps just huddle against the cold. They were three wet bushes shaking in the wind.

The music from radios suddenly stopped, and the deep voice of a newscaster began to speak in a solemn, determined, patriotic tone. The words were carried off by a gust of wind. The drenched stranger was trying hard to remember Etan R.'s directions. The bakery and the cypress trees were in the right place, but the long buildings deceived him. Instead of just two, there were four or five of them, all lit up like warships in a foggy port. Since the path broke off abruptly, he found himself having to slosh through flower beds. When a low branch struck him square in the face and showered him with sharp needles of water, the humiliation filled him with such anger that he stormed up the nearest flight of stairs to a porch. He stood shivering for a while before finally rousing himself and knocking lightly on the door.

It was there, outside the kibbutz secretary's front door, that the young man was at last able to make out what the newscaster on the radio was saying. "In response to the latest developments, an army spokesman announced a few minutes ago that our forces are prepared for all eventualities. Necessary though limited measures have been taken. Israel continues nonetheless to strive for a peaceful resolution of tensions. Prime Minister and Defense Minister Levi Eshkol cut short his vacation this evening to consult in Tel Aviv with a number of military and diplomatic officials, among them the ambassadors of the Four Powers, who have been asked . . ."

Azariah Gitlin tried to scrape the mud off his shoes, but in the end had to take them off. He knocked politely on the door a second time, and, after a brief pause, a third. It's the radio, he thought. That's why they can't hear. He had no way of knowing that Yolek was hard of hearing.

Dressed in pajamas and a dark blue woolen bathrobe, Yolek opened the door to carry out a tray with the leftovers from his supper. The meal had been brought to him from the dining room because of his illness. To his astonishment he saw a thin, wet, frightened-looking figure standing face to face with him. Startled eyes glittered at him. Yolek had a start himself, but managed a slight laugh, and inquired, "Srulik?"

Azariah Gitlin was taken aback. Dripping wet, chattering with the cold, soaked with sweat, he answered haltingly, "Excuse me, comrade. I'm not Srulik."

Yolek couldn't hear him above the sudden blast of music from the radio. He simply put his arm around the newcomer to steer him inside and jovially chided him, "Come in, come in, Srulik. Don't stand out there in the cold. All we need now is for *you* to get sick."

He raised his eyes, only to see a stranger.

He quickly removed his arm from the thin shoulders, but mastered his annoyance and spoke in his friendliest, most positive tones.

"Ah, please forgive me. Do come in anyway. Yes. I thought you were someone else. Is it me you're looking for?" He didn't wait for an answer but announced, gesturing imperiously, "Sit down, please. Right there."

Every winter Yolek suffered from back pains, but now he had come down with a bothersome case of the flu, which made him grimly depressed. He was a compact, very physical man, with hair growing out of his ears. From this graying, furrowed face, set off by a strong mouth, protruded an almost obscenely large nose, giving him the gross, grasping look of a lascivious Jew in an anti-Semitic cartoon. Even when his mind was far removed from practical matters, dwelling on youthful triumphs, on death, on his elder son, who kept getting more remote from him, his was a face that reflected no sorrow, no spirituality, but rather an odd mixture of lust and a patient, bridled craftiness that seemed to be biding its time for some pleasure to come. Sometimes a quick little smile unintentionally flitted across his lips, as though at that exact moment he had finally become aware of the vile machinations of the person he was talking to, who had been foolish enough to think that he could hide his plots from Yolek's probing eyes.

Yolek was used to talking a great deal, to addressing meetings, conferences, congresses, and committees of all kinds, and to doing so wittily. Whether making a point with a joke or with some paradox or parable, he was a master at putting words together in a powerful way, which gave him a secret pleasure. For six years he had represented his kibbutz in the Knesset, and for six months he had been a minister in one of Ben-Gurion's first cabinets. Among his friends in the movement and in the Labor Party he enjoyed the reputation of having a shrewd, almost clairvoyant intellect, one that saw things which others did not. He's a strong man, people said, a careful, clever fellow, honest to a fault, and totally devoted to the cause. If you're faced with a difficult decision, they said, you could do worse than visit Kibbutz Granot and spend some time sounding Yolek out.

"Excuse me," said Azariah Gitlin, "I'm afraid I'm getting everything wet."

"I'm the one who told you to sit, young man. Why are you still standing? Sit. Not here. Over there, by the heater. Why, you're soaking wet!"

Azariah Gitlin placed his guitar case by the chair Yolek pointed to and sat down stiffly and politely, taking care not to lean against its back. Suddenly he jumped up in alarm, removed his knapsack from his shoulder, and laid it with great care on the guitar case as though it, or the case, or both, contained some highly fragile object. Sitting down again as close as possible to the edge of the chair, he grinned at the sight of the puddle forming beneath him on the floor.

"Please excuse me," he began, "but *are* you Comrade Yolek? Could I possibly have a few minutes of your time?"

Yolek withheld an immediate answer. Gently, he settled his aching back into a padded armchair, stretched out his legs with infinite caution on a low footstool, and fastened the top button of his pajama top. Next he reached for the pack of cigarettes that lay on the coffee table to his right, extracted one of them, regarded it cunningly as if to show it he was nobody's fool, and then, with something like a wink, laid it back on the pack without lighting it. "Yes," he declared, turning his left ear toward his guest.

"I'm really not disturbing you? It's all right if I get right down, as they say, to brass tacks?"

"Please do."

"Well, then, first of all, please pardon my sudden appearance. My invasion, I should say. Not that I don't know that rules of formal etiquette have been abolished on the kibbutz, and rightly so, but I still must excuse myself. I came on foot."

"Yes," said Yolek.

"I walked all the way from the junction. It's a good thing no border raiders are out on a night like this."

"Yes, indeed," said Yolek. "So you're the new boy from the fruit-packing plant at last. Kirsch sent you to us."

"Not exactly."

"Eh?"

"I'm afraid I am someone else. I came to see about joining."

"What! You're not Kirsch's assistant?"

Azariah Gitlin looked down at the floor. Humbled. Disgraced. Lowest of the low.

"I see," said Yolek. "You are indeed someone else. I beg your pardon."

During the brief silence Yolek studied the pitiful creature seated across from him in wet socks, water streaming off it like sweat on a hot summer day. He noticed the long, sensitive fingers like those of a girl, the frail shoulders, the elongated face, the restless expression, the green eyes that betrayed some basic fear or despair. He reached for his cigarette once again, turned it around suspiciously to compare its two ends, and tamped it gently between his fingers. With his other hand, he pushed the pack toward the guest.

Azariah Gitlin snatched a cigarette, planted it in his mouth, thanked Yolek for it, thanked him once again for the lighted match he extended, and began to talk in a rush, swallowing his words, despairing of sentences halfway through and beginning new ones, gesturing continually with his hands, not daring to pause even to inhale. He was from Tel Aviv, a socialist by conviction, but sociable too, an orderly, hard-working type. His name, if he hadn't mentioned it yet, was Azariah Gitlin. A few weeks ago—three, or three-and-a-quarter, to be exact—that is, roughly twenty-three days ago, he had been discharged from the army. Honorably discharged. He had a document to prove it. In writing. No, he had never been to a kibbutz before, not even on a visit. Except once, when he happened to spend two hours at Kibbutz Bet-Alfa. But what were two hours? Not enough time to skin a cat, so to speak. Besides, he had had a good friend in the army, a young boy from Kibbutz Ginegar, who had tried to kill himself in the quartermaster's office and whose life he, Azariah, had saved at the last minute.

Not that any of this really mattered, by the way. All these details were, so to speak, incidental. The main thing was that he had developed an interest in the history of the kibbutz movement. He had talked to many people about it and had read a number of essays and even a novel—and, of course, Comrade Lifshitz's pamphlet *Facing the Future*—so that he was by no means a stranger to the subject and had some idea who he had the honor to be speaking with. Was he truly not disturbing him? The fact was that he felt nothing but contempt for people who made pilgrimages to famous men's homes simply to rob them of their time.

Family? No, he had none. That is, he had no brothers or sisters, and, for the time being, no wife or children either. When could he have had the time to start? All he had were some distant relatives, some refugees from Europe. No, he positively preferred not to discuss them. Some people were best not talked about. Mum's the word, so to speak. "The shorter the line, the straighter. The fewer the words, the greater." And so he would waste no more of them. He simply wished to be accepted by Kibbutz Granot. To strike roots in its soil, so to speak. That is, he wanted to be part of a communal enterprise. Incidentally, the day after his release from the army, three-and-a-quarter weeks ago, he had registered as a member of the Labor Party.

Yes, he had all kinds of ideas, he read a lot too, and he even had written a few things of his own. Nothing special. Poems, yes. Some prose. A few theoretical pieces. No, he hadn't tried publishing them. Still, the plain fact was that two days ago, well after midnight, he had sat alone at a table with a cup of coffee and had run his finger blindly over a list of all the kibbutzim in Israel. Wherever it landed, he had decided, was where he would go. "It's fate that steers the horse that veers." Take Spinoza, for example. A thousand years ago he had wisely written that although human beings come into this world ignorant of the reason for their existence, each one of them is born with the desire to realize what is best for himself. And that is how he had ended up this evening at Kibbutz Granot.

With all his experience in the realms of both ideology and practical politics, Comrade Yolek must surely have encountered events that seemed at first glance to be pure coincidence, yet that, once contemplated philosophically, revealed their predestined character. That too was an idea of Spinoza's. Need he, Azariah, apologize for using the arguments of a philosopher excommunicated by his fellow Jews?

"If you'll excuse me for saying so, Comrade Yolek, the ban

on Spinoza was an act of gross injustice, so to speak, whereas the kibbutz was established to put an end to injustice in all things."

A profession? In all honesty he had to admit he didn't yet have one. When could he have had the time to acquire one? He had only been out of the army for twenty-three days. It would make him happy to be taught some agricultural skill like wheat growing or wine culture that would allow him to contribute to society. Even the broken clock is right twice a day.

His job in the army? A technical sergeant, a specialist in halftracks, although, to be honest, that was not his official rank but only an acting one. Not that it mattered. By the way, he had no demands. A roof over his head and three square meals a day, as they say. Perhaps a little pocket money, as is customary on kibbutzim.

No, he knew no one at Granot except for a splendid young man who told him the way to Yolek's house with great patience. Yes, of course, he understood that a kibbutz was not a summer camp. The hammer that shatters glass tempers steel, as they say. In all honesty and frankness, he should point out that he was accustomed to the harshest conditions and most backbreaking work. Not only had he just left the army but as a child in Europe he had grown up under Hitler's boot. No job, if you asked him, could be too difficult in a place where one could go to work every day with a sense of joy and community. If he wasn't mistaken, that was the whole idea of the kibbutz. In a word, he would gladly do whatever was asked of him. He wasn't choosy or spoiled. On the contrary, it might well be said that he was tough as nails. During the war, Stalin had put it to the Russian people bluntly. "Each of you wants to eat, get off your butt and on your feet!" *Pozhalusta.*

"Yes, Comrade Yolek, yes, of course, I know that I have to be on probation first. You can't do a thing in the army either without going through basic training. Excuse me, I'm so sorry, I really didn't mean to get ashes on the floor. I'll clean them up right away. No, I beg your pardon, Comrade Yolek. It's my fault and I'll clean it up. And wipe up the water that's dripped from my wet clothes. Forgive me, though. Are you by any chance in a hurry? I know I've been talking a lot, and I'd better stop now before you get the wrong idea about me. Basically I'm a quiet, even introspective type. Just tell me when and I'll scram. A thousand years ago Spinoza wrote—I'm quoting from Klatzkin's translation—that love and generosity alone can conquer another man's heart. Well, it's finally stopped raining. Perhaps you would like me to leave now and try my luck on some other kibbutz?"

All this time Yolek sat there, shifting in his chair to find a more comfortable position for his sore back. Without forgoing his usual cunning look, he had listened tactfully to his guest's harangue. Now and then he interrupted to ask some brief, calculated question about the stranger's credentials. Whenever he failed to follow the verbal torrent, he would lean vigorously forward, turn his good ear to Azariah, and say, "Eh?" This inevitably made Azariah repeat himself and jumble things even more. With each new proverb or platitude, Yolek simply nodded, sometimes with a conspiratorial smile. He decided that the young man was nearsighted, although whether he made a habit of hiding his disability or had only removed his glasses upon arriving remained to be seen. In any case, Yolek resolved that this young man must not be allowed to carry arms under any circumstances.

Yolek was in the habit of cautioning himself against hasty generalizations about the human material that came knocking on the doors of the kibbutz these days. Each application, he believed, was a case in itself, and each applicant a world in his own right. When all is said and done, he rather liked this amusing young man, so different from the hulking, tongue-tied, thick-skulled Huns, Scyths, and Tatars who had grown up on the kibbutz acting as though they were merely the most recent of immemorial generations of peasants—until, that is, they came one fine day to ask for a special grant of public funds in the hope of wandering off somewhere to wallow in what they hideously referred to as their self-fulfillment. Say what one might, this eccentric character trying to claw his way into the kibbutz by hook or crook reminded him of those tormented soul-searchers from the small towns of Russia and Poland who had founded the first kibbutzim out of nothing, in the face of disease and desert heat. Although he found it hard to make up his mind, one thing was clear. The newcomer wasn't a scoundrel.

Thus, when Azariah fell silent after suggesting that perhaps he should try his luck elsewhere, Yolek said warmly, "Very well, then."

The newcomer's face lit up, and he laughed—an overly loud laugh.

"You mean to say I've convinced you?"

"Wait," said Yolek. "First you'll drink a glass of hot tea. Then we'll talk about the next step."

"Thank you."

"Yes, thank you, or no, thank you?"

"No, thank you. Not right now."

"You won't have any tea," said Yolek, surprised and disappointed. "What a pity. Be it as you wish. Though I had better tell you bluntly that if you don't drink a glass of hot tea now, you'll have to drink it later when my friend Hava returns. And now, let's switch roles for a while," Yolek went on. "I'll do some explaining and you'll listen."

Yolek's voice brimmed with sympathy and affection the way it always did when he spoke at a party or kibbutz meeting and wished to placate a particularly uncompromising opponent by making up to him and striking a chord of brotherly solidarity that would transcend all passing disputes. Azariah, for his part, nodded all the while Yolek was talking. At the same time he moved still closer to the edge of his chair, straining forward as if he had grasped the fact that Yolek was hard of hearing and, by a kind of somnambulistic logic, had begun to fear that he too might miss what was being said.

Yolek started out by explaining what winter meant on a farm. The earth was waterlogged. Hardly anyone could go out to work. The tractor drivers slept all day long. The field hands were sent off for courses in Judaism and Marxism and psychology and modern poetry. Even the citrus picking had to stop. Not to mention the problem of housing. There were young couples on the kibbutz who still had to make do with a single room without a private shower or bath until the new construction, also interrupted by the rain, was completed. This was no time for taking on newcomers. There was no work to give them, nowhere to put them up, and no one to be responsible for them. It was for this reason alone that Yolek couldn't recommend that Azariah be accepted for a trial period. Not, by the way, that he put much stock in trial periods. A trained eye could see at a glance what stuff a man was made of. And if it couldn't, that simply proved that the man had such a closed personality that ten years wouldn't help to figure him out. There were always, of course, exceptions, but exceptions on kibbutzim never lasted for long.

All this, needless to say, was on the level of generalities. "In regard to your specific case, I'm very sorry to tell you that at the moment we have no room for you. If you come back in early summer, when there's lots of weeding and fruit thinning to do, or even in midsummer, when we begin picking the grapes and the citrus fruit, I'll, of course, reconsider. Maybe we'll have some vacant rooms by then. Maybe some temporary help will have left. And maybe you'll have found another kibbutz, or changed your mind altogether. After all, life changes and so do we. And next time, if there is one, it would be a good idea to write to us first. Yes. It's half-past seven now. And talking so much is hard for me. I've got the grippe and some sort of allergy too. Soon my friend Hava will be here. She'll take you to the dining room for a bite to eat so that you won't leave on an empty stomach and all disillusioned with kibbutz life. She'll find a seat for you in the pickup truck that's taking some of us to a show in the city tonight. Are you sure you won't have a glass of tea first, though? No? No it is, then.

"Everyone has a right to his opinion, and we won't force anything on you here. And yet, my young friend, I must say that if everyone has a right to his opinion, not every opinion is right. Spinoza, now. Did you learn about him in school? Or did you discover him by yourself? In any case, perhaps you'll be so good as to allow me to correct you slightly. It hasn't been a thousand years. You said he lived a thousand years ago. But Spinoza died in Amsterdam only some three hundred years ago. That's a long time too, of course—but still.

"Eh? You'll walk? But why should you walk all the way to the junction in weather like this, and in the dark? Didn't I tell you there's a truck leaving for the city? Are you trying to punish us? There's no need to act foolishly. And you can see that it's starting to rain again. Look here, what's the matter with you? You surely don't expect me to keep you here by force? Suit yourself, though. Have a good trip. If you should happen to change your mind, you'll find the truck in the square in front of the dining room. And by the way, our own Maimonides and Ibn Ezra influenced Spinoza every bit as much as Plato and Aristotle and all those other non-Jews.

"I just wish you wouldn't be so stubborn. Please, go to the dining room, have a bite to eat, take the truck into town. We'll see about having you for a tryout this summer."

Azariah had risen from his seat before Yolek finished speaking. His socks left wet prints behind him on the floor. He picked up his guitar case in his right hand, hung his knapsack over his left shoulder, and bravely managed a polite, intimidated smile. Nevertheless, there was desperation and even terror in his eyes, the terror of a naughty child who has been caught in the act. Yolek, still in his armchair, cocked his head to look at him sideways as if something had just confirmed all his previous suspicions. The sense of having been right gave him his usual sharp pang of pleasure.

The visitor stumbled toward the door, grabbed hold of it, and furiously began pulling on a handle that was meant to open outward. His predicament temporarily dumbfounded him. Murmuring something that Yolek failed to catch, he put his guitar case down, figured out the secret of the door, and, once outside, cast back an anguished look.

"Goodbye," he said twice. "Forgive me."

"Just a minute," called Yolek. "Wait."

Panic-stricken, the young man turned around, bumping his shoulder against the door. There was a flare of fear in his green eyes, as though a trap had closed at the last minute, when escape seemed sure.

"Yes, sir."

"Did you say halftracks? What did you say you did in the army?"

"Nothing special. I was just a technical sergeant. Not exactly a sergeant. An acting sergeant, private first class."

"What exactly is a technical sergeant?"

"I'm not going back into the army!" Azariah Gitlin shot back fiercely, bristling like a cornered cat. "And no one can make me! I was honorably discharged three-and-a-quarter weeks ago."

"Easy there, young man. Easy there. Perhaps you could simply explain what a technical sergeant does? Anything to do with garage work?"

At once the lights were relit in the young man's face, as though, having abandoned every hope, he had been unexpectedly acquitted of all charges. Yolek felt his curiosity stir dimly. There was something about the newcomer that aroused his suspicion and approbation at the very same time.

"Yes, Comrade Yolek, yes, it's definitely garage work, and lots more too, armaments, combat gear, engine testing, everything, mechanics, automotive electronics, maintenance, repairs, even ballistics and some metallurgy, everything." He spoke at breakneck speed, in a single long breath.

"Eh?"

"Combat gear. I said armaments and combat gear."

"All right, all right, that's all very well. But do you know how to fix tractors and farm machinery or don't you? You do? Ah! We're singing in a different opera now. You saw my ad in the evening paper? You didn't? Honestly? No, no, there's no need to swear. I believe you. I believe everyone until I catch him in his first lie. I'll tell you what, though. This is one very strange coincidence. But first of all, come back inside. And please close the door. Good. Now for the plum I have for you. For the last six weeks I've been looking all over for a hired hand to work in our tractor shed. Sit down. Why didn't you tell me all this in the first place instead of lecturing me on Spinoza? Not that I regret one single moment of our conversation. You're not to blame for it in any case. Our two mechanics walked off the job at the same time and left us nothing but scorched earth. Itzik married a girl from Kibbutz Mizra and is fouling up the works in their tractor shed now. The other one, Peiko—really first-rate, that fellow—was hijacked from us by the central office. Move closer to the heater. You're shaking. Not that even a young man like Peiko can undo all the damage that's been done to the Party these past years. Everything's gone to hell there, just as in our tractor shed. But see here, you're getting sick. Your eyes look feverish. Don't worry, though. I've something stashed away that will nip whatever ails you. We're going to drink a little toast—a toastlet, maybe?—to Spinoza and the idea of kibbutzim. That is, if the thought of a wee bit of brandy doesn't frighten you off. What did you say your name was again?"

Azariah Gitlin repeated it, last name first.

"Meanwhile, here's some hot tea," Yolek said. "And don't tell me you don't want it because I've already poured it and don't get me angry. Here's sugar and lemon and here's the rotgut. You can either add some of it to your tea or drink it from a shot glass. You have your identity pass? Your army discharge? No need to jump up. I didn't ask to see them now. I just wanted to make sure you had them. Drink! Your tea is getting cold and the brandy will lose its aroma. I don't run a police station here. Your documents will be checked tomorrow and the necessary paperwork taken care of.

"No, kibbutzim don't distribute official membership cards. Why, here's Hava! Hava, I'd like you to meet Azriel Gitlin. He's a young volunteer, a gift from heaven, who may save our tractor shed in the nick of time and whom I in my infinite wisdom nearly chucked right down the stairs. Hava, would you please hand me a pair of clean socks from the drawer? The boy is all wet and may soon be sick himself. After dinner we'll invite him back here for another cup of tea and to talk about heaven and earth and all that's betwixt and between. This lad is a wonder—a man not only with ideas in his head but also, if he is to be believed, a crackerjack mechanic. One has to search far and wide these days to find anybody his age who isn't a hopeless Tatar."

"Comrade Yolek . . ." Azariah began, as if about to launch into a fervent declaration, but he broke off and fell silent, for Hava had chosen at the very same moment to ask a question.

"Do you play the guitar?"

"A bit. I mean I play a lot. Would you like me to play something for you now?"

"Perhaps later," said Yolek with one of his shrewd smiles. "Perhaps after supper. Or perhaps not. Perhaps we should postpone both our colloquium and your recital to another time. This evening—after you've eaten, of course—Hava will take you to Yonatan. Let the two of them meet, why not? Let them talk about the tractor shed or whatever they like. In the third drawer, Hava, you'll find the key to the barbershop. Yes, he'll stay in the barber's room, next to the Italian. There's a folding cot there, and blankets, and a kerosene heater. The barber, I'm sorry to say, comes only once every six weeks. There, young man, you can taste the life of the pioneers of old until we find you more permanent quarters. Oh, well. If I don't see you again tonight, I'll see you in the morning at the office. I do hope you won't decide to abscond on foot in the middle of the night, eh? *Na*, there's no need to answer. I was just making one of my old-fashioned jokes, and already you're on the defensive. Just pretend that nothing was said. Here, take a few cigarettes with you for the road. By the way, what do you have in that case, a violin? No? A guitar? We'll have to find some time to introduce you to Srulik. He's our head music man. And first thing tomorrow morning don't forget to come see me at the office. No, not about music—about the formal arrangements for you to stay. At the moment my elder son is running the tractor shed, and he'll explain all about it. If you can get Yonatan to talk, that is. And now, forward march, both of you. Go have your supper."

"All right," said Hava quietly, if with a kind of concealed hostility. "We will."

Tenderness or wonder made Yolek Lifshitz smile all of a sudden and declare, "Azariah!"

"Yes, Comrade Yolek."

"I hope you enjoy being here with us."

"Thank you very much."

"And welcome."

"Thank you very much, Comrade Yolek. I mean, I won't disappoint you. Never."

Hava turned to go and was followed by Azariah. She was a short, energetic woman with masculine, close-cropped, grayish-white hair and a clenched mouth. Overall her expression was one of a violently uncompromising good nature. Life, it seemed to say, is a vulgar, thankless, insulting business. Although scoundrels and swine are everywhere, I will not desert my post. I will do my duty without fail, devoted to the cause, to society, and to my fellow man, even if no one knows as well as I what a pigsty my fellow man is. As for the cause, the less I hear of it, the better. I've already heard and seen and smelled far more than I care to, but let it be.

"You said your name was Azariah? What kind of a name is that? Are you a new immigrant or something? Do you have parents? No? Then who brought you up? Look out, there's a revolting puddle over there. This way. That's right.

"And apart from everything else, you're also a young poet? No? A philosophist? Never mind. The only thing that matters is whether you're an honest man. I don't give a hoot for the rest. Here, bless their souls, we have all types. Once, when I was a girl, I read somewhere in Dostoyevsky that if a man wants to stay really honest, he'd better die before he turns forty. From forty on they're all scoundrels. On the other hand, they say that Dostoyevsky was a scoundrel himself, a drunken swine and a petty egotist.

"You can wash your hands over here. There's no hot water. The faucet isn't working. As usual. Here are the trays and over there the dishes and silverware and cups. Would you like an egg? Yes, I'm glad you think so, but that's not what I asked. I asked if you wanted a hard-boiled or a soft-boiled egg. Now sit yourself here and eat, and don't let anyone make you self-conscious. No one here is any better than you are. I'll be back in a few minutes. Don't wait for me. Just start eating.

"By the way, whatever Yolek told you is fine and dandy, but personally I'd advise you not to get too excited about it. Yolek has lots of ideas at night, but he always makes his decisions in the morning. Are you absolutely sure you don't have a fever? I've never believed in aspirin, but I'll bring you one and you can do what you want with it. Take your time eating. No need to rush. You're not going anywhere tonight."

She remembered the sobs and pleas of the young man who had loved her when she was young. On the threshing floor on summer nights the kibbutzniks got together to sing beneath the stars while the jackals wailed in the distance. "Her eyes outshone the morning star," they sang, "and her heart raged like a desert wind." In the darkness the young man who loved her put her hand to his cheek to let her know it was wet with his tears. I shouldn't have run down Dostoyevsky in front of a young man I don't even know.

Yolek didn't resettle himself in his chair until he heard the steps outside grow faint. He could feel the pain creeping up his back and along his shoulders and neck like a patrol sent out in advance of a full-scale attack.

Although he tried to concentrate on the news coming over the radio—something about troop concentrations along the northern border that had already been broadcast several times that evening—he found it difficult to grasp what this might portend. He felt sorry for Prime Minister Eshkol, undoubtedly sitting at this very moment in a closed, crowded, smoke-filled room, struggling to fight off sorrow and fatigue while trying to assess battalions of nebulous rumors and unconfirmed facts. He felt sorry for himself as well, ground down as he was on the kibbutz by endless trivialities, not to mention his aches and pains, when he should have been at Eshkol's side in that closed room, helping him to steer a moderate course. These hot-headed Huns, Scyths, Tatars surrounded him on all sides, pressuring him to do something melodramatic. Perhaps these aren't just ordinary back pains, thought Yolek. Perhaps they're a warning signal.

Quite apart from his physical woes, some obscure worry was gnawing away inside him. He felt he had forgotten some terribly important, even urgent, matter, one that was imperative to remember lest some great harm be done. Yet what it was, and why it was so urgent, he could not for the life of him recall. Could it be that he had left a door open or forgotten to unplug the electric kettle? But the kettle was unplugged, the doors were all shut, and so were the windows. Outside, the rain began to come down harder.

3

Yonatan thought of the words "beyond the call of duty." That was how the army magazine had described his conduct on the night of the raid on Hirbet Tawfik. In the hasty retreat from the enemy's position on those terraced, shell-blasted hills, lit by the hideous glare of Syrian artillery flares, he had carried on his back a bleeding soldier he didn't know, a squat man who kept gasping, I'm done for, I'm done for, I'm done for, the last word drawing out into a thin wail.

And you, you suddenly decided that you'd had it. I can't carry him another foot. Everyone else is already home safe except for the two of us lost in these hills with the Syrians breathing down our necks. If I just put the dying son-of-a-bitch down and let him die in peace among the rocks instead of on my back I may save my life, and no one will ever know, because there's no one to rat, and I'll be alive and not dead.

How the thought of that scared me. You're crazy, I said, you're out of your fucking mind, and I began to run like hell with that dying bastard on my back, and bullets and tracers and mortar shells exploding all over from that other Tawfik, the upper one, the one we never took, the one the Syrians held, and that fucker kept bleeding into my ear like a torn garden hose, screaming I'm done fo-o-or until he had no breath any more, and neither did I. My lungs were full of burned smells, burned fuel, burned rubber, burned weeds, burned blood. If I'd had a free hand, I'd have cut his throat with my hunting knife just to make him shut up, but I kept on running, bawling like a boy.

How we got through that mine field before Kibbutz Tel Katzir I'll never know. By then I was howling too, oh God save me, God come save me, I don't want to die, oh God I'm done fo-o-or. If only the bastard would die but not on my back before we reach Tel Katzir—he'd better not leave me alone here. And then this one crazy shell landed twenty meters off just to teach me not to run like a lunatic, to run more slowly. Oh God is he heavy, I can't go on any more!

But we'd reached Tel Katzir, we were in the middle of all this barbed wire, being shot at. Don't shoot, I began to scream, hey, don't shoot, can't you see we're dying, hey, can't you see we're dying, until they heard me and brought us to a field hospital in a bomb shelter. That's when they took him off my back at last. We were all glued together with blood and saliva and sweat and piss and all the fluids in our bodies like two newborn puppies, one blind filthy lump. We'd been soldered to each other, his nails stuck into my chest and back like staples. When they unpeeled him, there were pieces of my skin on him, and so soon as he was off me, I collapsed like an empty sack on the floor.

Suddenly in the badly lit bunker it turned out that I was really out of my skull, that it was all a mistake, that the blood which soaked through my clothes and my underwear and into my crotch and even my socks wasn't his at all. He wasn't even wounded, just in shock. All that blood was my own, from a piece of shrapnel in my shoulder, barely two inches from my heart.

They bandaged me up and gave me a shot and said as you'd say to a child, "Take it easy, Yoni, take it easy, Yoni," but I couldn't take it easy because I couldn't stop laughing. Someone said, "This man's in shock too. Give him ten cc.'s to calm him down." But even in the ambulance on the way to hospital as they kept asking me to calm down, to get a grip on myself, to tell them where it hurt, I lay on the stretcher and roared with laughter so hard that I began to choke. "Look at *him*," I gasped, "*he's* done for! Just look at *him*! *He's* done for!" all the way to the hospital. Then they put me to sleep for the operation and after that they published a story in the army magazine; I remember the title exactly: "Wounded Soldier Saves Comrade's Life."

That joker, the old-timers say when they talk about him, from three feet away he managed to miss a bull. And a bull, mind you, isn't a matchbox. But he managed to miss it, and, believe it or not, today he's the owner and president of the Esplanada Hotel chain in Miami Beach, Florida, where he lives like a lord.

After supper, Yonatan and Rimona returned home from the dining room. He couldn't remember what his mother Hava had asked him when she came over to their table at the end of their meal. He could only recall saying that tonight was out of the question.

The two of them stood for several minutes by the heater to thaw out. They were so close that her shoulder grazed his arm. He was enough taller than she to look down on her rain-drenched hair falling gently over her shoulders, the left one rather than the right. Had he wished, he could have stroked it. But he stooped and turned up the flame of the heater instead.

The room was lit as usual by the reddish-brown light cast by the heavy lamp shade. Everything was in its place. Everything was neat and tidy. Rimona had even folded the newspaper and stashed it on the low shelf where it belonged. Even the floor tiles gave off a subtle scent of cleanliness. Tia lay sprawled by the heater. It would have seemed a house at perfect peace had it not been for the crying of a child from the next-door apartment.

"These walls," said Rimona.

"What's wrong?"

"They're so thin. You'd think they were made out of paper."

It seemed a meaningful kind of crying, neither a whine nor a tantrum, as if the child beyond the wall had broken some toy that he loved and knew he alone was to blame. A woman sought to soothe him. Only the tone of her voice reached Yonatan and Rimona; the words could not be made out.

When Yonatan asked Rimona if she was busy, she wanted to know why he asked. Did he want to explain something to her on the chessboard perhaps? Although they never played chess with each other, she was always willing to sit with him for half an hour or so, the pieces arranged before them on the board, while he explained various strategies: the Nimzowitsch Opening, the King's Indian Defense, the flanking versus the direct attack, the correct way to play the Queen's Gambit, the sacrifice of this or that piece for the sake of a tactical advantage. Rimona found it pleasant to listen to such things. If he cared to set up the pieces, she added, she would make coffee, fetch her embroidery, and be with him in a minute.

Although Yonatan didn't reply, Rimona went to make the coffee. Like a soldier caught in a crossfire, he spun wildly around, stepped away from the heater, and crossed over to the bookcase, where he stood with his back to the room. His eyes finally fell on an old photograph of Rimona that she had framed and placed among the books, a black-and-white snapshot of the two of them taken on a hike in the Judean Desert. He was astounded to discover that they were not alone. Behind her, in the lower right-hand corner, appeared a strange, hairy, uncouth leg in short pants and army boots. Now was the time to make his move, to say or do that crucial thing. Doing his best to steady himself, he finally managed to say, angrily, "My cigarettes. Did you by any chance see my cigarettes?"

Rimona came into the room carrying a tray with two mugs

of coffee, some pastry, and a small blue Bokhara creamer.

"Why don't you sit down? You can pour the milk in our coffee while I get a fresh pack from the drawer. There's no need to be upset."

"Forget it!" snapped Yonatan. And then, bitingly, "Who the hell asked for a fresh pack? My cigarettes are over there. Look, right under your nose! On the radio. What did you say?"

"I didn't say anything. You were talking, Yoni."

"I thought you did. Maybe you started to and changed your mind. Or maybe you just meant to. Here, I'll pour'a da milk. That's how Bolognesi says it, 'pour'a.' I always feel I'm interrupting you, even when you're silent."

"How strange," said Rimona, though there was not the slightest touch of wonder in her voice.

"And maybe you'll be good enough to stop saying 'how strange' all the time. Everything seems 'strange' to you. There's nothing 'strange' about it. Why don't you sit down instead of wandering all over the room? Sit down!"

After she was seated before him, his eyes came to rest on the cleavage of her blouse and he thought of the rest of her—of her twelve-year-old's breasts, of the cold, dainty lines of the torso hidden beneath her clothes, of her navel like a shut sleeping eye, of her sex like some pious, genderless illustration in a facts-of-life manual for teenagers. It won't do her any good, Yonatan thought, nothing will any more, not her lovely red sweater, not her long blond hair, not even her bashful smile. The smile of a sweet little girl who's been naughty and knows that she'll be forgiven because everyone loves her and everything will be all right. Only this time she won't be forgiven and nothing will be all right. This time it's hopeless and everything is all wrong. Just look at her, that skin sagging on her neck, behind her tiny ears, underneath her adorable chin, all those places where she's drying out and cracking like weathered paint or an old shoe. It's the beginning of her old age and there's not a thing that she can do about it. Nothing can save her. The magic of Zanzibar is lost. Gone forever. The End. And I don't feel in the least bit sorry for her because no one in the world feels sorry for me. The only thing I feel sorry about is all the time that's been wasted.

"Did you forget?" asked Rimona, with a smile.

"Forget what?"

"I'm still waiting."

"Waiting?" said Yonatan in amazement. He felt a moment's panic. What could she mean? Waiting for what? Did she already know? But she couldn't possibly.

"I don't get it," he added. "Waiting for what?"

"For you to set up the chessboard, Yoni. And I'll turn on the radio. There's a Bach fugue on. I've already brought in my embroidery, and you told me not to bother about getting the cigarettes because you would, but you forgot. Don't get up. I'll do it for you."

Some minutes later they sat facing each other in the twin armchairs. Music came over the radio. Rimona hugged the coffee mug with her palms to absorb the warmth. For the last time Yonatan reviewed in his mind the words he had decided to use.

"I'm ready if you are," said Rimona.

Once, when he was on patrol and crossing the border at night into Jordan near the village of Tarkumiyya, Yonatan suddenly found himself scared to death for no good reason. The night seemed full of eyes. Among the rocks the darkness crackled with a wicked laughter. They're waiting for us. In some unaccountable way they know we're coming down this wadi tonight, and they're lying in ambush, as invisible as we are conspicuous, laughing to themselves because the trap is sprung.

A shadow passed over Rimona's brow. Through her slightly parted lips, Yonatan could make out the white tips of her teeth. He thought of expanses of white sand incandescent in the sun, blasted by the wild midday light of the Zin Desert near a bone-dry site that was marked on his map as Caravan Spring. The memory flooded him with a pain unlike any he had ever known, and the sharpness of it made him shut his eyes.

He recalled how their love began. He recalled the weeks before their marriage. The long ride by jeep through the mountains and down to the gray flatlands below. The campfire of dried branches that smoldered all night long. The sleeping bag they shared on that desert night behind the silent jeep. Her child's breasts caught in his heavy hands like two warm starlings. Her tears, her whispers. "Try not to mind it, Yoni. It's not your fault. You just go ahead and don't mind."

He thought too of how their love had ended. Three years ago at half-past-two in the morning when she said, "Look, Yoni, lots of girls are like that. You have to try not to mind."

He thought of her first pregnancy. And of the last one. Of the dead baby girl he had refused to look at in the hospital. And once more of her delicate body, that cold, exquisite slab of marble. Of his last, abasing attempts to arouse in that pale adamant some life, some pain, some injury or anger. So many days and nights, nights and days. And the distances. Her suffering that he could only imagine, and not even that. His aloneness. At three in the morning on a wide, arid sheet beneath a wide, arid ceiling with everything gleaming like the bones of a cadaver in the light of the full dead moon in the window, wide awake yet abducted by some white nightmare in a snowy polar wasteland, wide awake but alone with a corpse.

The shame of words. Of lies. Wastelands of unspoken truths. Sleeping. Waking. The pallor of her fingertips. The white tips of her teeth. The sight of her naked body, so fragile, chaste, and pitiable, in a cold shower on a summer day. The taste of her silence. Of his. The permanently dead space between his and hers. Her duplicitous, hollow beauty. Her feigned tenderness that mustn't be touched even when you felt most like touching. The rub of her small hard breasts against the skin of his face, the muscles of his belly, the hair of his chest. The patient, bitter beating against her, the more and more desperate search everywhere for some opening, with kisses, with caresses, with cajolery, with silence, with cruelty, in the darkness, in the half-light, in the hot light, on sultry afternoons, in the hours before dawn, in bed, in woods, in cars, in sand dunes, like a father, like a child, like a savage, like an ape, gently, despairingly, jokingly, pleadingly, obscenely, violently, servilely—all in vain.

The breath that whooshed out of his lungs like a sob each time that he came so loathsomely far from her and from himself and from any love, always stymied in the end by the same dead frozen silence on the same dead frozen lips. Her body as stiff as a corpse. The rustle of the sheets cold and venomous and between them the soft sibilance of thrashed silk. The fruitless movement of her lips in the hair of his chest, the vain meander of her tongue down to his groin, his hands with sudden fury grasping, shaking her shoulders, shaking her back, her whole body, as if it were a watch that had stopped ticking, even cuffing her face with the back of his hand, one time even with his fist. All in vain. Always the same creeping wanting, the same fear, the same regret, the same ruses, the same shame, the same suffocating venom welling up inside him like a scream being screamed underwater. And afterwards his questions. Her silence. Her questioning. His silence.

And, always and without fail, her insane baths and ablutions, as if she were scrubbing some filth or poison from her skin, extirpating the last of his and her body odor with hot water and suds, before getting back into bed suffused with the fragrance of the childish almond soap that he hated, all pink and clean like a baby, like a God's angel in a kitschy religious tableau. And falling asleep right away while he lay there listening to another woman's laughter through the wall or the whispers of couples on the lawns, drifting through the open windows on summer nights.

Once and for all to grab the bread knife and plunge it into her soft skin, into her veins and her arteries, and down deeper yet, to open her up, to rampage through the dark lymph of her and the fat and the cartilage, to the innermost nooks and crannies, to the marrow of her bones, to carve her till she screamed. He had had enough. He couldn't go on any more in such againstness.

Thus Yonatan, so far from forgetting the words he had prepared for that evening, was suddenly repelled by them, and, indeed, by anything that could be said in words. If only he could draw what he felt, or play it on an instrument, or jot it down as a simple equation in clear mathematical terms.

"The coffee you made me," he said. "I'm sorry. I forgot to drink it and it's cold."

"There's more hot coffee on the stove. I didn't drink mine either, because I was embroidering and thinking. I'll pour us both some more."

"What were you thinking about, Rimona?" Opening his eyes, Yonatan saw the flower of blue flame beneath the white-hot stove shield and, glancing down, the quick, nervous tremors that ran down Tia's spine as she lay with outstretched paws by the heater.

"I was thinking," said Rimona, "that maybe tomorrow they'll finally fix the steam boiler in the laundry room. It's been hard for us without it."

"It really is about time," said Yonatan.

"On the other hand," said Rimona, "you can't exactly blame anyone for it. Lipa has been sick. Your father's not much better yet either."

"My father keeps telling me I need a haircut. Do you think I do?"

"You don't, but if you want one, get one."

"I haven't been sick once all winter. Except for this stupid allergy. Sometimes it makes people think I'm crying. Praise'a God who dries'a the tears of'a the poor. That's what Bolognesi says whenever my eyes tear. Look at me, Rimona."

"The winter isn't over yet, Yoni, and you keep running back and forth all day from the tractor shed to the metal shop without a hat and with torn boots."

"You're wrong. Only one of them. Bolognesi said he'd fix the sole. You know, that whole tractor shed business isn't for me."

"But you once liked it."

"So what if I did?" snapped Yonatan. "So once I did and now I don't. What is it that you're always trying to tell me without ever saying it? Or if you do start to say it, you stop right in the middle. Why don't you come out with it and stop playing games? I'm asking you to talk. I promise not to interrupt. I'll be quiet as a mouse and listen to every word. Go on."

"It's nothing," said Rimona. "Don't be angry, Yoni."

"Who's angry? I'm not angry. I'm only asking you a question and hoping to get a straight answer for once in my life. That's all."

"Then ask it," said Rimona, bewildered. "You're angry that I'm not answering, but you haven't asked me anything."

"Okay. It's this. I want you to tell me exactly what you thought three, three-and-a-half years ago on that Saturday night when you decided all of a sudden that we were getting married."

"But that's not the way it happened," said Rimona softly. "And besides, why are you asking?"

"I just am. To get an answer from you."

"But why ask now? You never did before."

"Because sometimes I think . . . were you going to say something?"

"No. I'm listening."

"But I want you to stop just listening your whole goddamn life! Talk. Open your mouth. Say something. You're going to tell me right now why you married me, what you wanted from me, what was going on in that head of yours."

"All right, I will," said Rimona, adding after a brief silence, "Why not?" Almost smiling, she huddled in her armchair clutching her fresh mug of coffee with all ten fingers. Her eyes seemed to trace in midair the musical forms pouring from the radio. "Yes, I'll tell you. It was like this. When the two of us decided to get married we were each other's first. You were my first and I was yours. And you said to me that we would go on being first all our lives, that we wouldn't copy anyone, and that whatever we did, in the house, in the garden, anywhere, we would do as if no one had ever done it before. That's what you said. That we would be like two children who are lost in the woods but who hold hands tight and aren't afraid. You said that I was beautiful and that you were good, and that from now on it wouldn't embarrass you any more, because when you were little you were embarrassed that everyone, your housemothers and your teachers and your friends, always said you were good. You said that you would take me hiking in the desert and teach me to love it. And you did. And you said that I would teach you to be quiet inside and to love classical music, especially Bach. And I did. We thought we'd get along well together even if we never talked all day, even if we sat together a whole evening without saying a word. And we thought, both of us, that it would be best for us, and best for your parents, if we lived together instead of in separate rooms, you with Udi and Etan R., and I with those two visiting girls. Because once we were married we could live together and not have to meet out-of-doors in all kinds of weird places. And the summer was coming to an end. Do you remember, Yoni, it was almost autumn and then it would be winter, and in winter there would be no place to meet. And so we decided to get married before the rains began. Don't cry, Yoni. Don't be sad."

"Who's crying?" said Yonatan angrily. "It's just that fucking allergy of mine making my eyes smart. I've told you a thousand times that they sting and that you should stop putting pine branches in your vases."

"I'm sorry, Yoni. It's just that it's winter now and I can't find any flowers."

"And I've told you a thousand times too to stop saying I'm sorry, I'm sorry all day long like some waitress or a chambermaid in a movie. What you should be saying is 'What now?' "

"What now, Yoni?"

"I'm asking you what's left now. And I'll thank you not to

repeat all my questions but make a little effort to answer what you've been asked."

"But you know what now. Why ask? You and I have been husband and wife for years. Why are you asking me?"

"I don't know why. I just am. I want to hear an answer for a change. Look here, are you purposely trying to drive me up the wall? How long are you going to go on talking to me like a little moron?"

She glanced up from her embroidery and her eyes once again appeared to be tracing the music in the air. Indeed, at just that moment the fugue seemed about to overflow its banks, surging upward, beating against mighty walls. And right after that, a gentling took place. The melody relented, as though despairing of cresting the dam, and, surrendering at last, dove deep to burble beneath the foundations. The powerful current of the theme forked into several thin eddies, each flowing its own way, each oblivious of the others, but swirling about one another with bashful desire, and slowly overcoming their forlornness to build up passionately to yet another floodtide.

"Yoni, listen."

"Yes," said Yonatan, feeling his heart grow limp with the sudden evaporation of his anger. "What."

"Listen, Yoni. It's like this. You and I are together. By ourselves. Close to each other, as you said we'd be. You're good, and I try to be beautiful for you, and not to copy others, but still to be the first. We almost always get along. And if sometimes something goes wrong or annoys you, like a minute ago when I told you not to cry and you got angry, it's still all right. I know you'll calm down in the end and we'll feel good with each other again. Maybe you think new things should happen all the time, but that isn't so. I'm not telling you to look at other people, but if you do look at them anyway, you'll see that new things don't happen to them every day either. What should happen, Yoni? You're a grown man. I'm your wife. This is home. All this is us. And it's the middle of the winter."

"It's not that, Rimona," said Yonatan, almost in a whisper.

"I know. You suddenly got sad," said Rimona, running one finger along the table. Then, with an uncharacteristically rebellious movement, she rose and stood before him.

"Have you gone completely out of your mind? What are you undressing for?"

The rebellion ended. She blanched and dropped both arms.

"I just thought that maybe," she said, trembling.

"Put your sweater back on. No one told you to undress. I don't need you with your clothes off."

"I just thought," she whispered.

"It's all right," said Yonatan. "Never mind. You're all right." He nodded once or twice, as if in wholehearted agreement with himself, and said no more. Neither, seated across from him again, did she. The music grew soft and tranquil. In a minute it would fade away and be gone. Rimona reached for the cigarettes, took one, lit it with a match, and began to cough until the tears came, because she didn't smoke. With a gentle, careful movement she stuck it between Yonatan's lips.

"That's how it is," he said.

"What is, Yoni?"

"Everything. You. Me. Everything. Did you say something? No, I know you didn't. Then say something, goddamn it! Say anything, scream, tell me what's on your mind, if anything ever is. What next? What's going to happen to you? To me? What exactly is going on in that little head of yours?"

"The winter will end," said Rimona. "Then spring and summer will come. We'll go somewhere on vacation. Maybe to upper Galilee, or the seashore. We'll sit on the porch in the evening watching the stars come out or the full moon rise. Do you remember once telling me that the moon has a dark side where everyone goes when they die? You shouldn't frighten me like that, because I believe whatever you tell me, and I don't stop believing it until I hear you say you were only joking. And then at the end of the summer you'll be called up as usual to the reserves, and when that's over, you'll take two days off from work and tell me about the new people you met and the new equipment your unit has. It will still be hot, and when you're done working for the day, you can sit on the lawn with Udi and Anat and talk politics. At night they'll come over for coffee and two of you will play chess."

"And then?"

"Then it will be autumn again. You'll go to the all-kibbutz chess tournament and maybe win another medal. When you come home, it will be time for winter plowing. Your brother Amos will get out of the army and maybe he'll marry Rachel. You'll start picking lemons and grapefruit, and then oranges, and you and Udi will be busy all day getting the shipments out on time. But I'll ask you just the same, and you'll agree, to turn the soil in the garden so that I can plant chrysanthemums again, and other winter flowers too. And then winter will come back, and we'll light the heater and sit here together, and it can rain and rain all it wants and we won't get wet."

"And then?"

"Yoni, what's wrong with you?"

Yonatan jumped up from his chair and savagely stubbed out his cigarette in the ashtray. Tensing his neck, he thrust his head forward on the bias, a movement that resembled his father's attempts to hear. A cowlick fell into his eyes and he brushed it roughly away.

"But I can't take it any more! I can't go on like this!" His voice was choked and seemed on the verge of panic.

Rimona looked at him quietly, as if he had said nothing more than please turn off the radio.

"You want to go away."

"Yes."

"With me or without me?"

"By myself."

"When?"

"Soon. In a few days."

"And I'll stay here?"

"That's up to you."

"Will you be gone for long?"

"I don't know. Yes. For a long time."

"And what will there be for us afterwards?"

"I don't know what there will be for us. What's this 'for us' stuff? Who says there has to be anything for us? What am I, your father or something? Look. I can't go on like this any longer. It's that simple."

"But you'll come back in the end."

"Are you asking me or telling me?"

"I'm hoping."

"Then don't. You can stop hoping. It's a waste of your time."

"Where will you go?"

"Somewhere. I don't know. We'll see. What difference does it make?"

"Will you study?"

"I might."

"And then?"

"I don't know. Why keep asking? I don't know anything now. Stop grilling me as if I were a criminal."

"But you'll come sometimes."

"Would you like me to?"

"If you feel like coming, you'll come, and if you want to go again, you'll go. It can be whenever you want. I won't change a thing in the house or cut my hair as I thought I would do in the spring. Sometimes you'll want to come to me, and then I'll be here for you."

"No, I'll want to stay away. Maybe I'll even go overseas, to America or somewhere."

"You want to be far away from me."

"I want to be far away from here."

"From me."

"All right. Yes. From you."

"And from your parents and your brother Amos and all your friends."

"Yes. That's right. Far away from here."

Rimona lowered her shoulders. She slowly touched her upper lip with a fingertip, like a slow pupil working on a math problem. He bent over to see her tears. There were no tears. She seemed supremely concentrated, lost in thought. Her attentiveness had lapsed and wandered back to the music. It's that radio, thought Yonatan. All that music has completely spaced her out. Ever so quietly she's going out of her mind, or else she's been a total halfwit all along and I just didn't notice. She's not even listening to me but to the music. It goes in one ear and out the other like the ticking of a clock or the sound of the rain in a drainpipe.

"Turn off that radio. I'm talking to you."

Rimona turned it off. Irately, as if that were not enough, Yonatan yanked the plug from the socket. There was a moment's silence. The rain outside had stopped. From the neighboring apartment came the sound of something falling, as if a tower of blocks had collapsed on the rug. The neighbors laughed.

"Listen, Rimona," said Yonatan.

"Yes."

"I guess I should start explaining, why and how and since when. That's hard for me."

"You don't have to explain."

"No? You mean to tell me you're so smart you don't need any explanations?"

"Yonatan. Look. I don't understand what's the matter with you, but I don't want you to start explaining. People always want to explain and understand, as if life were just a matter of explanations and solutions. When my father lay dying in the hospital of cancer, and I sat next to him all day without talking, just holding his hand, the doctor came by and said, 'Young lady, if you'd care to step into my office for a few minutes, I'll explain the situation to you,' and I said, thank you, doctor, there's no need to, and he must have thought I was either callous or an imbecile. And when I gave birth to Efrat and they told us she was stillborn, and Dr. Schillinger in Haifa wanted to explain it to us, you yourself, Yoni, said, 'What is there to explain? She's dead.' "

"Rimona, please. Don't bring that up now. Not that."

"I'm not."

"You're all right," said Yonatan uncertainly, his voice betraying a momentary wave of affection. "You're just a strange girl."

"It isn't that, though," said Rimona. She stared at him, and then, as if fathoming the tip of some obscure idea, she added, "It's hard for you."

Yonatan didn't answer. He laid his broad, ugly hand on the table close to Rimona's pale, thin fingertips, taking great care not to graze them. The contrast with his own stubby fingers with their hairy knuckles and nails black from engine oil pleased and soothed him. In some enigmatic way it seemed not only just but comforting.

"When do you intend to do it?" asked Rimona.

"I don't know. In two weeks. Maybe a month. We'll see."

"You'll have to tell your parents. There'll be all sorts of meetings. Everyone will talk about it. There'll be lots and lots of talk."

"Let them talk. What do I care."

"But you'll have to talk too."

"I have nothing to say to them."

"And I'll have to prepare all kinds of things for you to take with you."

"Please, Rimona. Do me a favor. Don't prepare anything. What's there to prepare? Nothing. I'll just throw a few things in my knapsack and take off. I'll just pick up and go."

"If you'd rather I didn't, I won't."

"Right. All I want is for you to keep cool during the next

few days. And if it's not too much to ask, to try not to hate me too much."

"I don't hate you. You're mine. Will you be taking Tia?"

"I don't know. I hadn't thought about her. Maybe. Yes."

"Do you want to talk some more? No, you don't."

"Right."

She fell silent again. Yet it was not an ordinary silence. It was as if she were listening, as if now that the talking had ceased she could concentrate on hearing alone. After a brief interval she took his hand in both her own, glanced at his watch, and said, "It's almost eleven now. If you'd like, we can listen to the news and go to sleep. We have to be up early."

Yonatan felt her fingers on his wrist. A moment later he felt them on his shoulder, because he still hadn't answered. Was she saying, "Listen to me, Yoni, what I wanted to say was that it's almost eleven and you'll miss the news, and besides, you're terribly tired and so am I, so let's go to sleep"?

Her fingers were still on his shoulder. His hand reached out and groped for the coffee mug on the table, but when he raised it to his lips, it was empty.

When the baby was stillborn at the end of the previous summer, Yonatan drove straight to the hospital from the citrus groves in his work clothes and sat on a hard bench outside the maternity ward all afternoon and evening. When night came, someone said to him, "Why don't you go to sleep now, fellow, and come back in the morning." But he refused to leave and continued sitting there with a crossword puzzle on his knees that couldn't be solved because it had been misprinted, all its Downs and Acrosses confused. Close to midnight an ugly old nurse with a flattened nose and a hairy black mole like a blind, third eye stepped out of the ward. "Excuse me, nurse," he said, "maybe you could tell me what's going on in there." And she answered him in a voice rubbed raw by cigarettes and worries, "Look, you're the husband, you know your wife's not a simple case. We're doing our best but she's not a simple case. As long as you're here, you might as well make yourself some coffee in the staff kitchen. Just don't leave a mess." At three in the morning the same god-awful-looking woman appeared again and said, "Lifshitz, try to be strong. Women can have normal births even after more than one such mishap. Two hours ago we decided to get Professor Schillinger himself out of bed for you. He drove all the way from the outskirts of Mount Carmel just in time to save, I literally mean save, your wife's life. He's still working on her now. Perhaps he'll have a few minutes to talk to you when he's done, but please don't keep him too long. Tomorrow, I mean today, he has several operations to perform and he isn't a young man any longer. Meanwhile, make yourself another cup of coffee in the kitchen but please leave it clean."

Yonatan shouted, "What did you do to her?" The nurse replied, "Young man, I'll ask you not to shout here. Really, what's the matter with you? Stop behaving like a caveman. Try to think logically. You'll see that all that matters is that your wife is alive. Professor Schillinger literally revived her. Instead of being thankful for the blessing you've received, you stand here shouting. She'll be all right and the two of you are young."

Outside, by the hospital gate, the dusty, decrepit old jeep that belonged to the field hands was waiting for him. Completely forgetting that they would need it for work by four or four-thirty, he started it up and headed southward until he ran out of gas some thirty kilometers past Beersheba. A hot, sandstormy morning was breaking beneath a grimy sky. The desert was gray and shabby, its hills like garbage dumps, and beyond its huge mountain peaks like scrap metal running the length of the horizon. Yonatan left the jeep, walked a short distance, relieved himself, lay down, and fell fast asleep in the sand. Three paratroopers passing by in a command car woke him. Get up, you crazy nut, they said, we thought you'd killed yourself or been slaughtered by the Bedouin. Yonatan looked around him at the filthy, shifting sand dunes polluting the air with dust and at the hideous mountains in the distance.

Yonatan turned on the radio, but the station was off the air. He took a sheet and blankets from the linen chest, and went to the bathroom to wash up and brush his teeth. When he emerged, Rimona had already made their bed and was setting the clock by the twelve o'clock news from the army broadcasting service. The announcer expressed grave concern over the possible results of the conference of Arab military chiefs scheduled for the next day in Cairo. The situation gave signs of rapid deterioration. Yonatan said he was going out to the porch for a last cigarette and then forgot to do so. Rimona undressed in the shower as usual, reappearing in the heavy brown flannel nightgown that resembled a winter coat. When they woke Tia from her snooze at the foot of the table, she arched her back, shook herself, let out a yawn that turned to a thin whine, padded to the front door, and waited to be let out. A few minutes later she was let back in, and the lights were turned out.

4

That night, in the darkness of the barber's half of the shack near the farm sheds, Azariah Gitlin lay with open eyes, listening to the groans of the old, wind-tossed eucalyptus trees and to the tiny fists of rain on the tin roof while his mind whirred with musings about himself, his secret mission, and the love of the members of Kibbutz Granot that should and would be his as soon as they realized who he really was.

He thought of the kibbutzniks' eyes following his entrance into the dining room, of the old pioneers, their faces brown as mahogany even in the dead of winter, of the young men, so bulky and slow-moving that some of them seemed like drowsy wrestlers, and of the young women, whispering to each other, no doubt about him, as they watched him come in—buxom, golden girls who, for all their simple dress, brimmed with a saucy femininity that suggested a knowledge of things you never dream of.

Azariah longed to get to know all these people right away,

to talk to them, to win their hearts, to arouse their strongest emotions; to slip past their defenses and touch their private lives as profoundly as he could. If only he could skip over the awkwardness of the first few days and step right into the middle of things. He wanted to let them all know that now that he had arrived their life would never be the same. Perhaps he would give guitar recitals in the dining room that would stir the weariest heart among them. Then he would share the ideas he had suffered so hard to arrive at during his long years of solitude, his very own thoughts about justice, politics, love, art, and the meaning of life. He would make these people admire him, love him, for his passionate inner strength. Around him would gather the young ones whose spirits had been dulled by their humdrum lives and the toll of hard physical work. He would give lectures that would rekindle their enthusiasm. He would found a discussion club. He would write articles for their newsletter. He would astonish even Yolek with his historical insights into the Ben-Gurion era. His arguments would carry the day in every debate.

Before long, all would know that a rare soul had come to live among them. They would begin coming to him with their problems and with requests for his opinions. In their dimly lit bedrooms, they would talk about him in hushed tones. An uncanny fellow, they would say. And the loneliness in his eyes! the young women would add. They would choose him to represent their kibbutz. He would appear at movement conferences where he would blaze new trails and demolish old shibboleths. Oh, how he would astound them with the revolutionary power of his thought! His words would batter down the breastworks, as strangers he never had met would be discussing him in a hundred different places. At first they would say: You know who we mean, that new fellow who got up at the last conference and gave it to them but good in four brilliant minutes that they'll never forget. After a while it would be: Azariah? He's the latest discovery, a rising new star; we're sure to hear more of him.

Eventually people would ask: Can you believe that there are

still some old bags who refuse to accept the Gitlin approach? The leaders of the movement, still reluctant to commit themselves, yet consumed by curiosity and doubt, would declare: That's all very well, but why doesn't he come around for a serious talk? Let's have a good look at him and hear what he has to say. And when he had left their offices, they would confess: No question about it, he swept us off our feet. The boy's a real find. In time the press would sniff him out too. And the radio. Inquiries would be made and background information sought from the kibbutz. The mystery of his origins and life story would amaze them. How little is actually known about him, they would report. One winter night he simply walked in from the dark.

Crotchety reactionaries would argue with him in the weekend magazine sections. At great length they would attempt to squelch his explosive ideas but in vain. Four or five lines of rebuttal would suffice to crush them, such was the elegant but merciless juggernaut of his wit. Yet in closing, he would always pat their elderly shoulders: Nonetheless, I must credit my opponents for their contributions to the intellectual outlook of their own generation.

A nationwide debate would arise over the new concept, whose founder and leading spokesman was Azariah Gitlin. Fresh forces would rally around him. Young women would write letters to the editor in his defense. Budding poetesses would seek his company. One would even dedicate a poem to him entitled "The Eagle's Lonely Sorrow." Celebrities, famous pundits, representatives of the foreign press would come to exchange views. He would be referred to as a visionary for the times. And all the while he would stubbornly refuse to leave the barber's room or the shack. Repeatedly, to everyone's amazement, he would turn down the kibbutz's offer of a better room. In this ramshackle cabin, small groups of young activists would assemble from all over the country. How startled they would be to discover that Azariah Gitlin's sole earthly possessions were a metal bed, a wobbly table, a decrepit old chest, one chair, and a guitar. These and the numerous bookshelves lining the walls would bear silent witness to the ascetic severity of his life and to long nights of arduous thought. Why, the carpenter who volunteered one morning to make those shelves was the very same brusque young man who had been the first to encounter him upon his arrival in the kibbutz.

His guests would sit on the floor, hanging on his every word, only rarely interrupting to ask for a clarification. There was no way, the pretty girls would whisper to one another, absolutely no way to persuade him to move to better quarters. Here is where he was put that first night, and here is where he is going to stay. The man has absolutely no material wants. Sometimes, late at night, we wake and hear as in a dream the chords of his guitar. Between sessions, one of these barefoot girls would volunteer to make coffee for all of those assembled. With a generous smile he would thank her. Later, the visitors would take their leave, and a new group would arrive, some from afar, for inspiration, guidance, or simply to bask in his presence. He would exhort them all to prepare for a protracted struggle. He would preach the need for perseverance. He would reject out of hand all political gimmicks and tactical adventures.

Of course, he would make deadly enemies. He would take them on in the newspapers, compassionately yet ironically citing Spinoza or some other celebrated thinker, as required. His tone would be forgiving, as if the Old Guard consisted not of angry ancients but of hot-headed Young Turks, whose attacks on him he so pitied that he would not stoop to rub salt into their bruised and battered pride.

One day, perhaps even by next summer, Prime Minister Eshkol would inquire of his inner circle about this eighth wonder of the world. Why not bring the lad to see me so that I can size him up myself? When Azariah was invited to Eshkol's office, the secretary would allot him ten minutes. Half an hour later, Eshkol would order her to hold the calls. He would be sitting in his chair not uttering a word, overwhelmed by Azariah's analysis of the nation's affairs. From time to time he would dare to pose a question, jotting down the answers in pencil on little scraps of paper. The hours would go by. Evening would descend outside the windows, yet Eshkol would refrain from turning on the lights, so rapt would he be in the revelations of Azariah's monastic years. Finally, he would rise from his seat, lay his hands on Azariah's shoulders, and say, "*Yingele,* from now on you're staying with me. Consider yourself nationalized. As of seven o'clock tomorrow morning, your place will be here at my side, in that room over there that can be reached only through my private office so you'll be on tap whenever I need you. But for now, what I'd like to ask is your opinion of Nasser's true intentions and how we can rally our nation's youth around the flag."

It would be late at night before he finally emerged from the Prime Minister's office. Shapely secretaries would exchange whispers as he passed, his shoulders slightly stooped, his face exhibiting neither pride nor triumph, but responsibility tempered by sadness.

And one day Yolek Lifshitz, the secretary of Kibbutz Granot, would say to his friend Hava, "Well? Who was it who discovered our Azariah, eh? It was me, that's who, although I was nearly dumb enough to chuck him down the stairs. I'll never forget how he turned up here that winter night, a shady-looking character if ever there was one, and wetter than a drowned cat. Just look what's become of him now!"

The one thing Azariah did not think about was the work awaiting him in the tractor shed the next day. Since he had failed, after a desultory search, to find the light switch, the dusty, naked bulb still shone feebly from the ceiling. A haze settled over his mind. Unable to get warm beneath the thin woolen blanket, he lay shivering from the cold. Sometime after midnight he heard a monotonous chant from the other side of the plywood partition, a kind of shrill prayer or incantation in a language that was neither Hebrew nor anything else, its accents guttural like the desert's and as though risen from the depths of some evil slumber:

"Why do the heath'm rage 'n' people imag'm vain things 'bout God 'n' 'bout His Messiah . . . He was lowly 'n' we 'steemed 'm not . . . He was more hon'lable than thirty but he 'tained not to Thee . . . And King David 'pointed 'm over his guard . . . Asael brother of Yo-o-av . . . 'n' his cousin Elha-a-nan . . . 'n' Helez the Paltite . . . 'n' Ira son of Ikesh Tekoo-o-ite . . . 'n' Zalmon A-hoooo-hite . . . He was loath'en'd, he had'a no form nor come-leeee-ness. . . ."

Azariah Gitlin got out of bed and tiptoed barefoot to the partition. Through a crack in the plywood he glimpsed a tall, thin man sitting on a low stool, wrapped in a blanket reaching over his head, a needle in each hand and on his knees a ball of red yarn. He was knitting.

Azariah returned to bed and tried cuddling up beneath the blanket. The wind howling outside knifed into the shack through the chinks between the planks, and the rough woolen blanket scratched his skin. Desperately trying to reanimate the magical power of his thoughts he lay there half-awake and half-asleep until nearly morning, longing for the women who would come to love him, comfort him, and wait on him body and soul. Two of them, young and full-bodied, who would be utterly shameless about having him in their power, lying as he was on his back with his eyes shut tight and his heart pounding madly away.

The morning was vile. Misty vapors swirled among the houses. It was biting cold.

At half-past-six, as requested by a note slipped under his door, Yonatan Lifshitz arrived to take the new mechanic to work. He found him fully awake and engaged in light calisthenics. Over greasy coffee in a corner of the dining hall, whose fluorescent lights were already on because of the dimness of the morning, the newcomer talked a blue streak and Yonatan understood hardly a word. It struck him as comical that his charge had dressed for work in clean clothes and a pair of ordinary walking shoes. The questions he put to Yonatan were queer too. When and how had Kibbutz Granot been founded? Why had it been built on the slope of the hill instead of on the hilltop or in the valley below? Was there archival material available from its pioneering days? Was there any point in trying to get the founders of the kibbutz to talk about those times for the record? Would they tell the truth, or would they simply glorify their own works? And the price they paid: Did many of them really lose their lives to Arab marauders, malaria, heat stroke, killing work?

Most of these queries the young man answered himself, and with considerable astuteness, perhaps even some knowledge. Now and then he let drop some bon mot about the eternal, tragic conflict between high ideals and gray realities, or between the social vision of the revolutionary and the passions of the human heart. At one point Yonatan thought he caught the phrase "the clear, certain premises of our mental life," and he began to feel a weary longing for some clear, bright faraway meadow bathed in sunlight by the banks of a broad river, perhaps in Africa. Once that image faded, he had a faint desire to know what might be eating this young man so early in the morning. Yet this desire too faded rapidly. The rawness of the weather and his own fatigue made Yonatan bunch up inside his clothes. Water leaking through his torn boot was freezing the tips of his toes. What was there to keep him from proclaiming himself sick like his father and half the kibbutz and going back to his room this very minute? No. On a day that should have been declared an official bed day, he had to show this yackety mechanic the rounds.

"Let's go," he said, disgruntled, pushing away his mug. "Come on, let's head for the tractor shed. Have you finished your coffee?"

Azariah jumped up from his seat. "A long while ago. I'm one-hundred-percent at your service."

To this remark he added his full name, volunteered the information that the secretary of the kibbutz had told him that Yonatan's name was Yonatan and that he and Hava were his parents. He concluded by quoting some little proverb.

"This way," said Yonatan. "Watch out. These steps are slippery."

"The laws of nature are such," said Azariah, "that there are no accidents. Whatever happens is necessary and predestined, even slipping on these steps."

Yonatan did not reply. He neither liked nor trusted words. Yet he was well aware that most people were in need of more love than they ever received and that this sometimes made them try to make friends with total strangers in the most ludicrous ways, including talking too much. He's like a lost wet puppy, thought Yonatan, wagging not only his tail but his whole rear end to get me to like him and pet him. Fat chance! You're barking up the wrong tree, pal.

While the two of them passed farm sheds, navigated puddles, and sloshed through mud, the young man kept up his steady stream of talk. Yonatan withdrew from his silence only twice—once to ask the newcomer if he had been born in Israel, and again to inquire if he had ever worked on, or at least had a good look at, a D-6 Caterpillar engine.

Azariah answered no to both questions. He had been born in the Diaspora (it struck Yonatan as odd that he didn't say "abroad" or simply name the country he had come from) and knew nothing about Caterpillar tractors. Not that it mattered. In his opinion, backed by experience, engines everywhere, whatever their differences, were close relatives. Once you had doped out one, you understood them all. Anyway, he would do his best. The worm and the man both do what they can. Yonatan wondered where his father had ever managed to dig up such a creep.

The corrugated tin walls of the tractor shed only made the cold day worse. The slightest contact with anything metal froze one's fingers at once. Congealed oil, dust, mildew, and filth were everywhere. In the joints of the rafters, among the tool chests and crates of spare parts, even on the tractors, tribes of spiders had spun upside-down cathedrals. Tools were scattered, as if in anger, about an abandoned-looking yellow machine smeared with mud and black oil, its innards exposed. On the treads, on the tattered driver's seat, in the folds of the hood that had been thrown to the floor were wrenches, pliers, screwdrivers, bolts, and iron rods. A beer bottle half filled with some slimy liquid, rubber belts, torn sacks, and rusted gears lay all over. And the whole derelict place was pervaded by the acrid chemical smell of lubricants, burned rubber, and kerosene and diesel fumes.

Yonatan, whose mood blackened every time he entered the shed, glanced about with a sullen, defiant look. The new mechanic began hopping around the tractor engine in his spotless clothes like some sort of vainglorious grasshopper. Finally he came to a halt at the front of the engine, struck a pose as if for an official photograph, and joyously launched into a manifesto.

"A brand-new time, a brand-new place, and I'm brand-new too. Every beginning is a birth, and every ending, no matter what is ended, brings with it the taint of death. All things should be accepted calmly and with a light heart, because fate in its many disguises always stems from the same eternal decree, just as it must forever be the essence of a triangle that the sum of its three angles always equals one-hundred-and-eighty degrees. If you were to think about this fact for a minute, Yonatan, you would be surprised to realize that not only is it true, it can also give us the most wonderful peace of mind. To accept all things, to understand all things, and to respond to all things with perfect inner tranquillity! Mind you, I don't deny that a part of what I say comes from the philosopher Spinoza, who, by the way, was a diamond polisher by profession. Well, I've told you in a nutshell what I believe in. And you, Yonatan, what do you believe in?"

"I," said Yonatan distractedly, unintentionally kicking over an empty can of engine oil, "am freezing my ass off and getting sick. If you ask me, we should pour a little gasoline beneath that barrel of diesel oil over there, put a match to it, make a great big bonfire, and burn down this whole fucking tractor shed with all its fucking tractors once and for all. Just to get warm. Look, this is the patient. With a little good will you can get it to turn over, but after two or three minutes it conks out. Don't ask me why. I don't know why. All I know is that a note slipped under my door last night told me to take the new mechanic living next to Bolognesi to the tractor shed in the morning. If you really are one, why don't you see what's wrong with this damn thing while I sit down and rest my legs."

Azariah Gitlin complied with enthusiasm. Having rolled up his pants cuffs with his fingertips in a way that reminded Yonatan of a fashion model fingering the hem of her dress in a newsreel, the young man climbed gingerly onto one of the tractor treads to study the engine. From this vantage point, without turning around to face Yonatan, he posed two or three simple questions that the latter was able to answer. When he asked yet another, Yonatan replied from his seat on an overturned crate, "If I knew the answer to that, I wouldn't need you here in the first place."

Azariah Gitlin did not take offense. He nodded several times, as if understanding Yonatan's dilemma only too well, made some vague remark about the importance of creative intuition even in purely technical matters, and patiently blew a puff of warm breath across his musicianly fingers.

"Well, what do you say?" asked Yonatan indifferently, noting at the same time, much to his surprise, a glow of affection on the newcomer's face. For whom or what that affection was meant, however, he had not the slightest inkling.

"I have a big favor to ask of you," Azariah sang out.

"Yes?"

"If it's not too much trouble, could you please try starting it up? I want to listen to it. And, of course, to look too. Then we'll see what conclusions we can come to."

Yonatan's reservations, which had been growing steadily, now turned to outright distrust. Nevertheless, he climbed into the driver's seat and switched on the ignition. It took four or five tries before the staccato retching of the starter yielded to the hoarse, steady, ear-splitting roar of the engine. As though repressing some unconscionable desire, the ponderous engine began to shake and shudder.

Meticulously, taking care not to dirty his clean clothes, Azariah stepped down from the tread and backed away from the engine. Like an artist who retreats to the opposite end of his studio to get a better view of his canvas, he chose to stand at the maximum distance, in the far corner of the shed, beside the oil and fuel drums, flanked by some filthy straw brooms and a pile of old, used springs. Shutting his eyes in a gesture of supreme concentration, he listened to the raucous growl of the engine as if it were a madrigal sung by a distant choir, among whose myriad voices it was his job to pick out the only one that was flat.

As absurd as this performance seemed to Yonatan, watching from his seat on the crate, it was also somehow touching. Was it because the young stranger was so very strange?

A sharp, high whistle rose above the din. Like a public speaker suffering from throat strain, the tractor broke into a series of hoarse coughs. These were progressively stifled until brief stretches of silence could be heard. Finally, after five or six sharp backfires, the engine fell silent. From outside the shed, shrill, bitter, and piercing, came the caws of birds screaming in the wind. Azariah Gitlin opened his eyes.

"That's it?" he asked with a smile.

"That's it," said Yonatan. "It's the same every time."

"Did you ever try putting it into gear as soon as it starts?"

"What do you think?" said Yonatan.

"And what happened?"

"What do you think?"

"Listen," concluded Azariah. "It's all very strange."

"You're telling me." Yonatan said dryly. He no longer had the slightest doubt that the newcomer was not just another queer fish but an out-and-out imposter.

"What I'm telling you," said Azariah Gitlin gently, "is that curiosity may have killed the cat, but it's haste that killed the bear."

Yonatan did not reply.

"And now," said Azariah Gitlin, "I need some time to think. If you don't mind, I'll take a few minutes to do it."

"To think?" snickered Yonatan. "Why not? Be my guest." He rose, picked up a ripped, greasy sack, sat down again on the crate, wrapped the tattered burlap around his torn boot, and lit himself a cigarette. "Fine. You go ahead and think. When you're done, raise your right hand."

He had not yet finished the cigarette when, to his utter amazement, the young man declared, "I'm done."

"You're done what?"

"I'm done thinking."

"And what, may I ask, did you think of?"

"I thought," said Azariah hesitantly, "that maybe, when you finish your cigarette, we might start working on this tractor."

The entire repair job was performed by Yonatan himself and took no more than twenty minutes. Clean, pale, and alert, Azariah Gitlin stood looking on, telling him exactly what to do as if reading instructions from a manual, presiding over the operation from afar like one of those grandmasters Yonatan had read about who play blind chess without pieces or a board. Only once in the course of the proceedings did the young man bother to step onto a tread and peer into the bowels of the engine. Using the tip of a screwdriver, he adjusted a contact with a watchmaker's precision and then climbed down again, taking great pains to avoid the grime.

As soon as the tractor was started up, it began to gurgle steadily and softly like a purring animal. The gears were successfully tested. The engine ran for ten minutes without a hitch. At last Yonatan switched it off and said in a voice that sounded too loud in the sudden silence, "Yup. That's it."

He couldn't decide whether the newcomer was a magician or

a mechanical genius, or whether the whole problem had been so simple to begin with that he could have easily solved it himself had he not been so tired, cold, and preoccupied during the last few days.

Azariah Gitlin, on the other hand, celebrated his little triumph with a delirious outbreak, slapping his companion repeatedly on the back and singing his own praises until Yonatan was thoroughly revolted. He reveled in recounting the times he had miraculously confounded his enemies, among whom were an evil major called Zlotshin, or Zlotshnikov, a beautiful female officer in an army garage with deeply ambivalent feelings about him, and that Ph.D. idiot in engineering from the Haifa Technion who failed to come up with some mechanical solution that he, Azariah, had hit upon at once. He talked about his brainstorms, about the human brain in general, about Major Zlotkin or Zlotnik, who had been driven mad by envy, about her seductive advances, about some revolutionary technical device developed by him but cunningly pirated away by Major Zlotshkin's brother-in-law, who made a mint with it, and bought some nice little island in the eastern Aegean, from which he bombarded Azariah with letters full of threats, expressions of admiration, and offers of joint ventures.

Yonatan half listened to all this in ponderous silence. At last Azariah fell silent too, only to wipe off a bluish oil stain that had spattered on the tip of his shoe.

"All right," said Yonatan. "It's a quarter-past-eight. Let's go have breakfast in the dining hall. Then we'll come back and see what else needs to be done around here."

On their way to the dining hall, still compulsively talking, Azariah told two different jokes about passengers on Polish trains, one involving an anti-Semitic priest and the other a big fat general, both of whom, the first despite his great malice and the second despite his great strength, were outwitted by the Jews. He alone laughed at the punch lines, which caused him nervously to joke some more about all the old canards that no one laughed at but their tellers.

Yonatan noticed for the first time that the newcomer had a faint accent. It was so well concealed as to be barely identifiable. The "l's" were a bit too soft, the "r's" slightly prolonged, and the "k's" sometimes expelled from the palate as if he had swallowed something distasteful. Obvious effort had gone into overcoming this accent. Perhaps this effort, or the speed with which he spoke, was why Azariah so often tripped over his own words, nearly choking on some of them. At such times he would break off in mid-sentence, only to fling himself back into the breach at once.

No two lonelinesses are ever alike, thought Yonatan. If two people could really have anything in common, it might be possible for them to become truly close. Just look at this poor bastard trying so hard to cheer me up and make me laugh when he's so unhappy himself. You can see he's all twisted inside—too sensitive, too cocksure, too obsequious, and all at the same time. We get all kinds of strange types here, and they go on being strange to the end. Some of them go all out to make friends with us and fit in, but after a couple of weeks or months, they can't take it any more and they split. Either we forget all about them or remember them only because of something funny, like that middle-aged divorcée two years ago who decided to make a play for old Stutchnik of all people. Rachel Stutchnik caught them one night listening to Brahms in the music room, him in her lap. Easy come, easy go. Maybe he thinks that being the secretary's son, I've been appointed to look him over and report back. Why else would he be freaking out like this to make me love him at first sight? But who could love a weirdo like him? I'd be the last one to. Especially now, when I can't even stand my own self. Maybe some other time I might have tried to like him or get him to calm down. He'll climb the walls here, and when he's had it, he'll clear out. Relax, pal. Take it easy.

A light, pinpointy rain was falling. The wind sharpened the pins and sent them flying in every direction. The electric wires were pricked by them too and hummed an odd tune.

"After breakfast," said Yonatan, "you should go to the storeroom and ask for a pair of work clothes. You'll find Peiko's old boots in that crate behind the diesel oil. Peiko's the man who ran this place for years."

When the two of them stopped to wash up at the stand outside the dining hall, Azariah's long, wistful, delicate fingers caught Yonatan's eye. The sight of them made him think of Rimona. And at that very moment he saw her sitting with some friends at the far end of the hall, grasping a mug of tea with both hands. He knew that it was still full and that she was holding it, as usual, to warm her fingers. For a second he wondered what she might be thinking about this morning, but he scolded himself at once. What do I care what she's thinking? All I want is to be far away from them all.

Through breakfast Azariah Gitlin kept coming on strong, both to Yonatan and to the two other people who joined their table, Yashek and little Shimon from the sheep pen. Having introduced himself, he asked if he might have their names as well. Then, with a peculiar sort of merriment, he told them about his sleepless night in the barber's room, where, as if in some horror movie, a cracked voice on the other side of the wall began speaking at the stroke of midnight. He saw—waking or dreaming, he still couldn't say—a ghost mumbling all sorts of Biblical abracadabra in a dead tongue, Chaldean perhaps or Hittite.

He then related the tale of the tractor, fishing for compliments from Yonatan so that the other two men might be suitably impressed. Indeed, though less than a day had passed since his arrival in the kibbutz, and he had been urged to rest up for a few days before beginning work, a sixth sense had told him that there was no time to waste, which was why he rose early this morning and ran to the tractor shed, thus proving—or rather, demonstrating—no, the right word was justifying—yes, justifying the faith placed in him and the high hopes pinned on him. Of course, whatever praise he deserved was due to his intuition more than his knowledge or skill, since the minute he heard the sound of the engine he had had a brainstorm. As the saying went, "If his wagon is stuck in the mud, tell Ivan not to push but to put on his thinking cap."

Whenever one of his tablemates reacted to all this exuberance with a vague smile, Azariah guffawed loudly and redoubled his efforts. And when Yonatan poured two mugs of coffee and handed him one, he couldn't find enough words to thank him.

"A guiding hand brought Comrade Yonatan and me together from the start. You should have seen his warmth, his patience, his . . . when he broke me in on my new job. Such refinement, such tact! Why, he never says a word about himself."

"Knock it off," said Yonatan.

"What's the matter?" asked Yashek. "Why don't you let someone say a good word about you for a change?"

Little Shimon took a crumpled newspaper out of his pocket and turned to the sports section. The front-page headlines told of a brief, bitter battle between Israeli and Syrian armored forces along the northern border. At least three enemy tanks had been hit and gone up in flames. Syrian earthmoving equipment engaged in the Jordan diversion project had also been destroyed. A photograph showed the grinning general of the northern command surrounded by grinning soldiers in full battle gear.

Seeing this, Yashek remarked that he saw no end in sight.

Little Shimon, hiding behind the sports section, declared gruffly that if it weren't for the Russians he would take care of the Arabs quickly enough with one or two healthy kicks in the rear.

"We like to think everything depends on us. But it doesn't. Eshkol isn't exactly Napoleon. Some things don't depend on anyone," Yonatan said, more to himself than to the others.

At this point Azariah burst back into the conversation. He warned of the dangers of shortsightedness, explained where Ben-

Gurion had been mistaken on the one hand and Eshkol wrong on the other, quickly sketched the sinister mentality of the Russians while appealing to Svidrigailov and Ivan Karamazov, argued that Slavs were constitutionally incapable of moral inhibitions, and sought to cast a new light on the subject of Jewish destiny. Raising his voice insistently to court Yashek's attention and paying no heed to the glances being cast at him from neighboring tables, he undertook to expound the dialectic distinction between strategic ends and political means, and between both of these and the "national idea" that every civilization was based on. He predicted an imminent war, deplored the blindness prevailing everywhere, sketched possible international complications, suggested ways out of them, and, in light of all these factors, posed two basic questions for which he immediately volunteered the answers.

There was in all this an irresistible passion and a nervous power of imagination that, despite its bizarreness, caused even Yashek to nod twice and say, "That's so, that really is so." Thus egged on, Azariah launched into a fresh harangue on the wisdom of looking for what Spinoza called the "Ratio," that is, for the permanent laws underlying the multifarious phenomena wrongly labeled coincidence. But he soon noticed that the others had finished their breakfast and were waiting for him to pause for breath so they could get up and go. This realization, at the very time he was desperately trying to extricate himself from a lengthy sentence, led him to break off completely and turn back to his food. He began gulping it down so as not to keep anyone waiting, only to have it go down the wrong pipe and trigger an outburst of coughing.

"Take your time," Yonatan said calmly. "These two goof-offs are in a hurry because they haven't earned the salt in their salad yet, but we've already done a damn good job on that Caterpillar. Now we have all day." Outside, the gray rain continued to fall, stubbornly and insensibly, like a frozen madness.

That evening Azariah Gitlin, carrying his guitar, knocked on the Lifshitzes' door. Freshly shaved and washed, his curly locks dripping wet from the rain, he begged pardon for having come uninvited. Nevertheless, he had read somewhere that the kibbutzim had—and rightly so—done away with the rules of formal etiquette. Moreover, Yolek had suggested last night that he drop in on Yonatan and Rimona to get acquainted. Besides which, the room to which he had been assigned—the electric bulb was so weak he couldn't read a paper or book, much less write. And so he had decided to try his luck and drop by for a visit.

Yes, thank you, he would love a cup of coffee. There was an old Russian proverb that went, "The man who has no other friend will be the Devil's in the end." Not an exact translation, but at least he had preserved the rhyme. Were they sure he wasn't intruding? With their kind permission, he promised not to overstay his welcome. He had brought his guitar because it had occurred to him that Yonatan and his friend might like music, in which case he would gladly play a few simple tunes. Indeed, the three of them might even sing a bit. He had said "friend" rather than "wife" because that was the word, so right-sounding for a kibbutz, that he had heard Comrade Yolek use last night. How nice it was here.

Yes, their furniture was simple and comfortable, nothing fancy about it, and everything in the best of taste. Such coziness was just what his weary soul needed. He had no friends. Not one. For which he blamed only himself. Until now he hadn't known how to make friends and hadn't tried to find out. But from now on he would, so to speak, put his cards on the table and turn over a new leaf. And please excuse him for talking so much. Though the two of them might think him garrulous, they couldn't be more wrong. Yet the moment he set foot in the kibbutz he had felt himself among kindred souls, and this had made him open up. Everywhere in the world people were light-years away from one another, whereas here he felt such warmth, such togetherness. . . . Look, he wanted to show them his identity pass, not to prove who he was, but because of a pressed cyclamen between its pages that he had picked a year ago. He wanted to give this cyclamen to his friend Yonatan's friend. Please. It was, after all, only a token.

Rimona put the kettle on to boil. Yonatan set out a plate of small cakes and the Bokhara creamer. Tia shuffled over to the guest, pressed her nose against his knees, sniffed, sighed, and crawled off to lie beneath the couch, from where only her tail protruded; it thumped several times on the rectangular gray rug spread on the floor by the coffee table. Four carefully arranged rows of books stood on the shelves. Heavy brown curtains covered the window and the door leading out to the porch.

The whole room seemed to be at peace, even the picture on the wall, in which a dark bird perched on a red brick fence. Shamelessly piercing the surrounding murk like a golden spear was a diagonal shaft of sunlight. Lancing a brick at the bottom of the picture, it caused it to blossom into a nimbus of blinding light. The bird looked weary; its bill was slightly, thirstily agape, its eyes closed.

The electric kettle whistled. Rimona brought the coffee to the table. "You must like your new job," she said. "Yonatan tells me you're very good at it."

Careful to avoid her eyes, Azariah told her how happy it made him to have Yonatan as his first friend on the kibbutz. And of course, though two men stood no more chance of meeting than two mountain peaks if it wasn't predestined, he hardly need say that one's first encounters in a new place could be fateful. Incidentally, he once had read a fascinating article about the place of women in a kibbutz, but he did not agree with it. That is, he reserved his views on the subject. What did Rimona think? He himself suspected that the problem had yet to be solved.

"It's too bad," said Rimona, "that you came in the middle of winter instead of the beginning of summer. In winter everything is so sad and closed in. In summer the flowers are all in bloom, the lawns are green, the nights are much shorter and not so dark, and the days are very, very long. They're so long that sometimes a single one can seem like a week. And from our porch you can see the sunset."

"Except that by summer," said Yonatan, "we would have found someone else to work with the tractors and we might not have had room for you. The fact is that you came in the nick of time. To think that for three days I stood there like an idiot, staring at a simple gas block without realizing what the trouble was!"

"If you'll permit me to express a very different opinion," said Azariah, "I personally do not believe in chance. Everything that happens does so for a precise if unknowable reason. 'If the carriage is meant to break down, all the czar's coachmen can't get it to town.' Think, for instance, of an ordinary citizen named Yehoshafat Cantor, an arithmetic teacher, bachelor, stamp collector, and member of his building's tenants' committee. He steps out one evening for ten minutes of fresh air and gets in the way of a bullet fired accidentally, let us say, by a private detective cleaning his handgun on his back porch. The blast blows Cantor's head off. I say to you without the slightest hesitation that all the natural, social, and psychological sciences cannot begin to reconstruct the myriad events that conspired with uncanny precision to bring about this tragic death. Why, we're talking about the most incredible chain of circumstances, one involving infinitesimal fractions of seconds and millimeters, one composed of countless variables of time and space and weather, of optics and ballistics, of human wills and obstructions to those wills, of genetics, personal habits, education, of major and minor decisions, mishaps, errors, customs, the length of a news broadcast, the leap of a cat from a garbage pail, a child annoying its mother in a nearby alleyway, etcetera ad infinitum. And each single one of these circumstances has its own chain of causes going back to still other causes. All it takes is for one of these countless variables to be off, so to speak, by a hair's breadth to change the whole outcome. The bullet now flies in front of Cantor's nose, or passes through his sleeve, or parts the hair on his head. It may even blow out the brains of someone else—me, for example, or, perish the thought, one of you. Any one of these or other possibilities would in turn take its place in a new chain of circumstances leading to still other events beyond human ken, and so on and so forth.

"And what do we so cleverly do about it? In our ignorance, bewilderment, and fear—and perhaps, I should add, in our laziness and arrogance—we say that an unfortunate accident took place. And with this lie, this vulgar, ignorant falsehood we write the matter off.

"I can't remember when I last had such strong, good coffee. That may be one reason I'm talking too much. I've hardly said a word to a living soul for ages because I haven't had a soul to say one to. Even though the Bible teacher around whom I just constructed my little hypothesis may never actually exist, one grieves all the same for the death of a decent, dedicated man who may not have set the world on fire in the classroom, so to speak, but who never did the slightest harm to his country or his fellow man. These are delicious. Did you bake them yourself, Rimona?"

"They come from a box," said Rimona.

"I noticed this morning," said Yonatan, "that every little thing excites him."

"I'm sorry about that teacher," said Rimona.

"Yonatan," said Azariah, "has a sharp eye, so to speak. There's no point in pretending that I'm not excitable. Still, I'll say it again, my own governess never made pastry as good as this when I was a boy. I won't tire you now with stories about my governess, but sometime when your children are here I'll tell them all about her. Children love listening to me, especially the little ones. Maybe you know the legend of the Jewish peddler who came to a village of terrible Jew-killers and lured all their children after him with his flute until they drowned in a river. Little children would follow me through hell and high water, because I tell them the loveliest stories that are frightening but not too frightening."

"We happen," said Yonatan in a slow, sleepy voice, "not to have any children."

Azariah glanced up just as a profoundly bitter smile began to form around Rimona's lips without ever touching them. Before dying away, it momentarily reached her shaded eyes. Looking at neither of them, she said, "We had a little girl but lost her," adding, after a pause, "Whether or not it just happened, as you say, I don't know. But I'd like to know why it *had* to happen."

There was a silence. Yonatan rose, tall and very lean. He collected the empty coffee mugs and took them to the sink. While he was out of the room, Azariah noticed that Rimona's blond hair fell over her back and shoulders, more to the left than the right. He noticed the slender stem of her neck and the fine lines of her forehead and cheeks. She was, he thought, beautiful, and Yonatan was handsome, and he loved them both, even as he envied them. He winced to think of having pained them by mentioning children, and he felt shame and self-loathing to be almost glad to hear that they had none. I must make them happy now and always, he thought. I must get so close they'll never be able to do without me. Her pale, Christian beauty is so painful. I'll never let her know how vile I really am.

Azariah Gitlin vaguely began to hope that this girl might hurt him, do him some wrong, which she would have to make amends for. And yet he couldn't imagine how this might come about.

When Yonatan returned to the room, Azariah looked down at the floor and did not see him shut the copy of *Witches and Witch Medicine* that was lying open at the end of the couch. As he put it back in its place on the middle shelf, Azariah politely asked if he might smoke.

Yonatan took from his shirt pocket the pack of expensive American cigarettes that Azariah had given him that afternoon as a present and handed it to him.

"Long ago," said Azariah, "in ancient Greece, there was a

philosopher who believed that the soul resides in the body like a sailor in a ship. As lovely as that image is, it must be rejected. Another Greek philosopher wrote that the soul dwells in the body like a spider in its web, which in my own humble opinion is much closer to the truth. Using the powers of observation that I developed during my long, unhappy years of wandering, I noticed a good quarter of an hour ago that someone here must like to play chess. If I may be permitted to hazard a guess, that someone is you, Yonatan, not your friend."

As Yonatan opened the board and set up the pieces, Azariah delivered himself of a few boastful remarks, only to retract them at once and apologetically point out, "A great philosopher once observed that the winner of the Olympic medal was not necessarily the fastest man in Greece but simply the fastest man in the race."

Yonatan Lifshitz and Azariah Gitlin smoked and played in silence while Rimona sat by the radio with her bag of embroidery unopened in her lap, so intensely absorbed was she in a dream of her own. Yonatan's eyes kept filling with tears that he neither wiped away nor bothered to explain to his guest. Rimona had still not removed the pine branches from the vase since she had found no flowers to replace them.

After six or seven moves, Azariah blundered. He did his best to come up with a smile, remarking that, even though the game was as good as over almost before it had begun, for him it was no more than a first probe. Yonatan suggested that they begin again.

But Azariah refused. He blamed the thunder rolls outside for his inability to concentrate and, with a kind of irritable sportsmanship, insisted on playing to the bitter end. "He who has never tasted defeat will never know that triumph is sweet."

At this Rimona pressed her embroidery to her lap and looked up at him only to notice the many tiny, agitated wrinkles that came and went around his eyes. He had already single-handedly eaten every pastry on the large plate except for a sole survivor, a last concession to good manners that he kept absentmindedly picking up and putting down again. Once he even raised it all the way to his lips before giving a last-minute start and gently replacing it. Rimona opened her bag and began to embroider.

"That man you said was killed by the bullet. If he died instantly, that means he didn't suffer. Did you say his name was Yehoshafat?"

"That's right," said Azariah. "But I'm afraid I've only made you laugh at me. I always say the opposite of what I should."

"Your move," said Yonatan.

With a sudden burst of fervor, Azariah slid his remaining bishop along a diagonal that reached nearly from one end of the board to the other.

"Not bad," said Yonatan.

"Watch out!" crowed Azariah. "I'm just warming up!"

Indeed, within the space of a few moves, after recklessly sacrificing a knight and two pawns, the young man had reversed an apparently hopeless situation and was even threatening Yonatan's king.

"Do you see that?" he asked, flushed with success. At that exact moment, however, he seemed to run out of inspiration, unnecessarily losing another pawn and the initiative. Yonatan continued to play patiently, cagily, with calculated precision. Azariah, on the other hand, kept throwing away ingeniously gained advantages and committing mistakes that would have made a beginner blush.

Rimona put down her embroidery and went to open the window to air out the smoke-filled room. Tia rose too, arched her back, and moved closer to the table, panting in short, rapid breaths, her pink tongue hanging out, her eyes glued on her master and her ears cocked forward, as if straining not to miss a word or a move. Azariah Gitlin burst out laughing. "Give me time," he said, "and I'll teach your dog to play chess. You'd be surprised at what a dog can learn. Once, when I lived in a camp for new immigrants, I taught a Yemenite's goat to dance the hora."

Rimona shut the window, returned to the couch, and said, as if continuing her thoughts out loud, that it must be sad to have to spend so many hours alone in the barber's shack. In the bottom closet, she believed, was a small, unused electric kettle that they could lend to Azariah. Before he left she would also give him some coffee and sugar and a few pieces of the pastry that he liked so much.

"Check," said Azariah. His voice was cold.

"But what good does that do?" marveled Yonatan. "I can go here or here. Or here."

"I'm just pressing home the attack," said Azariah with a nervous giggle. "Thank you, Rimona," he added. "When you're being so nice to me, how could I possibly go and hurt Yonatan's feelings by inflicting, so to speak, a defeat on him."

"Your move," said Yonatan.

"As a gesture of friendship I offer you a draw."

"Hold on there," said Yonatan. "Why don't you first take a good look at what's happening to your rook. You're in bad trouble."

"If so, it's because I lost all interest in this banal, repetitious, and, if you don't mind my saying so, boring game at least ten minutes ago." Azariah's reply was almost a singsong.

"You," said Yonatan, "have lost."

"So I have," said Azariah, trying to force a comically gay expression.

"And I," said Yonatan, "have won."

"There now," said Rimona. "The kettle's boiling again."

They drank more coffee and Azariah demolished another plate of pastry. When it was all gone, he took his guitar out of its battered case, moved away from his hosts, and sat down on a footstool near the kitchen door. Tia went with him, sniffing at his shoes. At first he picked out two or three simple popular tunes, sometimes humming softly along, but then he started playing a melancholy melody that neither of them knew.

"That was sad," said Rimona.

Azariah flinched. "You didn't like it? I can play all kinds of things. Just tell me what."

"It was beautiful," said Rimona.

Thoughtfully, Yonatan gathered the survivors from the board and arranged them in two rows, black and white, on the table.

"That was just fine," he said. "I don't know much about music, but I could see that you played that piece very carefully, as if you were worried you might get carried away and snap the strings. It made me think of how quickly you figured out what was wrong with the Caterpillar. If you'd like, I'll say a word about you to Srulik. He's in charge of music around here. For now, though, we'd better think of going to the dining hall for supper."

"Comrade Yolek," said Azariah, "mistook me for that Srulik yesterday. I myself, of course, do not believe in pure coincidence. Everything happens for a reason."

Before he left, Rimona gave Azariah Gitlin the electric kettle, a bag of sugar, a can of coffee, and yet more pastry. Yonatan rummaged through drawers and found a new light bulb for Azariah's room. One look at it, though, was enough to establish that it wouldn't be any brighter than the old one.

Over supper Azariah once again began to lecture his hosts, which struck Yonatan as tiresome. He went on chewing in silence on a piece of bread while helping himself generously to the salad and a double portion of omelet. Rimona, however, listened attentively to every word. At one point, when she asked Azariah what he would do to stave off political disaster, it so went to his head that he forgot all about the vegetables she had just put on his plate. He began rehearsing an ingenious plan for engineering a big-power confrontation that would enable little Israel to slip safely away and even come out ahead.

During this recital, Etan R. stopped by their table and interrupted Azariah with a grin: "Well, well, I see you didn't get lost after all. I live in the last room by the swimming pool. If by any chance you find any justice around here, come tell me about it right away so we can nip it in the bud."

From across the hall, Yonatan's mother Hava waved hello. Little Shimon, mug in hand, came over to ask Yonatan to lend him the newcomer for a few days in the hope he might work some miracles in the sheep pen as well.

Before they parted and went their separate ways, Rimona invited Azariah, touching his elbow, to come again some evening to chat and play chess and to bring his guitar if he felt like it.

Once back in the barber's shack, Azariah thought of the picture that hung in Yonatan and Rimona's room, the dark, thirsty bird atop the brick wall, the surrounding murk, the diagnoal shaft of sunlight, and the flaming wound that shaft inflicted on a single brick in a lower corner. So I'm invited back to chat and play music and chess. She'll have to make up to me a lot more than that if she expects to be forgiven. Her baby girl died and now she doesn't even have that.

"He's a loudmouth, a cheat, a brown-nose, and a bullshitter," said Yonatan to Rimona, "and yet you can't help kind of liking him. I'm going over to talk to Udi about the fruit shipments. I won't be late."

A thick night hung over the kibbutz. The air was cold and raw, and the biting wind did not flag. It's a funny thing, thought Rimona, smiling in the darkness.

In the days that followed, Azariah Gitlin made still more repairs. His energy knew no bounds. He greased, tuned, and tightened; took apart and reassembled; changed dying batteries and readjusted fanbelts; washed, waxed, and polished. He undertook to reorganize the shed by arranging the work tools in a logical order, putting up a broad wooden board on which to hang screwdrivers, wrenches, and pliers according to size, labeling all the drawers and shelves, and scrubbing the filthy concrete floor with detergents. He persuaded Yonatan to climb up to the rafters to get rid of the spider webs and birds' nests underneath the tin roof. He catalogued the spare parts and took a full inventory. As a crowning touch, he clipped a large, colored photograph of the rotund Minister of Welfare from an illustrated weekly magazine and taped it to the wall. Every day from now on, plump-cheeked and jovial, Dr. Yosef Burg would look down on the men at work, imparting a self-satisfied bliss.

Azariah arrived early each morning in dark blue work clothes that were slightly too big on him and stood waiting for Yonatan to appear with the keys to the shed. Invariably, Yonatan would be sleepy, grouchy, and often teary-eyed, and Azariah would try to cheer him up with a story about one of the old grandmasters, giants like Alekhine, Capablanca, and Lasker, compared to whom such current aces as Botvinnik and Petrosian were, so to speak, abject nonentities. To be sure, his entire fund of knowledge on the subject came from the chess journals that Yonatan had lent him and that he studied exhaustively while lying in bed.

One evening Azariah made his way to Yolek and Hava's and harangued them from eight o'clock until nearly midnight on the cyclic nature of Jewish destiny, its recurrent pattern of destruction and redemption, repeatedly referring not only to his own ideas but to a number of articles by Yolek Lifshitz in issues of the Labor Party monthly that he had come across in the recreation hall. He also expounded on the place of the creative individual in kibbutz society. Though his knowledge was as limited as his fervor was unbounded, he did manage now and then to come up with an original enough thought to make Yolek remark after he was gone, "Take it from me, Hava. I'm rarely wrong about these things. That boy has a real spark in him. If he's lucky enough to find a good girl, something may come of him yet."

"He's very strange and very sad," replied Hava. "If you ask me, this will come to no good end. You and your big discoveries!"

Azariah managed to gamble away his last two packs of American cigarettes before he had a chance to give them as gifts to newfound friends. One night he landed in the last room adjoining the swimming pool, reintroduced himself to Etan R., met the two girls who had been living with Etan since the onset of winter, and began to talk about citrus fruit. When he claimed that a grapefruit was simply a cross between an orange and a lemon, Etan not only objected but challenged him to a bet. Azariah immediately appointed the two girls as judges, asked for their verdict, and deferred without protest to their lack of support, laying his two packs of cigarettes on the table. Before leaving, he promised to bring the relevant volume of the *Encyclopaedia Britannica,* for he intended to prove that there was a fruit, perhaps the tangerine, that was half a lemon and half an orange after all.

From Etan R.'s he went to pay a call on Srulik, the music man, for whom he played his guitar for a good ten minutes, smiling all the while but blinking frantically like a cat that wants to have its ears scratched. Indeed, the cat succeeded, for Srulik decided to let him try out for the kibbutz chamber quintet.

On Thursday he visited Yonatan and Rimona again to return part of the coffee and sugar they had given him. After all, he was now getting supplies from the kibbutz commissary in accordance with Secretary Yolek's instructions. He presented Rimona with a wicker shade he had made for the lamp, pointing out that it was only a token gift.

The next night a guest lacturer from the executive committee of the national trade union spoke in the dining hall on the plight of Soviet Jewry, reading from a large number of crumbling old letters that had reached him in devious ways from behind the Iron Curtain. His audience was composed almost exclusively of the older members of the kibbutz, the younger ones, with a single exception, having found other entertainment. Srulik the music man, who was sitting next to him, later swore to all his acquaintances that several especially heartrending passages had made the newcomer shed a tear. By the time the question period arrived, however, Azariah had either got a grip on himself or had had a change of heart, for he not only asked a question but refused to accept the answer given and continued to query the lecturer until a full-fledged argument broke out.

In one way or another, Azariah Gitlin was considered odd by most people who met him or who had heard about him from others. "Yolek's Spinoza," he was frequently called behind his back. High-school wits amended this to "Chimpanoza." Etan R. mimicked Azariah's manner and speech standing knee-deep in mud, dripping wet and orating about the nature of justice, which, after all, could be found only on a kibbutz, and at the same time demanding an urgent meeting with its "head." Yet not even Etan could help acquiescing, albeit with a shrug, when little Shimon claimed that the new mechanic could talk politics for hours and make them sound as thrilling as a detective or science-fiction story. There was nothing dull about him, provided, of course, that one had the time to listen.

Apart from an occasional smirk or snide remark, no one would have dreamed of hurting Azariah Gitlin. It took all kinds. If a bizarrely philosophical, overtalkative, and somewhat pathetic young man just happened to land among them, what harm was he doing? He worked hard, he did what he was told, and some said that he wasn't even half bad at it. Besides, you could see that he had had a hard life. Sometimes, during an argument in a committee, someone would cautiously poke fun at Yolek by saying, "Come on, Yolek, you're beginning to sound like that Spinoza of yours."

What was on most people's minds was neither Azariah Gitlin nor the headlines in the newspapers but the flooding taking place in the low-lying fields. The winter crops were in danger of rotting in the ground.

As for Yonatan, he returned to his silence. Rimona, too, never brought up the conversation they had had. She took to poring over a little English book from India about the depths of karmic suffering and the heights of astral purity. She had borrowed it from Azariah, and its margins bore his penciled comments in an agitated hand. Every evening, without fail, she sat down with it. The stove burned with a blue flame as always, and soft music continued to come over the radio.

All was calm between Rimona and Yonatan.

5

The land was calm, too. The fields were sodden and vapors rose from the earth whenever the winter sun emerged between one rain and the next.

One morning, as he was taking an early bus to Tel Aviv, where he was to attend a meeting of the Labor Party Central Committee, Yolek Lifshitz looked out the window at the washed pine trees whispering in the wind, redolent of peace and good will. All along the road running through the coastal plain new settlements had sprung up, gleaming white with roofs of red tile. All were constructed in straight lines, the houses equally spaced, as if designed by a bright, logical child. Between the houses the residents had already strung laundry lines, built shacks and storerooms, erected fences, put in trees and bushes, planted lawns, and hoed up beds of earth for flowers and vegetables.

Why, these are no less than the very things we set out to accomplish when we were young, thought Yolek. It's just that we gave them all kinds of high-flown names so that we could take ourselves seriously. We were coming to free this land of the primeval curse of its desolation, to tame its wilderness, to propitiate it, and to make it our home. Well, now the high-flown words are rooftops and treetops. Only why, O foolish heart, this shame of feeling poetic about it? Instead of meeting today in Tel Aviv, we should all, every last one of us, be getting together under the open sky and breaking out into song, into a mighty paean of old pioneers. We should come just as we are, cracked of voice, wrinkled of face, stooped of shoulder. And what if we're laughed at? We can join in the laughter ourselves. If there are tears, let there be tears. We did what we said we would. Here it is, all around us, but why, then, this chill in an old heart?

The previous night Prime Minister Eshkol had addressed the nation and assured it that things were looking up. He spoke in the future tense, predicting better times and general prosperity, made some humorous quip about great efforts being rewarded in the end, warned against impatience, called for perseverance, and did not minimize the dangers ahead but nonetheless concluded with an optimistic quotation from the poet Bialik. Immediately afterwards, a special feature was broadcast about the restoration of the newly settled Ta'anach region to its ancient fertility, followed by a program of old pioneering songs.

At each stop, men bundled in work clothes boarded Yolek's bus. From time to time, whenever the sun peeked through the thick clouds, a sharp change swept over the mountains and valleys to the east. No sooner did light touch their slopes than they turned to a vibrant, luxuriantly deep green. Atop a newly built fence in a newly built village perched a bird, soaking wet. A cat scrounging among nearby garbage cans whose lids had been blown off by the wind pretended not to see it. Throngs of children trooped by on their way to school, cheap imitation-leather briefcases strapped to their backs. A blue and red poster on a signboard promised one and all a gala evening.

We are halfway through the sixties, thought Yolek. It is a

long and rainy winter between wars, long enough for the people to fill their lungs with the scent of wet citrus groves and the fragrance of their fruit. When everyone is cultivating his garden, should not my task be to rejoice in our achievements and make others feel that joy too? Be not jaded, O foolish heart, but gala, and full of joy!

Nineteen sixty-five. A winter between wars. Before joy can prevail, all the nightmares, all the suffering, all the wounds must heal. But we're turning over a new leaf here. A safe haven for the Jewish people, that's what we used to say when we were young.

Yolek opened the window a crack, since the bus was full of cigarette smoke, to take a breath of fresh air. Ga'ash, Rishpon, Shefayim, the old village of Ra'anana—all these settlements along the road seemed to him like final, unchallengeable arguments in the age-old debate with ancient rivals that was still going on in his mind.

All around him, as if every minute were precious, settlers were digging into the flat, sandy strip of coast flanked by rocky mountains. Heavy equipment moved huge mounds of earth so that concrete foundations could be laid. Hilltops were being leveled every morning. Fields of weeds were being cleared, virgin brushland plowed, roads paved from village to village. Metals were being melted down to be cast in foundries. And all this while hordes of people were buying and selling, changing addresses and fortunes, scouting the lay of the land, searching for new opportunities. Apartments passed from hand to hand. Crafty maxims were rife. Strike while the iron is hot. Live by your wits. Don't look a gift horse in the mouth.

The people on the bus were reading newspapers in many languages besides Hebrew. Even the bus driver struck Yolek as being a recent immigrant, from Iraq probably, who had already managed to get ahead in life. All these desperate refugees, he thought. We gathered them here from the four corners of the earth. It's up to us to impart our dream to them and make it sing in their bones. Let not the warm but weary heart grow chill in these good times that we dreamed of through all those harsh years. Eshkol was right to have chosen last night to talk about the Ta'anach region. In this urban sprawl along the coast, building plots are selling like hotcakes. When the whole state of Israel seems on the verge of overflowing, why not the weary heart too? We still haven't said our last word. And that's how I'll begin today at the meeting. Without denying the dangers, without overlooking all that's wrong, I'll tell the party to open its eyes, to take a good look all about it, and rejoice. We've had enough gloom and doom.

Yet on these winter nights winds sometimes swept up the wadis and through the crevices of the mountains until you heard them break into a desperate howl right outside your window, as if they had been driven all the way from the snowy steppes of the Ukraine and still had found no peace. And right before dawn a formation of jets would sometimes shoot with savage furor across the low canopy of sky like a pack of hounds in heat.

In the central bus station of Tel Aviv, Yolek was witness to one of those perennial Jewish scenes that still persist and still wreak havoc. A man with a Hungarian accent who, so it seemed, had been caught in an act of petty theft, began to bellow like an ox being dragged to an altar when he saw a policeman approach.

"*Gevalt!*" he cried out in Yiddish. "Jews, have pity! *Gevalt!*"

Dismayed, Yolek bought an evening paper at a newsstand and sat down to read it in a small cafe not far from the station. Headlines announced that a conference of Arab generals meeting in Cairo had arrived at a number of secret decisions. The Prime Minister's speech was reported in a few brief paragraphs. In an adjoining column was a story about a pitched battle among new immigrants in a suburb near Nes Tsiyyona. Yolek could easily imagine it, this fracas of asthmatic, ulcer-ridden, sclerotic refugees, their feeble blows glancing off their antagonists with mounting hysteria.

Elsewhere, in the town of Bet-Lid, two middle-aged men had had to be tied down to be restrained from attacking each other with an ax and a hoe. The hoe-wielder was a baker from Bulgaria and the ax-swinger a goldsmith from Tunis. A settler in the Lachish region had walked out on his family of two wives and nine children, including two sets of twins, left a note that he was going to look for the ten lost tribes of Israel, and disappeared without a trace. A Persian faith healer from the village of Ge'ulim had been indicted for selling amulets to barren women, making them drink a narcotic potion, and, once they were under its influence, committing unspeakable acts.

Yolek thanked the waitress, paid for his coffee, and left. Tel Aviv was not in his opinion an attractive city, yet there was something intrinsically miraculous about it. Great pains had been taken to make day-old streets look historical. There were even green benches here and there that might remind one of Cracow or Lodz. Since his back was bothering him and party meetings never started on time, Yolek decided to sit for a while. A passerby soon recognized him, perhaps from a rally somewhere, or from an old picture in the newspapers in the days when Yolek had served in the cabinet. He wished him a good morning and even sought to strike up a conversation.

"Well now, Comrade Lifshitz, I suppose you find yourself worrying a lot these days."

"Worrying about what?" asked Yolek.

"Oh, things in general. The situation, you might say."

Yolek answered with a question of his own. "And when did we Jews ever have it better?"

On an inner page, Yolek came across a brief item about a man he had known in passing many years ago, an engineer named She'altiel ha-Palti, who had come to Palestine in the early twenties from the small town of Novozhivkov in Russia. This ha-Palti now claimed to have invented a top-secret, giant rocket that would ensure the state of Israel once and for all against any attack. His letters and memoranda on the subject having gone unanswered, however, the old man had irately turned up one day in the offices of the National Land Trust, slightly wounded a young typist with an ancient Italian revolver, and then nearly taken his own life in the mimeograph room in the basement.

We are a mob of the strangest individuals, thought Yolek, who ever pretended to be a people. To speak the same language. Exchanging old songs for new. Forever talking and writing of our hopes and longings as if mere longiloquence could still the promptings of one's inner voice. But why does the weary heart feel so chill?

In the basements of their new houses, these men and women build shelters just in case the bombs should start to fall. The army keeps beefing up its forces. Perhaps there's more than petty politics behind the disinterest in She'altiel ha-Palti's invention. Perhaps his rocket, or something like it, has already been built under wraps. Ben-Gurion always had a soft touch for scientific projects, and Eshkol, too, for the military ones. Who knows what goes on in the back rooms, what wild schemes are discussed by the generals and the savants, even as they are by husbands and wives in their beds at night? How will it all end? What will happen if, God forbid, things take a turn for the worse. Anything is possible. Everything has more than one interpretation. The shouting, the laughter, the curses, the fistfights, the nightmares, the horrid memories, even the war threats coming from Cairo. That's something I should say a few words about, too, when I take the floor. Here is Eshkol promising the nation its dreams are coming true, even if slowly. And there are the wise men of Zion bombarding us in article after article with their historical lessons, their cyclical theories, their grim musings about the common destiny. Is this, then, just an illusion, this winter slumber we're in? Beneath our quilts we are all tossing, turning, debating, wrestling with demons, fighting off legions of nightmares, making all kinds of desperate calculations. What man has never murmured to his wife, "Just in case. You never know. Why not be on the safe side? We have to be prepared for the worst"? And aren't Yonatan and his friends saying to each other: "For as long as we can. Who knows what's ahead"?

On the avenue behind the Habimah Theater, Yolek passed a group of old Jews huddled together on a bench. With their seemingly perpetual display of loathing, despair, and bitter mockery, they might have been drawn by Nazi cartoonists. No doubt worn out by endless argument, they sat in silence, chewing tobacco and staring out into space as if they had read the future there and fatalistically accepted what it foretold.

A religious Jew named Avraham Yitzhak Hacohen Yatom, the owner of a small washing-machine agency, had shut down his business and was now staging a hunger strike in front of city hall. That too Yolek had read in his newspaper. The man was threatening to starve himself to death unless the excommunication of the late philosopher Baruch Spinoza was rescinded. The mayor had sent a clerk down to negotiate, but rain began to fall, and the two men were forced to seek shelter inside.

In settlements along the borders, watchmen stared into the darkness only to see more darkness receding. Sitting on piles of sacks and drinking tea in their tin huts, they would murmur to each other in low voices:

"What quiet! Who would have thought it?"

"Maybe this is it at last."

"Who knows?"

"Anyway, it's quiet now. Let's wait and see."

Opening the party meeting, Prime Minister Eshkol declared, "We, comrades, may well be the craziest adventurers in all Jewish history. Which is precisely why, running as hard as we can, we nonetheless have to run slowly and very, very carefully."

Very, very carefully, thought Yolek Lifshitz. And that's precisely why the heart is so chill and will grow more chill yet, as each of us dies in his own corner without a chance to see the end.

When his turn came at last, Yolek spoke about the close relationship of international and domestic problems. While taking a few wry swipes at today's youth, he reaffirmed his faith in the people's ability to withstand all internal crises. He also stated his faith in their ability to withstand all external crises. What aroused his deepest anxiety was the prospect of being threatened by both at the same time. We must, he said in closing, remain alert and clear-headed. The younger members of the party must be asked to keep in mind the broader historical perspective. Countless centuries of Jewish history, Jewish suffering, Jewish yearnings, and Jewish tears are looking down, are shedding down, upon us.

It's not just that we will soon die, thought Yolek as he left the conference room for the bus station. It's that we ought to die. We have outlived our age.

He had known all along that the meeting would end without any dramatic decisions, merely with a vote to appoint yet another committee to examine the issues raised. Nevertheless, he had made two decisions of his own. The first was not to return home until the seven o'clock bus, and until then, barring rain, to stroll around the city a bit to breathe its sea air. The second was to investigate the story of the young mechanic, who had been taken on without a sufficient check. An army discharge, after all, could be forged.

Yolek walked slowly in a northwesterly direction toward the sea, into an unfamiliar neighborhood. A year ago, in the winter of '64, a new development had gone up here. Its residents had taken all their savings, borrowed more money, obtained mortgages, and otherwise swung things financially to be able to live in these blindingly white high-rise buildings, in luxury apartments that would have made the local moneybags in the shtetl they had come from—the moneybags who had laughed at their starry-eyed idealism when they set out empty-handed for Palestine thirty years ago—turn green with envy in his unmarked grave.

In vain, Yolek realized, had been the whole arduous attempt to rebuild Jewish life on a new foundation; in vain, the pioneers' tents and co-op restaurants; in vain, the creed of physical labor and life in the sun; in vain, the going barefoot, the peasant clothes, the shepherds' songs; in vain, the long nights of argument and debate. All these ex-pioneers who had skimped, saved, and borrowed to build homes, in each of them a living room; in each living room, a glass-paneled cabinet; in each glass-paneled cabinet, a fancy dinner service for twelve. "Keeping up with the Cohens," Eshkol had called it today.

Here and there, in earth trucked in from afar to cover the shifting dunes, a few pale saplings had been planted. No doubt the mayor had cut a ribbon and spoken glowingly of the future. Look at that little boy riding his bicycle down that lane. The wind is bringing him the same smell of fresh paint and whitewash that it is bringing me.

By four, the long evening had begun to set in, granting a kind of reprieve to the city of Tel Aviv. Alongside the new power station, where the Yarkon emptied into the sea, three fishermen were spreading a net. An old woman in charge of a kiosk near the last stop on the bus line looked suspiciously around and, seeing that no one was watching, treated herself to a soda from the tap. Between clouds the color of blood and clouds the color of fire, the sun was entering its last western lap. Far out on the horizon, more clouds shaped like dragons, crocodiles, whales, monstrous serpents were beginning to form. Perhaps, if his time had not run out, he should head west.

Yolek stood listening, but all he could hear from the distant buildings was a raucous whoop of children, spiteful and cruel like the sound of a lynch mob, but without the cries of a victim. Hedges trembled in the cold wind. Hibiscuses shed drops of water hidden in their leaves from the last rain.

Soon the moon would rise, distorting the rectangular roofs,

creating soft, free-flowing forms, silvering the laundry on the lines that had been strung across the streets. It was then that the middle-aged survivors who lived in those streets would put on their hats and coats and wrap scarves around their throats to go out for a stroll, stepping along like cosmonauts on a planet of undependable gravity, as dreamy as sleepwalkers. Should they pass a new office building, they would see it collapse. Should a car drive by, they would hear bombs. If music poured forth from a radio, the blood would curdle in their veins. If they looked at a tree, it would burst into flames.

Tel Aviv on a winter evening between wars. A forced gaiety stretching as far as the farthest suburbs. In it a hard-working carpenter, from Cracow, Munya Liberson by name, stayed up late in his fluorescent-lit shop. His glasses perched precariously on the tip of his nose. Now and then he murmured to himself as he carefully made a measurement or inspected a joint. The flowering of so many pretty Jewish girls outside his window seemed to him a cause for grave concern. And the clamor made by the city each night to drown out the outer silence. What would it all come to? Why so many new hotels going up along the shoreline? Why this bulwark between the city and the sea?

Lest worst should come to worst. Behind this western wall, the city cowered, cringing with fear of the open spaces that lay beyond. Even as a man turns his back to a strong wind, rounds his shoulders, tucks his head hard between them, and awaits a coming blow.

6

And then the winter rains stopped. Overnight the fog was driven eastward, and a blue Saturday broke with the dawn. With the first fingers of light, even before the sun had risen over the ruins of Sheikh Dahr, bird survivors began to discuss their luck with great excitement. As soon as the sun came up, they broke into demented screams.

The sabbath light was warm and crystalline. Every puddle, every window pane, every strip of metal glinted and dazzled. The air buzzed and flowed like honey. Figs, mulberries, pomegranates, almonds, and arbors of grapes stood bared in their ultimate leaflessness, huge droves of birds flocking to them all. All morning long a clear wind blew from the sea, wafting its salty smells.

Early that day the kindergarten children sent up a solitary kite. It climbed tenaciously to heavenly heights, at which it seemed to be a flying genie or sea monster. Don't believe any of it, it's a trap, thought Yonatan Lifshitz as he dressed, put water on for coffee, and went out to stand on the porch. They're just decorating your death with the crepe-paper of love. If you don't make tracks now like an animal, they'll trick you into staying until you relax and forget that your life is your own. "He who forgets abets," as that poor bastard would say. That must be one of his Russian proverbs.

Rimona was sleeping on her back, her hair spread over the pillow, on her forehead a spot of sunlight that had crept through the slats of the blinds. It was Yonatan who first heard the kettle whistle.

"Get up and see what a day we've got outside! It's just what you promised, you sorceress! Get up! Let's have coffee and go for a walk."

Rimona sat up in bed like a baby, rubbing her eyes repeatedly with her tiny fists. "Yoni," she said, as if surprised to find him there, "it's you. I dreamed I found a turtle that could climb walls. I kept trying to convince it that it couldn't until you came along and said that the two of us were being silly and that you'd show us something really new. And then you woke me. There's a fresh hallah from yesterday in a plastic bag near the coffee."

One by one each of Rimona's promises came true. By nine o'clock every window on the kibbutz was open and quilts, blankets, and pillows had been hung out to air. The riverine light deepened all their colors but positively set fire to blue pillow cases and pink nightgowns.

How dazzlingly white were the little houses in that storm of blue light, their tile roofs redder than red, each smoking with a thin mist. Far off in the east, the mountains seemed to levitate in the brilliance, as if they were but their own shadows. "Just look at that!" said Azariah Gitlin to his neighbor, the hired metalworker with the torn ear. "Just look—and, oh, by the way, good morning—how spring has won the battle with a single knockout blow!"

Bolognesi, he who pondered all statements at length looking

for a catch, stared hard at Azariah before answering humbly, "Praise God!"

Housemothers had already dressed their little charges in T-shirts and gym pants, placed them four abreast in the broad laundry carts, and begun to wheel them about the kibbutz. When Yolek, still in his heavy pajamas and fur-lined slippers, looked out the window at the teeming lawns and exclaimed, "What a carnival!" his wife replied through the bathroom door, "I didn't sleep again last night. And by five those birds were making such a racket I thought it was an air-raid siren. If it's not one thing, it's another."

Men and women peeled off layers of clothing, rolled up sleeves, opened a top button or two of blouses or shirts. Some of the men went so far as to step out-of-doors undressed to the waist, baring dense mats of hair, fine golden fuzz, or graying curls. The honeyed light pampered winter-weary shoulders and waterlogged front yards, glanced glowingly off the tin drainpipes, fondled lawns that had wasted in the long, frosty nights, and trickled off into cisterns of shade beneath the huge cypress trees.

Most amazing were the flies and bees, now zooming everywhere. Where had they been hiding from the cold and rain all winter long? And the white butterflies—flurrying in bright hot-spots of light—the snowflakes that fell on the high mountains to the east just four nights ago. Even dogs had run amuck and were racing back and forth across the lawns in crazy figure-eights. Were they trying to catch the bubbles of sunshine that, impelled by the soft sea breeze, speckled the grass, the lilac bushes, the dazzling bougainvillea, the hibiscus hedges, that caromed from puddle to window pane and from window pane to drainpipe, skittering wildly, evanescing, condensing, fissioning, fusing, and once again fragmenting brightly?

The real-as-rain smell of the earth and the wind-borne smell of the sea put a song on the lips of all, making everyone feel an urgent need to do something at once, to effect an immediate change, to paint a rusty railing, attack a clump of weeds with a hoe, prune a hedge, clear a culvert, shinny up a drainpipe to replace a cracked tile, or simply hoist a bawling infant high in the air. Or else, to forget about it all and instead collapse in a motionless heap like a lizard in the sun.

Most pleasant have you been to me, my brother Jonathan, thought Azariah, as he skipped across the puddles on his way to the Lifshitzes'. He planned to suggest a long Saturday hike, an offer they could not possibly refuse. Even if Yoni was too tired, perhaps Rimona would come. In the woods last night had she not already bandaged his wounds? But just when his dream had become too sweet to bear, he had opened his eyes only to hear his neighbor chanting in a tongue that resembled Chaldean.

"It could be a line in the movies," said Yonatan. "A husband wakes his sleeping wife in the morning, and what are the first words she says? *Is that you, Yoni?* Who did you think it was, Marlon Brando?"

"Yoni," said Rimona softly, "if you've finished your coffee and don't want any more, let's go outside."

Yolek Lifshitz, secretary of Kibbutz Granot, a man neither young nor well, groaned as he bent over to pull a folding chair from the small storage space between the posts supporting his house. Carefully he dusted it off, dragged it to the paved patio at the end of his garden, opened it gingerly lest he catch his fingers, suspiciously tested the strength of its canvas seat, sat himself down, and stretched out bare feet ridden by swollen, evil-looking varicose veins. Having left his glasses in his shirt pocket he had removed before stepping outside, he set aside his weekend paper, closed his eyes, and decided to concentrate on one or two matters that needed to be resolved. Time was short.

In a dream last night he had been asked by Eshkol to inform the Syrians about the flood damage without revealing its full extent. "We want them to think that things aren't so bad and that we can still take lots more punishment since time is on our side, although just between the two of us, Yolek, I'm telling you that it's urgent, in the worst possible way." No sooner had he left Eshkol's tent than Ben-Gurion, red-faced and terrible, had sprung at him from a nearby Arab well and roared in a voice as shrill as a madwoman's, "I don't want to hear another word about it! You'll shut up and kill if you have to, even with the handle of a hoe just as King Saul killed his own son!"

The cries of the birds across the blue caress of the sky were distracting. To his surprise, Yolek realized that the birds were not, as the poet Bialik had written, caroling. On the contrary, they were screaming at the top of their lungs. Especially unsettling were the complaints of pigeons coming from the roofbeams of the house. A ferocious dispute had broken out among them, and they were pursuing it in fulminous bass tones.

"Sha, sha," Yolek muttered in Yiddish. "Why do the heathen rage? There's no need to get so excited. Ben-Gurion may be up to his old tricks again, but we're not going to let them faze us." He soon dozed off, his heavy hands on his paunch, his mouth slightly agape. The circlet of gray hair around his bald head, which in this magical light suggested a saint's halo, ruffled in the breeze. Although the pigeons kept at their tirade, the shrewd, ugly man with the face of a beadle or a sad, clever court Jew had lost at last his ironic look, wary with the age-old caution of his race. Yolek was at peace.

"He's out like a light, our Yolek," laughed Srulik the music man as he passed by in his blue sabbath shirt and neatly pressed khaki pants, a ball belonging to the neighbors' children in one hand. Hava could not stand that unctuous German accent of his, that impertinently intimate smile. Look who's shooting off his big mouth, thought she. Just who does he think he is?

"Let him sleep," she bristled. "At least one day a week let him sleep in peace. Even the head guard in a loony bin gets a day off now and then. He stays up nights worrying about all of you, so why not let him rest now?"

"By all means, by all means!" laughed Srulik, who, whatever Hava might think, was a warmhearted man. "Let the Guardian of Israel sleep all he wants."

"Very funny!" snapped Hava. She was standing by the clothesline, hanging up flannel pajamas, linens, a nightgown, and some heavy sweaters. "I just want you to know that you're taking years off his life, all of you. And when he's gone, you'll put out a memorial booklet saying that Yolek Lifshitz never knew what it meant to be tired. Well, never mind. I'm not complaining. I stopped complaining long ago. I just want you to know what you've done. All of you!"

"Really, now," replied Srulik with a patience born of affection, "it's a sin to be so cross on a morning like this, Hava'ke. Just look at the light! Just smell the air! If only I dared, I'd pick a flower to give you."

"Very funny," said Hava.

Srulik made a motion as if to toss her the ball, smiled, almost winked, thought better of it, and went his way. Bitterly, Hava watched him go, her eyes like an owl's blinded by a beam of bright light. To herself she said, *"Shoyn."* Fine.

All the nights spent in bed alongside this thickening man, the smells of his illnesses, his nicotine breath, his snores in her face, the shadow of his crowded bookshelves made by the bathroom light that must never be turned off at night, his mementos on the shelves above the bed like a huge billboard announcing: *I am a national figure. I have been a minister!*

You are a national figure, all right, and I, Mr. Minister, have been your dust rag, your old socks beneath your long underwear. I've been your underwear too. By all means, Mr. Minister, you should work wonders, you should be a minister again, you should become President even, but I wish to God I'd been killed by those bullets of Bini's. He couldn't aim a gun to save his life, but he could play the flute, and he pastured the flock all alone by the edge of the wadi that autumn, standing so straight and so sad on that rock in his black Russian blouse with his black tousled hair, playing the flute in Ukrainian, to the sky, to the hills, until I begged him, Stop because I'll cry! He stopped because he loved me, that's why, but I cried anyway. Until that night when I saw him on that sweaty mattress through the chink in the partition, lying naked on his back and holding his tool as he held his flute, diddling it, crying, and the minister snored by my side till I woke him in a whisper and made him look at Bini squirming there before he turned over and came. That's when Mr. Minister appointed a committee to look into the matter discreetly, to let time heal all wounds, but by then I was pregnant and ever since I've been your pet bitch, *ty zboju, ty morderco!* Quietly you killed me, quietly you killed him, and now quietly you're killing your son, though I'll never give you the satisfaction of knowing if he's really your son or not. It's just as that fawning music man said, "Let the Guardian of Israel sleep in peace." Never mind, Hava'ke, never mind, never mind, she crooned to herself, as if to calm a child deep within.

"Hava," said Yolek, "you won't believe it, but I think I actually dozed off."

"Sleep all you want. I think Srulik was looking for you."

"Eh?"

"Srulik. I said Srulik was here."

"You're right," said Yolek. "Spring is really here."

"By all means," snapped Hava. And went off to make him tea.

Because of the mud, they couldn't take the short route, the one that followed the tractor path in an almost straight line through the fields, curving slightly only by the cemetery, until it reached the foot of the hill. The rain had turned it into a quagmire, forcing them to take a detour to the north along the narrow, unused, but still paved British road that looped twice around the hill before entering the ruins of Sheikh Dahr. Every winter the stiff asphalt crumbled a bit more, and a wild undergrowth of nettles, thorny burnet, and prosopis broke rapaciously through it, piercing its tarry cadaver with prickly snarls. Flood waters had caused the stone shoulders to collapse, and whole sections of the road had caved in and been swept away. Craters made by shells and mines in the '48 war gaped amid the rank foliage, marking where blood had been shed. Along a curve in the road stood the hulk of a burned-out truck, through whose empty headlight casings ferns were growing. The phrase "the wrath of God" crossed Azariah's mind.

At ten o'clock, Udi and Anat had joined Yonatan, Rimona, and Azariah, and they had all set out together for Sheikh Dahr. Udi was sure that the floods must have unearthed some of the ancient facing stones of the biblical Jewish village. He had a collection of stones like these in his garden, adding to them from time to time both for their beauty and for the feeling of vindication, or poetic justice, or biblical prophecy fulfilled, that their retrieval, or, as he preferred to call it, their "liberation," gave him. As soon as the tractor path was dry, he would hitch up a tractor and liberate whatever they might find today. "If we do find anything, that is. And if one of us happens to come across a nice old piece of Arab junk, we can take it home for a planter and grow a creeper in it."

Anat, for her part, was more interested in mushrooms. She thought the rocky slopes beneath the pine-reforested hilltops would be a good place to go looking for them.

Azariah Gitlin had volunteered to be responsible for the logistics of the party. Early that morning he took from the kibbutz kitchen some fried drumsticks left over from the Friday night meal and carefully wrapped them in plastic, not to mention potatoes, fresh vegetables, oranges, and cheese and hard-boiled-egg sandwiches. In honor of spring's arrival, he had put on his very best clothes, a striped red-and-blue shirt and a pair of smartly cuffed gabardine slacks that were a bit on the short side, baring his thin white legs above his green woolen socks and the pointy-toed, stylish, though slightly down-at-the-heel city shoes he'd worn to work on his first day in the tractor shed. After careful consideration, he had decided against bringing his guitar. "He who plays for applause, the muse in himself ignores." On his belt he had hung an army canteen borrowed from Etan R. Feeling in fine fettle, he had determined to evince from now on all the traits of sleepy superiority that he had also borrowed from Etan. No more of this sensitive, scared-adolescent stuff. Henceforth he would be the person he really was, a man who had seen much, suffered much, and learned to bear all in stoic silence. He had even adopted a new walk, whose nonchalant strides, with both thumbs tucked into his belt, had been casually picked up from Udi Shneour. He was determined to be as helpful as possible to the hiking party. If, for instance, they were to run into something unexpected or dangerous on the way, and all the others, so to speak, panicked, he wouldn't think even for a second about his own safety.

At the moment he was keeping a sharp eye on the movements of Tia, who repeatedly strayed from the road to blaze a disappearing trail through the thickets of high grass, thorn bushes, and wild oleanders, penetrating into the damp heart of the shady maquis and rustling about there for many minutes at a time as if on the spoor of some prey. She pawed up earth, chased invisible quarry, let out scared yelps that turned to wolfish howls, backed off with angry alarm, circled the field mouse, turtle, or hedgehog she had found to cut off its line of retreat, and finally, trailing feathers of fern and arrowheads of thorns, charged back to rejoin them as if newly born, only to wander off again.

"I tell you, she's on to something," said Azariah. "I tell you, she's found tracks and is trying to let us know. And we don't even have a gun."

"Take it easy," said Udi in his clipped, rough voice. "It's only a scalping party of Red Indians."

"At eight this morning I saw Bolognesi leave the kibbutz by the back gate and set off by himself in the direction of the old well," said Azariah darkly.

"Bolognesi is a good person," said Rimona. "And so are you, Azariah. And this is a good day for a hike."

"That's for sure," said Udi. "It's a damned nice day. The winter really overdid it this year."

"I don't know about that," said Rimona.

"About what?"

"About the winter already being over."

"I wish you'd stop talking about the winter," said Anat. "I'd rather hear about scalping parties."

They walked on in silence for a while until Tia bolted out of the bushes and jumped on Yonatan with her forepaws, as if to head him off or slow him down. Just then, three shots echoed softly in the distance, so muffled they might have been fired under a quilt, and a flock of birds circled high into the air, rapidly gaining altitude.

"When a blue Saturday like this comes along after weeks of wind and rain," said Rimona, "it makes you want to go right out and pick something fresh. Then at least there'll be something to remember it by if the rain starts up again. Like those olive branches up there, so dark green on one side and so pale silver on the other. Yoni's allergic to pine. It makes him cry. But who can pick them when they're still so wet? Just a touch will get you a cold shower down your neck."

Before she had a chance to finish, Azariah had bounded off the road and charged up the collapsing embankment at its side. Struggling through the mud, he advanced into a low thicket of gum trees from which, smiling modestly, he finally emerged with a bouquet of wet olive branches.

"I can pick more," he promised. "As many as you like."

"But you're drenched!" cried Rimona, the corners of her mouth smiling at him. She ran a hand over her cheek as if she were the wet one, wiped his forehead with the back of it, and took the branches with cupped palms. "Thank you," she said. "You're so kind."

"It was nothing," said Azariah, grinning.

"And there's water down your neck too. Give me a handkerchief. I'll dry it for you."

The promise of her touch and the lilt of her voice set Azariah to rummaging frantically through his pockets. He found a penknife but no handkerchief. Flustered, he couldn't find any cigarettes either. Yonatan, sensing what he was after, offered him a smoke and lit one for himself. I'll break every bone in your body, you little grasshopper, he thought, but reversed himself at once. Never mind. Tomorrow I'm taking off and leaving her behind. She'll be yours for the asking, you dumb grasshopper, because you'll be all that she'll have. And all you'll have is a stuffed kewpie doll.

"Those cigarettes you people keep smoking," said Anat, "are making you miss out on all the wonderful smells."

"Right you are," said Azariah, trying to roughen his voice. "I'm going to put mine out right now. It's too damned nice around here."

"How about that?" said Udi to Yonatan. "As soon as you get up in the morning, they're telling you what to do. No Smoking or Spitting Allowed. Oh well. Take a look at that landscape over there, Yoni. All the Arab terraces have been washed away, but that bottom course of stone still left down there must be from Second or First Temple times. Whatever Jews built, lasts. No flood can touch it."

"Once they talked of building a small dam here, you know," said Yonatan. "The idea was Yashek's, but my father laughed it off. He said this wasn't Switzerland and there wasn't any money to spend on fantasies of paddling swans serenaded by fräuleins with mandolins. That was strictly for pictures on bonbon wrappers. But after thinking it over for a couple of days, as he usually does, he began to wonder if it didn't make some sense. He even asked me and Little Shimon to check into it, that is, to form an ad-hoc committee, as he called it. It turned out that there would be so much seepage that the water in the dam wouldn't hold out after late April or early May. Yashek himself admitted that the whole thing was a pipe dream. Then my father, of all people, began insisting it was possible and that there wasn't any reason why we couldn't cover a couple of acres of ground with plastic sheets to make a real little lake. Right now he's still corresponding with a professor from the Weizmann Institute, who says one thing, and a professor from the Hebrew University, who says another. But what I really wanted to say, Udi, is that two or three hundred meters from here the flagstone path starts, where Abu-Hani used to have his orchard. Do you remember it, where that tree was that looked like a rhinoceros? If we find it, we can cut straight across to Sheikh Dahr without getting bogged down in mud. The odds are you'll find some of your biblical relics there too. Maybe the stone that Cain killed Abel with, or the bones of some crucified prophet. Down! Tia, you dumb beast! Hey, you're getting me all dirty! Down!"

All day long, thought Azariah, it's been just the four of them. I'm the spare tire nobody needs except to get scratched in the bushes and stuck in the mud and wet as a dog just for some olive branches. She wiped off my face like a person touching a person, not like a woman touching a man, but he was still so jealous he threw the match away as if he were throwing a punch. And he's my best, my only friend in the whole kibbutz, in the whole world! It's just that I'm better at losing, better at taking it on the chin than any of them, readier to die to tell them about the long arm of justice because all of us are armed, *the whole people is an army, the whole country is a front.* I'm the only civilian around here, just me and Eshkol, which is why the two of us alone know how serious things are. He just doesn't know that I know and can help him. There are things that have to be talked through, not just gabbed about with dead words, like saying it's a damned nice day. What's so damned nice about it? Dead words about landslides in this or that wadi, who cares? What's one more landslide when our whole life is sliding away every moment? Time is a landslide in itself.

After Udi and Yonatan go off to look for their biblical bric-a-brac, I'll be left alone with these two women. I swear to God that for once in my life I'll try not to tell any lies.

On the hilltop, against the sky, backed by blue clouds, stood the ruins of Sheikh Dahr, light slashing through the gaping windows like an eviscerating sword, the out-of-doors just as bright on one side of the smashed, charred, homeless walls as on the other. Rubble from fallen roofs lay in heaps. Here and there an unsubmitting grape vine had run wild, clinging with bared claws to a remnant of a standing stone wall. Above the ravaged village rose its shattered minaret. Across the way, a fiery bougainvillea climbed in crimson up the remains of the sheikh's house, as if still smoldering with the flames that had been put to this "murderers' den" that, as Yolek Lifshitz once put it, had exacted such a "cruel blood price."

"A cruel blood price," thought Yonatan. But from the ruins of Sheikh Dahr came not a sound of protest, not even the bark of a dog. Nothing but the silence of the earth and another, more subtle silence that seemed to blow down from the mountains, the silence of deeds that cannot be undone and of wrongs that no one can right. Also words he had heard from his father—or had he read them somewhere?

The other hikers fell silent too. Even Azariah said nothing. They listened to their steps echo from the sunken stone path and watched Tia nose through the muddy fields, where she seemed to be looking for some secret sign of life. The dripping olive and carob trees kept up a steady pitterpatter, as if the last word, one for which they were still groping, had yet to be said. Three crows waited on a branch. Far off, a hawk, falcon, or buzzard—Yonatan could not say—hung on the wind. No one spoke until Udi's sharp eyes made out an edible mushroom beneath a pine tree. Then Anat cried out, "And here's another! And over there lots more!"

"All right, then," said Udi, as though giving himself an order, "here we are. This is it!"

Without asking if anyone agreed, he proceeded to spread out a red-checked, captured Arab Legion *kaffiyeh* between two gleaming gray stones. The girls took the picnic basket from Azariah. At Rimona's beck, he ran to gather kindling for a fire to bake the potatoes. "Down!" shouted Yonatan at Tia.

Anat had already borrowed Azariah's pocket knife to cut up the vegetables for a salad. She was a plump, solid young woman with a bold chest and eyes that seemed always to be laughing at some salty joke she had just heard—a joke she could easily top at once if she hadn't preferred to leave an edge of anticipation to that pleasure. A sea breeze ruffled her brown curls and strove to whip up her flowery skirt. She took her time pressing it back against her thighs despite Azariah's stare. But to her husband Udi she said, "Why don't you come scratch my back like a good boy? Right here. And here too. It's itching like crazy."

The damp kept them from getting a fire started. First Yonatan erected a little wigwam of the twigs collected by Azariah and built a tripod of matches within. Although he shielded it with his body from the wind while he lit it, it didn't catch. "Come on," said Udi, coming to the rescue, "quit playing boy scout." He crumpled and then lit a piece of newspaper, but it immediately went out too. After a second fruitless try, he started cursing in Arabic and kept it up until all the matches were gone. Then, he turned savagely on Azariah, who all this while had been looking on with spiteful glee and declaiming yet another of his asinine Russian proverbs about someone called Ivan and a thinking cap.

"Why don't you shut the hell up, Chimpanoza! So we won't have a fire! Everything's wet as snot around here. Who needs those shitty potatoes anyway?"

Azariah jumped to his feet and broke a soda bottle over a rock. But he did not run at Udi with it. Rather, he turned his back to the group, leaned over the feckless fire, and thoughtfully experimented for a few moments with a thin sliver of glass until it caught the sun's rays. These he focused on a shred of newspaper until fine smoke began to rise, followed by tongues of flame.

"You owe me an apology," he said.

"We're sorry," said Rimona softly.

"Forget it," said Azariah.

When I was a kid of six or seven, the village sheikh once came to visit. His name was Hajj Abu-Zuheir, and he came with three other notables. I remember his white robe and their striped gray ones as they sat in the white wooden chairs in father's room around the white table on which chrysanthemums were growing in a yogurt cup. *"Hada ibnak?"* asked the sheikh, his teeth as big and yellow as corncobs. And father replied, *"Hada waladi wa'illi kaman wahad, zeghir."* The sheikh touched my cheek with a hand that was furrowed like the earth, and I could feel his mustache and his tobacco breath on my face. Father told me to introduce myself, and Abu-Zuheir ran his weary old eyes from me to the bookshelf and back to father, who was the headman of the kibbutz, saying to him gently, as if playing a modest role in some solemn ceremony, *"Allah karim, ya Abu-Yoni."* Then they sent me out of the room and began some long negotiation that little Shimon had to translate back and forth as father knew hardly any Arabic. It must have been Passover week, because someone brought matzos from the kitchen and a big jug of coffee. And now there's not a dog left in Sheikh Dahr and all of the fields, those that we quarreled about and those that we didn't, and all their sorghum and barley and alfalfa, are ours. Nothing is left now but those blackened walls on the hill and maybe their curse hanging over us.

Yonatan walked off and stood among some olive trees, urinating. His head was cocked to one side and his mouth slightly open as if working on a chess problem. His eyes fell on the easternmost mountains, which seemed in this flowing, honeyed light to be within shouting distance. A dim, steely blue the color of an autumn sea, they loomed like steep breakers that seemed so imminently about to tumble westward that Yonatan felt an urge to run at them at once and plunge in head first. Indeed, he suddenly began to sprint, followed by Tia, saliva dripping from her jowls, panting heavily like a sick wolf. He kept it up for about three hundred paces, until his boots began to sink deep into the mud, and water gurgled into his socks. He began climbing from rock to rock, collecting great globs of mud on his shoes, hobbling like an elephant until he was once more on dry ground, the words of that old poem "But Their Hearts Were Not True" running mockingly through his mind.

"Take this knife," said Rimona, "and scrape the mud off your boots. If you're through running."

He looked at her for a moment with a weary grin. Seeing only placid innocence in her eyes, he obeyed and sat down on a rock to clean himself off while the women struggled to carve the chicken and the new mechanic in his striped shirt and best pants bent over the fire that no one had believed he could light.

"I ran like an idiot," said Yonatan. "I'm talking to you, Azariah. I wanted to see if the winter had made me forget how to run. What about you?"

"I have run quite enough in my life," said Azariah, taken aback but with some semblance of self-respect. "I came here to stop running."

"Come on, let's race," said Yonatan, surprised by his own

challenge. "Let's see if you're as good at it as you are at chess."

"Azariah," taunted Udi, "only likes to run at the mouth."

"I hate to run," said Azariah. "I'm through running. And now you'd better leave me alone if you want to have a fire and your potatoes."

Expertly rolling the potatoes in the pockets of hot ash formed by the twigs, he kept his eyes facing Udi and Anat in order to avoid Rimona's, which he had felt resting on him from the moment of Yonatan's challenge. His flesh burned, for Rimona was looking at him not like a woman looking at a man, or even like a person looking at another person, but rather like a woman looking at a thing, or perhaps like a thing that is suddenly looking at you.

Rimona's corduroy pants clung to her trim, nubile body snugly but unobtrusively, and she had neatly knotted her shirt somewhere above the navel, baring a bit of flat stomach and slim waist. It's just her way of lying, though Yonatan. Only who cares?

"You can relax," said Anat. "The food is almost ready."

Butterflies frolicked around the pine trees and in the swatches of light between the umbrae of the olives. One, white like the others, hovered motionlessly in place, like a snowflake or an orange blossom. A sickly-looking gibbous moon hung caught in the boughs of an olive tree, like Absalom in his oak. Ringed by craggy branches, it could have been a pale Jewish fiddler trapped by a band of peasants in some distant land of exile.

"Dogs keep barking throughout the night, the moon keeps quiet but shines on bright" was Azariah's comment, even though Tia was not barking but resting peacefully on her side.

"We'll eat in just a minute," said Anat.

Yonatan squatted by Rimona's side on his haunches like an old Bedouin and helped slice the onions. When Anat once again let her dress play peekaboo with her solid thighs, Azariah was moved to remark, "I keep feeling that somebody's watching us. Maybe we should post a lookout."

"I am dying of hunger," said Udi.

"There's lemonade in Azariah's canteen," said Anat. "Someone can start to pour it. Let's eat."

They drank from the canteen cap, which went round from hand to hand, and plunged into the chicken, diced salad, baked potatoes, egg-and-cheese sandwiches, and peeled oranges for dessert. The conversation drifted to the village of Sheikh Dahr as it had been before the '48 war. They talked about the cunning of the old hajj, about what the Arabs would have done to us had they won, and about what Udi proposed doing to them in the next war. Yonatan took no part in an argument that soon broke out between Udi and Azariah. He was thinking of a picture in Rimona's album that showed a group of picnickers in the dappled light of a clearing in a thick oak forest. All the men in it were fully dressed, and among them was one woman, naked as the day she was born, to whom he had given the private name of Azuva, daughter of Shilhi. That joker, the old-timers said, he couldn't hit it from three feet away. And a bull isn't a matchbox! It's a huge target!

Yonatan imagined receiving a midnight phone call from his other father, the owner of the Florida hotel chain, that would suddenly open up all sorts of possibilities and places where anything might happen—terrible tragedies, sensational successes, unexpected romances, extraordinary encounters—and all of them far from here and from the evil ruins of this village and its antediluvian goat dung. Your passport, your ticket, and a handsome sum of cash will be waiting for you at the airport manager's office. Just tell them, Jonathan, that you're Benjamin's boy and leave the rest to them. You'll find your instructions in the inside right pocket of the custom-made suit they'll hand over to you.

On the ridge facing them a palm tree stood beside a leafless, twisted wild pear that looked like a blind old man who has stumbled by mistake into an enemy camp. Why all this sadness here unless it's a coded message from the dead who once lived upon this muddy ground? If you don't pick up and go right now, you'll never be on time for whatever is waiting for you and won't wait forever if you're late.

"Forget about the Bible and those Ay-rabs of yours for a second," said Yonatan, rousing himself from his trance. "Do you remember, Udi, how when we were little, the wind from Sheikh Dahr used to bring the smell of the smoke from their outdoor ovens at night? We'd lie beneath our blankets after lights-out in the children's house when all the grown-ups had gone, too scared to admit how scared we were of that smoky wind blowing through the east windows with that smell of kindling and dried goat shit that the Arabs burned for fuel. You know that Arab smoke smell. And their dogs barking and sometimes the muezzin wailing away at the top of the mosque."

"Now too," said Rimona hesitantly.

"Now too what?"

"She's right," said Azariah. "You can hear a sort of faraway wailing now too. And we don't even have a gun."

"It's the Red Indians," whooped Anat.

"It's the wind," said Rimona. "And I'm almost sure that the smoke is from your fire, Azariah."

"There's still some chicken left," said Anat. "Does anybody want it? And two more oranges. Yoni? Udi? Azariah? Whoever's still hungry can have more. There's plenty of time."

Udi managed not to return empty-handed from his ramble on the hillside, bringing back a rusty wagon pole found among the rocks, some remnants of a leather harness, and the skull of a horse grimacing with hideous yellow teeth. All three finds were intended to give his front yard what he called "character." He was even considering digging up the skeleton of some greaseball from the village cemetery, wiring it together, and standing it in his garden to serve as a scarecrow and shock the entire kibbutz.

"If you don't watch it, Udi," said Azariah, "one of the birds it scares may be the soul of a dead Arab and peck your eyes out."

They rested for another half hour or so. Udi and then Azariah took off his shirt and undershirt to bask in the sun. When a mild dispute broke out whether the three jets screaming southward overhead were French Mystères or Supermystères, Yonatan remarked that his father had once voted in the cabinet against the Franco-Israeli honeymoon of the fifties, or perhaps had merely abstained. Now, though, Yolek admitted that he had been wrong and that Ben-Gurion had been right.

"They've spent their whole lives being right, those old folks. Whatever my father says, even if it's admitting he was wrong, comes out sounding like he's the one who's right and you're the one who's wrong because you're too young. It's only the old folks who have the strictly logical minds and the infallible intuition and all that, while you're too spoiled, or too confused, or too lazy, or too superficial to think straight. It doesn't matter if you're thirty years old. They still talk to you like a grown-up being patient with a child who's only being treated like a grown-up in order to make him feel good. You can't even ask them for the time of day without getting a whole complicated answer full of explanations for everything, point by point, A, B, C, D, and all that, and without being told that experience is the best teacher and that there's always another side to the coin. What you think makes no difference because you belong to a generation that never learned how to think. You can't get a word in edgewise. It's like being checkmated by someone who's playing both sides of the board because you have no pieces of your own, just your tender soul with your psychological problems."

"You have no pity," said Rimona.

"I," said Yonatan, "cannot stand pity."

"Except when you get some of it yourself."

"That's enough of that!" snapped Yonatan.

"All right," said Rimona.

Udi turned the conversation back to jet planes, speaking enthusiastically about the new Mirages the air force was acquiring, more than a match, he was sure, for the latest MiGs the Syrians and the Egyptians were getting from the Russians. He happened to be high up enough in the reserves to know of a fantastic plan to finish off the greaseballs with a single blow if they so much as dared raise their curly heads.

Flouncing her skirt to cover her knees, Anat jokingly scolded her husband for giving away military secrets. Azariah took offense, insisting politely but firmly that there was no reason to refrain from discussing military matters in his presence. He was not a foreign agent. In fact, as a technical sergeant in the army he had dealt with some highly confidential matters himself. Regarding secrets, for example, he could tell them some fascinating things about tank warfare and General Tal's revolutionary plans. Incidentally, it was his opinion that the old folks Yoni was so annoyed with had more brains in their pinkies than all the brash young big shots had in their heads. They had suffered in the lands of Exile, rather than being born with silver spoons in their mouths like his and Yoni's generation, which at the worst had to endure the smoke from Arab villages and kill a stray Arab now and then. No wonder the younger generation was so closed-minded and always whining. Not, he hastened to add, that he was referring to anyone present. In fact, if he was thinking of anybody, it was only himself, although on the whole he was, so to speak, talking generally. Still, he felt obliged to ask them all for forgiveness, especially Yoni, whom he might have unintentionally hurt. Nor, by the way, was he happy with the phrase "lands of Exile." He promised to find a better one.

Azariah was again bewildered by Rimona's eyes, which were resting on him poignantly, as one is sometimes watched by a house pet who remembers some primordial truth beyond all knowledge or words. The corners of her mouth smiled at him, or seemed to in his imagination, as if to say, that's enough, that's enough, little boy, which caused him to flounder even more while trying to end with a joke.

"Azariah," said Rimona. "If you feel the need to talk, you can talk and we'll listen. But don't think you have to."

"Of course not, why should I," mumbled Azariah. "I mean, if you're bored and want me to make you laugh, I can be, so to speak, very funny. It's all the same to me."

"Go ahead, then," said Udi, winking at Yonatan, who was picking burrs and clots of mud from Tia's fur.

"Okay, take a baby, for instance," Azariah proposed, spreading his arms apart the length of an infant. "Take a little baby. I mean before it's born. When it's still a twinkle in its mother's eye. Once I used to think that all the family dead, the uncles and the grandfathers and the grandmothers and the cousins and even the distant ancestors, come to say goodbye to each baby before it's born, the way you say goodbye at the station to someone going on a long trip. And I'd imagine that each one of them asked it to take something of theirs along—a pair of eyes, or the color of somebody's hair, or the shape of an ear or a foot, or a birthmark, or a forehead or chin—because each of them wanted to send some little reminder or token of their affection to relatives still living. It's as if the baby were a lucky traveler who had received permission not just to go abroad but to cross an Iron Curtain that they know they'll never be allowed to cross, which is why they load it with as much as they can so that the people in the happy land it's going to will know that they haven't forgotten. The only problem is that the baby, being, after all, a tiny thing, has a strict baggage limit. At the most, say, one feature from its uncle and its grandmother's eyes, or perhaps an unusually thick thumb. When it finally arrives at its destination all of its relatives on the other side who are excitedly waiting to kiss it and hug it start arguing right away who sent what to whom. One of them says that the chin is without a doubt Grandpa Alter's, another that the little ears that look almost glued to the head belong to the twin aunts believed to have been murdered by the Nazis in the Ponar Forest, still another that the fingers definitely come from a cousin of father's who was a well-known pianist in Bucharest during the 1920s. All of this, of course, is simply, you understand, a parable."

"A Rumanian shaggy dog story," said Udi. "One of those that never get to the punch line."

"Why don't you leave him alone?" said Yonatan. "Quiet, Tia! Just a little more beneath the ear and we're done."

"All right by me," said Udi. "Let him talk. He can go on all day. And he will, that's for sure. Myself, I'm going up to that stinking village."

"I believe," said Rimona, "that he really had the two twin aunts who were killed. And you just have to look at his fingers to see that the part about the pianist in Bucharest is true too. But please, Azariah, don't tell us any more about youself now. Some other time. Let's sit quietly for a few minutes and see what we can hear. Then whoever wants can go to Sheikh Dahr and whoever is tired can rest."

Many birds were about, but none were singing. They were talking to each other in sharp, clipped tones that were neither joyful nor peaceful but quiveringly alive as if to announce some impending danger. Behind their raucous chatter the wind whispered conspiratorially, while something blew from the ruins of the village as light as a murderer's fingers, as hushed as a rustle of silk.

Azariah noticed it too and knew that it would be only a matter of hours before the winter returned. One night in his childhood, after they had slipped out of Kiev, when they were hiding in the dark cellar of an abandoned farmhouse before the long flight to Uzbekistan, they cooked and ate a little yellow cat. It was Vassily the Russian convert to Judaism who killed it with a blow of his fist when the animal rubbed up against him to be petted.

The blizzard outside and the damp within caused the fire to go out before the cat was done, and they had to eat it half raw. But crybaby Zhorzi didn't want to taste it even though he was hungry, and when Vassily said to him, "If you don't eat, you won't be big and strong like Vassily," he cried even more until Vassily finally clamped a large, red-freckled hand over his mouth and said, "If you don't shut up, Vassily will make you go fff-ff-f-t just like the cat. You know why? Because Vassily is hungry, that's why."

Suddenly, sickened by all his lies, the white ones as well as the black, Azariah confessed to himself that he too had eaten a piece of his own cat after all.

"Someone like you, Udi," he said, "doesn't have to go hunting for the Bible in old Arab villages. Just look at yourself in a mirror and you'll see the whole Bible from Joshua to the second book of Kings. As for the Prophets, Psalms, Ecclesiastes, and Job, though, this country still needs to wait a couple of hundred more years for them. I'm not really contradicting myself, although maybe I am just a bit, because history moves in cycles, and in zigzags too, as we were taught to run in the army, so that if you're aimed at while you're zigging, you've already zagged by the time the shot is fired, and vice versa. You see, when we went into exile, and even before that, we Jews began to hassle the world by telling everyone how to live, what they could do and what they couldn't, what was bad and what was good, until we got on everybody's nerves—just like that uncle of mine I mentioned, Manuel, the musician. He played in the Royal Philharmonic and was a professor too and such a bosom friend of King Carol's that the King felt he just had to give him a gold medal. Only right in the middle of the ceremony, Manuel began ranting like a mad prophet about all the decadence and corruption and recrucifying of Jesus each day by people who called themselves Christians. That's why the goyim hate us like poison and always will. As the Russians say, 'You can give Sergei a new suit of clothes, he'll still be the same wherever he goes.'

"It's only on the kibbutz that one sometimes sees a calmer, how can I put it, slower type of Jew. I swear I'm not trying to insult you. I mean Jews who have begun to learn the art of relaxing and the secret of sending down roots. They may be on the crude side, of course, but if you take, say, those olive trees over there, there's something crude about them too. What I'm trying to say is that we should learn to live without talking so much. If we have to talk, it should be like you, Udi, when you tell us in a few words, without preaching or promising salvations, that it's a damned nice day. Good for you, Udi! We should learn to live simply and to the point. To work hard. To be close to nature. Close, so to speak, to the rhythms of the cosmos. We should learn from those olives. We should learn from everything, the hills, the fields, the mountains, the sea, the wadis, the stars above. That's not my own idea. It's Spinoza's. In a word, we should relax."

"Then why don't you?" asked Anat, laughing as if someone had tickled her in the right place.

"I am only beginning to learn how to relax," Azariah apologized with a weak smile. "But if you mean that I should stop boring you, I'm already done talking. Or do you want me to make you laugh some more?"

"No, Azariah," said Rimona. "We want you to rest now."

With a small rock, Udi knocked over the empty canteen with a perfect pitch from twenty feet. "Come on," he said, "let's go."

Tia had finished gnawing the leftover chicken bones. They buried their garbage and shook out and folded the Arab Legion *kaffiyeh.* The girls plucked the stubble from each other's back.

"Who the hell's crying?" snapped Yonatan out of the blue, though no one had said a word. "It's just my goddamn allergy again. It starts up whenever anything starts growing. Azariah is right. I should go live in the desert."

"Excuse me. I said nothing of the sort."

"Maybe it was your Uncle Manuel, or whatever the hell his name was."

"Let's go!" said Azariah in a most down-to-earth manner. "My Uncle Manuel was killed, and we're out here today for a hike, not a memorial service. C'mon, let's go!"

The hikers split into two groups. Anat and Rimona went looking for mushrooms in the woods, while the men and Tia climbed the hill to poke about the ruins of the village. In no time Udi found the patterned neck of what had been a large earthenware jar and presented it to Azariah on the condition that he put an end to long speeches. "Fill it with soil and put a plate under it," he said. "I'll give you a cactus to plant in it." Azariah, in turn, gave him an old whetstone he found. A grindstone fragment that Yonatan came across had to be left for drier weather when a tractor and wagon could be used to haul it back. Suddenly, Azariah started and grabbed onto Udi's shirt.

"Watch it!" he whispered. "There's someone around here. I smell smoke."

"He's right. There's smoke coming from somewhere. I think it's from the mosque."

"Better be careful," said Azariah. "On the other hand, it could just be Bolognesi. I saw him leave the kibbutz this morning by himself."

"Hush up for a minute!"

"Or it could just be someone out for a walk. A nature lover. Or an amateur archaeologist. Or just someone wanting to be alone."

"I said be quiet! Let me listen."

But the only sound to be heard was borne on the wind from the far-off kibbutz. Its melancholy tones suggested a grave being dug. There was a rhythmic pounding, a feeble bleat, a faint clink of metal, the hoarse purring of a motor.

"The fact is," said Udi, "we don't know who might be skulking around here and we aren't armed. He could be very dangerous."

"Who?"

"That fellow. The escaped prisoner we were warned about a week ago. The strangler."

"Bolognesi?"

"Fuck Bolognesi! Yoni, instead of clearing out, maybe we should try taking him, huh?"

"Knock it off!" grumbled Yonatan. "We're not here to play cops and robbers. Let's pick up the girls and head home. It's time to call it a day."

"Why not? Don't forget, there's three of us and only one of him. It's a cinch if we're smart. The main thing's to keep him guessing. The bastard's probably asleep in the mosque."

"If I may make a suggestion."

"You may not! Calm down or you go right back to the girls. How about a little action, Yoni?"

"Why not?" said Yonatan with a shrug, as though he were giving in to a foot-stomping child.

"I'll make a dash for it first," volunteered Azariah.

"No one's dashing anywhere," Udi commanded coolly. "We're not armed. He may be. But he doesn't know that we're not or how many of us there are. Azariah, listen carefully. Don't budge from here. Pick yourself a nice big rock—that one over there will do—and wait in the corner behind the wall. Don't make a sound. If he comes running in your direction, wait till he's past you and brain him one. Is that clear?"

"Fantastic!"

"Yoni. Take the dog and cut off his retreat on the other side of the hill. I'll sneak up beside the door and holler at him to come out with his hands up like a good boy. And get this. The minute you hear me, make a racket. Get the dog to bark. Let him think we're at least two platoons."

"Fabulous!" shortled Azariah.

"If he comes out shooting, we all hit the deck and let him get away. But if he doesn't have a gun, I'll jump him from behind, and the two of you run to lend a hand. Ready? Let's go."

Why, we're brothers, thought Azariah with a proud, wild joy. We're blood brothers, and even if our blood is spilled, so what? Such is love, such is life! If we must die, die we must.

Enough, said Yonatan to himself. Enough. Who the hell cares anyway?

Far down the hillside, Anat and Rimona heard the long, savage shout. But whoever had been in the mosque was gone. There was nothing in its cold, damp, and dark interior but the embers of some smoking mossy twigs, a sour smell of urine, and a few freshly stubbed cigarette butts. Udi, poling about, managed to unearth a little tumulus of excrement that soon buzzed with green flies.

Yonatan, swept by an obscure longing, laid a pensive hand on Azariah's shoulder. "Well, that's that," he said. "Isn't it, pal?" Udi urged that they all hurry back to the kibbutz and report what they had seen to Etan R., who was in charge of security. Despite their haste, the hikers remembered to take along their mushrooms and relics, not to mention a small turtle found by Azariah after the storming of the mosque. Lovingly, secretly, he had named it Little John.

Etan R. telephoned the police, who immediately notified the border patrol and regional army headquarters. The Saturday ended in general commotion. Someone suggested asking the air force for a small observation plane while there was still enough light to see by. Before nightfall, patrols had been sent out to comb the deserted village, the orchards of the kibbutz, and the three wadis that ran down from it. The depth of the mud impeded the search, and by the time darkness came not even the bloodhounds had managed to come up with anything. Etan R. proposed pushing on with the aid of artillery flares. On Udi's advice, the kibbutz doubled its guard force and switched on the large searchlight atop the water tower.

"I'm the one," said Azariah, "who first realized he was out

there. Don't forget I warned you the very minute we set out."

"With a little luck we could have bagged him easy," said Udi.

"We could have," said Yonatan, "but we didn't."

"You're all tired," said Rimona. "Let's get some rest."

At three o'clock that same afternoon, before the first of the border patrol's olive-green jeeps had arrived, the hikers had sat down to drink coffee at Udi and Anat's before turning in for a sabbath nap. Udi did most of the talking, conducting a post-mortem of his unsuccessful blitz. The whole thing, he estimated, had taken no more than forty seconds. Rimona listened as if following another story altogether. She sat quietly on the mat, absorbed in herself, the calves of her bent legs resting against Yonatan and her shoulders against Azariah, who strove furtively to match her slow breathing with his own.

Around them, weedy plants grew from empty shell cartridges. Copper coffee mugs of all shapes and sizes, some sooty black, some silvery bright, stood on the shelves. An ancient nargileh adorned the coffee table, as did a charred helmet, from which there branched a wandering Jew. Several curved, oriental daggers jutted out from the inside of the front door. Hanging from the ceiling on a machine-gun belt was a chandelier of three light bulbs set in defused hand grenades. The mats and low stools were of wicker. A copper tray ornamented with Arab calligraphy, set on an old ammunition box, served as a table. Anat served coffee in little black cups that gave off a steamy smell of cardamom.

Even though he put little hope in its success, Udi intended to join the manhunt that was getting underway. If the man in the mosque had indeed been the escaped prisoner, he could easily have reached the main road long ago and hitched a ride to Haifa. On the other hand, if he was an Arab infiltrator, he had no doubt slipped back across the border. You could count on that nebbish of a Prime Minister, Eshkol, that nothing would happen to him there. He was probably sitting right now in his nigger hole and laughing his nigger laugh. Suddenly Udi's thoughts turned to money matters. He spoke of the profits from last year's cotton crop and of how the cowshed, always in the red, was only kept up because of old Stutchnik. Maybe Azariah had a Russian saying for such madness? No?

Instead, Azariah offered to amuse them with a spoon trick. Sticking the utensil deep into his throat, he proceeded to pull it out of the cuff of his gabardine slacks with a sheepish smile.

"But he does," said Rimona.

"Does what?" asked Anat.

"Have a saying for it," said Rimona. And without looking up she recited under her breath, "He who has never tasted defeat will never taste of triumph's sweet."

"That's enough magic of Chad," said Yonatan. "Let's go take a nap. You can rest at our place, Azariah. On the couch. Rimona won't mind. Let's go."

"All right," said Rimona, "if that's what you want to do."

It wasn't yet four o'clock when they left, but a dirty gray canopy of light already grazed the roofs of the small, white, symmetrically aligned houses. All the blinds had been drawn and the bedding hastily taken from the laundry lines. Not a soul was to be seen. A stealthy wind from the northwest blew in short, sharp gusts. A clap of thunder pealed far away like a piece of bad news, followed by a savage bolt of lightning that streaked across the whole firmament. The brief silence in its wake was shattered by an avalanche of thunder. Almost as soon as the first drops began to fall, the earth was lashed by ropelike whips of rain. Wet and out-of-breath, the three of them reached the house. Yonatan kicked the door open and slammed it behind them.

"I told you we wouldn't beat the rain," boasted Azariah. "Never mind. It doesn't matter. I've brought a present to cheer you up. Here, it's yours."

"Poor little turtle," smiled Rimona, taking it into her hand. "Just don't try climbing any walls."

"Leave it alone, Tia!" shouted Yonatan. "Rimona, we'll have to put it in that empty cardboard box on the porch. Come on, you two. It's time to take our nap."

"It's pouring," said Rimona.

The bottom of the blind banged against the window sill, spattering water across the pane. I, thought Yonatan Lifshitz, could have been on the road by now. I could already have been on the Bay of Biscay, where storms are really storms. And then it occurred to him: The dog stays with them.

The rain refused to stop, and the three of them had to eat supper inside—a meal of yogurt, omelets, and a salad. Through the streaming windows they could see people with raincoats pulled over their heads, running like hunchbacks with bundles of children in their arms. Of all the morning's birds only one could still be heard, its high, steady chirp like an automatic transmitter signaling from the site of an accident. Now Azariah regretted the lie he had told them: he must confess it right away, even if they laughed at him. Even if they asked him to leave. And they would have every right to. He would just go back to his tumbledown shack next door to Bolognesi where he belonged.

Yes, he had lied to them that morning. That is, about the cat.

What cat?

Why, the cat that Vassily the convert had cooked and they had all eaten on that Russian winter night in the abandoned farmhouse when he was a child. It was all a fraud. Not that it wasn't true that he had cried as he had never cried in his life; not that Vassily hadn't threatened to kill him, or that everyone, himself too, wasn't so hungry that they had taken to peeling the moss from the cellar walls and gorged on it until they gagged. Still, what he had told them that morning was a contemptible lie because he had eaten that cat just like the rest of them.

"But you didn't," said Rimona. "You never told us about any cat."

"Maybe I just wanted to and was afraid," said Azariah, taken aback. "That makes it even worse."

"He's crying," said Yonatan. After a moment's silence, he added, "Don't cry, Azariah. Why don't we play a game of chess."

With a quick, precise movement, Rimona lightly brushed her chill lips against the middle of Azariah's forehead. Azariah grabbed for his plate and raced with it out into the rain, stumbled, righted himself, splashed through puddles, trampled bushes, sank into mud, and fought his way out of it again until he reached Bolognesi's shack, where he found the Tripolitanian snoring loudly beneath his rough army blankets. He set down the plate at his side, tiptoed out again, ran all the way back to the Lifshitzes' door, pausing only to remove his dirty shoes, and announced triumphantly, "I've brought my guitar. We can have some music and sing if you'd like."

The storm raged all night. The army patrols gave up their search and returned soaking wet to their bases. In the end the electricity failed. Azariah kept on playing in the dark.

"In the morning," said Yonatan firmly, "we'll let our turtle go free."

That same night, at about one, having despaired of falling asleep and engulfed by dreary premonitions of death, Yolek rose, wrapped himself in a flannel bathrobe, and put on his slippers with a groan. He was furious with Hava for having turned out the night light in the bathroom, and his fury did not abate even when he realized that the power itself had failed. In Polish, he swore at himself and the drift of his life.

It took no small effort to find and light the kerosene lamp without waking his wife. He sat down at his desk, hating the sootiness of the wick as he adjusted it and the need to refrain from smoking lest it disturb Hava's sleep. Finally he put on his glasses and, in the next two hours, passionately composed a letter to Levi Eshkol, Prime Minister and Minister of Defense.

7

My Dear Eshkol,

Just receiving this letter will no doubt astound you, to say nothing of what's in it. You may even be angered with me. Well, I beg you not to be. In more than one debate between us, having run out of other arguments, I've heard you defend yourself with the old rabbinic saw "Judge not your friend until you have been in his place." This time, with your permission, it is I who will resort to this *argumentum in extremis* against you. So please bear with me.

Writing these lines is a painful business for me. Yet I am confident that you, who have always had the time for a comrade in distress, will not be put off even if you are surprised. Only a few days ago, at our party meeting in Tel Aviv, you took advantage of an empty seat in the sixth or seventh row to sit down beside me and whisper more or less these words: "Listen here, Yolek, you old turncoat, I sure as hell do miss you right now."

To which I, incorrigible sinner that I am, answered something like "I'll bet you do—like a hole in the head." Followed in low tones by "Just between the two of us, Eshkol, if I were back in the saddle these days, the first thing I'd do would be to take a stick to those rednecks who are swarming all over you and making your life so miserable." *"Nu?"* you asked jokingly. After which you sighed and added, more to yourself than to me, *"Nu, nu."*

Which is still the tone between the two of us after more than thirty years, thirty-six to be exact—in fact, closer to thirty-seven. And by the way, don't think I've forgotten the first time we met that October, or was it November, of 1928, when I came to you in despair. You were treasurer of the League of Kibbutzim, and I begged you, quite literally, for a small handout for one of our communes that had just arrived from Poland and was stranded up in the Galilee without a penny to its name. "You won't get a red cent from me!" you roared, then explained apologetically that charity began at home and sent me to Hartzfeld. Ah, well! Hartzfeld, of course, sent me right back to you. At which point you relented and agreed to make us a loan of what you humorously called "hush money." I haven't forgotten. And neither—please be so kind as not to play the innocent—have you.

In a word, that's been the tone between us all these years. Thirty-seven of them. And, by the way, we haven't many more left. We've almost reached the bottom line. Not that you and I don't still have a mutual reckoning to make for a long list of sins and transgressions committed against each other. Ah, well! I trust that you'll forgive me for all of mine. Believe me, I have already forgiven you for yours (except, that is, for the Pardes-Hanna affair, for which there can be no forgiveness this side of the Pearly Gates). But the ledger is nearly full and I feel a great weight on my heart. Our time is up, Eshkol, and—forgive me for talking this way—we're simply so much dead wood now. It can't be helped. If only what promises to come after us didn't give me gooseflesh, no, worse yet, the blackest of nightmares.

Wherever you look, in the party, in the government, in the

army, in the kibbutz movement, everywhere, there's nothing but Scyths, Huns, and Tatars closing in from all sides. Not to mention the plain ordinary scoundrels who have begun cropping up all around in alarming numbers. In a nutshell, no one knows better than you what an ill wind is loose in this land. Only what have you done about it? Stayed in harness, gritted your teeth, and said nothing, or at most sighed into your sleeve. And yet, if we were to use the last of our strength, we could perhaps still wield some influence, could perhaps still, ancient as we are, stem the tide. Well, I don't mean to write a polemic. We're old men, my dear friend and rival. We're living off the capital now. Pardon me for saying so, but we're on our way out. And I need take only one look at you to see how the state of things haunts and torments you. Believe me, it makes me shudder too. And by the way, forgive me for saying so, but you've also, as the Bible says, waxed fat and grown thick quite alarmingly. Physically, I mean. Why can't you take better care of yourself? Why can't you realize that *après nous,* as the French have it, the deluge?

Na. I'm getting carried away. Listen to me then. I'll try to make it as short as I can. It's time I got to the point. Only what, in God's name, is the point? It's precisely over this question that I agonize. It's a winter night, long past midnight, and a torrential rain out there is ruining the crops that are already rotting from a surfeit of heavenly bounty. And just to make things worse, the electric power is off too, so that I'm writing you by the light of a smoking kerosene lamp, which, whether I like it or not, brings back old memories that, I am not ashamed to admit, make me feel very close to you. You do know, don't you, that I quite literally loved you. Not that this made me anyone special. Who didn't love you in those days? You were once, if I may be forgiven for saying so, a gorgeous young fellow, tall, dark, handsome—in fact, the only tall member of our whole short, squat crowd—a gypsy at heart, half Ukrainian peasant, half Don Juan, with a glorious tenor voice to boot. Just between the two of us,

I may as well admit that we were all madly jealous of you. The girls said you were Eros incarnate and swooned when they spoke of you. Hartzfeld, behind your back, used to call you "that Cossack."

I myself, I must confess, was never much of a Valentino. Even then I must have had my nasty intellectual face. Oh, how I loathed it!

All said and done, though, I must say that time has been a great equalizer. You, if you'll pardon my saying so, have lived to become a fat, bald old buzzard, and so have I. What a pair of respectable old fogies we two are, both of us with glasses! We may still be a bit suntanned, but from the inside out our bodies are cankered by disease. There's hardly a sound bone left in them. We're on our last legs and the Scyths are already lining up to pounce. By the way, "a nasty intellectual face" is my friend Hava's phrase. A difficult, very peppery lady, although idealistic beyond all words. Once, in her salad days—I can't recall if we ever discussed this—she conceived a passion for a criminally insane lad but had enough presence of mind to extricate herself from his clutches and enough ambition to attach herself to me. I, as is my custom, forgot and forgave long ago. The problem is that to this day she can't forgive me for having forgiven her.

I won't deny that I'm a wicked man, as wicked as they come, yes, wicked to the very marrow of my old bones. In fact, I may even be one of the thirty-six perfectly wicked men on whom our world depends. I mean one of those wicked enough to have sold their own souls on behalf of the cause we held sacred from the time we were young, one of those whose wickedness alone enabled them to preach and practice the faith and all its many commandments. Nevertheless, my dear Eshkol, wicked as we were, we did do a bit of good along the way that the Devil himself cannot deny us. It's just that we were wicked even then, and cunning too, even if it's only lately that the fools and our enemies have begun to realize what deceitful old men we really are.

All our plotting, all our conspiracies—why, it was never for our own pleasure or profit, but only to do good. Not, if truth be told, that we shunned the public limelight then any more than we do now.

And yet, in the last analysis, our wickedness, if you will, was almost religiously selfless. We served the cause with both the good and the bad in us, and that makes us a thousand times better than this new race of rascals that's sprung up around you, and around me, and everywhere you look. Ah, well! It's all over with now. You, if I may say so, are a fatter, more bloated old dotard than even the cartoonists make you out to be, while I'm a hunchback curmudgeon with—it shouldn't happen even to you—a bad ear in the bargain. And quite ill as well, by the way.

But this isn't the point either. Believe me, for once I'm not writing to you in order to quarrel. We've already quarreled more than enough, the two of us. On the contrary, it's high time we made up, you and I, from the far ends of our two vast deserts of loneliness. That's why I'm not going to have it out with you again over the Lavon affair and all that. Whatever I have to say on the subject has already been said, both to your face and in the press, and deep down in your heart you know only too well that you'll broil on a low flame in hell for your part in the whole charming episode. *Finis.*

The main thing is that we are defeated, my dear Eshkol. Defeated once and for all. My hand rebels against writing these words, but the truth takes precedence. It's two o'clock in the morning now, the rain keeps falling like a curse, and it's all over with, the whole long journey. In vain, my friend, was all our devotion, in vain all our dreams, in vain all the years we plotted with subtle cunning to save the Jewish people—*na,* these Yids of ours—from their own hands and those of the Gentiles. An ill wind is tearing it all up now. Pulling it up by the roots. I tell you, it's the end of everything. The cities. The towns. The kibbutzim. And worst of all, of course, the youth. The Devil has had the last laugh. We simply carried the virus of Jewish exile with us to this country, and now we see a new exile sprouting right under our nose. We've gone from the frying pan to the fire, I tell you.

Please forgive me for writing all this. There's such thunder and lightning in the window right now and the electric power, I've already told you—or have I?—has failed. By the way, writing by this lamp is very hard for me. The cigarettes I smoke choke the last breath out of me, but without them I nearly go mad. I do believe, though, that I'll drink a little glass of brandy—just a wee drop. To the Devil's health right now! Cheers!

My dear Eshkol, do you, too, tonight in Jerusalem, hear from the depths, from the belly of the storm, the wail of a freight train in the dark? Do you? Or don't you? Because if you do you'll understand better the frame of mind in which this pitiful letter is being penned. Just now, my good friend, I thought of some lines of the poet Rachel that you used to recite with great feeling and pathos: "Or was it no more than a vision I saw and you but a dream that I dreamed."

Na. It's an old, old story: the dreams, the fire in the breast, the selfless devotion—and the cunning, old age, and disillusionment too. An old story indeed. And now our time has come to die, unless, *pace* Gogol, we are already dead souls. Please forgive me for venting all this spleen on you. What, if I may ask, are your daughters up to these days? Ah, well! You needn't answer, and you can forget that I asked. With sons like mine, in any case, one certainly can't found a dynasty. Far from it. One has the green bile and the other the black. And a bug in his head—self-fulfillment, self-fulshmillment, doing his own thing, having his own fling, getting his whatsis together, all the possibilities he's missing in the big world out there, and the Devil knows what else. (Incidentally, I assume you do too.) And that long hair of theirs! One might think every last one of them was an artist. A whole generation of *artistes*! Half-asleep all the time too, the whole lot of them. And—there's really no contradiction—mad about sports. Who kicked whose ball, who tripped whom, and all the rest of it. *A groysser gesheft.*

Ben-Gurion once said in one of his dithyrambic moments that here in this country we made a nation out of the human chaff of the Jewish people and turned the Worm of Jacob into the Lion of Judah. That's no more than to say that you and I were worms and chaff, and these long-haired cretins are the lions that we prayed for. How did Alterman once put it in a poem? "As wondrous as the butterfly's birth from the worm." It's enough to bring down the house, I tell you. Why, the thought of this tiny, ugly, airless, poor man's America of ours doing its own banal thing . . .

And you, by the way, you're to blame too. Nor can you be forgiven. If it had been up to me, I'd have clamped down with an iron fist long ago on all the yowling, all the commercials on the radio. From morning till night this country is being flooded by the most apelike, positively murderous Negro sex music, jungle drums, jazz, rock-and-rock, as if we had come to this land to live in the jungles of Africa and turn at long last into cannibals. As if none of us had ever heard of Chmelnitski and Petliura and Hitler and Bevin and Nasser. As if the last remaining Jews had gathered here from the far corners of the earth for the sole purpose of having an orgy.

Ah, well! This is no time for settling old scores. You too have wearied of tilting against an ill wind. Why, just the other day my older son came to inform me that working in the tractor shed is not for him. And that the kibbutz is not for him either. And that the state of Israel, with all due respect, is just a little corner of a big, wide world. And that he wants to see that world and have all kinds of experiences in it before settling down. In a sudden philosophical epiphany, he came to the earthshaking conclusion that life is short and that one only lives it once. Quote, unquote. And that his own life belongs to him—not to his people, not to his kibbutz, not to the movement, and not even to his parents. *Na.*

Good morning, Mister Whiz Kid, I said to him. Where have you been taking a crash course in philosophizing? In the sports pages? With some disc jockey? Watching the movies?

Na. He just shrugged and turned to stone.

Let me add that I'm not excusing myself either. *Mea culpa.* I did him and his brother a great wrong. All through their childhood I was so busy bringing about the kingdom of heaven for the party and the movement that I left their education to the kibbutz. Not, incidentally, that you have any right to talk. From what I hear, you haven't fared much better. Well, we sowed the wind and we have, as it was written, reaped the whirlwind. But the true, the one real culprit is none other than Ben-Gurion. He and his lunatic Canaanite theories about the new generation of biblical Gideons and Nimrods that we were going to raise here, a pack of wild prairie wolves instead of little rabbis. No more Marxes, Freuds, and Einsteins; no more Menuhins and Jascha Heifetzes; not even any more Gordons, Borochovs, and Berls—no, from now on nothing but sunburned, ignorant, illiterate warriors, Joabs and Abners and Ehuds.

And what came out of all this hocus-pocus? Nabal the Carmelite, I tell you, and all the other little pisspots we see on all sides. You yourself are surrounded by these gangsters—wild-eyed kulaks plucked by Ben-Gurion from behind the plow, Jewish Neanderthals, Cro-Magnon heroes, moronic rednecks, circumcised Cossacks, biblical Bedouins, Tatars of the Hebrew faith. To say nothing of all the calculating, diplomaed, foppish young scoundrels with their expensive suits and silver tie clips, all those decadent Anglo-Saxonish dandies and their flashy American elegance. What a far cry they all are from the provincial scoundrels, the mystical Jewish cutthroats, the somnambulists in love with ideas that you and I were! *Na.* That's just the tone that's between us. Don't you be angry with me. I'm writing from the depths, and they are seething.

Not that I'm looking to pick a fight with you. We've fought more than enough, you and I. Although, to tell the truth, I don't envy you. Yet maybe things would be better if I were in your place. You're too quick to give in and forgive. Whereas I'm just wicked enough to squelch this wild bacchanal once and for all. Still, I don't envy you. On the contrary, my heart goes out to you. Thank God I'm not responsible for this mess and can, biblically speaking, sit quietly beneath my grape vine and my fig tree. Something tells me, though, that deep inside you, you too are heartsick with weeping for Rachel's lost dream. For, though it dare not speak out, the heart knows that we have been hopelessly, irrevocably, eternally defeated. All is lost, Eshkol. *Geendikt.*

Enough beating about the bush. Time to get down to what's really on my mind—my son.

Look at it this way. No one knows better than you do that in all these years Yolek Lifshitz never toadied up to you for a single personal favor. On the contrary. Often enough I spooned you out wormwood and vinegar. During the Great Split I even published an article against you and cruelly called you a *jongleur.* And, more recently, during the Lavon Affair, I wrote that you, Levi Eshkol, had sold your soul to the Devil. Nor, God help me, do I take a word of it back. May He before Whom there is neither foolishness nor levity forgive us, my dearest Eshkol. The truth of the matter is that we were all *jongleurs.* We honestly did sell our souls. Not for filthy lucre, to be sure, or for our own worldly pleasure or comfort. We sold them, if I may say so, for the sake of heaven. And that brings me back to what I said about the thirty-six wicked men on whom the world depends. *Na.* I'm digressing again.

Allow me to return to my son. That is, to my elder, Yonatan. And allow me, too, to make a long story short. The boy was raised here on Kibbutz Granot with more than his share of vitamins and sunshine, yet somehow managed to grow up to be a sensitive, shy young man, a real *feinshmecker.* As for the rest, you can easily imagine it. A politician with high principles for a father, and for a mother—*nu,* Hava. Perhaps you've met her? A shattered soul, that one, a walking hornet's nest. Incidentally, we'll all fry over a low flame in hell for what we've done to our women. All our revolutions and utopias have been carried out on their backs. And they were the only ones who paid the full price.

On top of everything else, this young man suddenly went and fell in love with a strange, apathetic creature, one who—mind you, I write this for your eyes alone with the utmost confidence in your discretion—may even suffer from some slight mental retardation. And the two of them set up house. I must say I don't understand the first thing about modern love. And then they had some sort of gynecological tragedy. I won't go into the details. Of what help could you or I be in such matters anyway?

In a word, they have no children, no great love for each other, and apparently no real happiness together either. And now, how shall I put it, the young man is looking for some purpose in his life. That is, he's planning a long trip overseas to "find himself" or "fulfill himself" or whatever it is they call it. The Devil alone understands them. The whole thing devastated me. Why, here I was, about to lose my elder son. The boy too was lost! You can imagine that I didn't give in without a fight. I reasoned with him all I could. I tried being nice and I tried being harsh. I clung to him with every ounce of strength I had. And our strength, Eshkol, is nearly gone. You yourself know how true that is. What are we to them even now but pig-headed old men, old buzzards who have lived too long, power-hungry old tyrants? In short, the boy refuses to budge. He's determined to make some radical change in his life.

You'll want to know what stuff he's made of. Well, I'll answer that as simply as I can. He's got a good head, a good heart, and a good soul. He's missing only the spark that could set him off. Please, don't smile at this point in your usual, heartily cunning way as if to say, "Witness dismissed. What else can you expect of a doting father?" I beg you to believe that I can see my son quite objectively. That much credit you still owe me. And forgive me if I seem at the same time to be writing all this with my own heart's blood. Oh, yes, I forgot. The boy plays chess too. He's even tournament caliber. In other words, he's not just another dumb yokel.

My dear Eshkol, you're a wise man. Please don't think the worse of me for this. My hand shakes as it writes. It's a terrible thing for me to have to come to you after all these years and ask for a private kindness. To tug at your sleeve, as it were, and beg you to remember what the rabbis said about the man who saves a single soul, etc. I place my firstborn in your hands. You know his family. You know his paternity. Be so good as to find him some suitable novitiate.

I hang my head before you. *Nolo contendere.* We may be old men, Eshkol; we may have had our fill of being spat at and insulted; we may have committed every sin in the book; but he—I mean my son Yonatan—is no scoundrel. You have my word on that. I'll even swear to it on the Bible, if you like. The boy is no scoundrel. Far from it. He won't disappoint you. He won't try to take you for a ride or stab you in the back. It was you who once said to me, "After all, a man is only a man—and even that only rarely." Well, than, take the boy and you will not live to regret it. A man may be made out of him yet. He still hasn't been totally ruined by the ill wind that's decimated his generation.

It's nighttime now, my dear friend and old rival, and the storm is still howling outside. The elements themselves have conspired to bring the grim tidings to us. And Death is breathing down our necks. We who gave the pillars of the earth a good shaking are now being hush-a-byed like babes. The incorruptible usher has come toward us down the aisle. Already he's tapping our shoulder and requesting us, politely but firmly, to tiptoe out of the hall without much fuss. Well, then, it's time to go. Not on tiptoe, though. On the contrary, let's walk out proudly and with our heads held high—as high, that is, as your corpulent, and my decrepit, body will permit. We have nothing to be ashamed of, you and I, who in the course of our lives accomplished one or two worthwhile things that our ancestors never dreamed of. You know that's the truth as well as I.

By the way, I'm not ashamed to admit that it grieves me to think Ben-Gurion will apparently outlive us. Forgive me for being wicked to the last, but just between the two of us, what did he have that we didn't? Only that he, and he alone, was the demiurge behind the ill wind! Let that be as it may, though. I won't pick another quarrel now. I know that you still refuse to agree with me on this, and insist that we are pygmies compared to him, etc. As you wish. When I wrote in my last pamphlet (*Facing the Future,* 1959) that Ben-Gurion had left an indelible stamp upon our lives "for better and for worse," you even reprimanded me in public. "You should get down on your knees before him, Yolek," you said. But I won't pursue the matter any further. In the meantime you've felt his sting too, which made me both grieve for you and—why bother to deny it?—experience sweet feelings of malicious joy. Let's not argue any more about Ben-Gurion. Deep in your heart and in your gut, you old buzzard, you know as well as I do that I'm right.

Let me tell you about a curious incident. Several weeks ago a bizarre young man—a bit of a sensitive plant, and a musician and philosopher to boot—turned up at our kibbutz and asked to be allowed to stay. I had my doubts about him. Another eccentric was not exactly what we needed at the moment. On second thought, though, I decided to risk it and take him on. He is the kind of human material one doesn't see any more, a genuine dreamer and intellectual, if rather confused. In a word, he might have been one of us had he not been born in the wrong generation. "The forest's too deep for small boys and sheep," he tells me, quotes copiously from Spinoza, and suddenly stops to opine that Ben-Gurion is out of his mind. I hardly need tell you that I gave him a good dressing-down, but to myself I said, using a favorite phrase of yours, *"Nu, nu!"*

And by the way, to change and stick to the subject at one and the same time, a few days ago I noticed an odd item in the paper about an engineer named She'altiel ha-Palti. He supposedly sent you a memorandum about some revolutionary military rocket he claims to have invented. It may interest you to know that this She'altiel ha-Palti is none other than our old friend Shunya Plotkin, who was once a mounted guard in Nes Tsiyyona. One of the last Mohicans and no doubt as sick and weary at heart as you and me. Please, at least take the trouble to answer him kindly and in person. Who knows? Perhaps there really is something to his fantasies. Why not look into it? And don't answer me with "Another lunatic is not exactly what I need at the moment." Allow me to convey to you what I've learned from long experience. Whoever is not a partial lunatic is a total scoundrel. Simple as that. Either/or. And we certainly don't need any more scoundrels, do we?

Well, it's time to end this letter with comradely greetings. It's still storming outside and dark as the ninth plague of Egypt, and my only light is this smoking, flickering lamp. It's as if Death itself were pounding his fists on the window pane and refusing to put up with any more of my tricks or procrastination. I believe I'll drink another little glass of brandy to the health of the Devil and, with your permission, go to bed. Please answer posthaste about my son. You can easily plant him in your garden. You must. And by the way, I beg you not to take personally what I said about you at the meeting in Tel Aviv. You are very dear to me. Especially when I think of the Tatars looking over your shoulder.

Oh, yes, one last thing. Whether it's the brandy or the smoke from the lamp that's addled my brain, I have an idea. A proposition for you. Because you too must be passing a dreadful night in Jerusalem. And you too must be having trouble sleeping. Well, then, listen here. If there really is anything to this business of a world to come, and if it is, as our forefathers believed, a world of pure delight, how about agreeing to be my roommate? That is, if you think you could put up with me. The two of us might ask to share a tent together. We'll rise early every morning for work. We'll ask for and receive a little plot of rocky ground to clear and dig wells in and we'll plant grape vines, hoe irrigation courses, and fetch water in tin cans on donkeyback. And we'll quarrel no more, you and I. On the contrary. Every evening we'll light a candle or two in our tent and have a heart-to-heart talk. Whenever we disagree, we'll thrash it out between us, and when we've had enough of that, you'll play the harmonica and I'll sit down in my undershirt to compose a political tract. From time to time I'll ask your advice, and, even if I don't always take it, you'll bear with me. Maybe we'll find some heavenly terrace from which, at dusk, we can look down on this land. The two of us standing there barefoot in the breeze, keeping watch over our children. Who knows? Perhaps we'll even manage to wield some influence, to organize, manipulate, or wheedle the authorities into granting a reprieve, a commutation of sentence, a softening of the decree.

Because that decree is quite horribly grim. God forgive me for saying such a thing—my hand rebels against writing it—but you, Eshkol, know as well as I do that it's true. Or have I simply taken leave of my senses? I've been so ravaged by physical pain, and you too, if I'm not mistaken, have not been in the best of health. Take good, good care of yourself, then, and be strong.

Your
Yolek

He put down his pen and for a moment sat lost in thought. On his old face, by the waning light of the lamp, entrenched lines of irony, of love, of kindness, of suffering, of anger, and of cunning fought with one another to gain the upper hand.

Suddenly he changed his mind. Carefully tearing the pages of his letter from his writing pad, he fastened them with a paper clip and placed them at the far end of his desk. Then, reaching for the pen and beginning again, he wrote:

Dear Eshkol,

I need to ask for your help in a strictly private matter concerning my son. Can I meet with you sometime soon to discuss it in person?

Yours with comradely greetings,
Yisra'el Yolek Lifshitz

He rose from his chair with a groan, shuffled over to the bookcase, and opened a small panel between two shelves. With an unsteady hand he slipped the first draft of his letter into a bulging brown envelope that bore the heading "Personal/To Be Opened Posthumously" and shut the panel. Then he folded the second draft and put it in a plain envelope, which he addressed to Prime Minister and Defense Minister Levi Eshkol, The Government Compound, Jerusalem.

He extinguished the dying lamp, returned to bed, and lay there aching. The rain kept falling.

8

Now they're both fast asleep, and it's funny, because one fell asleep on the couch in the living room, burrowing beneath the pillow with his head to make himself a cave, and the other did just the opposite, sprawling on the bed in the bedroom without even taking off the cover, spreadeagled on his stomach. Watching anybody sleep makes you pity him. When you sleep, you look like the child you once were. In that book on human sacrifice in the Congo, it said that sleep is sent to us from the place where we were before we were born and will go back to after we die.

Both doors are open. The house is quiet. And so are we three. From where I am, I can see them both, one long and thin, one short and thin. Both absorbed in the same quiet. Not winning or losing any more. Not even at chess. This quiet comes from me. I have put Efrat to sleep, too, and now I am all alone. It is pitch dark through the window, but not so dark as in the two rooms where they are sleeping. Without jealousy. Without lies. Without moving. The one weak light comes from the kitchen, from me. Because that is where I am now, juicing grapefruit by the sink. Some of my light trickles over them through the open doors. They are both weak and good. That is how you are when you sleep.

I have my flannel bathrobe on. The brown one. It's winter outside. On the jacket of *The Magic of Chad* is a picture of a black warrior spearing an antelope. But a warrior spears only himself. A dead antelope will run like the wind at night, run to the meadow, to the forest, run all the way home. Because all of us do have a home.

I showered and shampooed to look my best for them. My hair is wet and loose. When they wake, I will give them juice to drink because they have both been down since yesterday with a fever, headache, and cough. All winter Etan has been living with two girls in his room by the swimming pool. Since the day before yesterday I have been living with Yoni and the boy.

I'm not the only one awake. Tia, at the far end of the rug in Azariah's room, is quietly snapping at whatever is burrowing into her fur. Snapping and snapping because she can't reach it. But she won't give up. For a second I heard Efrat cry far away. Now she's gone back to sleep. It is even quieter than before. The refrigerator has stopped humming.

I'll finish up in the kitchen and sit down to embroider.

There's the news again, on the neighbors' radio. Through the thin wall I can hear that Damascus is once again making threats. That's the kind of thing they both like to hear. That there have been grave developments. That things have taken a turn for the worse. That tensions have mounted. News like that makes Yoni clench his teeth and his eyes get narrower and darker. Zaro's eyes glow but first he turns pale, then he becomes flushed, then he starts to talk a blue streak. Just a rumor or a whiff of war is enough to make them both more dangerous, more handsome, more passionate, more alive to me. Like when they want to have sex and feel shame.

When Yoni can't hold it in any more and starts to come, he beats his fist on the sheet and bites my shoulder. And makes an animal sound in a hoarse bass voice like an echo in an empty house. Zaro gives a quick yelp like a dog that's been wounded. Then his mouth and nose drool and then there are tears. Their sleep comes from me. I accept them both. They are mine. The antelope is asleep. And the spear and the black warrior. When you sleep you are weak and good. I will wear my blue corduroy pants and red sweater and my hair is clean and light and I smell of almond soap and shampoo.

What is Damascus threatening? I can't hear because little Assaf is playing his toy xylophone. He taps his stick. Tin-tin. He stops to listen. Tin-tin-tin. He stops again. And yet another time. It must be a cold rainy windy night in Damascus too.

Something with wings is flying around. Maybe it's a moth. Around and around the overhead light. Burning itself each time and flying away. But each time wanting or having to come back. And burning itself again. Wanting what it does not have or need. Its shadow keeps flitting over the marble counter. Over the cabinet. Over me. Pretty little moth by the light, why don't you listen to me and take a rest.

The cut on my finger smarts from the grapefruit. When I suck it, it feels better. Saliva disinfects. And heals. I read in a book that white scientists in Mozambique learned from village doctors to treat wounds with saliva. Once I saw Yoni's mother sitting on her porch at the end of a blue summer day, sucking her thumb. Like Efrat. Sleep, Efrat. Mommy is here, watching you.

He's talking in his sleep in that cave of his. Saying something like rrrrrrr. Tia is saying rrrrrrr too. Be quiet, Tia. It's nothing.

What's funny is that now the turtle has started scratching in his box. Maybe he finished the cucumber I gave him this morning and wants to leave. Don't be afraid, little turtle. You're as snug as a bug in a rug. And so are you, little Efrat. Because I am.

There's a wind but no rain now. Telling us to be good. And we will be, so we can rest. It's so cold and wet out there. And so good that we're all in here. Except for the cypress trees bending in the wind. There's no way for them to come in. As soon as they have straightened up, along comes the wind and forces them back down. It's the wounded antelope again. That won't give in till it's reached home.

In winter we're shut up indoors. But soon it will be summer again. Whoever wants can lie in the grass. Whoever wants can swim in the pool. And then Yoni will go to play chess in the tournament. And to serve in the army. And tell me new things when he comes back. And Zaro will write me a poem. And go into politics and become famous and important.

It's so sad and cold to be young and a man, especially in the winter. They have this thing inside that's always hungry and thirsty. Always gnawing at them. And making them suffer. It's not just wanting to have sex. It's something else too. Something harder and more lonely. Because the sex part is simple. It's over with the minute they come, like a wound you heal with saliva. But this other thing is cruel. It hardly ever leaves them alone. Maybe only when they fall asleep. Or when there are grave developments and they smell a whiff of war. The smell of death makes up for what they're missing. It gives them some kind of pleasure. But what can it be that is always so hungry and thirsty. That has to spear antelopes over and over again. As though they had been given a promise that was never kept. A promise by an evil wizard who won't and can't keep it. And it's not just Zaro or Udi or Yoni. It's Yolek too. And my father when he was alive. And Ben-Gurion shouting over the radio.

And even Bach, the tears in whose music I love. How bad,

how sad he feels because he too was made that promise that wasn't kept. When I listen to Cantata 106, it's like being a child alone in a dark, deserted house without its mother. In a forest. In a wilderness. In the taiga, in the tundra, as Yoni says. First begging, come back, how could you leave me, then ashamed to be begging and boastful. What do I care, if I have to be alone, then I will be, I'm big and strong enough to spear an antelope. Just at the end there's that part where he almost seems to touch himself, where he murmurs, don't cry, don't cry, everything has a reason, soon pa will come to explain, soon ma will be home.

I brought kerosene. I lit the heater. And now it's burning with a lovely blue flame in the room where Zaro is sleeping. It has a nice crackle too. Just as the ad said. The Whispering Stove, it was called.

Azariah's hands are digging deeper into the cave beneath his pillow. He likes it when he's called Zaro. But there isn't any heater in the bedroom where Yoni is sleeping. I'd better cover him with another blanket. And feel his head. It's hot. And dry. And Zaro's nose is all stuffed. I'm a little chilly myself. I have this habit of pulling my hands into my sleeves to keep them warm. If Efrat loses her bottle and looks for it in her sleep, a black sorceress will come and put it ever so gently back in her mouth. Go back to sleep, my little Efrat.

I pour the juice into two tall glasses, and cover each glass with a saucer, and slice the yeast cake I baked yesterday. Whoever wakes and wants can eat and drink. Because there's plenty.

And there will be tomorrow too. I take out a glass bowl and pour a cup of sugar. Quietly, so as not to wake them. And crack four eggs and stir them into it. And slowly add half a cup of flour, stirring all the time, and half a cup of sour cream from the refrigerator, stirring all the time, and a grated lemon rind, stirring all the time. And all the time purring to myself. And now, but not all at once, two-and-a-half cups of flour, still stirring strongly to break up the lumps. And pour it out slowly so that it doesn't spatter into the electric baker that I greased with margarine and plugged in with the heat on medium. I have forty minutes to wait for it to brown.

I fixed Yoni's brown jacket while he told me about the taiga and the tundra. And then he said he was going away. But he never went. Yoni, I said, I can listen while I embroider. And there's a concert on the radio too. And I told them both what I read about the Kikuyu, who put out jugs of water when the moon is full to catch and save its reflection for the dark nights to come.

I've washed and dried the dishes and put everything away in the closet. The match I stuck in the cake didn't come out dry, so I'll let it bake some more. Meanwhile I'll see who needs to be covered. It's good that they're both down with fever. It's high time. And have to stay in bed. And put up with some peace and quiet. And stop climbing walls like little turtles. Because when we went on that hike two days ago with Udi and Anat, and they attacked the village on the hill and captured that mosque with no one in it, they all came down with the flu.

Now the cake is done. Anat told me that Udi's sick too. I'll sit down to embroider. And play a record softly so they don't wake up. If they do, there's cake and juice. Whoever wants can eat and drink. Maybe Albinoni? No, not him. Maybe Vivaldi's *Four Seasons*. Or else more Bach.

Yesterday was Arbor Day. Yoni's mother came by, all upset. What's the matter with you, you haven't even come to see how Yolek is, he's had these terrible pains. The doctor gave him two shots. The first was mild but the second knocked him out. She saw Azariah. And that made her even madder. What would people say? He's ill, I said. Just like Yoni. And if people talk, they talk about you, too. About things that happened before we were born. That tragic love of yours. You're a little cuckoo, Rimona, she said. I'm sorry, Hava, but it's so cold and damp in that shack of his, and there's no one to take care of him there. And the barber is supposed to come after Arbor Day, and whenever he comes he stays in that room next to Bolognesi. And it's raining, so Yoni asked Azariah to stay because Azariah gave him a little turtle. I swear you're a little cuckoo, Rimona. And she left and slammed the door. And the turtle is scratching again in his box. What does he want, want, want?

I'll dust the floor and the bookcase. I'll make myself some coffee too. They're both so sound asleep. So weak and good. Without spears or antelopes. And the funniest part is that I'd like to put them both together in the double bed and sleep out here on the couch by myself. Or else be between them at night. Touching them both.

It was an Arbor Day without any planting of trees or festivities. Just the rain coming down all day. And the wind sweeping in from the mountains to bend the cypresses in the garden. Letting out a long wail as if it were thirsty and wanted to come inside.

If she cries at night, I'll gentle her so that she doesn't wake them. I'll take her and lay her on my stomach with her bottle. Somewhere I read that the mother's heartbeat soothes the baby to sleep. Because it remembers it from the womb, the rhythm of the heart. In Namibia you're born to the rhythm of tom-toms.

I have a little cat and its name is Efrat. A sleepy little cat and that's that.

Once I read that Bach had ten or twenty children and that they all lived in a little red-brick house in Germany. Don't be sad, Mrs. Bach may have said to him, you'll see it will all be all right. And he said, yes, yes, though he hardly ever believed her, and helped fetch the coal and tend the fire and wash the dirty diapers and sing the sick baby to sleep. But sometimes when he was up late at night with a German rain falling outside, the spear and the antelope got to him too. He wanted a hug. Or a touch. Or a word. None of which Mrs. Bach could have given him even if she tried. His mother, he wanted his mother to come. To take him down from the cross. To wash the blood from his wounds.

And what came instead? The usual. Another war. More bloodshed.

The water is boiling again. I'll make them tea with lemon and honey in the big thermos. And fill the little one too. They'll have it to drink tonight when their throats hurt. How dark that rain is in that dark window!

When I was little we planted trees on Arbor Day. Once I even planted a little black rubber ball in our garden. It didn't take root and neither did the trees.

I am Rimona Lifshitz. I am Rimona Fogel. This is my daughter Efrat. This is my husband Yoni. This is my friend Zaro.

I left work early today to take care of my two sick men. Lipa fixed the boiler in the laundry that was broken when he was sick. Now he's all better. He told me a joke in Yiddish. After I showered, I put my hair up so they could see my long neck. But then I thought, it's nicer when it's loose and tumbling down.

No, they're not waking up. One's curled up like a fetus in *Healthy Pregnancy,* and the other just turned over and groaned. He's on his back like the crucified Bach in the jacket picture on the *St. Matthew Passion,* his arms spread wide and his hands balled into fists. Who gave me a cyclamen pressed between the pages of his pass book. Who wants to go to the tundra, to the taiga, to hunt for the whales that the newspaper said will soon be extinct. And to leave me with Efrat and Azariah. And with Tia. While we all wait for him.

That's why I'll change from this bathrobe. To look my best.

Whoever wakes can have juice and cake or else bread and sour cream. And have his temperature taken. And an aspirin. Zaro will play his guitar. Or else the three of us will play a game if we want.

Yoni's game will be to pretend he's a brave sailor hunting for whales or for desert islands in the South Seas. Far away at home I have to wait for him and trust him. In the end he'll come back with a bullet wound in his shoulder and be written up again in the paper. And he'll want to make violent love right away. And I'll say yes.

With Zaro it's mother and child. And because he's so shy, it will be up to me to help him without his knowing that I am. From the first caress to the last little yelp, I'll teach him not to hurry like a sneak thief because he isn't stealing a thing and there's nothing to be afraid of.

What I did for Azariah today was to wash and press his shirt and his gabardine slacks that got all muddy from our hike. And what I did for Yoni was to take his torn boot to the shoe shop and have Yashek fix it. So that it won't annoy him any more or laugh at him.

You can see the clearing in the jungle on the banks of a blue river just as it says in *The Blue Nile.* Efrat's crawling on all fours, the golden sand around her warm and clean. And the moonlight swaddles her with silver webs. From the empty depths behind her comes soft music. And African women in the whitest of white clothes are singing songs without words to their children in a language they call Amharic. And plucking hollow reeds from a shallow spot in the waters of the blue, blue Nile. And among them, dressed in white too, is Yehoshafat the teacher, who was hit in the head by a bullet while playing a tom-tom with the most delicate touch.

Blue-blue, blue-blue goes the heart. Blue-blue, blue-blue, in Africa there lived a gnu. Hush, little baby, don't you cry, lu lu lu lu lu, you'll see your daddy by and by, lu lu lu lu lu. Gnus, leopards, giraffes, lions, ostriches, hush, go to sleep, don't cry. Don't be sad, says Mr. Yehoshafat, it's wrong to expect new things all the time, new antelopes, new spears, new wanderings, new wars. Whoever is tired will rest. And whoever has rested will listen. And whoever has listened will know that it's a rainy night out. And that beneath the rain the wet earth lies quietly. And that beneath the wet earth the strong rocks are sleeping, the rocks on which light never shines. And that up above the clouds, up above the air, all is quiet too, the quiet between the stars. And that beyond the last star is the last quiet of all. What do they want from us? Not to disturb, not to make noise because nothing untoward will happen if we keep still.

Vassily the convert did not mean to harm Mr. Yehoshafat with the pistol he had cleaned and oiled. Now he has come to ask for love and forgiveness because his intentions were good. He gave me a pressed cyclamen. And a little English book from India about karmic suffering and astral light.

They are both asleep now. One hardly talks because it makes him sad to be like all the others, and one talks all the time because it makes him sad to be different. I accept them.

All that night after our hike when the power was off, he kept on playing and singing. He didn't dare stop out of fear we might say, thank you, good night. Until finally I said to him, let's go to bed now, Zaro, you can play some more tomorrow.

Never mind, Yoni said, he can sleep right here on the couch. Yoni, Zaro, I said, off to bed with you both. And because there were no lights, I lit a candle in the corner of the kitchen and another by the radio. Yoni fell asleep in his clothes on our bed, and I was left with the boy.

Excuse me, I said, I'm getting undressed and going to sleep. He was frightened and begged me in a whisper to forgive him for being so vile. But you're not, I said, you're good. Don't be sad.

He turned his face to the wall and lay all night wide awake on the couch, hating himself for something he wasn't to blame for. I couldn't sleep either. And when it was almost morning, the thunder and lightning woke Yoni, and Tia wanted to go out. So Yoni got up and saw me sitting in my nightgown, thinking. You're crazy, he said. Then Tia scratched to come back in. And Yoni went to open the door while Zaro lay there without moving, almost without breathing, that's how scared and embarrassed he was. And Yoni grabbed me by the shoulders and took me and threw me on the bed like a sack and did it to me all clumsy and wrong and so mean that it hurt. Yoni, I whispered, stop, he's awake, he can hear, don't do this to him. Fuck him, whispered Yoni, what do I care? This is it because tomorrow I'll be gone. How can you go when you're sick? Just look how you're burning with fever. Tomorrow I'm taking off, you crazy woman. If you want that crazy nut, I don't care. He's all yours, enjoy him, I've had it. Yoni, can't you even see that you love him a little yourself? But I'm sleeping, Rimona. You can get up and go to him dripping with my sperm, what the hell do I care? Fuck it all! So I went to him dripping and sat down on the floor by his side and said I had come to sing to him. Then I put my hand on his cheek and it was burning too. Don't talk now, child, give me your hand and see what I have, don't say a word. Until a dirty light came through the slats of the blinds and Arbor Day began. I took a hot shower, dressed slowly in the shower stall, and went to work in the laundry. When I came home, the two of them were down with a high fever. I gave them aspirin and tea and covered them and put them to sleep. Black women by the blue Nile will change Efrat's diaper.

Now they're waking up. One is squirming, the other tossing from side to side. I'll put away my embroidery.

Good night, Efrat, good night, Mr. Bach, good night, Mrs. Bach, good night, Mr. Yehoshafat. Yours, Rimona Fogel, says do not worry because everything is for the best. Whoever is sad will be happy. There is a mercy to be found behind all this rain. The refrigerator is humming because the power is back on. We will all be good.

9

In the winter of 1965, Yonatan L. decided to leave his wife and the kibbutz on which he had been born and raised. He resolved to pick up and walk out and start a new life. For years on end he had been told what was right and what was wrong. He could barely grasp what those words meant. Sometimes, when he stood by himself at the window toward the close of day, to watch the sun fall, watch the deep, bitter night descend over the fields, envelop the land, like a disaster, to the end of the hills to the east, he calmly conceded that the night was right.

One evening he told his wife that he had decided to pick up and walk out. Life, he said, must go on; suppose I was killed.

He first waited for the rain to stop, for the political tension to ease, for the thunderstorms to subside, for the tractor shed to be taken over. Thus, the year '65 had passed and the year '66 had begun.

It was a long, hard winter.

Yolek Lifshitz announced at a general meeting of Kibbutz Granot that he would soon be resigning the post of secretary and that it was not too soon to start looking for a successor, perhaps Srulik the music man. Gossip had it that he was scheming to return to a position of power in the party and perhaps even to a cabinet seat. The wilder speculation was that he was cunningly counting on some crisis, factional rift, or war of succession to propel his name to the fore as a dark-horse candidate who might prevent a party split. It was Stutchnik, in fact, who stopped Yonatan Lifshitz on the path between the tractor shed and the metal shop to inquire in a cordially sly manner about his father's plans. Yoni shrugged. "Lay off, for God's sake. What the old man wants is grandchildren. So he can found a dynasty." His reply only confirmed what Stutchnik and others had already begun to suspect.

Amos, Yonatan's younger brother, a sturdy, curly-headed, keen-witted prankster who was also a champion swimmer, took part in a retaliation raid into Jordan and received a medal from his paratroop commander for bayoneting two Arab Legionnaires in hand-to-hand combat. Indeed, there was no choice that winter but to strike across the border every few weeks and punish the enemy for the murderous raiders crossing from Jordan almost nightly.

For his part, Yonatan went on waiting in silence for some turning point, some change or omen to mark the beginning of a new era. Yet the days remained all rainily alike and Rimona too. Azariah had taken to dropping in on them practically every night, frequently sleeping on their living-room couch. Yonatan thought, so what? I'll soon be gone. Besides, Rimona's not exactly a woman, and he's just a poor homeless guy. He plays the guitar and a little chess, even if he usually loses. He takes care of Tia now and then. He helps Rimona clean house every week and does the dishes. What the hell! As soon as winter is over and I'm my old self again, I can beat the crap out of him if I feel like it. In the meantime, let him be. As that poor jerk said in one of those Russian proverbs of his, even a broken clock is right twice a day.

At the Lifshitzes' the music sometimes went on until late in the night. From outside came the groans of the wind and the muffled lowing of the cows. In the living room, the blue flame of the heater flickered cheerfully. Rimona sat curled up in her armchair, her feet tucked under her, her hands pulled up in the sleeves of her nightgown, as if pregnant with her own self. Yonatan smoked with eyes closed or else built and demolished match castles on the table. Azariah, at the far end of the couch, played to all hours and now and then sang along softly.

We might as well be in a forest, thought Yonatan. I promised her a child and I've found her one. Now I can go. Etan has those two girls Smadar and Brigitte in his room by the swimming pool and doesn't give a damn what anybody says. Udi is going to bring an old Arab skeleton from Sheikh Dahr in the spring, wire it up to make a scarecrow, and tell whoever doesn't like it to fuck off. And so if the three of us, being of sound mind and body, have decided to start our own little commune, it's nobody's business but ours. Where does it say we can't? Let the rest of them talk themselves blue in the face. Let that voice from the past sneer all it wants at the joker who couldn't hit a bull. For once our heart is true and to hell with the rest. I'll be gone before long and whoever wants to file a complaint can look for me a hundred thousand miles away. To quote that jerk again, "The dogs keep barking all the night, the moon keeps quiet and shines bright."

In our little cottages amid their frost-stricken yards the alarm clocks go off at seven. Reluctantly, we rise grumbling from beneath our warm blankets to don our work clothes and battered old coats and jackets that are no longer good for anything else. Running irritably through curtains of rain, we arrive out-of-breath in the dining hall to eat our thick slices of bread spread with jam or cheese and drink our cups of greasy coffee before trudging off to work. The dining-room crew removes the remains from the sticky tables, cleans each table first with a wet rag and then a dry one, and stands the chairs upon it with their legs in the air, to mop the floor. *And ye shall redeem the land,* proclaims a cardboard sign on the wall, left over from Arbor Day.

On winter mornings like this, conversation is kept to a minimum. Come here. What is it. Where did you put it. I don't know. Then go look. You're in my way.

Once, long ago, there was a time when all things done here were done with devotion, even with a kind of ecstasy, sometimes with enormous self-sacrifice. But then the bold dreams came true.

Dead silence and a sleepy sadness everywhere on the kibbutz. Except for the birds screaming in the cold. Except for the forlorn barks of the dogs. Every man an island.

At eventide, beneath a drippy chinaberry tree on his way to the Jewish philosophy group in the recreation hall, Stutchnik sorrowfully unburdened his thoughts to Srulik.

"Things are going to the dogs, my friend. Why don't you open your eyes? If you're going to be our new secretary, you'll have to do something about it. For all his big talk, Yolek never got off his butt to do a damn thing around here. Everything in sight is falling apart. The kibbutz. The country. The youth. I don't want to stoop to gossip—I've avoided it all my life like the plague—but just take a look at what's going on with a certain Very Important Person's son. *For the Lord hath created a new thing in the earth, one woman shall compass two men.*

"Total anarchy! Look at what's happening with the schoolteachers or with our own steering committee. Look at the government. Were all the foundations rotten to begin with, Srulik, or is it only now, after the fact, that the dialectical contradictions we kept swept under the rug all these years have begun to emerge? You're not answering, my friend. Naturally. That's the easy way out. Soon I'll stop talking myself. One heart attack is enough for me. Not to mention my rheumatism and this whole depressing winter in general. I swear to God, Srulik, you can't look anywhere these days without getting sick to your stomach."

All the while, Srulik had been nodding sympathetically. Now and then he smiled. When Stutchnik finally paused, he put in a word of his own.

"As usual, you're slightly exaggerating. Looking through dark glasses, you might say. There's no reason to despair. We've been through worse times, and thank God we're still here. There've always been crises and always will be, but don't think for a minute we've reached the end of the road."

"*Na!* You're a regular saint. You needn't talk to me the way you talked to the schoolchildren at that assembly. I can do without the propaganda. My eyes are wide open, and it's time yours were too. Besides, you're crazy to be out without a hat on. Who walks around like that in the middle of winter?"

"I'm not walking around, old man. I'm on my way to our group. Just don't forget that the days you're so nostalgic for weren't always so great either. We had our share of failures and embarrassments and even scandals. You are right, though. Why are we standing in this freezing wind? Let's go see if anyone remembered to light the heater in the recreation hall. Maybe our guest lecturer has arrived. I believe he's talking about Martin Buber. Look how dark it is at four-thirty! Worse than Siberia!"

Every evening it was the custom of some members of the kibbutz to gather in various study groups or participate in meetings that deliberated at length about the budget, education, health services, housing, and acceptance of new members, seeking modest ways to make gradual improvements without rocking the boat. Still others spent the evening with their hobbies—painting, embroidering, or stamp collecting—or dropping in on their neighbors for coffee and cake and a discussion of the latest politics and gossip. There were also, however, singles and young couples who preferred staying up late while passing around a bottle, playing cards or backgammon, and telling salty jokes enlivened by old war memories.

On one such night Udi said to Etan R., "Good for them! Bravo! Why shouldn't they? Isn't the Bible full of such stories? To say nothing of our own old folks when they were young. When they weren't draining the desert or watering the swamps and all that. Life isn't a fairy tale. Yoni once said that the most colossal fraud in the world was Snow White and her seven dwarfs. I mean the lies they told us when we were little about what went on between them after she'd spaced out on that apple. So what do you want of Rimona? After all, she's just started on her second dwarf. Come to think of it, Etan, how about bringing your private harem over there one night, letting me and Anat join you, and all of us having a ball together?"

"From the minute I collared him by the cowshed the night he arrived," said Etan, "I've had a bad feeling about that dwarf. And Rimona's not quite all there either. The one I really feel sorry for is Yoni. Yoni was once a damn good fellow. Now he's turning into another Chimpanoza and walks around all day long as if he'd been conked on the head. How about a little more arak? Anyhow, if only Eshkol had any balls and weren't such an old yenta, he'd take advantage of the Egyptians being bogged down in Yemen and kick those Syrian sons-of-bitches' asses in. That'd solve the Jordan water problem once and for all. For half an hour yesterday that Azariah may have chewed my ear off with his philosophy and proverbs about Eshkol and Khrushchev and Nasser, but basically the kid is right. In fact, he'd have a good head on his shoulders if only it hadn't been screwed on wrong. A king with any brains always has a court jester, and Yolek—Stutchnik says he's next in line for the throne—has his Azariah. What makes it so tragic is that Eshkol is his own court jester. Will you listen to what a god-awful night it is out there!"

One evening when Yolek was on the mend from his illness, Hava took it upon herself to let fly.

"Why on earth don't you speak up? Why? Do something! Involve yourself! Make your voice heard! Or do you love that circus clown more than your own son? I suppose it was me who put out the welcome mat, who let him come barging into this booby hatch like some kind of wild animal. Hold it a second! Don't answer yet! I'm not finished. Why do you always interrupt me in the middle of what I'm saying? Why do you always try to gag everybody? Why must you always work out in advance your logical answers with all their pros and cons and ifs and buts before you've even heard what's being said to you? Oh, yes, you try to look tolerant. You pull that patient, politic face of yours as if you were really listening, but you're not listening at all, because you're too busy thinking of your next squelch, with its firstly and its secondly and its thirdly, and all its quotes and bon mots. For once in your life, shut up and listen, because I'm talking about Yoni's life and death, not about the future of the labor movement. And don't try to butt in, because there's no answer you can give. I already know by heart the one you're about to give me. I know your whole repertoire. If it weren't so pathetically disgusting, I'd recite the whole text of it, complete with the corny jokes and the pauses for applause. The smartest thing you can do right now is waive your sacred right of reply and shut up. As if it weren't already written all over your face, the whole shyster spiel. Oh, when it comes to that, you're a champion all right! A champion? You are God Almighty! But the fact that Yoni's life is being ruined right in front of your nose—about that, Mr. God Almighty, you couldn't care less! You never did care and you never will. If anything, it's you who planned it in cold blood. Because Yoni is a blot on your lily-white escutcheon, isn't he? Because he's too confused, and too nihilistic, and too inarticulate. While that clown you've dragged into his life is God's gift to man, a gift you'll promote bit by bit, as they say in your trade, until you can put him to your own use. And find a chance to dump Yoni. Why, if we all dropped dead tomorrow—not only Yoni but Amos, and me too—you'd carry on as usual so quick the whole world would pass out with admiration for your courage. You'd even write some heartrending piece for the papers and make political hay out of it, wouldn't you, because who could be cruel enough to attack a poor bereaved widower and his halo of grief? We'll lie rotting in our graves, and you'll be more of a martyr than ever. You'll even be able to adopt that little cockroach legally. What do you care as long as you have your spotless reputation? You, and your big fat ideas, and your place in history, and all your j'accusational speeches! A nasty, wicked old man who saw his own son being carved up in front of his eyes and never even bothered to—"

"Hava! What exactly are you getting at?"

"Shut up is what I'm getting at! For once in your life let me finish a sentence before you start a speech that lasts all night. You've made far too many speeches already. And I've heard far too many of them too. And so has your precious history. You've been preaching to it for the last fifty years without letting it get a word in edgewise or ever stopping to hear what it might have to say for itself. But this time you're going to hear me out to the end. And spare me that 'can't-you-see-I'm-deaf' look of yours, because I know you'd rather not hear a word. And that "please-all-the-neighbors-will-hear-you" look too. What do I care about the damn neighbors? I wish they *would* hear. I wish this whole stinking kibbutz would hear, and the party, and the government, and the Knesset, and the whole United Nations! Let them! What do I care? I know I'm talking loud—that's because you're deafer than God himself, but I'm *not* screaming. And if I want to scream, you're not going to stop me. I'll scream until they break down the door to see if you're murdering me. That's how I'll scream if you don't shut up and let me talk for once in my life."

"Hava! Please. You can talk all you want. No one is stopping you."

"Again you're interrupting when all I'm begging you for is the chance to finish a sentence, because it's a life-and-death matter, and if you interrupt one more time, I'm taking this can of kerosene and pouring it on the floor and putting a match to it and burning down the whole house with all your precious letters from Ben-Gurion and Berl and Erlander and Richard Crossman and the King of Siam. So shut up and listen carefully to what I say because it's the last time I'll ever say anything. I'm telling you now that you have until noon tomorrow to get rid of that psychopathic pervert whom you brought here in cold blood to destroy your son's life, and had accepted by the kibbutz, and even invited to my house to talk about justice and philosophy and give his damn music recitals. Either he's out of here and out of Yoni's life on his rear end by tomorrow, or I'll do something so terrible you'll wish you'd never been born. You'll feel sorrier than you ever felt in your big fat life—even sorrier than you were after your glorious resignation from the cabinet that you're eating your heart out over to this day. And I hope you go on eating it out until there's nothing left but a shell! *Ty zboju, ty morderco!*"

"Hava! That's not something I can just go and do on my own. You know that as well as I."

"Oh, I do, do I?"

"There would have to be a meeting. Of the steering committee. To discuss it. We're talking about a human being."

"Sure. A human being! As if you knew what those words meant. As if you ever did. A human life? Human filth, you mean."

"Excuse me, Hava. You're so upset you're contradicting yourself without even realizing it. Think about it. It's been thirty years, but to this day you've never forgiven me for throwing that comedian of yours out of here when he tried killing half the kibbutz, including you and me."

"Shut up, you murderer! At least you've finally admitted it was you who made him go."

"I didn't say that, Hava. Far from it. You surely can't have forgotten with what patience and tolerance, with what forbearance I tried to get him the social and psychological help he needed before he went berserk. And even after. And you know as well as anyone that it was he who ran off as fast as he could right after his shooting spree, and it was I who had to use all the influence I had and pull every string I could to keep the British police out of it, to avoid an internal Haganah trial for criminal misuse of underground arms. And it was also I who spared him the humiliation of having to face a general meeting of the kibbutz, which would undoubtedly have booted him out in disgrace and perhaps even handed him over to the authorities or some mental institution. On top of which, it was I who managed to spirit him out of the country."

"You?"

"I and no one else, Hava. It's time I told you what I've kept to myself all these years despite the endless abuse from you. Yes. It was I who helped that poor maniac get safely out of the country. There were comrades who insisted I call in the police. What right do we have, they asked, to give carte blanche to every straitjacket case to go out and shoot anyone he pleases? And I, Hava, I and no one else, had to scheme in a thousand different ways to stall off the kibbutz and the Haganah until I could find him a berth to Italy on one of our boats—and that only by pulling strings and running all over the map. Do I really deserve to be the object of such spite for all that? After the man seduced or tried to seduce my wife? And almost murdered her and me and the darling son she was pregnant with? To this day you've harbored the most vicious hate for me because I didn't let that madman stay, and now you come and tell me I have to give the bum's rush to a boy who hasn't even—"

"*You?* You made Bini leave the kibbutz? And the country?"

"I didn't say that, Hava. You know as well as I do that he left of his own accord."

"*You?* By pulling strings? By scheming?"

"Hava! You always complain that I never listen to you. But here you are, hearing the exact opposite of what I am saying."

"You poor fool! Your poor idiotic fool. Have you gone off your rocker completely? Did it never occur to you that the child I was pregnant with might be his? Didn't that cross your mind at least once in your whole phony life? Did you ever once bother to take a good look at Yoni and another at Amos and another at yourself? How stupid can the great ministerial mind be? Just shut up about Bini! That's not what I was talking about. Don't put words in my mouth and don't interrupt me now, because it's time I had my say. You with your strings and your influence and your tricks! I've never said anything about whose son Yoni is. That's the brainchild you dreamed up to have an excuse to kill him. The only thing I've said is that I want that nut of yours out of here by noon tomorrow, and don't argue with me or try to intimidate me with your renowned rhetorical talents. I'm not your Ben-Gurion, or your Eshkol, or a tribunal of your peers, or an assembly of your admirers, or a group of pilgrims come to pay you homage. I'm nothing. I'm less than that. I'm a poor deranged female, a psychological millstone around your precious national neck. I'm not even a human being. I'm just an evil old monster who happens to know, but I mean *know,* who you really are. And I'm warning you—don't you dare answer me now!—I'm warning you that if ever I decide to open my mouth and tell a tiny fraction of what I know about you—not only what both of us know, but what you, Mr. God Almighty, don't even know about yourself—if ever I start to talk, this whole country will go into such a state of shock that you'll drop dead from shame on the spot. Did I say shock? Why, it'll split its sides laughing before puking its guts out. This is the Yolek Lifshitz we've all worshiped and adored? This is our pride and joy? *This?* And I, Mr. National Figure—and you'd better not forget it—I'm already a corpse, so I've nothing to lose by finishing you off once and for all. The only thing is that I'll be merciful. I'll do it in one blow, not little by little as you've done it to me, day after day and night after night. For thirty years you've kept turning the knife in me, and now you've brought in a little murderer to kill off your son the same way—though you'll never know if he's your son or not—a little bit at a time, the way you murdered me, the way you murdered Bini, with your strings and your schemes and your marvelous connections. Anything to avoid a scandal or, perish the thought, any tarnish on your esteemed public image. Why, you're the conscience of the Labor Party! You're purer than a baby's behind! No, Mr. Minister, I am *not* crying. You, Mr. Minister, will not have the satisfaction, you will not have the pleasure of seeing me cry the way you saw Bini cry night after night at your feet, washing them with his tears and begging you to—"

"Hava! Please! It's time you got over this whole Benya Trotsky business. No one knows better than you that you never loved him in return, that you chose of your own free will—"

"That's a filthy lie, Yolek Lifshitz! In another minute you'll be telling me how noble you've been for forgiving me from the bottom of your heart. Why don't you look yourself in the face for a change? Why don't you try honestly remembering who Bini was, you who schemed to murder him in a thousand different ways—those were your exact words, a thousand different ways—don't try denying them now! The same as you murdered me, the same as you're murdering Yoni, and don't think I haven't noticed how you've avoided discussing him and purposely kept bringing the conversation back to Bini in order to torture me. But you won't have the pleasure. I'm not going to give it to you. You're going to think about Yoni for a change, not history. This isn't some seminar or Labor Party panel. I'm not going to let you play the martyr here. Oh, don't I know what all your martyrdoms amount to and all your holier-than-thou-ness! Well, you can take your moral rectitude and your historical contributions and shove them! I spit on them the way you've spat and trampled all these years on my grave! For your own good, don't even try to answer me now. Either you send that little stinker packing by noon tomorrow or you're in for a big, big surprise. The radio and every newspaper in this country will be falling all over themselves to announce that, believe it or not, Yolek Lifshitz's wife, of all people, has put a torch to herself—unless the opposite happens, and she puts the torch to her national figure instead. I'm telling you, Yolek, that will be the living end—not mine, because that happened long ago—but yours, Mr. National Figure, with the whole country rolling in the aisles and gasping: 'What? *That* was our paragon of virtue? *That* was our model leader? *That* was our public conscience? That cold-blooded murderer?' I'm warning you right now, you'll smell so bad that your party won't touch you with a ten-foot pole, because I swear I'll make you stink to high heaven. All you'll have left to do with yourself is sit here and knit socks like that Italian murderer until you finally croak like a sick dog the same as I did. And I'll dance at your funeral the way you danced at mine long before you even began to screw around with all those bitches of yours at all your conferences and conventions and God knows where else. I won't mention any names, but don't think a little bird didn't tell me who His Highness shacked up with for two weeks, and who he shacked up with for two nights, and who he gave just half an hour, like an animal, between this motion and that vote. All it will take is a little acid to throw in your famous face, unless I drink it instead, though ordinary sleeping pills will do nicely too. And don't you dare say to me, Hava, don't scream. If you say that just once more, I really will—not that I have to, because I could just as easily give a perfectly ladylike interview to some popular magazine. They could call it 'Comrade Lifshitz in His Underwear' or 'The Private Life of Labor's Conscience.'

"You have until tomorrow to make up your mind and act. Till twelve noon. And remember that I've warned you. And don't try to answer me now with all your firstly's and secondly's, or even without them, because I have no time to listen. You've already made me late for my education committee meeting. So instead of composing answers in your head, I'll advise you, Yolek Lifshitz, to sit down quietly by yourself tonight and think things over very, very carefully—the way you're so good at doing whenever you have a political problem on your hands. Your medicine is in the blue bottle in the refrigerator. Don't forget to take two teaspoons at ten-thirty. Make sure they're full ones, not halves. And your pain pills are in the medicine cabinet in the bathroom. Don't forget either that you're supposed to drink a lot of tea. I'll be back by eleven-thirty, quarter-to-twelve at the latest. Don't wait up for me. Get into bed and read a paper until you fall asleep. Just have yourself a good think first—not how to answer me, I know I may have put things a bit strongly—but how to do what any true father who doesn't want his son to suffer would have done long ago. I'm sure that, as usual, you'll find a tactful, diplomatic, clearcut solution that won't cause any unpleasantness. Good night. My, I really am late. And don't you dare touch the brandy. Remember what the doctor told you. Not one drop! You may as well know that I've marked a line on the bottle. You're best off getting into bed with your paper. And you shouldn't be smoking so much either. Goodbye. I'm leaving the light on in the bathroom for you."

Once Hava had gone, Yolek rose from his chair. He shuffled over to the bookcase, reached with cautious fingers for the brandy bottle, studied its label craftily, shut his eyes pensively for a moment, smiled the faintest of mockingly sad smiles, poured himself a full glass of brandy, and set it on his desk. He then took the bottle to the kitchen and filled it with tap water up to the line that Hava had penciled on it. Back at his desk, he opened his appointment book to write: *See about Gitlin. Check regulations for temporary help. Compensation? Insurance?* And then added: *Have Udi S. fill in for him in tractor shed?* He lit a cigarette and inhaled deeply, took a tiny sip from his glass followed by two gulps, and with a steady hand began to write on a sheet of stationery, whose upper-right-hand corner bore the printed message *From the desk of Yisra'el Lifshitz*:

Mr. B. Trotsky
Miami Beach, Florida
U.S.A.

Dear Benyamin,

I'm writing to answer your letter of several months ago. Please forgive me for taking so long. I have been besieged by problems, both public and otherwise, which is the reason for the delay.

Regarding your offer to donate a sum of money for the construction of a public building in Kibbutz Granot, firstly, let me express my own and our members' gratitude for both the proposal itself and the generous intention behind it. Secondly, permit me the liberty of pointing out that the idea itself is not without its difficulties, some of them rooted in principle. No doubt you can imagine the existence of certain long-held feelings, sensitivities, and questions concerning both your present situation and events of the distant past that are best left unmentioned and forgotten. A word to the wise, etc. The rub is, Benyamin, that there are among us, I'm sorry to say, some stubborn souls who insist on raking up that past and opening old wounds. Besides which, to be perfectly candid with you, I too find myself in a quandary, seeing as how I, so to speak, was on the butt end of it all. In light of which, it may be that your kind offer needs to be given more thought. See here, Benya. Why don't we agree to put the whole matter aside for the moment and do some plain speaking with each other. I want you to tell me something. Please. In two or three lines. On a postcard. Or even a telegram. Just answer me yes or no. Have I in any way wronged you? Yes or no? As God is my witness, how have I sinned against you? What strings, as it were, have I pulled to your detriment? Of what intrigues against you am I guilty? Granted, it was not with malice aforethought that you fell in love with my friend. Who purports to plumb the vagaries of the human heart? And she—let's face it—suffered, frightfully, until she made up her mind. But make it up she did. I did not, after all, bludgeon her into doing so.

Does anyone seriously think I could have kept her by force had she really preferred you to me? Honest to goodness, Benya, was I really the villain of the piece, and she and you, as it were, the helpless victims? The crucified saints? What, in the name of God, did I do to the two of you? What made me deserve to be treated with such savage rancor? Do you mean to tell me that I was the Cossack with the whip and you my innocent whipping boy? Which one of us, may I ask, pulled a gun as his final argument? Was it me? Was I the murderer? Did I really destroy a grand passion, so to speak, by snatching her from your arms? Was it I who turned up uninvited one day and took all of us by storm with my shepherd's pipe and my Russian peasant's blouse and my romantic airs and my wild head of hair and my erotic bass voice? Why then should I be spat at and reviled? Why should I be punished all my life? What are she, you, and the boy continually tormenting me for? For having tried to behave decently and rationally? For not having reached for a knife or gun myself? For having kept you from being handed over to the British police? For the six English pounds I stuck into your broken-down suitcase at the last minute when you couldn't close it that morning and I had to tie it together with rope before you hit the road? For what? Is it just for the nasty intellectual face I had the hard luck to be born with?

Benya, listen. I wish you well. Wherever you are. I'm willing to let bygones be bygones. But for heaven's sake, stop hounding me. Let me live too for once in my life. And above all, keep your hands off the boy. If there's any fear of God in your heart, cable me at once just four words, *Yes, he is yours,* or else, *No, he is mine.* So I needn't go on being poisoned by doubt until the day I die. Not that that will help much either, because there isn't such a natural-born, poetic, ingratiating liar in the whole world as you. Still, Benya, if there is anything at all to our ancestors' belief in the life hereafter, they're sure to have an information desk where I can get a straight answer about the real father. Except that now I'm really writing poppycock, because by any standard of justice Yoni is all mine and you have no possible claim on him. What the devil difference does it make whose filthy fluids he came from? A vile droplet of pus is not what makes the man. If it is, this world is really a sorry jest.

Benya, you listen to me now. The boy is my son, and if there's a shred of human decency left in you, you'll tell me so. Yes. In a telegram.

Not, incidentally, that when all is said and done, it doesn't come to the same thing. Share and share alike, as we once used to proclaim. What a nightmare, Benya! What a bad April Fool's joke! He's not really mine, and he certainly isn't yours, and he's not poor Hava's either—in fact, he barely even belongs to himself. Still, I want you to know that if by any chance you are in cahoots with that obsessed woman of mine to lure my son to America with all kinds of goodies and make a degenerate, money-mad kike of him there, I'm determined to fight you with every means at my disposal until I've obliterated that web of deceit. Believe me, when it comes to playing dirty, I've learned a trick or two myself in this life. And just in case you need a hint to get the real picture, I don't mind giving you one. There's no reason why Hava should be above a full medical examination in order to establish her true mental condition. And don't delude yourself, either, into thinking your America is, so to speak, an impregnable Shangri-la. With a little spadework, it should be easy enough to discover exactly how you came by that bonanza of yours and to find a suitable ear into which to whisper the charming tale of your hot-blooded youth. A word to the wise, etc. I will *not* let my son join you in America even if you are so swimming in money, as they say, that you can send a gold-plated airplane to fetch him.

I suppose you must have a mirror of some sort at home. Why don't you look in it for a minute to see if you can stand the sight of the loathsome guttersnipe, the repulsive sewer rat you've become. Goddamn your hide, you bloodthirsty, blood-sucking vampire, it's you and your ilk who've defiled and fouled up everything. Where were you while we were giving our life's blood to water this land and rebuild its ruins and those of the Jewish soul? Play-acting! Clowning! Piddling around! Piddling with Plekhanov, and piddling with Lenin and the October Revolution, and piddling some more with Zionism and a midsummer night's flirt with pioneering in Palestine. And once you'd sown your wild oats here, turning tail as quickly as you could to sell out to the Golden Calf.

It's not Hitler or Nasser but you and the likes of you who will be responsible, I repeat, *responsible*, for the destruction of the Third Temple. No power on earth can possibly forgive me for the moronic pity I showed in not digging your grave thirty years ago, when you were still just a kinky little syphilitic, sniveling insect. You are the lowest of the low. It's people like you who've been the poisonous cancer in the body of the Jewish people for generations. You're the age-old curse of the Exile. You're the reason the Gentiles hated and still hate us with an eternal, nauseated loathing. You with your money-grubbing, you with your Golden Calf, you with your foaming lechery, you with your swank way of seducing women and innocent goyim with sweet-talk, stopping at no betrayal, sleeping on your filthy ducats that spread like germs from country to country, from exile to exile, from racket to racket, homeless, conscienceless, rootless, making us a laughingstock and a pariah among the nations. And now you reach out your sticky paws to make off with our children just as you tried to make off with our women, to seduce and corrupt them until they've sunk as low as you are.

But why deny it, Benya? The fault is mine. *Mea culpa!* I'm to blame for it all, because I didn't do what any Ukrainian peasant worth his salt would do if he caught his wife in the haystack with some kike peddler—one blow of his ax and *finis*! I'm to blame for not remembering what our ancient rabbis always taught. He who pities the brute is brutal to those deserving pity. I spared you like a mooncalf, Benya, like the good compassionate Tolstoyan I once was. I handed you your life on a platter. I helped you get away by the skin of your teeth, and now Hava calls me a murderer. Which I am indeed, because you with your three-ring circus and she with her black widow's poison are planning to hypnotize my son into joining you in Florida. No doubt you'll send him a ticket and a sack stuffed with dollars and take him into your business to be a racketeer like yourself, after which you'll have a good belly laugh at how you made a monied gentleman out of Yolek Lifshitz's son, one just like his mother's father in the shtetl, that pot-bellied swell with his thumbs stuck in his belt on both sides of his paunch. My Yoni, in whom I hoped to see our dreams come true, the first of a new line of Jews whose children and children's children would grow up in this land to put an end to the malignancy of the Exile. And now the Exile is back again, masquerading as a rich uncle. You traitor to your people, you. Goddamn your soul, Trotsky, may it rot in hell! And about that donation, the answer is, forget it. You can keep your filthy money.

Yolek Lifshitz tore this letter into little pieces and threw them into the toilet, which he carefully flushed twice. Wasn't it the Romans, by the way, who first said that money has no smell? If he wants to make a donation, by all means. All kinds of strange people give money to Israel without having their credentials checked first. We even accepted reparation payments from the Nazis. Yolek donned his winter coat and put a cap on his head. He decided to take a walk to cool off.

Halfway along his planned route he decided he must go see Yonatan and Rimona immediately. Almost at once, however, he recalled that that Gitlin fellow often spent his nights with them, and, changing his mind with a shrug, he resumed walking downhill in the direction of the cowshed and the chicken runs. The grounds were deserted as only village paths on a winter night can be. The rain had stopped. The wind had died down.

Three or four stars peered coldly through racks of tattered clouds. Twinkling. For a moment, Yolek thought of them as no more than pinpricks, little moth holes in a heavy velvet curtain, beyond which shone a vast, terrible illumination, a blinding, molten incandescence. And the stars themselves, it seemed to him, were but the faintest of allusions to the great storm of light raging behind that veil. As though the vats of heaven had sprung a few tiny leaks and several drops of bright liquid clung glistening to their black undersides. Yolek found comfort. He walked slowly, thoughtfully, breathing deeply of the sharp, keen air, taking in all the barnyard smells, charged with the heavy sensuality of a caress. When had he last been caressed like this? Long, long ago, not counting the few politically active widows or divorcées who had dragged him almost forcibly to bed, and that far from recently. Nature alone, so it seemed, cared enough for everyone, even a nasty intellectual, to ensure them all a few years of mother love. The whole thing is very strange and rather pathetic, thought Yolek, recalling that his own mother was the last person really to fondle him. Starlight on a winter night was no doubt to be taken auspiciously, but life was basically a rum business.

Thick, sour fumes steaming out of the chicken run. Sheep giving off a warmish odor of manure. A stream of liquid compost flowing out of and back into the darkness from the sopping hay. The breathing of the cows. The calm, drowsy, winter-night thereness of the farm animals.

Have I wronged my son, too, then? Am I really the cause of his suffering? Whatever made him choose a woman like Rimona? Was that his idea of punishing someone? Himself? His mother? Me? So be it, thought Yolek. Each of us will have to bear his own cross. Though if it weren't for that tragedy I'd be a grandfather now. Every day at three-thirty I'd arrive at the nursery ahead of all the parents to have the boy to myself. I'd take him on my shoulders to the swings. To the fields. To the orchards. To the lawns. To the sheep pen and the chicken run and the cowshed. To the peacock cage by the swimming pool. And shower him with candy, whole bribefuls of it, endless heaps of hush money despite all my principles. And kiss him quite shamelessly in front of everyone, toe by toe on his little feet. And frolic with him on the grass like a boy myself on summer days. And spray him with water from the garden hose and get as good as I give. And make him funny faces as I never did for my own sons. And moo and miaow and bark, all for the price of one little caress. And make up no end of stories about animals, and ghosts and goblins, and trees and stones. And rise at night long after his parents are asleep and sneak like a thief into the nursery to kiss him on his little head.

Far away, across the border, lights twinkled in the mountains. Yolek Lifshitz raised his coat collar, pulled down his cap against the cold, and stood looking at them. For nearly ten minutes he did not budge, entirely drained of the old passions and high principles that had guided him all his life. As though the answer had been obvious from the start, he had suddenly made up his mind. Frosty, hushed, and desolate the night, pinioned against the sky and earth. Yolek waited so until he saw a falling star. And begged for mercy.

10

Tia lay sprawled beneath the couch with only her hairy tail sticking out, now and then thumping the rug. The heavy brown curtains hid the window and the door leading out to the porch. All was at peace. The heater was lit, as was the reading lamp at the head of the couch. The overhead light was off.

"Hey, Azariah. Tell me something. What's that book you've been reading all evening?"

"The letters. In English. It's a philosophy book."

"The letters. To whom?"

"All kinds of people. Letters that Spinoza wrote."

"Okay. Get back to it. I didn't mean to disturb you."

"You're not disturbing me, Yoni. Not at all. I thought you'd dozed off."

"Who, me? Some chance. That's something I only do at work, when you're performing your miracles with the tractors. Just now I was thinking about that knight. I've got a simple solution."

"What knight?"

"Yours. The one you lost in our game yesterday after you were a rook up. She should be back soon."

"Is she at a meeting? Or is tonight choir rehearsal?"

"She's serving coffee and cake to the study group. To Stutchnik, Srulik, Yashek, and the rest of them. What does it say in that book?"

"It's about philosophy. About different ideas and points of view. As stated by Spinoza. Yoni?"

"What?"

" 'A little fink.' That's what they used to call me in the army. Do you think I'm a little fink? Or a cheat? Or a jerk?"

"Come off it, Azariah! Tell me something. Don't you ever feel like just picking up and taking off for some faraway place, some strange big city like Rio de Janeiro or Shanghai where you can be all alone, a total stranger who doesn't owe anybody anything? Where you can spend whole days just walking the streets, not talking to anyone, without any plans or even a watch on your wrist?"

"In Russia they say, 'The man who has no other friend will be the Devil's in the end.' That's a proverb. I've had enough of being by myself, Yoni, with no one to talk to. First in the Diaspora and then here. And all the time somebody was out to kill me. Not just Hitler. Here too at first, in the immigrant camp. And the enemies I had in the army. You can never be sure. Maybe even you wish to get rid of me, though you are my big brother and though I'd go through hell and high water for you."

"What kind of hell? Just listen to that rain outside! Wouldn't you like to take off for Manila, or Bangkok, say, right now?"

"Me? No way. I want to stay safely put. Without anyone after my scalp. Even if that means making concessions to Nasser. We can afford some. What I want is to spend my life with good friends. With Jews. With my own brothers. And to play music that will make people feel good and to write down my thoughts so that they can be of some use or comfort to someone. To shape up. So that I'll finally be accepted and not just put up with as some little fink. Or as some unavoidable nuisance, because as long as I'm that, I'm still no good. If life on the kibbutz doesn't change me for the better, the best thing I could do would be go live as a hermit in the mountains, where I'd grub for mushrooms and roots and drink stream water or melted snow. And though I'm afraid to ask, she always says, 'Zaro, stay, you're no bother to me or Yoni at all.' "

"That's true. As far as I'm concerned, anyway. As a matter of fact, I get a kick out of seeing my dear parents having conniptions over you. And the whole kibbutz too. Anat, for instance, grabbed hold of me the other day and wanted to know in her sugary voice if I wasn't just a little bit jealous. 'Thank you, it's my pleasure,' I said to her. She's a little brain-damaged herself, you know. As far as I'm concerned, you can stay here until moss grows on you. You're not in my way one bit."

"Thank you. Yoni? Do you think I could ask you a personal question, as they say? Just one. You don't even have to answer it. I guess I'd better keep my mouth shut, though. The more I open it, the more hot water I get into."

"Why don't you cut out the blah-blah and just ask?"

"Yoni. Tell me. Are you . . . my friend? A little bit?"

"I don't know. Maybe. I haven't thought about it. Actually, you know what? Yes. Why not? Only it won't do you any good, because I'm not really living here any more. Besides, there are times when I feel like choking the two of you. I mean strangling you both slowly but surely with my own hands. Or skewering you on a bayonet, just as my brother skewered those Jordanians, which won him a medal. But okay. Let's say we're friends. Even more than that. I, for instance, intend to leave you all my clothes, except for what will go into a small suitcase. No suitcase. A knapsack. And my chess set and chess journals. And my parents at no extra charge. And my screwdrivers and my hammer and my pliers. And my rake and my pitchfork, so that when summer comes you can make her the flower beds in the garden that she likes.

They're all yours. Don't mention it. Even Tia. Maybe my shaving kit too, because I feel like growing a beard. What else would you like? Just say the word. My toothbrush maybe?"

"Thanks."

"And remember that saying of yours I've heard at least a thousand times, 'He who forgets, murder abets.' "

"Yoni, listen to me. I . . . seriously, I want you to know that I'll never disappoint you. Not ever."

"Cool it, philosopher. Stop sounding like Memorial Day and put some water on for tea. No, wait a minute. Who wants tea? Go to the third shelf over there, behind those books, and bring me that bottle of whisky Rimona won at the Hanukkah raffle. We'll have a drink before she gets back. Do you love her?"

"Look, Yoni, it's like this: I . . . I mean, we—"

"Forget it! I wasn't looking for an answer. On the whole, maybe it's time you shut up a little, Azariah. All day long all you do is talk. At six in the morning in the tractor shed you're already making speeches about justice with a capital J—what it is, where to find it, what all those philosophers have said about it. Why don't you just drop it. You know what? I'll tell you once and for all where justice is. It quit the cabinet and the Knesset long ago. Now it's about to stop being secretary of the kibbutz. And it's already eating its heart out. Listen, what goes on between the two of you is none of my goddamn business. Because I'm clearing out of here tomorrow. You heard me. Taking off. That's it. What does it say in that English book?"

"I already told you, Yoni. It's a book of Spinoza's letters. With his ideas. All sorts of theories and hypotheses. The kind of stuff you can't stand. About God, for instance, and the nature of His being, and the errors made by human beings because of their affections. By that he means feelings and passions. Things like that."

"Just like Bolognesi. He also starts up with his God-bless'a-God-who-wipes'a-da-tears-a-da-poor. And my father, too, keeps lecturing me about the purpose of life and all that. And Udi Shneour says that all that counts is who's holding the gun. You want to know something? I listen to it all like a good little boy and don't understand a thing. Not one fucking thing. Just listen to that turtle scratching in his box. Not a thing. I don't even understand a simple fuel block any more. It takes an undernourished-looking runt like you to come and explain it to me, because I'm getting dumber day by day. Freaking out, as they call it now. So pour us some of that whisky and let's drink a toast—to the fink and the freak! Cheers! How about reading me from that book so I'll know what it's all about."

"But it's in English, Yoni."

"Then translate it."

"I'm in the middle of a passage. It's in a letter that's part of a debate between Spinoza and a scholar, and it's very difficult to understand what he's getting at unless you know what he means by axioms and lemmas and—"

"Knock off the bullshit and just read."

"All right. Just—"

"I said read!"

"Right. All right. Here. 'To the Right Honorable Hugo Buxhall. How hard it is for two people who adhere to different principles to agree and find common ground in a matter so bound up with other things.' "

"You can skip the introduction. Get to the point."

"I will, Yoni. It takes time to translate. Listen. 'Your view that the world was created by accident—' "

"I don't understand. What's he getting at?"

" 'That there is a necessary and predetermined order to the world, and that this order—' "

"Is one big fucking mess, Azariah! What order are you talking about? Where the fuck is it? Once, in a raid against the Syrians, we knocked off a few of their soldiers. We set up an ambush for their relief force, and they walked right into it with their jeeps and armored cars like flies into a jam jar. When it was over, we took a dead one—only he wasn't just dead, his body had been blown in two exactly at the waist—and we put him in the driver's seat of a jeep with his hands on the steering wheel and a lighted cigarette in his mouth and we called it a great big joke. To this day everyone laughs when they think of it. I wonder what your Spinoza would say about that. That we were animals? Murderers? The dregs of humanity?"

"You'd be surprised, Yoni. Most likely he'd point out calmly, without even raising his voice, that you did what you did because you had no choice. And neither, by the way, had the Syrians."

"Of course he would. What else would you expect? That's exactly what the whole world has been giving us from the day before we were born, our parents and our housemothers, and our teachers, and the kibbutz, and the army, and the government, and the newspapers, and Bialik, and Herzl—the whole lot of them. All they've ever done is scream at us that we have no choice but to work and fight for our country because our backs are to the wall. And now you and your Spinoza come and tell me the same goddamn thing. Welcome to the party! And while you're at it, pour me some more whisky. Pour'a a little more'a. Thanks a lot. That'll do for now. So what else do the two of you have to propose?"

"Excuse me?"

"I asked what the two of you propose. You and your Spinoza. If there's never any choice and our backs are always to the wall, what do you propose that we do about it? If everything's so hopeless, why did he bother to write that book and why do you bother to read it like a jackass?"

"Look, Yoni. Everything isn't hopeless. That's not what Spinoza says. On the contrary. He specifically stresses the idea of human freedom. We're free to recognize Necessity and to learn to accept calmly, even lovingly, the powerful, unspoken laws underlying the inevitable."

"Hey there, Azariah!"

"What?"

"Do you really love her?"

"Now let me tell you, Yoni."

"Yes or no?"

"All right. Yes. And I love you too. Even if I am a fink."

"And you love the whole kibbutz?"

"Yes, I do."

"And this country?"

"Yes."

"And this whole fucking life? And this rotten rain that's been falling on our heads like God's own piss for half a year already?"

"Yoni, forgive me and don't be mad at me for saying this, but she'll be back soon and I think—or rather, as they say, I propose—you shouldn't drink any more because you're not used to it."

"You want to know something, Azariah baby? Let me tell you something."

"Just don't get mad at me, Yoni."

"Who the hell is mad? Now you listen to me. You're as much of an asshole as I am. And a little crazy to boot. You, Spinoza, and she are one fucked-up threesome. Come over here! Now if you'd only let me crack open your ugly puss with a good right to the jaw, believe me, it would do both of us a world of good. C'mere!"

"I'm sorry, Yoni. I've already asked your forgiveness for everything, and now I'll pack up right away and clear out of this house and out of this kibbutz for good. I'd be kicked out before long anyway. The way I always am. Because I'm just a little stinker who should be finished off, which is what they said in the army and probably say behind my back here too. And she's older than me, she's so beautiful and saintly. And I am just so much filth. Only I do believe in justice. And in the kibbutz. And in having our own country and all the rest. Please, Yoni, don't hit me!"

"I won't, pal. You needn't be afraid. I'm not a Nazi. Though you never know. It's just that you get on my nerves. See, I think there *is* a choice. And that I'm not up against any goddamn wall. Spinoza can go fuck himself! You know something? You honestly do *deserve* her. Let's shake on that, philosopher. Bottoms up!

Meanwhile do me a small favor and spare us the gab. Or better still, why don't you go get two butcher knives from the kitchen and we'll see whether or not you are a real man."

"Whatever you say, Yoni. Just don't drink any more. You know I love you dearly, as they say in Russian, and I beg forgiveness for everything I've done. If you'd like me to get down on my knees—I'm down on them. If it would make you feel better, you can beat me. I'm used to it by now."

"Get back on your feet, you crucified Christ, and give me a cigarette. You're some clown, all right. Look how nervous you've made Tia. Tia, wha'sa matter? That's jus' Rimona coming back."

Rimona served tea and cake, and turned down the beds for sleep.

Bolognesi sat on his bed, his back erect. One ear was torn. His lips moved as if in prayer. Twenty years had passed since the day he beheaded his brother's fiancée with an ax. Although the details of the story were not known to the kibbutz, everyone had his own version, all equally gory and all totally contradictory. Though quiet, well-behaved, and useful, a man who had not harmed a fly since the day of his arrival, the looks of him—jaws tightly clenched like a wretch who has eaten something foul and can neither swallow nor spit it out—gave the women and children bad dreams.

For all his having become a pious Jew while in prison, his religious observance had lapsed, and he devoted himself now to the art of fine knitting for these very same children and young women of the kibbutz. He never took a day off from work, never got sick, and refused to accept any pocket money. No one from outside the kibbutz ever came to visit him, nor, except on official business, did any of its members ever drop by to see him in his shack. No one had anything more to say to him than a perfunctory "Good evening," "How are you?" "How's it going?" or "Thanks for the lovely new scarf." To which he would reply, "Why do the heath'm thank'a me when I have quiet'a my soul?"

Now on these cold winter nights Bolognesi sat by himself in his tumbledown, tarpaper shack, listening to the rain beat down on the roof. Often he had been asked to move to a small bachelor room, and each time he had mumbled a refusal, though the singles committee had voted to give him a kerosene heater, an old radio, a reproduction of Van Gogh sunflowers, an electric kettle, a black plastic cup, and a ration of instant coffee. At the moment he was busy knitting a red shawl for Anat Shneour in a bold Spanish style. The needles flew in his hands. The heater crackled on the floor. In low, monotonous tones he droned on and on, "I moan'a and make'a complaint. Horror overwhelm'a me like'a water off'a da sea. Selah. Yea, though I walk in the valley of the shadow of death I will fear no evil."

It was pouring again. The deluge battered the tin roof and slashed at the wooden walls. Thunderclap followed thunderclap, as if a mighty tank battle were being fought in another world.

Bolognesi rose from his seat. With steps as dainty as Dresden china, he went to the window and with his prim fists beat frantically on the pane.

11

At ten minutes after two in the morning, Yonatan woke from a troubled sleep. A bloody, faceless corpse had been brought into the tractor shed on an army stretcher. It's your father, buddy, the corps commander said, tapping Yonatan on the shoulder. He's been hacked to death with a dagger by two-legged beasts. But my father is a sick old man, protested Yonatan, trying to talk or bargain his way out of the truth. Your father was butchered with biblical cruelty, barked the corps commander. Instead of just standing there answering back, why don't you get off your ass and try to patch him together.

The words "biblical cruelty" struck Yonatan with a frothlike fury, as if he had been spat on in disgust. He shrank back, murmuring, okay, okay, dad, just don't be annoyed, you know I'm doing my best. The prostrate Yolek ignored this plea. His voice rang out like a gong. You evil seed! You generation of vipers! You degenerate race of Tatars! You will counterattack and retake

Sheikh Dahr this very hour regardless of losses. You've got to get it through your thick skulls that this is a life-and-death battle. If we lose, not only you but the entire Jewish people will die like dogs. But if they do, you boys must see to it that this time we take the whole wicked world down with us. Remember, we're counting on you. I'm sorry to have to say this, dad, said Yonatan, but aren't you dead? At that, the bloody, faceless corpse leaped from the stretcher and advanced on Yonatan with arms open to embrace him.

Dressed in his undershorts and a gray T-shirt, Yonatan rose with a start from the living-room couch he had been sleeping on. His head weighed a ton. He gasped for breath from all the cigarettes he had smoked. Once, in a movie, he had seen condemned men led from their cells to the scaffold in the middle of the night. Now, frozen and only half-awake, he felt almost without regret that his time too had come.

He went to the bathroom barefoot to pee and missed the bowl, wetting not only the seat but the floor around it. Idiot! he thought, what got into you to drink all that whisky and blab your head off? And how the hell did you end up sleeping like a stiff on the couch?

Through the open bedroom door, by the bathroom light, he could see Rimona asleep on her back and their young guest on the rug at her feet, curled in a fetal position, his head buried deep under a pillow. You son-of-a-bitch, you! What a fucking whorehouse! Yonatan struggled into his khaki army pants and shirt, began to fight his way into his patched work sweater, confused the sleeves, and had to fight his way out of the tangle and start all over again. He stepped out on the porch to breathe the clean night air. Tia followed him. In the wet, black hush Yonatan lit a cigarette.

Downhill, around each of the perimeter lights, shimmering circles of mist gave off a strange, sickly glow. A frog croaked in a puddle and then broke off. A barren sea breeze blew through the shadowy branches of the pine trees. Yonatan Lifshitz silently began to drink it all in. The vastness of the waiting night. The terrifying spaces that stretched darkly away, devoid of a human presence. The emptiness of the bunkers, the trenches, the fortified positions, the mine fields, the burned-out armor, the no-man's-land, the border posts left unguarded. And the earth itself conspiring slowly upward in the soft swell of its hillocks, in the humps of its hills, in its jagged faults that thrust skyward until it suddenly writhes in a spasm of mountains, range after range, chains of wild peaks, cliffs, canyons, ravines, tunneled gorges flooded by darkness—and beyond these the first desert plunging down to the long Jordan Rift, with yet more mountains on its other side, the high peaks of Edom, of Moab, of Gilead, of the Golan, the Hauran, and the Bashan, and fast upon them great tablelands of desert again, wilderness upon wilderness of sand and stone, a huge, dark stillness over all—here and there a lone rock, and another, and yet another, and on and on and on, for no purpose, for no person, untouched by human hand since the beginning of time and to be touched by none until its end, an illimitable wasteland consigned to howling winds. And after that still more mountains, their snow-capped summits eternally lashed by storms, with slopes where no foot has ever trod, gullies where no man has ever gone, gulches ripped by cascades, beneath monstrous outcroppings of basalt and pillars of granite. And beyond these the endless uninhabited prairies; the huge rivers coursing stilly in the darkness, tearing out their banks as if with fangs; the age-old rain forests, their ferny mosses twining up the tangled boughs of massive trees; the broad, unpopulated valleys; the empty brushland; the steppe after steppe stretching forever in the breathless wind; and finally the enormity of ocean, the cold, befogged, writhing seas and all their dark, indifferent waters. Behold the whole wide world—upon whose fullness a molten biblical wrath once upon a primeval time spilled like a geyser of lava.

And now all is over but the silence, brooding, as if in the presence of an unspoken illness, over a planet that bristles like a crouching beast to which nothing matters any more, not ourselves, not our homes, not our women, not our children, not our thoughts, not our words, not our never-ending wars of life-and-death. All is the same to the immense indifferent earth beast, the sleeping soundless earth corpse, devoid of hate, devoid of love, forever estranged from human suffering and from man's own estrangement. And over it a sky that is just as indifferent, without one living, sensate thing as far as the farthest galaxy in the lockers of space. One would have to be worse than a fool to go looking in all this cold nothingness for some sign of intimacy or warmth, much less for the magic of Chad. It will all be in vain. For even if there are other worlds, how will they differ from the one that starts at this porch? In them, too, death will skulk, like a sleeping mastiff.

"Well, that's the end of this one, Tia. Let's go inside. It's time to hit the road." Yonatan threw the burning butt into the bushes, muttered an Arabic curse, spun wildly around as if caught in a crossfire, and stepped back into the house.

Carefully climbing on a stool so as not to wake the sleepers, he took down a pair of battered paratrooper boots with thick rubber soles from the closet above the shower, then clumsily began stuffing his army knapsack with underwear, handkerchiefs, socks, and a leather folder with 1:20,000 maps. Two army shirts, a large flashlight, his army dogtag, and a compass were next. And last, a sealed, sterile army bandage left over from a stint of reserve duty.

He went to the bathroom and gathered up his toilet articles and allergy pills, taking care not to disturb Azariah's shaving gear or Rimona's almond soap and lemon shampoo. The face that stared out at him from the mirror gave him a start—a thin, dark, unshaven visage with gray bags beneath squinty red eyes, in which flickered a glint of pent-up violence, above them a wild shock of hair springing forward like the horn of a charging animal.

He left the bathroom to rummage through the closet, gritting his teeth until he found the old windbreaker that was coming apart at the sleeves and tore it savagely from its hanger. Into its pockets he stuffed a pair of leather gloves, an odd-looking woolen hat, a switchblade, a roll of flannel strips for cleaning his rifle, and a wad of toilet paper. From a small drawer he took an imitation-leather wallet that Rimona had given him the year before and took it to the bathroom to check its contents by the light. His identity pass, its pages slipping from their tattered binding. His reserve officer's passbook. A photograph of himself and his brother Amos as small boys, their hair slicked back, and dressed in their day-in-the-big-city outfits of pressed white shirts and shorts with suspenders. A faded snapshot of himself in army uniform, clipped from a yellowing page of the army magazine. In the money pocket he found some small change and sixty-odd pounds. He jammed the wallet into his back pocket.

His last foray was to open a locked metal chest at the bottom of the closet. From this he took a captured Russian Kalashnikov rifle, three bullet clips, and a bayonet and stacked them on his knapsack. Feeling tired and out-of-breath, he stirred some raspberry squash into a glass of water, gulped it down, and wiped his lips with the back of his sleeve.

One last glance at the two sleepers. The young man on the rug at the woman's feet, her blond halo of hair like a ripple of gold in the pale light on her pillow. The little mechanic curled up in a ball like a wet puppy, his head out of sight.

Yonatan winced. His flesh crawled and he shuddered, trying to fight down the memory of the free-for-all in the big double bed a few hours ago. The sweat, the sordidness, the anger, the relentless sperm, the shout torn from his chest, the boyish sobs, the soft beating of fists, the silent submission of the woman, like earth giving way to the plow.

A wave of burning revulsion. A biblical abhorrence of uncleanliness. The voice of his father Yolek welling up to stick in his throat. And the voices of all his dead forebears, coming to barrage him with a storm of stones.

All it takes to blow the two of them to pieces, and myself, and this whole stinking cesspool, is one little burst from the Klash. Tak-tak-tak-tak-tak.

"Get set," he said to Tia in a whisper. "We're off."

He bent over and petted her roughly, against the lay of her fur, then slapped her twice on the back. If I'm not going to get rid of them, I might at least leave them a note.

But what could it possibly say? Never mind. Let's just say I was suddenly killed.

He bent over to shoulder his knapsack and gun, adjusted the straps, then spoke to Tia again, this time almost gently, "All right, we're really off this time. Not you, Tia. Just me."

Goodbye, Azuva daughter of Shilhi. Goodbye, baby fink. Yonatan's finally picked up and gone. His life is about to begin. What he needs most now is to be serious. From now on that's what he's going to be.

There was a first glimmer in the sky, a misty light from the horizon beyond the eastern hills. The little cottages, the gardens, the winter-stricken lawns, the bare trees, the tile roofs, the chrysanthemum beds, the rock gardens, the porches, the laundry lines, the bushes—all were coated more brightly each passing minute with a fine, merciful radiance that was as pure as a wish. A cold wave of delicious night air rinsed Yonatan's lungs. He gulped deeply and cut across the kibbutz with long, gangling strides, slightly bent beneath his load, hunching his right shoulder, which carried his bulging knapsack and his rifle from a frayed strap.

On reaching his parents' house, he paused, ran his free hand through his mop of hair, and started to scratch. A bird chirped briefly, its song melting the darkness. A dog growled from its refuge beneath a porch, began to bark, then thought better of it. From the direction of the cowshed came the faint plaint of the cows and the rattle of the milking machine.

Father. Mother. Goodbye. Forever. I'll never forget that you meant well. From the time I was an infant you were so good and so horrible to me. You dressed yourselves in rags, and ate dry bread with olives, and worked like coolies all day long, and sang yourselves hoarse every night, and lived in an ecstatic trance, and gave me a white, white room with a housemother in a white, white apron who fed me white, white cream to make me a clean, honest, hard-working Jewish boy with a soul of forged steel.

You poor, suffering heroes, you miserable messiahs of the Jews, you tame-souled tamers of the wilderness, you crazy saviors of Israel, you fucking maniacs, you tyrants with diarrhea of the mouth! Your souls are seared into me like a branding iron, but I am not one of you. You gave me everything and took back twice as much, like loan sharks. Call me no good. Call me a traitor. Call me a deserter. Whatever you call me must be true because you've tamed the truth as you tamed the wilderness. It, too, eats right out of your hands. May you suffer no more, my good people, my monsters of redemption. Just let me clear the hell out of here in peace. Don't try to restrain me. Don't haunt me to the ends of the earth like avenging angels. What's it to you if there's one less scumbag around here, one less filthy stain on your snow-white honor. From your loving son who can't go on any more, farewell.

Yonatan.

Who's there. What's going on.

It's your father. Come over here at once!

What do you want.

Come here, I said. You look a sight. That's the latest thing, I suppose. May I ask where you're bound?

Outward.

What's the latest?

It's of a personal nature.

Eh?

Of a personal nature. Something strictly private.

Meaning?

That I'm hitting the road.

Well, good morning, my genius. I take it we're not good enough for you here.

Father. Hear me out for once. Everything here is just fine. I have no complaints. Hats off to all of you. You're the glory of the human race. You built this land out of nothing with your bare hands and saved the Jewish people in the bargain. Agreed. It's just that I—

You? You'll kindly shut up and get back to work. What, may I ask, will become of us if every mixed-up young fellow around here decides to take off whenever he feels like it?

Get out of my way, father. Get out of my way quick before I put a clip in this rifle and do what you taught me to do with it. Just do me the favor of dying peacefully, and I'll run like a zombie to trash Sheikh Dahr all over again, or grab a hoe and root out every weed and clump of crab grass from Lebanon to Egypt until not a blade remains. I'll throw myself like a madman on any patch of wilderness. I'll plant all the trees you want. I'll marry Jewish girls from the four corners of the earth to enrich the national gene pool. I'll make you twenty grandsons, each tougher than nails. I'll plow the rocks and then the sea, anything you say. If only you were already dead and could watch me take charge, during an assault, say, when the officers have all been killed and some shitass squad leader turns into the big hero and saves the day. Take my word for it, father. Everything will be just as you planned. I guarantee it. Just do me the favor of dying first so your son can start to live.

Yonatan turned his back on the sleeping cottage, stooped to pick up one of his father's stocking caps that had fallen to the ground, rehung it on the laundry line, and moved on. Near the bakery, he turned left to take the muddy shortcut leading to the front gate.

On reaching the bus stop just outside the kibbutz, he realized he had forgotten his cigarettes. Well, who needs them? As of this minute I've stopped smoking. Enough. No looking back.

Yonatan stood by the roadside for some twenty minutes, waiting for an early riser in a car, truck, or army vehicle to give him a lift. The first full rays of sunlight dawned over the hill of Sheikh Dahr. He swung his rifle to the east to mow down the sun with a hail of bullets the minute it dared lift its fiery head. A cockadoodle of roosters broke out in a rah-rah chorus of joy over the coming of the new day, the new day, the new day. "Shut the fuck up!" snapped Yonatan out loud, and laughed. Shut the fuck up, dear comrades, we've heard enough out of you. Morning bells are ringing, ding dong ding. Whoever's good and washes after weewee will get a cup of hot chocolate. And who is not here today, boys and girls? Little John is not, teacher. Little John went to bed with his stockings on. One shoe off, one shoe on. And now he's gone. Diddle diddle dumpling, my son John.

When, as in a child's drawing, the sun finally poked its head over the hills, Yonatan did not shoot. He bowed low in mocking obeisance instead and politely inquired if he might be of help.

Morning bells were indeed ringing out, on a lovely, rosy-cheeked winter's day. The owl, the raven, and the bat were coming off the night shift at Sheikh Dahr. Foxes were heading home to hit the sack in their crannies, caves, or holes. The ghosts who ruled the ruin by night were beating a hasty retreat. A few last tatters of fog were being put to flight by the bracing cold wind. Sleep tight, little foxes. Sleep tight, dear owls. Sleep tight, sweet ghosts. Yonatan's off to the races at last.

What qualm now kept him from taking one last glance at the place where he had been born and raised? At the commune his parents had built on a godforsaken rocky hill and turned into a demi-Eden snuggled by greenery and woods? Nearly all its members were asleep. Let them sleep. In kibbutzim everywhere, dear comrades were still in bed—virtuous housemothers, balding, good-natured organizers, middle-aged field hands, chicken growers, gardeners, shepherds, men and women from a thousand remote shtetls who had come here to turn all things upside down, themselves included, and build a new world. And elsewhere, too, all over this country. How gentle they all are when they sleep. Like my former wife, who was always gentle because she was never awake.

The best thing about sleep is that it allows everyone to be off by himself at last, a million miles away from all others, even the sleeper at his side. No committees to attend, no jobs to be done, no pressing calls to duty, no challenges to be met. The law that demands you love your neighbor is suspended. Everyone is secure in a world of his own. Those in need of love get just as much as they require. Those who need to be left alone are left alone. Those who deserve to be worried, regretful, or punished are punished and will toss for it. The oldest, most arthritic, hemorrhoid-ridden geezer with a stroke or two to his debit is free to be a young cavalier again or even momma's little boy. Whoever craves pleasure is rewarded, and those who crave pain may suffer without ceasing. The sky's the limit. If you want your past back, you can have it. If you long for a place you've already been or have never been able to visit, you're transported in a trice, all expenses paid. If you're frightened of death, you get it in small doses every night to build up your resistance. If you want a war, you get one de luxe. If you pine for the dead, just whistle, and they'll appear.

In fact, maybe I should go back right now, wake up Azariah, and shout out, hey, pal, I've got the answer to the question your Spinoza and his Right Honorable Hugo Buxhall and all your head-in-the-cloud philosophers have been asking forever—the one about is there any justice in the world and where can you find it? Top of the morning, Azariah, get up! And you too, Rimona, put the kettle on! Because I've been up and around, and, lo and behold, I've found justice. It's all in our dreams. Justice for everybody, more than enough to go around, to each according to his abilities and needs, the land of the true kibbutz. Not even a general can tell me what to do in my sleep because he can't tell himself what to do in his. He sleeps like a pussycat, without bars, without stripes, without medals, blanketed in his private justice. So go to sleep, comrades, if you want justice, because that's the only way you'll ever get it.

As for me, I intend to stay up all by myself and have fun. Because I'm not looking for justice. I'm looking for life—which is the exact opposite. I've slept my fill, and now I stay awake. I'm through with crazy old men, with their looniness, with their dreams. I'm through with their wacky utopias and their creeping justice. Let them sleep all they want, bless their souls. I'm awake as I can be and about to get on board a vessel of my own.

It was only then that Yonatan turned to take one last look at the place he had once called home. The perimeter lights had gone out. The kibbutz seemed to float on a cushion of milky gray mist—the water tower twined with green ivy, the hayrack, the cowshed, the teenagers' and children's houses, the spires of the cypress trees around the white dining hall, the little red-roofed cottages with their blinds still shut, the hillside above the swimming pool, the basketball court, the sheep pen, the old guardhouse, the auxiliary shacks.

Yonatan's sleepy, bloodshot eyes narrowed, like those of a small animal sensing the approach of hunters. Stop it. Stop it. Don't fall into it, pal. It's a trap. The cunning of nets fine as a spider's. Just because I sat singing here on this lawn all night long, propped against a friend or a girl. Just because here I was loved and kissed and scolded and taught to drive a cow and a tractor. Just because here good people live who will come to my aid if any harm befalls me, who, even if I steal or commit murder, even if I were a quadruple amputee, would take turns standing watch in the jail or hospital to guard me day and night. Don't fall into it, pal. The posse is already hot on your heels and you've not yet flown the coop.

How many minutes have passed? I'm still stuck here. What if someone sees me? The light on those hills is strange—blue, pink, and gray all at once. And nothing's coming but that freight train traveling south, its engine bleating for dear life. Those barking dogs inside the fence must think I'm the enemy. I am. One burst, tak-tak-tak, and they've had it.

But something was coming down the road. A truck. An old Dodge. And stopping. The driver was a portly, middle-aged man with cherubic cheeks and amiably glittering glasses.

"Hop in, young fellow. Where to?"

"It doesn't matter. Anywhere will do."

"But which way are you heading?"

"More or less south."

"Good! Just shut the door tight. Slam it. And press down that button next to you. Maybe you got hit with a reserve call-up, eh?"

"You could say that."

"Okay, okay, I'm not asking you to give away any secrets. Might you be a paratrooper?"

"Something like that. In reconnaissance."

"And you've got some little operation in the works, huh?"

"I couldn't tell you. Maybe. Why not?"

"Did you say you were heading south?"

"More or less."

"Right you are! You don't have to tell me a thing. Why risk it? Although let me tell you, I've been a Labor Party member for twenty years and a regional defense head for two, and I know how to button my lip. I also happen to know secrets I bet you've never dreamed of. That was south you said?"

"If it isn't going out of your way."

"May I ask your final destination?"

"I have no idea."

"Listen here, young fellow. Secrecy, shmecrecy, that's all very well, but there's a limit. Back in the days of the underground, there used to be a joke about Sha'ul Avigur, who was a big shot in the Haganah and a great stickler for security. Once, when his driver came to pick him up—would you mind wiping the windshield a little? That's the ticket, thank you—Avigur said to him, 'Step on it, I'm in a hurry!' 'Where to?' asked the driver. 'Sorry, that's confidential,' answered Avigur and wouldn't say another word. Maybe you've already heard this one. Never mind. As long as the bastards get it in the balls, and then some, and you all come home safe and sound. I don't mind telling you we get a big bang out of you boys today when we compare you with what we were then. What we paraded around and sounded off about at the top of our lungs, you do with your little pinky and no fuss. Moshe Dayan couldn't have put it any better when he said that all our operations in the underground didn't amount to what one squad in the regular army can do today. God bless you all! Maybe you'll at least agree to tell me where you want to be let off?"

"The farther south, the better."

"Eilat? Ethiopia? Capetown? Don't mind me. I'm only joking. Couldn't you whisper into just one of my ears where you're going to let them have it tonight? I promise to forget it instantly."

Yonatan smiled and said nothing. The blue of the sky that grew deeper by the minute, the low hills about to turn verdant, the soft light of the wheat fields with their promised ears of grain, the secretive light of the citrus groves, the bare light of the orchards, the flocks of sheep with their shepherds in khaki and visored caps—peaceful and lovely the country lay before him, sprinkled with white villages, crisscrossed by footpaths through the fields, embraced by the shadows of mountains, cooled by the chill sea breeze—lovely and yearning for his feet to tread on. We have to love and to forgive, thought Yonatan. We have to be good. And if I leave all this, let it be without forgetting and without the fear of the nets of longing. Only where to, goddamn it? Where am I running to?

"You dozing off there, young fellow?"

"Not at all. I'm awake as hell."

"Are you from Kibbutz Granot?"

"You bet."

"How are things there?"

"Terrific. Fantastic. The magic of Chad."

"Excuse me?"

"Nothing. It's not important. Just some verse I happened to remember from the Bible."

"Take a look on the seat between us. Have some coffee from my thermos and go on reciting the rest of the Bible for me. You're not by any chance a wilderness buff, are you?"

"Am I? I might be. Why the hell not? Thanks for this coffee. It's damn good."

Just then, as swiftly as flame, a flash of piercing joy shot through him such as he had not felt since he was wounded in the raid on Hirbet Tawfik—a wild, exquisite joy that percolated through every cell of his body to its very nerve endings, that made him feel a sweet tremor in his knees, a warm lump in his throat, a transfixing dilation in his chest, and an allergy of tears in his eyes—for at that exact moment he understood at last where he was going, and what it was that was waiting for him, and why he had taken his gun and was heading south to that place beyond the mountains from which legend had it no one had ever come back alive, and that he would be the first to do so, not only alive but flushed with triumph. And having done the thing that he had to do because it summoned him from the depths of his soul, he would take to the skies and cross the seas. Why hadn't he done it long ago? Crossed the southeastern border all by himself, slipped past the Jordanian patrols, eluded the rapacious Bedouin of Wadi Musa, and reached the rose-red cliffs of Petra, the city half as old as time.

Part 2

Spring

12

Wednesday, March 2, 1966, 10:15 p.m.

There was no rain today. And no wind. A clear, fine winter day. And very cold. The windows are shut tight and the electric heater is on, yet the smell of wet leaves, of wet soil permeate the air. The very smells of my childhood. Thirty-six years on this kibbutz haven't made me any less of a European. Not that I haven't bronzed in the sun and lost the sickly pallor of my father, a middling Leipzig banker. But I still suffer in the summer and feel more at home here when it rains.

I am ashamed to admit that after all these years intimate contact with all these high-strung Russian-Polish men and women is still a strain for me.

But I have no regrets. Nearly everything I ever did in my life has been done with a clear conscience. Then what troubles me? Perhaps a vague sense of not belonging. Of homesickness. Of a sorrow that has no address. In this odd place without rivers, without forests, without churchbells. Without all those things I loved. Nevertheless, I'm perfectly capable of drawing up the most coldly objective historical, ideological, and personal balance sheets, all three of which tell me the same thing—that there is no mistake. Every one of us here can take a modest measure of pride in what we've done, in our long, dogged struggle to create out of nothing this attractive village, even if it looks as if it had been built out of blocks by an intelligent child. And in our struggle to create a better society without shedding blood and with virtually no infringement on anyone's personal freedom. Detached as I am, I approve of this achievement. We haven't done a bad job. And to some extent we have truly made better people of ourselves.

But what do we really know about ourselves? Nothing. Now, on the verge of old age, I understand even less than I thought I understood when I was young. And I don't believe anyone else understands anything any more than I do. Not the philosophers. Not the psychologists. Not even the heads of the kibbutz movement. When it comes to our own selves we know less than scientists do about the secrets of nature, or the beginnings of the cosmos, or the origins of life. Which is nothing at all.

One Saturday, when I happened to be on lunch duty with Rimona Lifshitz, she serving the food and I the drinks, I asked her out of sheer politeness whether she wasn't finding it hard going and perhaps might need some help. To which she replied with her lovely, inscrutable smile that I shouldn't feel sad because everything was looking up. Those words were almost like the touch of a warm hand. Some say she's an unusual girl. Others think her phlegmatic or far worse. For my own part, ever since that Saturday, I have made it an unwritten rule to give her a little smile each time we meet. And now, early this morning, her Yonatan disappeared without a word, leaving me with the task of finding out where he is and deciding what should be done. Where and how to start looking for him? What does a man like myself, a fifty-nine-year-old confirmed bachelor who happens to have acquired from others a modicum of trust or even respect—what do I know about such things?

Nothing. Less than that. My ignorance is total.

As it is about our youth in general. Sometimes, when I look at these young men who have been through wars, and have shot and killed and been shot at, and have plowed fields by the thousands of acres, they make me think of wrestlers lost in thought. You can't get a word out of them. At most a shrug of the shoulders. Their entire working vocabulary consists of yes, no, maybe, and what difference does it make? Inarticulate peasants? Roughhewn warriors? Just earthen clods? Not necessarily. Sometimes, passing by late at night, you come across four or five of them sitting and singing like a pack of wolves baying at the moon. For what? Or now and then, one of them shuts himself up in the recreation hall and scrimmages savagely with the piano. Technically clumsy he may be, but you can hear the longing in it. For what? For the overcast lands of the north abandoned by his parents? For strange cities? For the sea? I have no idea. For the past nine years—ever since I stopped working in the chicken coop on doctor's orders—I've been keeping the kibbutz books, and now I've been given a new and unwelcome responsibility. Whatever made me accept it? That's a good question. I need time to solve it, though.

"Solve." How odd this verb sounds to me. We have spent our entire lives in this place, coming up with one solution after another. To the youth problem, to the Arab problem, the Diaspora problem, the elderly problem, the soil and water problem, the guard duty problem, the sex problem, the housing problem—every conceivable problem under the sun. It's as if all these years we've been painstakingly seeking to inscribe a few ingenious formulae on the waves of the sea or to make the stars line up in the sky by threes in drill formation.

And now back to today's events. It's late, and tomorrow is another day. On my own initiative, and without bothering to explain, I called off tonight's rehearsal by leaving a laconic note on the dining-hall bulletin board; I didn't think any of us was able to concentrate on music. The whole kibbutz is in an uproar. And everyone expects me to know what to do. Which is—what? The quintet will have to wait for a calmer night, when all of us are less preoccupied.

Correction: I personally need some music right now. In private. Brahms perhaps. My door is locked. I'm wearing my pajamas and over them the heavy sweater Bolognesi knit for me six or seven years ago. I've made some tea with lemon. I am jotting down a few pages in my journal. Then I'll go to bed and try to sleep. What I must do is write down the events of the day and one or two thoughts of my own. Some sixteen years ago I took it upon myself to keep a daily record of life on the kibbutz, even though I haven't the vaguest idea who on this kibbutz, or anywhere else in this world, for that matter, will take an interest in it. Who indeed?

(A somewhat theological aside. The dogs are barking, the night birds are screeching. The silence is hovering over the darkness—in the valleys, in the mountains, on the sea—mutely but insistently demanding a response from us all, man, dog, bird. And it's up to us to make ourselves understood.)

From a purely technical point of view, Yolek Lifshitz is still secretary of this kibbutz. Officially I won't assume office until after the vote at the general meeting scheduled for Saturday night. Practically speaking, though, for the past several days I've been acting as secretary. I feel I have no choice. When it comes to emotions, my own or anyone else's, I'm at a total loss. They're a closed book to me, an enigma within a mystery. And though I've done my share of reading in my solitary years, whatever I've found there, whether fact or fiction, has only made the enigma more enigmatic and the mystery more mysterious. First Freud comes along and says one thing. Good enough. Only then along comes Jung and says something else and no less plausible. And Dostoyevsky was no slouch either at showing us other abysses of the soul. Well, more power to them all. Yet I am not convinced. I have my doubts.

Not one of them can enlighten me on where young Yonatan Lifshitz might be right now. Is he sleeping in some abandoned house or shack? Outdoors? In a city? On an old mattress in a deserted watchman's hut? In a tent in an army camp? Or is he wide-awake and desperate, still on the move? Is he in a car? A plane? A halftrack? Is he looking for a streetwalker in the alleys of south Tel Aviv? Or is he navigating by the stars in the wilderness of Judea or the Negev? Is he serious, or just playing a practical joke on somebody? Is he taking revenge, acting the desperado, or simply being a spoiled child? Is he looking for something or running away from it?

The responsibility is now mine. It's up to me to decide what must be done. Call in the police? Sit tight and wait it out? Make discreet inquiries in the neighboring villages? Treat the matter as urgent? Or try to take it in stride?

Just who are these youngsters anyway? What is going on in their heads? They're first-rate farmers, no doubt about it. What we ourselves did with enormous effort, they toss off without any sweat. Presumably they're brave and proficient soldiers. Yet always with an air of melancholy about them. As if they stemmed from another race, an entirely different tribe. Neither Asiatics nor Europeans. Neither Gentiles nor Jews. Neither idealists nor on the make. What can their lives mean to them, raised in this whirlwind of history, this place-in-progress, this experiment-under-construction, this merest blueprint of a country, with no grandparents, no ancestral homes, no religion, no rebellion, no *Wanderjahre* of their own? With not a single heirloom—not a chest of drawers, not a gold watch, not even a single old book. Growing in a place that was hardly a hamlet, in tents and shacks, amid pale young saplings. Just a fence and searchlights, howling jackals and distant shots. What got into you, Yonatan?

How little good I was able to do today. And even that just by groping in the dark. Perhaps I managed to soothe a soul or two. And take a few steps I thought were called for. And all on my own because there's no one here to consult with. Stutchnik is a nice fellow. More or less a friend. Warmhearted, demonstrative, but unruly. Just the way he was when I first met him in the youth movement forty years ago. He is stubborn and opinionated, incapable of listening. I have never heard him admit to being wrong. Not once. Even in the most picayune matter. One time he wouldn't speak to me for half a year because I proved to him with a map that Denmark isn't a Benelux country. Six months later he sent a note to inform me my atlas was "badly out-of-date." And yet in the end he decided to make up and brought me a lambskin rug for the foot of my bed.

As for my good friend Yolek, far be it from me to judge his contribution to the nation or to the kibbutz movement. Who am I to say? His enemies accuse him of talking like a prophet but carrying on like a small-time politician. To which his supporters reply, "Oh, he's cagey, all right, but the man has imagination and vision!"

(In passing, let me remark that I personally can do without either imagination or vision. I have lived my life here to the music of a marching band, as if death had already been abolished, old age eradicated, suffering and loneliness ridden out on a rail, and the whole universe nothing but a giant arena for political and ideological quarrels. In short, imagination and vision are not my cup of tea. Long ago I gave up on ever getting Yolek and his fellow travelers to show a little compassion. Not uncritical compassion, to be sure. There has to be a limit. But compassion nonetheless. Because we all need it. And because without it, vision and imagination begin to turn cannibalistic. Which is why I'm determined to try to be compassionate as secretary of this kibbutz. And not cause unnecessary pain. Indeed, if I may insert another theological aside, of all the commandments in the Bible, of all our latter-day commandments—kibbutz-movement, national, socialist—the only one that still matters to me is the one against pain. No rubbing salt into wounds. *Thou shalt not cause pain.* Not to oneself either.) So much for that.

And now back to the events of the day. It was a clear morning. A cold blue sky. Not even as a boy in Europe have I seen such a glorious sight. It makes one feel slightly intoxicated and happy to be alive. Reading the headlines this morning about troop concentrations in the north, I had the childish fantasy of setting out for Damascus and convincing the Syrians to chuck this futile nonsense, to sit down with us in the sunshine to settle our problems once and for all.

Instead, of course, I went to the office and pored over the slipshod bills of lading that Udi Shneour stuck into my mailbox last night. From seven to nine I tried making some sense out of the bills and the chaos that's overtaken the citrus groves. After which I had intended to answer some of the mail that had been mounting on Yolek's desk. The more urgent letters, because I'm always perfectly content to put off till tomorrow what needn't be done today in the hope it will either take care of itself or go away. Officially, of course, since I'm not even in office yet, there's no need to rush.

At nine or nine-fifteen, a grim-faced Hava Lifshitz burst into the office. In a hostile, schoolmarmish voice she exclaimed, "Have you no sense of shame?"

I put down my pencil, pushed up my reading glasses, wished her good morning, and invited her to sit in my chair. (A few days ago someone walked off with the only other chair and never bothered to return it.)

No, she would not sit down. She simply could not grasp, she said, how anyone could be so insensitive, although nothing surprised her any more. She had come to demand that I do something, or, as she put it, that "you make this your business right now!"

"Excuse me," I said, "but exactly what is it that I'm supposed to make my business right now?"

"Srulik," she snapped, as if my name were a dirty word, "would you tell me whether you're a complete numbskull or just pretending to be one? Or is this simply your sick sense of humor?"

"That could be," I said. "Anything is possible. But I can't give you an answer until I know what the question is. And I suggest that you consider sitting down after all."

"Do you really mean to tell me you know nothing about what's happened? That you've seen no evil and heard no evil? That while the whole kibbutz has been talking about nothing else, Your Royal Highness has been spending his morning on the dark side of the moon?"

The two of us were staring at each other across the desk. I couldn't suppress a slight smile.

"Something terrible has happened," said Hava.

I apologized at once. I explained to her that I truly had no idea what she was talking about. The fact is that for the past several years I've been skipping breakfast in the dining hall and getting by until lunch with tea, crackers, and yogurt in my office. Was anything, God forbid, wrong with Yolek?

"He's next!" said Hava, bubbling with venom. "Troubles always come in pairs. But this time it's Yoni."

"Hava," I said, "I'm not clairvoyant. Please try to tell me exactly what happened."

With a sudden, jerky motion, as if she were about to scatter my papers or slap my face, she collapsed into the chair I had offered her, shielding her eyes with one hand.

"I don't get it," she whispered. "You've got to have the heart of a murderer to treat me like this."

I couldn't understand who was the murderer—her husband, her son, or me—or why I put my hand on her shoulder and called her softly by name.

"Srulik," she said, looking up at me, "will you help?"

"Of course I will," I said. And though, for many years now, physical contact with anyone has been difficult for me, I left my hand where it was. I may even have touched her hair. I wouldn't swear to it, but I think I did.

Yoni had left home sometime during the night, Hava said. He might have taken a gun with him. That feeble-minded wife of his had remembered this morning that he had been talking about traveling abroad. "But no one knows better than I do that you can't trust a word that demented child says. Whatever he may have been planning, it would take an imbecile to assume that he left with no passport or money, only with his gun and army uniform. Srulik, you know you're the only one here I can talk to. The rest of them are all just petty, narrow-minded, and selfish. Deep down, they're thrilled to bits because they know this will be the end of Yolek. They've been out to get him for years. I've come to you because you're a decent man, if no genius. A *mensch,* not a monster. He might as well have murdered his father with his own hands. Yolek will never survive this. He's in bed with pains in his chest, having trouble breathing. Blaming himself for everything. And that moron Rimona, who took in that filthy little murderer to destroy Yoni, says to me in cold blood, 'He left because he wasn't happy. He said that he would and he did. I don't know where he went. Maybe he'll come back when he feels better.' I should have slapped her face then and there. I didn't say a word to that skunk, that diabolic smut pusher who probably knows everything. Oh, I'll bet he does and is laughing up his sleeve and won't tell us a thing. Srulik, I want you to go right this minute and *make* him tell you where Yoni is. And don't be squeamish! Take a pistol if you have to. What are you waiting for? For God's sake, Srulik, the last thing I need now is a cup of coffee and a speech. You know I'm made out of iron. All I'm asking is for you to go right now and do what has to be done. You can leave me here. I'll be fine. Just go!"

The water, however, had already boiled, and I went ahead

and made the coffee whether she wanted it or not. Urging her to remain in the office and rest in my chair, I excused myself, put on my hat and coat, and went out to look for Rimona. On my way I stopped at the infirmary and asked the nurse to look in on Yolek and stay with him until I arrived. People kept stopping me to give advice, ask for the latest news, or spout all kinds of wild stories. I told them all that I was sorry but I had no time. Except for Paula Levin, whom I asked to check up on Hava and keep everyone else out of the office.

I tried my best to set my thoughts in order. The trouble was, I hadn't the foggiest idea where to begin. Of course, I had already heard some of the gossip about young Gitlin, who was said to have moved in with Rimona and Yoni. All kinds of insinuations, snickers, salacious innuendos. Until now I hadn't felt any need to take a stand on the matter. A society that prides itself on living by enlightened ideals must restrain itself—or at least so I think—from intruding into anyone's personal life. What goes on between a man and his wife, or between friends of whatever sex, is a strictly private affair in my opinion and deserves a *Keep Out* sign. And now along comes Hava insisting that "something terrible" has happened. Who's to say? Certainly not I. Anything having to do with sex, or the emotions, or the connection between the two, is *terra incognita* to me.

Once, as a boy in Leipzig, I fell in love with a dreamy high-school girl, but she much preferred a young tennis star—of the type then popularly called a "blond beast"—who was also a great fan of Hitler's. I pined away for a while but managed to get over it. Around that time, one morning at five o'clock, the family maid stepped into my room and into my bed. Not long after I joined a Zionist pioneering group in Poland and came to Palestine. Once here, some twenty-five years ago, I fell in love with P. In fact, I may still be in love with her in my fashion, but I've never let her know. Now she has four grandchildren to her credit, and I'm a confirmed bachelor. Of my few casual, awkward, acutely embarrassing sexual liaisons the less said the better. Sorry, unaesthetic affairs all of them, and instantly regretted. The whole business, as far as I can see, involves a great deal of pain and human degradation in exchange for a very few moments of pleasure—keen pleasure, I'll admit, but far too brief and meaningless to be worth the effort. Of course, it's only fair to point out that my experience is too limited to generalize, but I will allow myself one observation here. Built into this world is an irremediable erotic injustice so great that it makes a mockery of all our attempts to construct a better society. This is not to say that we mustn't set our sights beyond it and keep trying, only that we should do so without any grand illusions. On the contrary, as modestly, cautiously, and unpretentiously as we can. But now I'd better turn over the record, because this is most definitely a night for Brahms and still more Brahms.

And what comes next? Oh yes. Rimona, once I found her, remembered that when she got back last night from serving refreshments to the members of the Jewish philosophy group ("When was that?" "Late." "Yes, but when?" "About three-quarters of the way through the rain"), she found the two of them awake. A little tired though. Kind to each other, "like two little boys who have fought and made up." They were kind to her too. And then went to bed. As did she. (Whether they were kind to each other after that as well, I didn't try to guess. What do I know?)

"And when did Yoni leave?"

"In the night."

"Yes, but when?"

"Late. When he had to."

I asked her what had happened in the morning. Azariah woke up. He thought he'd heard shooting. He wakes up often thinking he hears shooting. Sometimes she thinks she hears, too. When they saw that Yoni was gone, he began to run all over.

"Who did?"

"Zaro. Yoni wouldn't have. Yoni takes his time. He never runs."

"What makes you say that?"

"Yoni is tired."

In short, Azariah dashed to the tractor shed, and to the dining hall, all over. And what did Rimona do while he was running? She checked to see what Yoni had taken and what he had left behind. He took what he always did when he gets called by his army unit in the middle of the night. Because sometimes that's when they come for him. Why then was she so sure that the army hadn't called for him last night too? I couldn't get a straight answer, only "This time it was different."

What did she do then? She sat and waited. Then she dressed, and made the bed, and cleaned the room. And didn't go to work in the laundry. And gave Tia her breakfast. And waited some more. What was she waiting for? She was waiting for it to be seven-fifteen. Why seven-fifteen? Because that's when Hava and Yolek get up. And that's when she went to tell them that Yonatan had left in the night. And that they shouldn't be upset.

And then what happened? Nothing. Nothing? Nothing. Hava was upset. And what did Yolek say? What did he do? He hid his face in his hands and sat quietly in his chair. And Hava stopped talking too and looked quietly out the window. That's when Rimona left quietly and went to look for Zaro.

"Rimona," I said. "I want to ask you something. Please try to concentrate before you answer me. Because it's important. Do you have any guess where Yoni might be now?"

"He's gone."

"He certainly is. But where?"

"To look for something."

"To look for something?"

A brief silence, followed by a smile, a calm, autumnal smile, as if to say the two of us knew things other people have never dreamed of. I smiled back at her and said, "Rimona. Please. This is serious."

"I'm thinking," she said.

"What are you thinking?"

"That he left because he said he would."

"But left for where? Why?"

"To wander," she said. "Perhaps."

In the early 1940's the kibbutz had made an arrangement with a pair of dentists, a husband and wife, Dr. Fogel and Dr. Fogel. They had recently arrived from Poland and offered to treat us at lower rates. The two of them never learned any Hebrew. Anyone who had a dental problem made a trip to their poorly equipped clinic in town. Until the wife was killed in an accident and the husband contracted a fatal disease. In return for a fixed annuity, we agreed to take their only child into the kibbutz. A sweet, self-absorbed little girl, very neat and orderly, although a bit slow and withdrawn. When she reached draft age, Yonatan Lifshitz married her. Every cabinet minister and party leader attended their wedding, and not a few members of the Knesset. Afterwards she began to work in the laundry. And became pregnant. And apparently something went wrong. Now and then people talked about her. I tried not to listen. What does a man like me have to do with gossip. Or with pretty girls. Or with anyone's psyche.

"Rimona," I said. "One more question. And this time you needn't answer, because it's of a personal nature. Did Yoni suffer from, or complain about, or seem hurt in any way by . . . your ties with Azariah Gitlin?"

She paused. "But they like to."

"Like to what?"

"Suffer."

"I'm sorry. I don't understand. Who likes to suffer?"

"These people. Not everyone. Some do. Hunters who spear antelopes do."

"I'm afraid this is beyond me. Who likes to suffer?"

"Yoni. And Zaro. And my father too. And Bach. And Yolek as well. Lots of them." Then her strange smile reappeared, and she added, "Not you."

"All right. Let it be. But what do you suggest we do now?"

"Whatever has to be done."

"Like what?"

She couldn't answer.

"Should we wait?"

"Wait."

"Or should we look for him?"

"Look for him. Because Yoni sometimes likes danger."

"Rimona. I need a straight answer. Should we wait or should we look for him?"

"Look and wait."

One last thing: Did she need anything? Any help from the kibbutz? The question seemed to confuse her. Any help? Oh, yes. Perhaps I could see to it that Zaro wasn't picked on, though he always asked for it. Just not make him leave. He's good.

"Tell me, Rimona, where are you going right now?"

"To see if he's had breakfast. And to make sure that he does, because all morning long he's been looking for Yoni. He even went to Sheikh Dahr, but he'll be back soon. Then, I don't know. Maybe to the laundry. Maybe not."

I finally found Azariah sitting by himself in the empty recreation hall. I must have given him a start. He was sorry, but he simply couldn't go to work in the tractor shed today. I had his word of honor that tomorrow and the next day he would work overtime to make up for it. He had already looked everywhere on the kibbutz, in all the orchards, as far as the ruins of Sheikh Dahr, but no trace. Now he wanted to die because he was to blame for everything. "Srulik, maybe you should get Little Shimon, he's in charge of exterminating stray dogs around here, and that's what should be done with me. Only you have to let me find Yoni first. I'm the only one who can. And lots more. Just give me a second chance, and you'll see what I can do for this kibbutz."

There was a panicky glint in his green eyes, which refused to meet mine, and frightened lines at the corners of his mouth. Yoni, he promised, would be back by this evening. Or, at the latest, by tomorrow or the day after. Or sometime soon. His intuition, which had never failed him, told him so. There were only two things that Yonatan had been missing. One was love. The other was purpose. Some Jewish ideal, if one might still put it that way, because something had died inside him. Unlike himself, Azariah, who had resolved to devote his life to the kibbutz, to society, to the country.

And what exactly was he doing alone in the recreation hall? He was trying, I might as well know, to put together a statement. Or a poem. A strong one. Something with the power to console and to rekindle the flame. (By the way, he really is a good guitarist. That much I've discovered at our rehearsals.)

"Azariah," I said. "Listen, please. If you really want to help, there's something I'd like you to do for me. First, calm down. It would make life easier for all of us if you tried not to be so emotional. And second, I'd like you to spend the day at the switchboard. I want you to make sure that the line is free as much of the time as possible. Someone may try to get in touch."

"Srulik, excuse me for saying so, but I feel I must tell you that I appreciate you greatly. Not appreciate. That's a ridiculous word. On the contrary, I respect you and wish I could be like you. In control of myself. While I agree with practically everything Spinoza ever said, I haven't been very good at living up to it. I keep catching myself all the time in the ugliest lies. Not ugly really. Unnecessary and low. Lying only to impress, though in the end I achieve the opposite. Yet I want you to know I'm working on myself. Little by little I'm changing. You'll see. And when Yoni comes back—"

"Azariah, please. We can discuss all this some other time. Right now I'm in a hurry."

"Of course. Excuse me. I just wanted you to know that, how should I put it, I'm entirely at your service. And at the kibbutz's. Twenty-four hours a day. I may be a fink. I definitely am.

But I'm not a parasite or a leech. And I am going to marry her."

"You're *what?*"

"Because that's what Yoni wanted, I swear. And if it will make Yolek happy, because he's been like a father to me, and Hava, and the rest of the kibbutz, then that's what I'll do, marry Rimona. And now I'm off to tend to the switchboard. To keep the line free day and night. Srulik?"

"Yes. What?"

"They don't come any better than you, if you don't mind my saying so."

Azariah spoke these last words with his back to me and set off on a run. Yoni, Udi, Etan, and that whole crew strike me as a strange tribe. They will never accept Azariah, and yet he isn't strange to me. In fact, he seems almost intimately familiar, yet he doesn't have a chance of fitting in. I never did believe a Jew could really and truly assimilate. That's what turned me into a Zionist.

After I returned to the office, I finally managed to get through to Yonatan's army unit. No, there had not been a call-up last night. They knew nothing about it, and since when was such a thing a fit subject for a telephone conversation anyway? As a special favor, however, they were willing to promise me that Yonatan Lifshitz was not on the base. Of that the young female soldier at the other end of the line was "one-hundred-and-one-percent sure." They were all one big family there, and she knew everyone who came and went. I thanked her but persisted: could I possibly talk with an officer called Chupka? (Rimona had recalled that this was the name of Yonatan's C.O.) I was asked to hang on but was then cut off. I dialed again, battling all the gremlins at different exchanges along the way, until finally I got the same young clerk. Chupka, I was now told, had left the base that morning. To go where? Hang on for a second, will you? And again I was cut off. And again I fought back with the patience that I've learned from a lifetime of playing the flute. And again I got the same girl, who this time, in a fit of pique, demanded to know just who I thought I was and who had authorized me to ask such questions. Without batting an eyelash, I immediately fired off three lies. That I was Yonatan's father. That my name was Yisra'el Lifshitz. And that said Yisra'el Lifshitz was still a member of the Knesset. Whether out of respect for Yisra'el or the Knesset, she finally consented to reveal the dark secret. Chupka was on his way, already in, or on his way back from, Acre, where he had gone to attend the circumcision of the son of one of his soldiers, whose name she gave me.

Right away I dialed Grossmann in Acre. (An old friend from my days in Leipzig, who works for the electric company.) An hour later he called back. Chupka was taking a nap, apparently at his sister's home in Kibbutz Ein-Hamifratz.

Two-and-a-half hours had already passed in the Great Phone War. I would have missed lunch if Stutchnik's wife, Rachel, hadn't been considerate enough to bring me a covered plate from the dining hall. I ate the meat croquettes, squash, and rice without ever once putting down the receiver.

At a quarter-to-two, I managed to get through to the office at Ein-Hamifratz. It was not until about four o'clock, however, that I got hold of Chupka himself. He said he hadn't a clue where Yonatan might be and promised that if "it turns out to be serious," I could count on him and his men to find their missing friend even if he was "on the far side of Bab Allah." I asked whether he thought Yonatan might do something rash.

"Let me think," he replied in a hoarse, fatigued voice. After a brief silence he declared, "Why ask me? Anybody is liable to do something rash." (Incidentally, he couldn't be more right.) In the end we agreed to keep in touch.

All the while I was playing detective on the phone, Udi Shneour and Etan R. were, at my request, combing those surroundings of the kibbutz that were too muddy to be negotiable by jeep. With no results. Then, once more at my prompting, Etan took Tia around on a leash to try to pick up a scent. Also without results.

I couldn't make up my mind whether it was necessary or desirable to call in the police at this point. The reasons for doing so were obvious. The reason against it was that if the whole affair turned out to be nothing but a lark, Yonatan would most likely be angry that we had involved the law.

By five o'clock I had finally decided I would talk to Yolek after all. Earlier in the day I had suggested to Hava that she call any friends or relations with whom Yonatan might be staying. She took this task upon herself with a look of genteel revulsion, leaving me with the feeling that, even though nothing else could be expected from an incompetent like me, any measures I had taken so far were perfectly brainless. Her only insistent request was that I place a transatlantic call to Benya Trotsky in Miami. This seemed to me rather pointless, but I agreed without disclosing my true feelings.

Thirty-nine years have gone by since my first encounter with Yolek Lifshitz. There was something offhandedly domineering about him that made me feel like an underling. He was a cautious, keen-witted man with not a youthful bone in his body even then, when we were all very young—as if he had come into this world as a fully formed adult. To this day I feel intimidated by his presence. It was he, incidentally, who first taught me how to harness a horse.

Frankly, I had expected him to go straight into his *mea culpa* routine, but he didn't. Assertively absorbed in his cigarette and staring at the ceiling, he thanked me for what I had done, the expression of his face reminding me of the times I had seen him faced with a critical political decision, his nostrils flaring, his huge, profligate nose eloquent with a profound contempt. He talked sparingly and unemotionally, as if his mind were made up to take some dramatic, irrevocable step. Like a general or head of state who has just pronounced the secret code word for crossing some fatal Rubicon still undisclosed to his entourage and who now sits waiting, exuding something that might be called serenity were it not for the chain smoking.

"Yolek," I said. "I want you to know that we're all behind you. The whole kibbutz."

"That's good," said Yolek. "Thank you. I can really sense it."

"And that we're doing all we can."

"Of course you are. I never doubted that."

"We've combed the area. We've contacted the army too. And made a discreet check of friends and relations. So far, no results."

"Well done. And I'm glad you put off going to the police. Srulik?"

"Yes."

"Some tea? Or a little brandy?"

"No, thank you."

"By the way, that boy needs to be watched and kept out of harm's way. He's in bad shape."

"Who is?"

"Azariah. You mustn't let him out of your sight. He's a precious young man who may be meant for great things. He needs to be watched around the clock because he blames himself for all this, and there's no telling what he may do. As far as Hava is concerned, do whatever seems best. I'll keep out of it."

"Meaning?"

"That she'll play this to the hilt. She will insist that Azariah move back to his room, and most likely that he leave the kibbutz altogether."

"What should I say to her?"

"I think that you're a great fellow, Srulik, and a first-rate bookkeeper to boot, but some questions are better not asked. Why don't you just consider it for a while. Yoni, I'm sorry to say, is a damn fool, but he isn't a scoundrel. And not just another dumb yokel either."

I apologized at once. Yolek made a weary gesture and assured me that he bore no hard feelings. He too thought we should get in touch with Trotsky to see if he had had a role in the affair, but that this needed to be done prudently, perhaps even indirectly. We were, after all, dealing with a pathological liar, an international crook who would stop at nothing. It might perhaps be worth putting out feelers in America. Not that there weren't advantages to a more straightforward approach.

I had to confess to not knowing what he was talking about.

Yolek, however, simply made a face and let drop some remark of Nietzsche's about begetting children and giving hostages to fortune.

I rose to go. My hand was on the doorknob when his cracked but commanding voice overtook me. He was almost glad that the weather was good. It would be too horrible to imagine Yoni wandering about in a drenching thunderstorm. The damn fool! Perhaps he was holed up right now in some old ruin or dinky gas station, no different from when he was a boy, full of self-pity and feeling angry at the world. Should he suddenly decide to return, we would have to play the whole thing down to spare his tender soul. It was a nasty business. But one way or another, whether from America or a gas station, the boy was sure to come back. True enough, we would have to get him out of the kibbutz for a year or two. Perhaps to study somewhere, or to work for the movement, or to engage in anything that would allow him to feel he was doing his own glorious thing. If he insisted on going overseas, we would find him something overseas. The boy was a spoiled brat with a head full of worms, but then the whole lot of them were soft in the brain. I myself—I trust you to keep this a secret—I had already decided to accommodate him because I saw how miserable he was. I even wrote to Eshkol. But where did we go wrong, Srulik? How did we ever manage to raise such a collection of halfwits?

All the while I kept thinking Scyths, Huns, Tatars, etcetera, and left with the promise that I would drop by again as soon as I could.

Does he love the boy? Detest him? Both? Want to mold him according to his will? Found a dynasty with him like some Hasidic rabbi? I understand nothing. Nothing at all. There is a poem of Bialik's in which he asks what love is. If Bialik didn't know, how should I?

Once more let me make a more or less theological observation. About fathers and sons. Any father and any son. King David and Absalom. Abraham and Isaac. Jacob, Joseph, and his brothers. Each, as it were, trying to make of himself a fulminating Jehovah. Complete with thunder and lightning. Hailing fire and brimstone.

Not that I have the slightest notion of who young Yonatan Lifshitz really is. Yet writing these words I feel a sudden concern for him. That he may be at the end of his rope. Maybe I was mad not to have gone to the police immediately. A human life could be at stake. Or perhaps we should simply sit tight. A young man wants time out to be by himself. It's his right. He's not a child, after all. Or is he? I don't know.

I will say this much, quite honestly. More than once, at some intense moment of loneliness in my own life, whether sorting eggs into cardboard trays for hours on end in the chicken run, or sitting on my little porch of a summer evening and listening to the families enjoying themselves on the grass, or lying awake until morning in my creaky bed while the jackals howl in Sheikh Dahr, or seeing the moon appear in my window like some drunken, beet-faced stormtrooper, more than once I've thought what Utopian bliss it would be to pick up and take to the road. To start a new life, anywhere, either by myself or with P. Leaving everything behind me, for good.

So why these pangs of conscience? What moral reason or obligation can there be to turn loose the police or his army-scout friends on Yonatan? On the contrary, if he felt he had to go, why not let him go in peace? It's his life. And, incidentally, I see nothing at all wrong in Azariah's marrying Rimona. Why shouldn't he? Just because of the lethal hatred of that hard woman, or the public image of an old tyrant? Are the two of them sufficient reason for me to launch a manhunt? To force the bird back into its cage?

And while I'm at it, being secretary of this kibbutz is simply not for me. Let them ask my good friend Stutchnik. Or Yashek. Or bring Yolek back by popular demand. I, in any case, am the wrong choice. It's all a mistake.

At seven this evening, I arranged for the telephone to be manned through the night. Etan, Azariah, Yashek, and Udi agreed to take three-hour shifts until seven in the morning, when I'll be back in the office to decide what to do next. At eight-thirty I went back to my room, showered, and took my medicine. At nine-fifteen I was urgently called to the office. Miami on the line at last.

"Yes, this is his personal assistant speaking. Mr. Trotsky is out of town. I'm sorry, but he cannot be reached. Can I take a message?"

I tried to phrase it as carefully as I could. I am calling from Israel. I am the acting secretary of Kibbutz Granot. A young man named Yonatan Lifshitz may contact, or may already have contacted, Mr. Trotsky. He is the son of old friends of his. If Mr. Trotsky hears from him, could he please get in touch with us right away. We would be most grateful.

And then back to my room again, where, like a faithful wife, my accustomed solitude waited. Have a seat, Srulik. You had a hard day today, didn't you? Come, let's light the electric heater and put on some water for tea. And slip on that nice old sweater of yours over your pajama top. And let Brahms play for us. And light the desk lamp. Rather than feel sorry for ourselves, though, we have written this report.

This entry has certainly dragged on. It's after midnight, and tomorrow won't be any easier. I'll wash up and lie down to read until I fall asleep. Bone up some more on my ornithology. In

German, English, and Hebrew I've been learning all about the birds, another subject I understand next to nothing about. Good night. Let's see what a new day brings.

Thursday, March 3, 1966, 4:30 p.m.

No news. No Yonatan.

The phone was manned in shifts all through the night. Chupka called. Sometime today he will try to drop by to see me.

Yolek is feeling worse. The doctor came to give him a shot and recommended hospitalization, at least long enough to give him a thorough checkup. Yolek thundered, banged his fist on the desk, and drove everyone out of the room.

My official position gave me the courage to go to him despite the general rout. He was seated regally in his armchair, holding an unlit cigarette that he was studying shrewdly, comparing its ends.

"Srulik," he said. "I don't like the looks of this."

"You shouldn't smoke," I replied. "And you must listen to the doctor."

"Out of the question," he said calmly. "I'm not budging from here until we hear something."

"Maybe we're making a mistake," I said hesitantly. "Maybe we should call in the police after all?"

He took his time answering. A sphinxlike smile played briefly over his face.

"The police," he said at last, lifting his left eyebrow, "means the press. And the press means a scandal. The boy has his pride. By wounding it we may cut off his line of retreat. No, I'm against it. We'll wait it out. Srulik?"

"Yes."

"What do you think?"

"That we should do so. Right now."

"Eh?"

"I think we should inform the police. And not wait a moment longer."

"Go ahead. You're the secretary," said Yolek, taking a long puff from his unlit cigarette. "You have the right to make your own mistakes. What did you tell Hava?"

"About what?"

"About Azariah. And, by the way, why hasn't he come to see me?"

"From what I've heard, he was up all night. Hava hasn't approached me about Azariah at all. Neither has Rimona. As far as I know, she went to work today in the laundry."

"Tomorrow's Friday, isn't it?"

"Yes."

"Why don't you inform the police tomorrow. Not today. Tomorrow. After forty-eight hours, I believe there's even a procedure for tracking missing persons. There's been no word from Trotsky?"

"Nothing yet."

"Of course not. I never thought there would be. Between us, I have my own suspicions. You must promise not to breathe a word of this. Is that clear?"

I said nothing.

"Hava's behind the whole mess. In cahoots with that Trotsky. I won't spell it out any further. It's her way of getting back at me."

"Yolek," I said. "Believe me, when it comes to human emotions I don't understand a thing, but that theory strikes me as implausible."

"A genius you never were, Srulik, but still the very soul of decency. Do me the favor of forgetting what I just said. All of it. Would you like some tea? A little brandy? No?"

I thanked him but urged him once again to go to the hospital as the doctor had advised.

Craftily, like a degenerate old philanderer, he suddenly winked at me with a lewd smile. "On Sunday, if Yoni still hasn't turned up, I'm going to go get him. The doctor be damned! Listen to me, Srulik. None of what I'm going to tell you is to leave these four walls. I'm flying there on Sunday. I've already booked a seat. And I'll bring him back. They're not going to get away with this. And don't try to talk me out of it."

"But I don't understand," I said. "Where are you flying on Sunday?"

"Not a genius is an understatement. All right, I'm going to America. By myself. Without telling Hava or anyone else."

"But Yolek, you can't be serious."

"But I can. And I am. And my health is not a topic for discussion. So don't argue. It's pointless. I wish to be left alone now, Srulik, and remember to keep your mouth shut."

After lunch I returned to my room. I seem to be coming down with the grippe. And so I've got into bed in my long underwear and put on a Bach fugue. And written a few more pages in this journal. On Saturday night I will be officially elected secretary of the kibbutz unless I have the gumption to announce that I'm not a candidate. Determination has never been a trait of mine, though, and people will think badly of me. So we'll have to wait and see. Could it possibly be that I'm the only sane person in all of this? Father, son, mother, Azariah, even my precious Rimona, to say nothing of Stutchnik—there's something strange about every one of them. True enough, a genius I never was. Twice this morning I picked up the office phone to call the police, and once even dialed the number, but changed my mind both times. I'll put it off until tomorrow after all.

Meanwhile I have read a suggestive passage in Donald Griffin's *Bird Migration,* from which I quote the following lines:

> Many species of birds begin their spring migration when the weather is still very different from that prevailing in their

> nesting areas. Species that winter in tropical islands, for example, where climatic conditions are highly stable, must leave such regions by a given date if they are to spend the short-lived summer in the far north.

And this as well:

> Whatever informs a bird in a tropical rain forest in South America that the moment has come to fly north if it is to arrive in the Canadian tundra just in time for the spring thaw?

I've copied out these lines because, absurd as it may seem, if even a great man like Yolek can allow himself to believe in the most crackpot hypothesis, why shouldn't I try out my own modest powers of divination, no matter how wild the hunch?

Roughly an hour-and-a-half ago, at about twenty after two, while I was lying in bed, reading Griffin, there was a knock on my door. Before I could answer it, the door burst open. It was Hava. She had to have a serious talk with me. At once. This minute.

That she found me in my long underwear, a tattered woolen scarf wrapped around my throat, looking like a refugee from the underworld, didn't faze her one bit or make her feel the least need to apologize. She marched across the room in a huff and sat down on my unkempt bed. I fled to the bathroom, locked the door, and dressed hurriedly before emerging.

An obviously aging woman, her hair braided in a circle around her head, a Polish severity about her, a wispy mustache above lips perpetually pursed, righteous to her fingertips but determined to be tolerant as a matter of principle, having no choice but to put up with the despicable weaknesses of others.

How, I asked, might I be of help? She would try, she said, to control herself. She would not even begin to tell me what she really thought. Now all she wanted from me was to act. If I didn't want to be haunted all my life by what was about to happen to Yolek, whose state was far worse than I thought, I had better get that sewer rat out of here this very day. Every extra hour was a knife in her back and in Yolek's sick heart. Not just because of the publicity—why, any moment the hyenas from the press might arrive—but because Yoni must on no account find that creature here when he returned. Didn't I realize what was going on? Was I an imbecile like the rest of them? That little turd was living as merrily as you please in Yoni's room, and even sleeping in his *bed.* Who in the world would put up with such a sick scene? Not even cannibals in the jungle. And I was supposed to be secretary of the kibbutz. Well, that was what always happened when little men try stepping into shoes too big for them. But never mind. I would pay for it dearly, with interest. For what I had put Yoni through and for whatever happened to Yolek. Either I made up for at least part of the harm I had done by giving that worthless bum the heave-ho, or I would never hear the last of it from her. Today! The doctor, by the way, had expressly said that he was afraid it was the heart this time. She wanted me to know she could see right through my manipulations. At least I might stop playing the village saint. Because she had never misjudged a person yet. And she hoped that I didn't expect her to believe that I had really done all I could to get in touch with America. What kind of monster was I, lying here in bed like a country squire and snoozing away the afternoon? At which point she rose and stood facing me, taut and breathless, as if declining with stoic fortitude to strike back at her enemies.

"Hava," I said. "You're not being fair."

"Then throw him out of here!" she snapped, her eyes flashing. "This very minute!"

With a gesture of offended gentility, she turned to go.

"I'm sorry," I said. "You'll have to give me time to think about it. I do promise, though, to talk to Rimona and the young man. I think he can be persuaded to return to the barber's shack.

But first we must concentrate on Yoni. There's reason to believe he'll come back soon. You have my solemn pledge that once he's safely home I'll convene a meeting of the family life committee. If it decides that action needs to be taken, I won't hesitate to do so. Hava. Please."

"I want to di-i-i-e-e!" she suddenly wailed in the shrill, piercing voice of a spoiled child who has been crushingly humiliated. "Srulik, I just want to die."

"Hava," I said. "Do try to calm down. You know we're all behind you. The whole kibbutz. Believe me, I've been doing, and will continue to do, everything in my power."

"I know," she sobbed, her face hidden in a white handkerchief. "I know you're a dear. And I'm just a horrid old witch gone completely out of her senses. I hope you'll forgive me, Srulik, though I've no right to ask after all my insults. I just want you to know I feel ashamed and want to die. Could I please have a glass of water?"

And after drinking it, she began again. "Srulik, tell me the whole truth. I'm tough as nails. I can take it. Tell me what you think. Is Yonatan alive? Yes or no?"

"Yes," I said quietly, with uncharacteristic firmness, "he's alive and well. He's been unhappy lately and just decided to go away and be by himself for a while. I've often thought of doing the same thing. And so have you. We all have."

She lifted her streaming face to me. "In this whole madhouse you're the only one who remained human. I want you to know I'll never forget it. That there was one feeling person among all those murderers and I attacked him like a beast and called him the most awful names."

"Hava," I said. "Don't be angry with me for saying that you need to rest a bit. There's already enough pain in the world. Let's try to keep as calm as we can."

"From now on," she said, like a mollified child, "I swear I'll do everything you tell me. I'm going to go back home right now and rest. You're my good angel. But I still don't think he should be living at Yoni's. And sleeping in his bed. It's indecent."

"You may be right about that," I said. "I think you are, but there's reason to believe he won't refuse to move back to his old room. After that we'll see. And Hava, if Yolek isn't feeling well, please let me know right away. Try to convince him to take the doctor's advice."

"But I'm not speaking to him any more. He's a murderer, Srulik. Are you asking me to throw myself into a murderer's arms?"

Once Hava was gone, I forced myself to spoon up half a container of yogurt and take an aspirin. I wrapped myself in my coat and went to look for Azariah Gitlin. I found him sitting at the switchboard. He was still so distraught that after sleeping for less than two hours he had got up and run back to his post.

He cringed when I walked in and hurried to offer me a cigarette—in fact, a whole pack, because he had another in his pocket. I had to remind him I didn't smoke.

"A thousand apologies, Comrade Srulik. Cigarettes are the most revolting poison. I beg your pardon. 'Stepan gave Alyosha his most precious stones; Alyosha got mad and broke Stepan's bones.' In Russian, Stepan actually gave Alyosha his silver spoon, but I changed it to stones to maintain the rhyme. I'm ashamed of myself, Comrade Srulik, for causing you all this trouble. Yonatan's the only friend I ever had in the whole world. But his going away—I mean this trip of his—I had absolutely nothing to do with it. Whatever you all may be thinking is the exact opposite of the truth. Because I want you to know, Comrade Srulik, that it was Yonatan who invited me into his home. It's as simple as that. You can even announce it at the next general meeting. He wanted someone to be there. He even showed me where he kept all his tools so I could replace him. Just as you've replaced Yolek. There's no embarassment like a bad comparison, as the saying goes, but you're all making the mistake that Spinoza called the confusion of cause and effect. Yoni didn't decide to go away because I moved in. He had me move in because he had decided to go away. It's a perfect example of mistaking the effect for the cause. Are you, Comrade Srulik, an admirer of Spinoza?"

"Of course I am," I said. "But let's leave Spinoza for less troubled times. Meanwhile, let me ask you a question and perhaps a favor too."

"Of course, Comrade Srulik. Anything you say. Your wish is my command."

"Azariah, if only to spare certain people a lot of heartache, would you agree to move back to the barber's shack until all this blows over?"

A cunning light flared and went out in his green eyes. "But she's *my* woman now. Not his. I mean in principle."

"Azariah, I'm asking for a favor. It's only for the time being. I'm sure you know the state of Yolek's health."

"Are you trying to say I'm to blame for that too?"

"No, not exactly. Maybe in part."

"For *Yolek*?" exclaimed Azariah with impudent glee, like a prisoner who has slipped a pair of handcuffs on his jailer's wrists. "Get this, Comrade Srulik, because I have news for you. Yolek himself sent me a message just ten minutes ago to come see him this evening to have a little chat—and to bring my guitar. Yashek even told me that the brandy bottle would be out. Besides, Comrade Srulik, the only fair thing to do would be to ask Yoni if I have to leave his house. And since that's impossible, why not ask Rimona? You're in for a big surprise. The way I see it, you have every right to ask me to leave the kibbutz altogether. Whenever you like. Go right ahead. But no one can ask me to leave my woman. That's against the law."

I'd like once more to set down for the record what I wrote yesterday and the day before and will no doubt write again tomorrow. I don't understand a thing. It's all a closed book to me.

It's ten o'clock now. Etan R. is on duty at the switchboard. Azariah and Rimona have gone to visit Yolek. Maybe Azariah is giving a recital there. Anything is possible in this world. Still no sign of Yoni. Tomorrow we'll call the police and ask Chupka and his scouts to start looking for our prodigal son.

Hava Lifshitz is with me now. She has made us both tea and brought some honey for my throat. She's sitting on my bed and listening to the music. Brahms again. It's been ages since a woman was in my room at such an hour. I shall quote another passage from Griffin:

> During a long flight, therefore, enormous quantities of body fat are consumed, just as they are on a cold winter night when a small bird is likely to burn most of its fatty tissue simply to maintain its body temperature until morning.

Meaning? Enough for tonight. I'll stop here.

Friday, March 4, 1966

It's evening now and raining again. Only a handful of people seem to have gone to the dining hall to hear a guest lecturer discuss Yemenite folklore. And still no word from Yonatan. The police chewed me out roundly this morning for taking so long to get in touch with them. They're already on the case but have nothing to report thus far. Chupka was here too. He listened carefully to what I told him, drank two cups of black coffee with Udi Shneour, said no more than nine or ten words at the most, made no promises, and departed. This afternoon we received a telegram from Miami. Mr. Trotsky intends to come as soon as possible, perhaps even by next week.

I also had a peculiar conversation with Rimona. When I asked her whether, when Yonatan came home safe and sound, she didn't think that Azariah would be best off living by himself, she replied, "But I have room for them both. And they both love and so do I." Did she understand the possible consequences? She smiled. "Consequences?"

I was at a total loss. Perhaps because of her beauty or simply because I'm not the right man for this office. For example, I couldn't muster the will to drop in on Yolek today. I was told that the doctor found him slightly better and that Azariah spent a good deal of time there. Playing the guitar, philosophizing, arguing politics, and God knows what else. Certainly I don't. Is that my job too, to know everything?

Besides, I'm sick with a high fever, chills, a cough, and a bad earache. Everything keeps swimming before my eyes. Hava has been taking care of me, insisting I stay in bed. "It won't do that lousy Stutchnik any harm to have to run around for a few days in your place." And on Sunday Trotsky will arrive. Or on Monday. Or never.

This evening I decided on my own to let Prime Minister Eshkol know that Yolek's son has disappeared without a trace and that we're worried about him. And now I'll sign off because I'm hallucinating a bit. Every time I close my eyes I have nightmarish visions of Yonatan in dire peril. And we have done nothing.

Saturday, 12:00 midnight

Not a word from Yonatan, the police, or the redoubtable Chupka. Toward evening the Prime Minister talked to Yolek on the phone and promised to extend all possible help.

I spent the day in bed with a temperature of one-hundred-and-four and assorted aches and pains. This evening the general meeting of the kibbutz elected me, *in absentia,* to be the new secretary. Stutchnik brought the news and carried on and on about how I was praised to the skies. The vote was virtually unanimous.

Hava has almost nothing to say. She knows about the telegram from Miami, as does Yolek, but neither mentions it. I don't think they've spoken to each other since yesterday. Stutchnik told me that Rimona and young Gitlin are taking good care of Yolek. And Hava sat up with me all night. My Florence Nightingale. I am wiped out. In my mind I keep seeing Yonatan wandering about, but something tells me that he's all right. I don't know what makes me feel so sure. I also don't know why I told her, my pen poised above this page, that Rimona might be pregnant and that either one of them could be the father. Have I gone out of my mind? The secretary of the kibbutz. I couldn't have made a worse blunder. My fever is way up again. Perhaps I shouldn't go on with this report tonight. I don't trust myself. Everything seems so complicated.

13

But what, after all, is the magic of Chad? Maybe no more than spending a few hours of this bright, lovely winter day sitting in a cafe on some street in Beersheba without a care, and with all the time in the world. And ordering soda. And an egg sandwich and a cheese sandwich. And some Turkish coffee. And another bottle of soda. With everything you own beneath the table at your feet. Your beat-up knapsack. Your gun. And the canteen you just bought at the PX. And the sleeping bag you swiped without thinking twice from the dusty pile lying by an army truck on a corner of the main street. What's one sleeping bag more or less? They can do without it. It's amazing what you can do without.

Just sitting with your legs stretched and watching the customers come and go through a door that hardly ever stays closed. Without a thought in your head. Like Tia. In a place where nobody knows you and you don't know anybody. Although everybody looks just like you. Tired, grizzled men in desert clothes, in army boots, in battle gear, with battered packs at their feet. Soldiers in khaki. Farmers in khaki. Quarrymen. Roadworkers. Surveyors. Hikers. With eyes red from the dust and a gray film of dust on their faces and in their hair. Nearly all of them with guns. And all of them, including yourself, belonging to the same distinct tribe, marked by chronic lack of sleep.

And what a relief. For the first time in your life you're not being watched by a soul. A total stranger, not a blip on somebody's radar screen, because no one in the whole world knows where you are. From the day you were born until this morning every single minute of your life was chartered, but that's all over with now. No more timetables. No more zero hours. No more assembly points. Light. Loose. And a little sleepy too.

With a lazy desert feeling trickling like wine through every cell of your body. And a smile winking on and off inside you. I shook them. I did it. There's no one to tell me what I can or can't do any more. If I want to go, I can go. If I want to stay, I can stay. If I want to mow them all down, I can do it with one beautiful burst and vanish into the desert forever. Just three hundred yards from here. The magic of Chad. And this is just the beginning.

A Bedouin was standing by the counter, a lean, bony, swarthy man in a striped robe and over it a tattered suit jacket. His long, dark fingers were crawling with lizardlike life. In a silken Hebrew he asked for a pack of cheap cigarettes. The counterman, apparently a friend of his, an excitable-looking Jew with a Rumanian accent and a rumpled plain white shirt beneath a checked apron, laid a pack of cigarettes on the sticky marble counter, swarming with flies. Adding a box of matches, he volunteered, "Go on and take 'em, they're on the house." A single gold tooth flashed in his mouth when he smiled. *"Nu, vus hert zach, ya Ouda? Keif el hal?"* "What's doing down your way these days?"

The Bedouin weighed the question at length, as if deliberating how it might be answered with no slight to either the truth or good manners. At last he said modestly, "We are doing okay, praise God."

"And that sorghum of yours, it's okay too?" asked the counterman, who sounded disappointed. "That sorghum of yours that they confiscated, you think you'll get it back in the end?"

The Bedouin was occupied with making a small rectangular incision just big enough to remove one cigarette from a corner of the pack. Then he tapped the bottom of the pack with a stiff finger as though performing a parlor trick, and a cigarette popped up like a gun muzzle in front of the counterman's eyes. "That sorghum? Maybe yes, maybe no. Help yourself, please, Mr. Gotthilf. *T'fadal.* Have a smoke."

At first the counterman declined with an ineffably Jewish gesture that signified, *What, me smoke one of those?* A moment later, however, with a second gesture that meant, *Ah well, if I have to, I have to,* he accepted the gift, thanked the Bedouin, and stuck it behind his ear. Then, after pulling down the handle of the espresso machine, he pushed a little plastic cup of coffee across the counter, sending a flurry of excitement through the convocation of impolitic flies. "*Efsher* you'll *tishrab, ya Ouda?* How about some coffee? And why don't we sit down for a few minutes and you tell me the *gantse mayse* of the sorghum. Maybe I can put in a good word for you when I see Major Elbaz?"

The two of them went to have a brotherly smoke at the table nearest the counter. The Rumanian dropped his voice to a whisper. Yonatan, who had been folding a paper napkin into the shape of a little canoe, now shot it across the table with his finger, scoring a direct hit on a saltshaker. Praise God, he murmured to himself. We are doing okay.

A noisy busload of American Jewish tourists burst into the cafe. Though most of them were elderly, they carried on like a group of schoolchildren whose teacher has stepped out of the room. On their heads, apparently freshly taken out of storage, were bell-shaped Israeli hats of blue cotton. Front and back, they bore the inscription, in Hebrew and English, TENTH ANNIVERSARY OF ISRAEL, HAVEN OF THE JEWISH PEOPLE.

In urgent need of cold drinks or the bathroom, they either fell upon the counter to banter with the Rumanian in Yiddish or threaded their way between the tables, struggling to squeeze by the ragged soldiers, the miners, the farmers in work clothes, the truck drivers, all engaged in the tribal pastime of feasting on grilled lamb, roasted drumsticks, french fries in pita bread, and plates of sesame dip washed down with an American cola or local soft drink. Now and then someone banged a saltshaker on a tabletop to free its clogged openings. Sometimes a roar of savage laughter would erupt from one of the corners.

Yonatan's eyes narrowed like gunslits. The counterman's Bedouin friend, he noticed, was wearing sandals made of rubber tires tied with rope. From his leather belt hung a curved dagger in an ornamental silver sheath. The skin of his face was pulled tightly back over his prominent cheekbones as if sculpted of flint. His dark hands, one of which sported a bright gold ring, were covered with a fine desert powder. His mustache was clipped smartly, but the matted hair on his bare head seemed to have been washed with cheap cooking oil, perhaps even, Yonatan thought, with camel piss. You never knew. Now he was standing with his back to the counter, watching the entrance with beady eyes to see who might pass through next. Watch out for Udi, pal. That's a friend of mine who wants to make a scarecrow out of you so that you can keep the birds off his garden and be the talk of the kibbutz. And forget about your sorghum.

Yonatan, craving a cigarette, rummaged through his pockets. Finding none, he went to the counter, where he stood scratching himself fiercely as he usually did when at a loss. Nevertheless, he managed not to take his eyes off his belongings for a second. Whatever wasn't nailed to the floor in a place like this had a way of walking off by itself.

"Yes, soldier boy. Anything else?" Mr. Gotthilf was too busy stacking coins on his sticky counter to look up. Behind him, on a shelf lined with candy and olive and pickle jars, was a photograph of a heavyset, coarse-looking woman in a tastelessly low-cut dress. A necklace of tear-shaped beads fell from her throat and vanished into the cleft. On her knees she held a small child with neatly combed hair parted in the middle, glasses, a tie, and a three-piece suit, with a handkerchief in the breast pocket. A black mourning ribbon cut diagonally across a bottom corner of the picture, which had been framed in a kitschy, fake mother-of-pearl. Why was it that other people's sorrows so often seemed just so much soap opera while our own always strike us as terribly poignant? What was the reason for all this suffering no matter where you looked? Even in this pathetic dump! Maybe it's a lousy cop-out to run away. Maybe my father and that whole chorus line of old men are right after all. Maybe I should go right home and devote my life from now on to the War on Suffering.

"Yes, soldier boy. Anything else?"

Yonatan hesitated. "Right," he said in his low voice, "you can give me some chewing gum. And I think I'll have a cup of espresso too."

He took his purchases back to the table as if his sally to the counter had cost him the last of his strength. Never mind, though. Everything was going smoothly. They could look for him all they pleased. The whole bunch of them. And bring the police and the border patrol with their bloodhounds. Why shouldn't they? Suppose I'd been killed. Let them comb the wadis. Let them look for my corpse. Why not? I'm already a million miles away. And they're never going to find me. Because I'm off to where I'm being waited for.

Two officers entered the cafe and sat down at a nearby table. Do I know them? Who could remember every face from the whole goddamn army? From some chess tournament, maybe, or that farm machinery course? Everyone here looked like everyone else. The safest thing to do is to keep your head down, your mouth shut, and clear out as soon as you've finished your coffee. Damn! I forgot to tell them to watch out for that cracked electrical outlet near the porch door. You can get a shock from it. I didn't even leave a note.

One of the two officers—a kibbutznik, Yonatan guessed—had a beautiful baby face, with ruddy brown cheeks, a classical nose, and cherubic blue eyes. He was wearing a patched army jacket and sneakers without socks. Smiling with milk-white teeth as if all too aware of his good looks, he was addressing his companion. "They just slay me, the two of them. That Shiko and his Avigayil. The minute she said she was leaving him and told him the whole truth about me and her. It must have been at least two in the morning, because she had just come back from my place, and it was cold as hell out, with a fog you couldn't see the tip of your nose in, but right away he jumps up and runs straight out into the wadi. . . ."

"We've heard it, Ron, we've already heard all of it a hundred times," interrupted the other officer, laying a hairy, freckled hand on Ron's shoulder.

What was Shiko doing in the wadi in the middle of the night when he found out that Avigayil had decided to leave him? And why had she? And what had Ron's friend already heard a hundred times? Yonatan was too tired to pursue it. Besides, it was too noisy to try to pick up the rest of the conversation because a many-wheeled truck that looked more like a freight train was struggling to maneuver its way into the narrow side street.

The turn was too sharp for it. Its gigantic wheels had chewed up the curb, and now one of its sides was crushing a municipal garbage receptacle hanging from a green metal post. The air brakes let out still another whoosh. A crowd began to form and to shout their advice, censure, and ridicule, all of which the driver, high in his cab, chose to ignore. Furiously the vehicle sought to fight its way into the street, uprooting a traffic sign and scraping a wall like a bull in heat. The sandstone of the damaged building poured down in a granular cascade. At this point, or so it seemed, the driver began to consider a retreat. He struggled with the gears and pulled as hard as he could on the wheel, as if tugging at the bridle of a recalcitrant animal. All of a sudden the monster lurched backward, and the crowd let out a gasp—less than a hair's breadth now separated the back of the truck from the window of a pastry shop across the street. Once more the driver grasped the wheel and, breathing hard, wrested it all the way in the opposite direction. Gripping it tightly to prevent it from getting away, he battled the shift stick until he finally got the truck into gear, and the beast lurched forward only to become stuck, with either end smack up against a wall.

The steadily growing crowd surged around it, swearing at the driver or kicking the truck's tires, clucking its collective tongue, calling out its brainstorms, inspirations, ingeniously improvised solutions. At last, as a long line of backed-up traffic began rending the air with deafening honks, one resolute bystander stepped out of the throng to take the bull by the horns. This hero, who looked like a cowboy and was none other than the rude-limbed, rough-voiced, sun-scorched officer who had been sitting in the cafe with his baby-faced friend, pulled himself up the side of the truck by the door handle and, shouldering the driver aside, forced his way into the cab. Once there, he calmly stuck his neck out the window to survey the battleground below. He looks just like a water buffalo, thought Yonatan, and laughed quietly to himself. He didn't give a hoot about any of it.

What time could it be? His watch had stopped running, though, judging by the light, it must be close to noon. A large, good-looking woman, brown from the sun, had just stepped into the cafe and sat down by herself at a small corner table. Her fingers festooned with many rings, she lit herself a cigarette. The Rumanian counterman came running and, with a great show of courtesy, placed before her a glass of tea, a spoon, a sugar bowl, and a slice of lemon on a dish. "Mr. Gotthilf," laughed the woman in a low, throaty voice, "Mr. Gotthilf, what's wrong with you? You look like a ghost. I hope to God you're not getting sick."

"Only of life," joked the counterman. "That's the one sickness we're all one-hundred-percent sure to die of. Would you like something to eat, Jacqueline?"

The woman shook her head. She had ceased concentrating on Mr. Gotthilf because she had become aware of Yonatan's glances and decided to return them with a mocking, sideways stare that seemed to say, All right, mister, it's your turn. Let's see what you can do.

And all the while customers kept coming and going, all suntanned and windburned, all eating and drinking and guzzling away, all talking in loud, rasping voices. A goddamn good place to be by yourself. And a goddamn good thing that your watch has stopped and that you feel a little sleepy too. Can it be one o'clock? Two? Two-thirty? What difference does it make? From now on, all hours are going to be the same.

The hubbub outside had ceased. The cab of the truck was now at right angles to its trailer. A sweating policeman hopped around it like a cricket, trying to direct traffic, while Captain Water Buffalo and the truck driver sat smoking by the exhausted engine like two comrades-in-arms gone down to a joint defeat. Apparently they did not blame each other but rather some unfriendly act of God. There was nothing to do but wait. Besides, they're sure to build a highway here some day and all these old Turkish buildings now in the way will be shipped off to Saudi Arabia. Till then, what's the rush?

14

Yonatan rose and paid his bill, muttered something to the counterman, and forced himself to say "See you, baby," to the good-looking woman but grinned at the floor as he did so. Everything was right on schedule. The desert was still waiting for him. He hoisted his gear onto his back and walked out of the cafe with leaden strides. Was he really all that tired? Not really. In fact, quite the opposite—groggy but rested, as if he'd just slept for twenty hours straight. Why, he had slept away all the years of his life like a log and now he was awake as all hell. There must be a Russian saying for it. What the hell? Not *mea culpa.*

At an army hitchhiking post at the edge of town Yonatan was greeted by a smell of sweat, smoke, rifle oil, and dry urine. On the asbestos wall of the shelter someone had scratched a crude pair of fat, outspread thighs and, between them, a floating penis that resembled a mortar barrel but had an open eye in the act of shedding a tear. Above it the artist had scratched the words GOOD TO THE LUST DROP.

Yonatan, who was the only one waiting for a ride, eventually decided that this caption needed correction. He first thought of scratching on the penis, with the sharp corner of an ammunition clip, FUCK EVERYTHING. And then, over the whole drawing, MEA CULPA. Or THREE CHEERS FOR JUSTICE. In the end, he contented himself with crossing out GOOD TO THE LUST and inserting the word DEAD after DROP. As he did so, two ragged-looking reservists pulled up in a decrepit old command car, one wearing a heavy army overcoat, the other with his head and shoulders wrapped in a gray blanket. Without a word Yonatan clambered in the back, dumped his gear on a pile of similar belongings, cuddled up in his windbreaker, and squatted comfortably on a stack of greasy tarpaulins. As soon as they set out, the increasing speed of the vehicle hammered exhilaratingly in his veins. He narrowed his eyes against the wind and gulped its cold, astringent blows deep into his lungs. Gritty particles picked up from the road slashed at his face. In his hand, he held firmly the ammunition clip with which he'd recaptioned the lewd drawing in the shelter.

For a long while out of Beersheba, the fringe of the desert sprouted with fields of coming Bedouin wheat, as though its soft hills had been tinted by a brush as far as his watering eyes could see—a lovely pastel green, rippled now and then by the wind, gleaming here and there with dazzling pools of rainwater, growing fainter as it stretched to meet the pale blue horizon, where a transcendent compromise seemed to have been reached between the color of the sky and the color of the grain. A promised reconciliation.

Far away, in a place where the heavens descended gently on earthly fields, there was love in this world. All would end happily there. A perfect peace.

Between him and that place endless waves were billowing across an endless expanse. Field after lonely field. Flat earth bounded by soft hills, flat earth stippled by droplets of light, all the way to the edge of the world, with only a single road to spear it like a black arrow, answered only by the roar of a motor. This is life. And the world. And me. And love. Just wait peacefully and you will receive it. Just go on resting and all will be given you. Everything is waiting. All things are possible. The magic is on its way.

Here and there his squinting eyes made out some dismal signs of life. A few goatskin tents that suggested a dark stain sprayed against a gleaming canvas of sand. A slowly disintegrating tire abandoned between nowhere and nowhere. A bullet-pocked fuel can rusting away in a downpour of winter light. Sometimes the clear purity of the desert air was violated by the stench of a dead camel or donkey, or by the mingled smells of smoke, gasoline, and engine oil. Yet time and again, it reasserted itself.

Here and there, too, were signs of a military presence. A lone antenna protruding from a distant hilltop. The chassis of a small truck by the road. Three, no four, jeeps passing on their way from the far south, their machine guns cradled on rests welded to the engine hoods. His lips were dry, his throat was parched, his eyes kept watering, but Yonatan had never felt better. As the sun dropped lower in the sky, the earth developed fissures where the desert began to fall away to the great rift valley below. The wheat had thinned out until there were only a few haggard-looking strands of it, and an occasional field of barley, to dapple the treeless stretches of scattered shrub. The gray-brown slopes of gravelly flint on the hillsides broke sharply eastward. From a high curve in the road, Yonatan caught sight of the peaks of the mountains of Edom shrouded in a veil of blue haze. A band of titans from some distant star who had lost their way and sunk down at last in this place, flashing blindingly from the sun-drunk surface of the Dead Sea. Were they able to rise at night from their lassitude and, stretching themselves to their full height, touch the farthest galaxies in the skies? Yonatan almost winked at them.

He let them have the barest of waves. Hey, you, wait for me.

He recalled how his father loathed the desert. The very word made Yolek grimace, as if it were a dirty word. It often catapulted him into one of his taming-the-wilderness spiels. Deserts were a badge of shame, a mark of inequity, a disgrace to the map of Israel, an evil presence, an ancient enemy that must be subdued by armies bringing tractors, irrigation pipes, and fertilizer sacks until the last of its surly acres had been compelled to bear. *And the desert shall rejoice and blossom like a rose. For in the wilderness shall waters break out and streams in barren places.* Jewish water engineers would turn the parched ground into fountains and the thirsty land into springs. *Come, comrades, let us set the earth ablaze with a bright green flame.*

From deep down in his blanket, the soldier at the wheel called out, "Hey, buddy, where to?"

"Down south."

"How about as far as Ein-Husub?"

"Sounds fine."

Then silence again, and wind.

Hello there, desert! I happen to know all about you. I know your red cliffs and your black cliffs. I know the mouths of your wadis and their gravel beds, your rock ledges and the secret pools of rainwater in your crannies. Since I was a child I've been told how good I am. And all my life that's what I've been embarrassed to be—good. But from now on, all that changes. From now on, I really will be good. To begin with, I've given my wife away to an immigrant kid. I wish him lots of happiness with her and an end to all his troubles. And I've solved a twenty-year-old problem for my parents, because when they got out of bed this morning, the problem was gone. The best of luck to them. And I've handed Rimona a brand-new husband on a platter. He'll be the perfect little boy for her to baby and bring up. And left them Tia too. And my bed. And the chess table I carved out of olive wood. That's how good I am. And always have been. Because it's our duty to be as good as we can until the suffering stops. Srulik once said to me that there's enough pain in this world as it is and our duty is not to cause any more. And I said to him, hey, why don't you cut out that Jewish bullshit. A dumbass thing to say, because it was bullshit straight from the heart.

Eshkol and my father and Srulik and Ben-Gurion, the whole bunch of them are the most wonderful Jews who ever lived. You won't find any better in the Bible. Even the prophets, with all due respect to them, talked a nice line but never did a damn thing about it. But these old men suddenly figured out fifty years ago that the end was in sight and the Jews were up against the wall, and so they took their lives in their hands and ran with them together straight at that wall, do or die, and came busting out the other side and made us a country, for which I take off my hat to them. And cheer at the top of my voice.

Now hear this, you desert, hear this, you mountains and you wadis, hear it once and for all, hats off to Yolek Lifshitz and to Stutchnik and to Srulik. Hurrah for Ben-Gurion and Eshkol. Three cheers for the state of Israel. Berl Katznelson's little pinky is worth more than me and that asshole Udi and Etan and Chupka and Moshe Dayan all put together, because they're the Saviors of Israel and we're the Scum of the Earth. There's no one like them in the whole world. Not even in America. Take a kid like Zaro, for example, a miserable little fink, from the day he was born the whole world ran after him with a hatchet to kill him and almost did—the Germans, the Russians, the Arabs, the Poles, the Rumanians, the Greeks, the Romans, the Pharaohs—falling on him like a pack of wolves. Imagine slaughtering a sensitive kid like that who plays the guitar and has all those beautiful, poetic thoughts. If it hadn't been for my father, and Berl, and Srulik, and Gordon, and all the rest of them, where could he have run to? Where in this whole fucking world would he have been taken in with no questions asked and given work and warmth and a room and self-respect and a lovely woman and a brand-new life?

Hurray for Ben-Gurion and Eshkol. Hurray for the kibbutz. Hip, hip, hurray for the state of Israel.

If only I were the man I should have been and not just a spoiled turd of a Scyth or a Tatar, I'd have gone to my father tonight instead of taking off and said to him, I'm at your command, sir, send me wherever you like, sir. Say the tractor shed, and the tractor shed it is. Say the army, or a new kibbutz right smack in the middle of these salt flats, or a secret mission to Damascus to knock off the gynecologist and the ophthalmologist together, and it's as good as done. But what I'm afraid I'll have to do after that, sir, once I've given you my all, is to go tonight or tomorrow night to Petra and die there for the good of the cause. Just like that shitass son of King Saul in the Bible who wasn't good enough to be king or good enough for anything except to get himself killed in a war so the torch could be passed to the better man who could be of service to his country and even make a distinguished contribution to the Bible. Hats off to you, Little John, slain upon the high places, and hats off to you, David, for writing such a terrific eulogy straight from the heart and being the Savior of Israel. And please excuse me, Professor Spinoza, for being a little slow to get what you meant when you so wisely said that everyone has a role in this life and that the only choice we have is to understand what our role is and to accept it gracefully. Why, the smell of this wind alone is enough to make you grow up to be a man, to honor the darkening sky, the towering wilderness, to honor thy father and thy mother, to be good at last, as Azariah says, as Spinoza says, as you wanted to be and were too embarrassed to be because of your longing. Because longing of any kind is a poison.

The last light was fading when they reached Ein-Husub. Yonatan thanked the two reservists and shouldered his gear. The lights of the perimeter fence were already lit. The place seemed to be half army camp, half tumbledown frontier settlement. Yonatan knew that a Druse unit belonging to the army or the border patrol used it as a base for its patrols. Visible as well were an odd smattering of reservists, miners traveling to and from the copper works in Timna, a few hikers and nature lovers, Bedouin working for the military, and a tall bushranger of a civilian with bright blue eyes, skin dark as an Arab's, and a long Tolstoyan beard hanging down to the white hair of his naked chest. "I arranged to meet some pals of mine here" was going to be his alibi should anyone ask, but nobody did.

Yonatan threw his things on the ground, scratched himself, and looked about him. The shadow of the mountains cut the moonlit sky. Dogs barked hoarsely. In the nearby darkness some girls were singing. A smell of campfire smoke drifted among the tents and shacks. With a muffled drone punctuated by little backfires a generator throbbed away. Yonatan had been in Ein-Husub before, once with a hiking party and again two years ago, when his unit reassembled here after a nocturnal sortie into Jordanian territory near As-Safi, at the southern end of the Dead Sea. Even if someone around here knows me, he thought, they'll never recognize me now. But just to be on the safe side he put on his old woolen cap, pulled it down over his eyes, and raised the collar of his jacket almost to his ears.

For a few minutes Yonatan stood motionless beside a filthy ditch running between two prefabs. He looked like a cross between a soldier and a gypsy. Yellow lights shone far off in the darkness. He tried to think ahead. First find something to eat and drink and water to fill his canteen. The second thing was to crawl into this ditch or find some trees somewhere where he could unroll his sleeping bag. Before sacking out, though, he'd better swipe a couple of blankets because it would probably get very cold here tonight. Tomorrow he would have the whole morning to kill. He would have to go over the map carefully to make sure of the safest route to take. His best bet would be to leave Ein-Husub at about two in the afternoon, hitch a ride south to Bir-Meliha, and then head eastward on foot into Wadi Musa, in the general direction of Jabel Harun. There must be some old guide-book available around here that would tell all about Petra. He should oil his gun too.

And I've already gone seventeen hours without a cigarette! That means everything is shipshape and right on schedule. All I need right now is food and blankets. C'mon, pal, let's see some action.

"Hi, baby."

"Yes, sweetheart?"

"Are you by any chance from around here?"

"I'm by any chance from around Haifa."

"But you're stationed here?"

"May I have the pleasure of knowing who's asking?"

"That's beside the point. The point is that I'm about to perish from hunger."

"That's all very well, sir, but maybe you'd like to tell me just who you belong to anyway."

"You're going philosophical on me. But if you're really interested, and provided you give me something to eat first, I'll be happy to give you a short course on Justice and the theory of who we belong to. What do you say?"

"Did anyone ever tell you you've got a sexy voice? The trouble is, I can't see the rest of you in this darkness. Oh well! Go ask Jamil if he has any cold potatoes left. If you'd like some coffee to wash them down, I'm afraid you've got a problem. So long."

"Hold on, baby. Where are you going? Your name isn't Ruti, by any chance, is it? Or Etti? Mine, by any chance, is Udi. And you might as well know the statistics. Reconnaissance officer. Five-foot-ten. Likes chess, philosophy, and farm machinery. Stuck all alone here at least until tomorrow morning. Is it Ruti or Etti?"

"Michal. And I'll bet you're a kibbutznik."

"Used to be. Now I'm a wandering philosopher, looking for signs of life in the wilderness. And hungry as hell. Michal?"

"Yes, *sir*!"

"Has anyone ever told you what a terrific hostess you are?"

"Sorry, but I don't get the hint. All I'm getting is colder and colder."

"I'm more than willing to trade you warmth for food, baby. I'm all alone here, see, and I've got half-a-ton of gear on my back. Have you ever heard of the word 'compassion'?"

"I already told you. Try Jamil up there. He might have some cold french fries or something else left over."

"Some hospitality! You're a real sweetheart, baby. I can't tell you how nice it is of you to offer right in the middle of the desert to take a total stranger to the kitchen for a banquet and a hot cup of coffee. Especially since I haven't the foggiest idea where the kitchen is and wouldn't know Jamil if I tripped over the guy. Okay? So give us a hand. Right! That one. Now let's take me to the grub."

"What's going on here, mister? Second-degree rape?"

"Right now it's only an obscene act. But if I enjoy it, we can take it from there. On a full stomach. Did you or didn't you tell me how sexy I was?"

"Your name's Udi? Then listen, Udi. I'll take you to the kitchen to eat and get you some coffee, but first you've got to take your hands off me, and pronto! And if you've got any other ideas, you'd better ditch them right now."

"Are you a redhead, baby? Just a tiny bit?"

"How could you possibly tell?"

"It's all in Spinoza. That was one hotshot philosopher. After you've fed me and let me have my coffee, I'll give you a crash course. And if you've got any ideas of your own, don't forget them, baby. It's cold as hell around here."

He had never before made love like this. Not humiliatingly, not resentfully, but fiercely and tenderly, and with a fine, delicate precision, again and again all night long until dawn. As if he had found a twin whose body had been cast in the matching mold of his own.

After the Spam, the cold french fries, and the sooty, disgustingly sweet coffee, the two of them went arm-in-arm to her room near a wireless shack. There they found a highly superfluous Yvonne. Michal, without batting an eyelash, sent Yvonne off to sleep with Yoram, "because what's about to happen in this room is going to be strictly X-rated."

The bed was a hard, narrow military cot. A freakish desert moon shone in the curtainless window. There was a baying of dogs, and Yonatan suddenly felt choked by an ancient rage. Whatever happened to that poor bastard Shiko, who ran out into the wadi just when the flash flood hit? But the rage gave way at once to a feverish tenderness. In my whole goddamn life I've never been so goddamn alive. And with a woman in my hands.

The room was so shiveringly cold they didn't bother to undress. Fully clothed and laughing, they slipped between her prickly woolen blankets. Yonatan propped himself on an elbow to study her face in the moonlight. He kissed her wide-open eyes and raised himself on his palms to get a still better look. "You're so handsome and sad-looking," she said, "and such a terrible liar too." With a fingertip he traced her lips and the fine line of her jaw until she took both his hands in her own and placed a breast in each. He felt no urge to make haste. Step by silent step he caressed her body, as if trying to find his way across unfamiliar terrain in darkness, until, burrowing into his uniform, Michal found his sex and took it out. She kissed it in the moonlight and laughingly addressed it with his very own words. "You wandering philosopher, you, let me know when you've found signs of life in the wilderness." His fingers worked their way to the treasurehouse of hers at once, where slowly, almost thoughtfully, they picked out a tune so compelling that she arched roundly against him. With a mock guffaw, he blurted, "Hey! What's the big rush?" Her answer was bites and nips and scratches. "Your name is Woman," he said to her, in his basso profundo, "and mine is Man."

And he undid the buttons of their bulky uniforms and cupped

first one breast and then the other with such tender angry choking passionate fierce gentle precise persuasion that she begged him to come to her. Come you crazy I can't take it any more. Shut up he said what's the rush while his sex beat about like the cane of a furious blind man, crawling and slithering among the layers of her clothing, coiling and lunging at her belly at her mons veneris until all of a sudden the cane slipped into place and slid home. Honeystruck, it paused and there was a lull. And a trembling. And a movement beneath him like a sea.

And she bit his ear and raked his back with her nails inside his clothes and groaned come quick I'm dying and her match made Yonatan catch fire and drive home again and again, hammering away inside her, snorting and thrashing and lashing and butting as though battering impregnable walls and so overwhelming her that it tore a sharp cry from her gut, and then another, and suddenly, like a dog shot in the dark, let out a cry himself and burst into a flood of tears and sperm as if every wound in his life had opened at once and the very blood of that life was pouring out. Never had he opened up like this to anything, nor anything to him. The ineffable ecstasy jarred the root of his sex and ran from there to his gut to his back up his spine to the scruff of his neck to the roots of his hair sending a shiver through the soles of his feet so that she said you're crying real tears look you have goosepimples your hair is even standing on end and kissed him on the mouth and all over his face while he gasped I'm not done I have more. You're crazy she said you're stark raving mad but he silenced her at once with his lips and came within her a second and a third time. You madman I have no more strength for you.

Woman he said woman I never knew that a woman could be like this. And then they lay in each other's arms and watched the moon wander from their window.

"Are you rejoining your unit tomorrow, Udi?"

"I have no unit. And my name isn't Udi. But I do have to go somewhere."

"And then you'll come back to me?"

"Look, Woman. That's a question I happen to hate."

"But you must have a home, or at least an address somewhere."

"I did. Not any more. The Himalayas, maybe. Bangkok? Bali? Who knows?"

"I'd go with you. Would you take me?"

"I don't know. Maybe. Why not. Michal?"

"What, child?"

"Don't call me child. Because my name once was Yoni and now I have no name."

"Shhh. Don't talk now. If you're still, you'll get a kiss."

They curled up in their blankets and slept until an hour or two before dawn, when she woke him and whispered, laughing, "Come on, Man, let's see what you're really made of." And when he took her this time it was not in an iron drive like a plow breaking earth but with a wistful yearning, like a small craft upon a smooth sea.

It was still dark outside the window when Michal rose from the cot, put on her uniform, and bade farewell. "Goodbye, Udi Yoni, I have to catch a jeep to Shivta but if you're still around when I get back tonight, maybe we can have a little talk." Yonatan groaned, or grunted, in his sleep and did not awaken until roused by the first fingers of daylight and the unhappy howl of a stray dog. He dressed, contentedly fingering his growing stubble of beard, fixed himself some coffee in a tin cup, haphazardly made the bed, and took from the shelf above it an army booklet entitled *Sites in the Arava and the Desert.* From the other bed he filched without a qualm a gray army blanket, flung open the door, and, standing in the doorway, had himself a long pee with his head cocked to one side and his lips parted like those of a dreamer in an untroubled sleep.

The dawn chill was sharp but bracing. Yonatan put on his jacket, wrapped himself in the blanket with the solemnity of a

Jew donning a prayer shawl, and stood with his face to the mountains in the east. Thin and hazy like ancient glass, the air exuded anticipation. The lights of the perimeter fence were still on. Here and there a few heavily clad figures scurried about the tents and shacks. Beyond the camp stretched the desert vastness, serenely attending night's end. Yonatan squinted into the wind, pulled down his woolen cap, and lifted his jacket collar. His nostrils flared, like those of an animal feeling the call. His whole body was being swept away by an urge to set out at once, to the mountains, the wadis, the canyons, the steep, slippery rock ledges, the dwelling places of the deer and the mountain goat, the lair of the wildcat, the mighty pinnacles where nested the vulture, the griffin, and the lammergeier, where twisted and swiveled the efa and the horned viper. Names known by heart from maps, from years of army maneuvers, took on magic. Mount Ardon. Mount Gizron. Mount Lotz. Woody Mountain, on which no wood ever stood. Mount Arif. The Tsichor Range. The Shizafon Plateau, on which, a thousand years ago, Rimona and he had once sighted four or five stray camels wandering like specters on the horizon. The Ye'elon Plateau, its treeless, shrubless, lifeless canyons broiling in the sun without a penciling of shade. Uvda Canyon. Scouts Canyon. The broad shingle flats. Yes, even that remote stretch of level ground north of Ramon Canyon, Demons' Plain.

What have I done with my life all these years? From the citrus groves to the dining hall, to a dead double bed to this committee, to that meeting. Here, praise be, I've come home at last. Here, I'm no longer theirs. Thank you for all this beauty. For Michal. For every breath. For the very sunrise. I should break out in applause without further ado—or make a deep bow.

The advance guard of sunlight flared on the western hills behind him. And then, in a nascent halo over Edom, in an ancient script of molten violet and lime green, in an unearthly Roman candle of awesome fiery gold, a toothed arc on the horizon burst into flame, splitting the sky as a spear as a wound as a blood-red sun.

This is my last day. By sun-up tomorrow I shall be dead, and that is just what I should be, what I've waited for all my life, and here, at last, it is. How cold I feel in my bones.

But just look at what a show the sky, the mountains, the earth are putting on for you. What you have to do now is find that Jamil and put something in your stomach. And clean and oil your gun, and then sit down somewhere for a couple of hours to study your maps and pick the route that makes the most sense. A cigarette sure as hell would hit the spot right now, but you don't smoke any more. And maybe you ought to write a note to Michal and leave it on her bed. But you don't have anything to say to her, or to any man or woman in the world, and you never did. Except for thank you. That's a pretty dumbass thing to say if you do say so yourself. Let Azariah say it for you, because he and your father and Eshkol and Srulik and all the rest of them are so impossibly good at it.

You bet your sweet life I'd have hit it from a pace-and-a-half if I'd wanted to. Only their hearts were not true. Hurrah for Saint Benya, who didn't spill a single drop of blood. But my heart is true as hell. And all this holy light is starting to glare. May He be exalted? And sanctified? In His great name? Is that what you say over an open grave? I can't remember the rest of it. I don't have to. They'll never find me in any case. Not even my corpse. Much less my shoelaces. I've been around long enough to see that it isn't for me. Whatever I've touched has gone wrong. Still, I am grateful for all this beauty and will say again, if no one minds out there, thanks for everything.

And now you'd better find something to eat and get organized. It must be six o'clock at least. Or even seven. Your watch has stopped again because you forgot to wind it.

15

"A glass of tea? Or some brandy?" asked Yolek. "Mind you, it's only my allergy acting up again. Otherwise I haven't popped a tear since it happened. I don't deny that when the door opened and you suddenly walked in and hugged me and said what you did, well, my emotions just got the better of me for a second. But there now, I'm over it. You remember Hava, don't you. And sitting here to my left is Srulik. My replacement. Our new secretary here on the kibbutz. And a saint in disguise. Give me ten men like him and I could move the world."

"Good to meet you, Srulik. Please don't bother getting up. I'm no longer one-and-twenty, and believe me, this is the first time in memory that I've ever heard a good word from Yolek Lifshitz about anyone. As for you, Hava, words simply fail me. I embrace you in my thoughts and have nothing but admiration for your courage."

"Hava, if it's not asking too much, please make Eshkol a strong glass of tea. Never mind what he says. And give our good friend Srulik some too. And Rimona and Azariah. None for me. If Rimon'ka will be gracious enough to pour me a sip of brandy, I'll make do with that."

"My dear friends," said the Prime Minister, who, squeezed and crumpled though he was into the narrow kibbutz chair, was still a commanding presence, a tall, broad, heavy, gullied mountain of a man, a protuberant outcropping of superfluous bulges, sagging rolls of flesh, and improbable pouches of skin, a cliff partially collapsed by a landslide. "I want you to know that what you've been going through has been continually on my mind these past two days. Just thinking of you makes my heart ache and my head feel like a jar of scorpions. From the moment I heard the sad news I have been beset by anxiety."

"Thank you," said Hava from the kitchenette, where she had been busy herself setting out her very best china on a tray, arranging quartered oranges on a plate in a chrysanthemum pattern, taking out her fancy paper napkins, and entrusting Rimona with a fresh white tablecloth. "It's very kind of you to have taken the trouble to come."

"Oh, don't you go thanking me, Hava. I only wish I could have come as a bearer of good news instead of like someone paying a condolence call. Now, my friends, perhaps you should give me a blow-by-blow account. Do you mean to say the boy just got up and left without so much as a by-your-leave? *Na. A shayne mayse.* In Yiddish you say, small children, small *tsuris,* big children, big ones. Hava, please, no tea for me, or anything else. And you've heard nothing from him since? *Na.* A fine young upstart! And if Yolek will forgive my saying so, or even if he won't, the son of an upstart too. God only knows what must have driven him to do a crazy thing like that. Why not tell me what happened right from the word go."

"My son has disappeared," said Yolek, gritting his teeth like a man trying to bend an iron bar with his bare hands, "and I'm to blame."

"Yolek, please," Srulik intervened warily. "Why cause yourself even more pain with such talk?"

"The man is right," said Eshkol. "Let's have no foolishness. And none of your Dostoyevskyizing either, Yolek. It won't do us any good. I'm sure you've already taken all the necessary measures. Let's wait a few more days and see what happens. I myself have already been in touch with one or two people in the right places and told them in no uncertain terms to treat the matter as if the boy were my own son. Or theirs. And I also went down on my knees before those hooligans from the press and begged them to control themselves and not splash this all over the front page. Maybe they'll have enough heart to lay off until the boy—what did you say his name was?—comes safely home and all ends happily."

"Thank you," said Yolek.

"His name is Yonatan," Hava was quick to chime in. "You were always a good person. Not like some people I've known."

"That," joked Eshkol, "is something I wouldn't mind having from you in writing."

Hava carried in the tray, and Rimona helped her arrange the refreshments on the plain, square table. With a housewifely fussiness that made Srulik suppress an incipient smile, Hava inquired whether the guests wanted tea or coffee? Sugar or saccharine? Milk or lemon? Cookies, tangerines, orange-and-grapefruit salad, or homemade cream cake? All the while, a large green fly kept banging against the window pane, outside of which a bottle-green day lay drenched in sunshine.

Yolek's eyes, looking away, fell upon the ancient, bulky brown radio that stood on a low shelf within arm's reach. He suggested that they listen to the hourly news. By the time the set had warmed up, however, the news was almost at an end. In a speech at Aswan, President Nasser of Egypt had scoffed at the delusions of the Zionist dwarf-state. Opposition leader Menachem Begin had once again accused the government of appeasement and turning the other cheek to the Arabs and called for its replacement by a strongly patriotic government. The weather: continued clearing with possible light rain in the Galilee.

"Business as usual," sighed Eshkol. "The Arabs curse all of us, while the Jews curse only me. Ah, well, let them enjoy it. They can sound off as much as they like. Between you and me, though, you're looking at a very tired old man."

"Then rest," said Rimona. As if heeding her own advice, she laid her head on the shoulder of Azariah, who was sitting beside her on the couch.

"Enough of this!" said Hava. "Turn off the radio."

Azariah's eyes fell upon Yolek's books, which stood in long rows on their shelves, with photographs tucked here and there among them. Of Yonatan and Amos. Of Yolek with various socialist leaders from all over the world. Of five thistly strawflowers blossoming eternally in a porcelain vase. He felt that there was an unforgettably tormented, Ozymandian majesty about these two old men who never looked each other in the eye, who sat facing each other like two fallen Prometheans, like the ruins of two ancient castles in whose darkest keeps secret life lingered on with all its old battles, its exquisitely refined tortures, its witchcraft and foul play, its nightjars, owls, and bats. Like moss growing over a crack in a wall, an illusory peace stretched its tentacles between these ravaged citadels. Sunk in slumber, their remaining might still filled the room with an aura of palpable grandeur. A secretive, intricate, elusive current ran between them when they talked or even kept silent. The rancor of some old love, the last weary vestiges—like distant, receding thunder—of a great potency that Azariah craved with all his being to touch and be touched by. There must be a way, he thought, of penetrating this fatally charmed circle and rousing them from their repose.

He narrowed his green eyes and fixed them on the Prime Minister in a long, piercing stare of the kind that had the power (so he had once read in some book of Hindu lore) to make a person feel another's eyes upon him. How desperately he wanted to cast his spell on Eshkol in just this kind of way, to make him look up at him or even speak to him, if only to ask the most banal question—to which his own reply would be so astoundingly momentous that the Prime Minister would want to hear more and still more.

The air of weary authority, the spellbinding ugliness of this man whom Azariah had known until now only from flattering photographs or from unkind cartoons in newspapers—the hamlike, liver-spotted hands resting limply on the arms of a chair, one of them loosely dangling a large, yellowish wristwatch from a frayed band—the swollen, cadaverish fingers—the leathery, lizardlike skin—all of this aroused in him a febrile excitement that was almost carnal.

"Now look here, Eshkol," said Yolek after a long silence, "this may not be the time or place for it—"

"What's that? Who? What did you say?" Eshkol, having dozed off, opened his eyes.

"I was saying that this may not be the time or place for it, but I've been wanting to tell you for quite a while now that I owe you an apology. For what I said about you at the last meeting. And for other things too. I was too hard on you."

"As usual," noted Hava dryly.

Srulik smiled ever so faintly to himself, that secret, slightly melancholy, inscrutably Buddhalike smile arrived at so long ago.

"Azoy," said Eshkol, the sharp, humorous look in his eyes belying the catnap he had just taken. "Of course you should feel sorry, Reb Yolek. And how you should! And I, quite honestly, should have whipped you to within an inch of your life long ago. So come on now, you bandit, how about the two of us cutting a deal? Suppose you cut out feeling so sorry for yourself and I cut out wanting to punch you in the nose, eh? *Gemacht,* Yolek? Can

we shake on that?" In a different tone of voice, he added, "Stop being such a damn fool."

Everyone laughed. In the ensuing silence, Srulik put on his suavest smile and suggested politely, "But why not? Azariah and I will move all the furniture aside and you two gentlemen can square off once and for all. Go to it! And take as long as you like!"

"Don't listen to him," Rimona said softly. "He was only joking."

"You sweet girl!" roared Eshkol, pointing a pale, fat finger at her. "Don't be afraid, *krasavitsa.* The two of us, I'm sorry to say, are just a pair of old con men who do all our fighting with our mouths. The days are long gone when I could deliver a decent uppercut. And, whatever he says, our friend Yolek here wouldn't know how to apologize if his life depended on it. In this regard, by the way, he's just like Ben-Gurion—that is, in excellent company. Thank you, I don't take sugar. I drink mine plain."

Don't be afraid. Now is the time to speak up. About everything. They've fallen asleep on their feet. In a burning house, these horrid old godfathers frump around as pleased as punch with themselves, cracking their inspid jokes, so bourgeois you could puke. Burned-out souls, both of them. They'd have been the death of Yoni too if he hadn't got away just in time to save the bright first principles of his soul. Totally rotten they are from all their wheeling and dealing with shabby little intrigues, the flabby syphilitic old bastards, all bloated and gassy from their own dyspeptic hatreds, lost, creaky-souled Jews who can't even smell the sea any more, who haven't seen a star or a sunrise or a sunset or a summer night or a cypress tree swaying in the moonlight for a thousand years, dead Molochs devouring their children, insatiate schemers swamped by stale affections, weaving their hideous spider webs around us, deader than dead. One a big blob who looks like a putrescent dinosaur, the other a stoop-shouldered gorilla with the head of a mangy lion and arms as hairy as a caveman's. Not even a mad dog would expect any love from these two, would even wag his tail for them. I'll bang on the table! I'll make the walls blanch with fright! I'll flabbergast them down to their bootsoles! I'll tell them that all is lost, that Yonatan, and they'd better believe it, ran for dear life because he saw the ship going down. How I wish I had a cigarette. Good God, he's fallen asleep again.

"If I may express an opinion," said Srulik, "I don't think the boy has left the country. I can't prove it, but something tells me he's alive and well and wandering about right here in Israel with no clear destination in mind. Which of us has never secretly thought of dropping everything and taking off just as he did?"

"Mazel tov!" snorted Yolek, his face the very mirror of disgust. "A new psychologist is born. Before you know it, he'll be defending the latest Tatar fashion of doing your own thing too." For some reason or other, he'd chosen to pronounce the word "psycho*lo*gist."

"Comrade Eshkol," said Hava. "Why do you think he took a gun with him?"

The Prime Minister let out a sigh. His eyes closed behind their thick lenses, as if Hava's question were the final straw. Ponderous, much too big for his chair, dominating the room without a word or even a gesture, his shirt hanging out over his carelessly buckled belt, his shoes spattered with mud, his face like a knotty whorl in the bark of a hoary olive tree, the weary old sea-turtle finally managed to reply, almost in a whisper, "That's a hard one, Hava. And not only that. Everything seems hard nowadays. Not that I'm drawing analogies, but everybody seems to want to reach for a gun. Something's gone wrong somewhere. Maybe our whole way of thinking had a fatal flaw hidden in it right from the start. But you mustn't think I came here to burden you with my own problems. On the contrary, I wanted to cheer you up. And now, without meaning to, I've just rubbed salt in your wounds. All any of us can do these days, I guess, is to grit our teeth and plug away and keep on hoping. No, thank you, young beauty, no more tea for me. I can't drink another drop, even though that first cup was heavenly. On the contrary, I have to be off at once. Actually, I was just passing by here on my way to the Upper Galilee. Tonight I'm sleeping in Tiberias, and tomorrow I'm supposed to have a look at the Syrian border and hear what all my clever generals have to say about the situation. And also listen to some of our good people who live up there and, so help me, do what I can to encourage them. The Devil alone knows with what. The truth is, I don't know whom to believe any more and whom to trust. Everyone talks like a prophet and acts like a comedian. I'm not kidding when I say it's just one big comedy wherever I go. Yolek, you joker, stop looking at me like that. The big genius. His own skin he saves and leaves me holding the bag. The Devil only knows what they're cooking up for us in those palaces in Damascus, much less how we can keep from eating crow. My handsome generals have a unanimous one-word answer, and they serenade me with it all day long: Bang! And to tell the truth, when all the pros and cons are toted up, I tend to agree that it's time we let them have it in the teeth even if Ben-Gurion—and perhaps you too behind my back—keeps telling everyone I'm a senile old man. Ah well! Thanks for the tea, Hava. God bless you all. And let's hope we'll be hearing good news soon. How old did you say the boy was?"

"Twenty-seven. This is his wife, Rimona. And the young man next to her is a friend. Our younger son is serving in the paratroops. It was good of you to trouble yourself to come."

"I'll have him sent home right away. Your younger son, I mean, of course. If you'll just jot down his name and unit on a piece of paper for me you'll have him back before the night is out. I'm sorry, but those shmendriks in the car outside are sure to be swearing at me for being, as they say, behind schedule. You needn't envy me, Yolek. You're welcome to both the honor and the power. I'm worse off than a slave, and little children do lead me. If I'm in their good graces tomorrow afternoon on my way back from the Galilee, perhaps they'll allow me to stop by here again. Maybe it will all have ended happily by then, and we can hug the lost lamb and think aloud together how we can set things right. Be well!"

He rose heavily from his chair, stretched himself to his full height and bulk, groaned, and reached out with an ugly hand to pat Yolek on the shoulder and Hava on the cheek. Putting an arm around Rimona, he added, as if for her ear alone, "My heart goes out to you, my friends. At most, I can have only the tiniest inkling of what you must be going through. In any case, you have my solemn word we'll do all that is humanly possible to get the boy back to you. And now tell me, *krasavitsa*, were you really and truly afraid that Yolek and I were about to slug it out? *Na*, let me give the bandit a good hug so you can see for yourself how we feel. And goodbye to you too, young man. Don't get up, for heaven's sake! Yolek, be strong. And you too, Hava. And cheer up, my dear young woman. You'll have your true love back in your arms soon enough. Goodbye to you all."

"Your Excellency," burst out Azariah, making a sudden dash for the doorway to block the guest's path with his own skinny frame. Like a raw recruit coming to attention, he drew himself up stiffly with his hands at his sides. His voice, tinged with both arrogance and despair, quivered with his challenge. "Mr. Prime Minister, sir, if you'll permit me just two minutes of your time, I have an observation to make. I know that it says in the Bible that the poor man's wisdom is despised, but I'm sure Your Excellency must also remember the verse just before that one. All I'm asking for is two minutes."

"Speak now or forever hold thy peace," said Eshkol, coming to a halt. He smiled and his entire expression underwent a change. It was that of a warmhearted, good-natured, venerable Russian peasant stretching out a gnarled hand to stroke the mane of a frightened colt. "Ask for half of my kingdom, young man, and it shall be yours."

"Mr. Prime Minister. You'll have to excuse me, but I want you to know that you haven't heard the whole truth."

"I haven't?" replied Eshkol patiently, leaning slightly toward the trembling young man.

"No, Mr. Prime Minister, sir. You've been misled. Perhaps not deliberately, perhaps only out of respect for your station, but misled all the same. A minute ago you said, sir, that you didn't understand how it was possible for her to be left alone. I'm referring to Rimona."

"Well?"

"That isn't true, sir. It's just a front. Everything you've heard here is a front. As you yourself said, sir, you've been watching a comedy. The truth is that Rimona has not been left alone. Not for a single minute. As usual, Mr. Prime Minister, you've been lied to."

"Azariah!" snapped Yolek Lifshitz, crackling with anger. "That will be enough out of you!"

"I'm afraid," said Srulik gingerly, "Comrade Eshkol is in a hurry. We have no right to detain him."

"Your Honor," insisted Azariah, leaning forward as if he were about to throw himself off a cliff. "I promise not to detain you, sir, for any more than exactly forty seconds. Haste, as they say, killed the bear. And it's your right to be in possession of all the relevant information so that you can consider the matter rationally and come to your own conclusions. Yonatan Lifshitz, sir, was the only friend I ever had. He was a big brother to me. In Russian you say, 'A friend in need is a friend indeed.' Maybe, sir, you've forgotten what it means to be someone's blood brother. Through hell and high water. Till death do us part. Never mind who I am. Let's even say I'm a fink. Or a clown. That's all strictly beside the point, so to speak. Perhaps I'm just a poor slob. But that's what people call you too, sir. Behind your back, of course.

What you have to know, Mr. Prime Minister, is that Yonatan set out to look for the meaning of his life. Not the meaning. The purpose. He did so because every last one of us is born free. Nobody is public property. Or the property of his parents, or of his wife, or of his kibbutz, or even—please excuse me, Your Excellency, if I'm being presumptuous—the property of the state of Israel. Truth before manners. The fact is that an individual belongs only to himself, if even that. That's what Jewish ethics have to say about the matter, and we Jews, sir, have made that principle into a universal rule. You surely don't need to be reminded of our prophets and all that. So what's wrong with his having decided to go off somewhere? Is that a crime? And if he preferred not to leave a forwarding address, what law did he break? I can't believe, sir, that all of life is like being in the army. He just wanted to go away. It's as simple as that. So why don't you call off your dogs? This isn't a matter for state jurisdiction. Your Honor, too—I heard this from Yolek himself—ran away from home to come to Israel. I'm sorry if 'ran away' sounds invidious. I'll take it back if you'd like. But nothing else. And in one of your debates with Mr. Ben-Gurion, sir, you said in so many words that a man's personal decisions must be honored. That was concerning one's relationship to the party, I'm sure you remember it, sir. Yonatan went where he did of his own free will, knowing exactly what he was doing, and before he left, he entrusted to me—or rather, I should say, he gave me—his wife. So that now she's mine. I admit that, morally speaking, Hava and Yolek are my parents, and that Srulik is also like a father to me too, but the truth comes first. They have no right to hound Yoni and no right to demand of me that I give up my woman. There's a limit to making concessions. A red line, so to speak. I'm quoting what you, Mr. Prime Minister, said the day before yesterday in the Knesset, and you were one-hundred-percent right. As you generally are, sir, because it's not you, but Mr. Ben-Gurion, who is the enemy of freedom. We don't live in a jungle. We live in a

Jewish state. You should be consistent, Your Excellency. Meaning that you should back me up on this. Because she's mine. De facto, of course, not de jure. This isn't a matter for the police, or for the law, or even, with all due respect, sir, for the Prime Minister and Minister of Defense. No one can try to take her from me. Please explain that to them, Mr. Prime Minister, before you leave. Tell them the facts. And since you're on your way to the Syrian border, where you'll be fed all kinds of lies, or at most a lot of half-truths, let me suggest to you—"

"Azariah! That's quite enough of your buffoonery. Stop it at once."

"Comrade Yolek! Comrade Srulik, Hava, Mr. Prime Minister, I'll have to ask you please to stop trying to silence me, because with all due respect I'm afraid I'm the only person in this country who's willing to tell the whole truth. I've already promised not to take more than a minute or two of your time, and I won't. What do you all take me for? A chiseler? A cheat? You know they don't come any more idealistic than me. And what are two minutes? No more time than it takes to skin a cat. To get to the point, Mr. Prime Minister, I have to warn you that you've been sold a bill of goods, so to speak. If you'd like, I'll be happy to say a few words about the Syrians, and Nasser, and the Arabs in general, and the Russians too. You can either hear me out or not, sir, and afterwards, of course, you're free to decide what the country should do about it."

"The boy is a tragic case," apologized Hava. "He's a Holocaust survivor whom we've tried to take in here. Naturally, it hasn't been easy, but we haven't given up on him either."

"Hava," interrupted Yolek. "Please be so kind as to stay out of it. There's no need to explain. Eshkol can manage without your help."

The Prime Minister made a weary gesture but did not alter his engagingly warm smile.

"Never mind. Those shmendriks out there can wait in the car

a little longer. They don't own me yet. And the Upper Galilee is not about to run away. Let's let the young troubadour finish his ballad, but he'll have to stop calling me Your Excellency and to talk a language a man can understand. Don't be afraid of me, young fellow. Feel free to speak your mind, but try beating about the bush a little less."

"But the Galilee *will* run away, sir!" Azariah cried out. "The Galilee, and the Negev, and all the rest. There's going to be a war. We'll be taken by surprise, fallen upon as in a pogrom. They're already sharpening their knives. That's why Yonatan walked out of here with a gun in his hand. It can break out at any time."

"Zaro," said Rimona. "Don't get worked up."

"You keep out of this, Rimona. Can't you see that it's me against the whole world? Does the woman I love have to take their side too? I've warned Comrade Eshkol that there's a war on the way and that even if we win, it will be the beginning of the end. I've said what I have to say. Now I'll keep my mouth shut."

"You know," said Eshkol, "the boy may be right. Down in my gut the whole thing scares me, and I don't want to win any war. Ah well! A fat lot of good we've done each other today. What did you say your name was, young man?"

"Gitlin. Gitlin, Azariah. And I pity us all."

"You do? Perhaps you would be so good as to tell us why we're all so deserving of your pity?" A mischievous glint flashed behind Eshkol's thick lenses.

"Quite simply, sir, you'll need all the pity you can get," continued Azariah, "because this country is surrounded on all sides by such bottomless pits of hatred. And has such bottomless pits of loneliness, because no one can stand anyone else. And this, if you ask me—I mean all the loneliness, the backbiting, and the hatred—is not only the very opposite of Zionism, it's a sure prescription for disaster. No one loves anyone. No one even loves you, sir. They make fun of you behind your back. They say you're a patsy, a half-and-half, a sell-out, a nebbish, a sissy, a finagler. They talk about you like Nazis. Even using anti-Semitic language. A shylock. A hymie. A cheap Jew politician. That's how they talk about me too. Don't you interrupt me, Comrade Yolek! You should be glad I haven't told Eshkol the things *you* say about him. And I pity you too because everyone hates you as well. There are people on this kibbutz for whom you couldn't die too soon. Most of Kibbutz Granot, and even one or two people here in this room, call you Yolek the Monster. They even say it was you that Yoni was running away from. So you better let me talk, because I'm the only one on this whole kibbutz, if not in this whole country, who still knows the meaning of compassion. It's the heart of darkness, I tell you, all this hatred and backbiting. And all along you've been lied to and kowtowed to. No one loves anyone, sir, not even on a kibbutz, any more. It's no wonder Yoni cleared out. The only one who loves all of you is myself, and Rimona loves me and she loves Yoni. When you were tastelessly joking a few minutes ago about knocking each other's teeth out, you were simply telling the truth. Because you hate each other's guts. Yolek is green with envy of you, Mr. Eshkol, just as you are green with envy of Mr. Ben-Gurion. If we Jews hate each other so much, why be surprised that the Gentiles hate us? Or the Arabs? Srulik is dying to be Yolek. Yolek would do anything to be Eshkol. Eshkol would give his right arm to be Ben-Gurion. Hava would gladly murder you all if only she could get up the courage to poison your tea. And then there's Udi and Etan and your son Amos, who do nothing all day but talk about killing the Arabs. This is a snake pit, not a country. A jungle, not a commune. Death, not Zionism. When Hava calls you all murderers, she knows what she's talking about because she knows the truth about every one of you. Not that that makes her less of a murderess herself. She'd kill me right here and now if she could, like a bug. And that's all I am. But not a murderer. No, sir. Maybe you've forgotten that Rimona and Yoni had a baby girl, Efrat. She died because death has been rampant here. But I'll give them a new child. Rimona and I still haven't forgotten what love is. And it's only because I love you all so much that I'm telling you there'll be a war soon and that the writing is already on the wall."

"Amen," said Eshkol, his smile frozen on his sallow face. "Faithful are the wounds of a friend. I'm afraid that for the moment, however, I'll have to waive the right of reply. Should you ever find yourself in Jerusalem, young man, drop by and we'll pick each other's brains. And now, be well, all of you. If the prodigal son turns up, please be so good as to inform me at once, even if it's the middle of the night. As for writings on the wall and all that, I never did put much stock in them. I say build our strength, keep a stiff upper lip, and go on hoping. God bless you all. Goodbye."

On his way out, the Prime Minister absentmindedly patted Azariah, who had finally stepped aside from the door to let him pass, twice on the back. He was flanked by two good-looking, smoothly shaven young bodyguards, who, with their blond, American-style crewcuts and wide, conservative ties appeared to be cut from the same cloth. The wires of their earplugs vanished discreetly into the collars of their blue suits. They opened and shut the doors of the car, which departed immediately.

"Come with me, Azariah," said Srulik. "I want to have a talk with you right now."

Amused but excited, Yolek objected. "What's wrong? Frankly I'm delighted Eshkol was subjected to that fusillade. It couldn't have done him a bit of harm when you think of that crowd of apple-polishers and diplomaed scoundrels he's surrounded with. Azariah gave him some piss and vinegar to drink, and it did my old heart good. Leave the boy alone, will you? Come over here, Azariah, you've earned yourself a shot of brandy. Bottoms up! To the health of the Devil! Quiet, Hava. Nobody asked you. The murderers are having a little nip. Did you get a good look at Eshkol? Why, it frightened me just to watch his face. He looks like death warmed over. Don't listen to her, Rimon'ka! Leave that bottle where I can reach it. And a cigarette might be a good idea now too."

"You're lunatics," said Hava. "All of you."

"Zaro has a fever," said Rimona. "So does Srulik. Yolek's heart is bad. And Hava hasn't slept a wink for two days. We've been talking for a whole hour, and now we should all rest."

She cleared the table, wiped it, and left the room to do the dishes. At that very moment, the front door opened again and another visitor walked in.

16

Sunday, March 6, 1966, 10:30 p.m.

Where should I begin this evening? Perhaps I ought to mention that sometime between yesterday and this morning I got over my grippe entirely. And that today was my first official day as secretary. I still can't help feeling slightly ridiculous each time I write down, *I am secretary of Kibbutz Granot.* Although I missed the general meeting last night that elected me almost unanimously, it wasn't just my fever that kept me from putting on a coat, making an appearance, and saying quite simply, Comrades, I'm truly sorry, I've thought the whole thing over and come to ask you to withdraw my candidacy. I'm not the right man for the office.

Well, now that the position is mine, I'll have to stick it out and try to do my modest best. At the moment Hava Lifshitz is asleep here—in the next room, of course. She's been sedated by the doctor, and I shall have to look after her, as I will look after the whole kibbutz. How strange to think of a woman in my bed! Just writing it makes me want to stifle a laugh, like a schoolboy. Someone might get ideas. I, of course, shall sleep on a mattress in this room. I've arranged for our nurse, Rachel Stutchnik, to sleep at Yolek's place. The doctor is worried by his EKG and his blood pressure, but Yolek is still adamant about not going to the hospital. Tomorrow it will have to be decided whether he must be taken there against his will. *Will have to be decided?* What a shock to weigh those words. After all, the responsibility is now mine. Tomorrow I shall drag him to the hospital whether he likes it or not.

What a confused, troublesome turn of events, not to say what a wildly grotesque one. But in point of fact, most situations seem grotesque to me, whereas nothing ever seems fantastic. Anything, I'm convinced, is possible. There is nothing human beings are incapable of.

Perhaps if I try to write it all down as it happened, something may yet become clear to me. I'll try, as usual, to be as straightforward as possible.

At 3:30 this morning I woke up in a sweat from all the aspirin I took Saturday night. My grippe was gone, though I still felt weak and dizzy. By the light of the reading lamp I put a bookmark in my Donald Griffin, which had fallen on the blanket beside me, put the book on the night table, donned Bolognesi's old sweater and my bathrobe, turned on the electric heater, and sat there for a moment thinking that on just such a winter morning as this Death may come for me as I'm pulling on my trousers or making my bed. For that matter, it could even come this very moment so that my life would stop without my having managed to understand a thing. What a pity! After thirty years of playing my flute, the two of us haven't experienced even one moment of total harmony, much less ecstasy. After twenty-five years of loving P., I still haven't given her so much as a hint. I'm still alone, and she has four grandchildren. Yes, it will probably be on a morning like this that I'll keel over right here and die.

And so I made myself a glass of tea with honey and lemon and took it to the east window to await the first light. Something inside kept telling me that Yonatan was in trouble but unharmed, that Rimona was pregnant, and that the father could be either of them. What made me so sure? But then, who'd ask an inner voice for logical demonstrations at four o'clock in the morning?

Far off in the darkness a cow lowed. Something moved outside the window, perhaps Tia, patiently snuffling among the hibiscus bushes, exploring the thicket of bougainvillea, pushing on into the honeysuckle arbor deep in the garden and vanishing there. I moved the electric heater closer because I was having a slight chill, then returned to the window. A light, grayish rain coursed down the pane against which my forehead was pressed for a good ten minutes. A freight train hooted in the west. Roosters crowed from the far end of the kibbutz. How desolate this garden looks on a winter day before sunrise. The puddles of muddy water. The sopping wet garden table, its chairs upended on it, their legs in the air. The thick-fallen leaves of the grape vine. The dripping of the pines in the fog as in some Chinese painting. And not a living soul.

By six or six-fifteen the light had become a bit stronger, although the sky was still overcast. The refrigerator yielded up some yogurt that Hava had left for me yesterday, which I ate with crackers. Then I made the bed and shaved. Meanwhile the water had boiled again and I made myself more tea. Perhaps I should have stayed in bed for another day or two, but I didn't think twice about it this morning. By seven I was already in Yolek's office, answering the backlog of letters from the ministry of agriculture, from the regional planning council, from the central bureau of the kibbutz movement. Trying to put the place in a little order, I threw out the old newspapers in the drawers of Yolek's desk and came across an old pocket flashlight that I stuck in my pants pocket for some reason. Next I had a look at the minutes of last night's general meeting. (One-hundred-seventeen members were apparently convinced I would make a good secretary. Three were not. Nine could not make up their minds. How did P. vote?)

By now the kibbutz was fully awake. Etan R. drove by the office window on a tractor, pulling a wagonful of fodder to the cowshed. Friend Stutchnik trudged wearily by in the other direction on his way back from the night milking, his boots heavy with mud.

Suddenly Hava burst into the office. Had I gone out of my mind? A man with a hundred-and-four fever running out naked in the middle of the night to go to work! What was wrong with me? Where were my brains?

I asked her to join me for a glass of tea and let me explain her errors one by one. In the first place, it was not the middle of the night, but half-past-seven in the morning. Second, my fever was gone, and I didn't feel all that bad. Third, I hadn't gone out naked, but fully clothed. And besides, I had walked, not run. I had work to do, though my brains for it, I agreed, left much to be desired.

"So tell me, Srulik, you must like it here, sitting like a big shot at Yolek's desk in his swivel chair and going through all his papers. It's not such a bad life after all, is it, now."

Her eyes flashed. She was convinced she had found my weak point. I wasn't a saint, after all. I had my little human frailty, and it could be mounted on a pin in one of her albums and used against me should the occasion arise.

"How is he?" I asked. "How did he spend the night?"

"He's a monster!" she snapped. "Can you imagine? The very first thing this morning he wanted me to get Rimona and her sewer rat to keep him company. And I'm going to do it. Why not? Let them put on a show, all three of them. The skunk can strum, the moron can dance, and the murderer can give the curtain speech. Let them enjoy themselves because I'm taking my toothbrush and my pajamas and getting out of there. Today."

"And where will you go, may I ask?"

"I'll move in with you. Will you take me?"

Her face was as puckered as an infant's. She was close to tears. "Will you?"

God in heaven, I thought. But I said yes.

"You're a magnificent man, Srulik. Humanly speaking, I mean. I didn't sleep a wink all night. I was thinking of you and Yoni. If there's anyone in this whole world besides me who really wants him back and is trying to save him, it's you. The rest of them are all murderers. They'd just as soon never see him again. Don't argue with me. Instead of arguing, I want you to make an announcement to the press this morning. I want you to lie. You can say that his wife has been committed to a mental hospital. Or that his father is critically ill. A white lie, that one. Or better yet, announce that his father has died and that he's being pleaded with to come for the funeral. That ought to bring him back. And don't forget to have it broadcast on the radio too."

"Hava," I said with unaccustomed firmness, "you're being ridiculous. I must ask you to excuse me and leave me alone for now. Please go home or to work. You're no help at all to me here."

I waited for the fireworks, but to my great surprise she obeyed at once, though not before begging me to forget her outburst, swearing she had faith in me "as in an angel of God," promising to bring a better electric heater for my office, and ordering me to continue taking aspirin. From the door she exclaimed, "You're a dear."

I wish she hadn't said that. That's no way to talk to me.

As soon as she was gone I panicked. Had I actually invited her to move in with me? Suppose she took me up on it? Was I out of my mind? What would I do with her? What would Yolek say? What would the whole kibbutz say? What would P. think? Madness.

In any case, I didn't have long to regret it. Within a few minutes a police van pulled up in front of the office. Out of it stepped a captain and a sergeant, who asked to talk to the secretary.

"The secretary is indisposed," I said.

The captain was insistent. "This is an urgent matter. Who's in charge here?"

"I beg your pardon. I am. I was referring to the former secretary. It's he who is sick. I'm the new secretary."

Well, then, it was me they wished to talk to, as well as a member of the family. They were already at work on the case. Yesterday they had picked up a young man roaming the beach at Atlit, but he had turned out not to be our client. From Ashkelon there had been a report of a suspicious individual who had slept half the night on a bench in the bus station but he disappeared before the police arrived. Yesterday and this morning, too, they had combed the ruins of Sheikh Dahr. If I'm not mistaken we had a call from you people about some suspect sign of life there a few months ago, didn't we? What we need now, however, is as much accurate background information as we can get. Was there a family quarrel? Any emotional disturbance? Other problems? Did the young man have a previous history of disappearing? Where did he get the weapon he took with him? Were there any reliable full-face photographs of him available? Did he have any identifying marks? What was he wearing when he left? What exactly did he take with him? Did he have any known enemies? Could we draw up a list of the names and addresses of friends, relatives, or acquaintances with whom he might be staying? Did he have a passport? Did he have family abroad?

I rose to open the window, letting in a biting draft of air. Udi happened to be passing by outside, and I asked him to find Rimona and have her come to the office. By herself, I stressed. While waiting for her, I tried to answer a few of their questions as best I could. The sergeant wrote down everything I said.

"This is strictly confidential," said the captain, "we received an urgent phone call this morning from the ministry of defense.

Mr. Eshkol's military attaché personally asked us to go all out on this case. I take it that our party's father is in the Knesset? A good friend of some very important people?"

"Thank you," I said. "I'm sure you would have done everything possible in any case."

When Rimona arrived, she helped me serve my guests coffee, smiling her incongruous, wistful smile at nobody in particular, her dark eyes glowing, her blond hair covered by a kerchief. Noticing that a calendar on the wall was hanging crooked, she straightened it before sitting down. Her answers, or so I thought, must have made a rather strange impression on the two officers of the law.

"Lifshitz, Rimona?"

"Yes, that's me." She smiled as if astonished that they should have known.

"Pleased to meet you. My name is Inspector Bechor. And this is Sergeant Yakov. Our sympathy. We hope to have good news for you soon. You have no objection to our asking you a few questions?"

"Thank you for coming to visit. And for your sympathy. It's Yonatan who needs the sympathy, but he is away now. And Azariah needs it too."

"Who's Azariah?"

"Yoni's and my friend. There are three of us."

"What do you mean, three of you?"

"We're three friends."

"Please, Mrs. Lifshitz. Try to keep your answers to the point. That way we can be the most help and the least bother to you."

"Everyone is being very kind and helpful. Srulik, and you, and Yakov. And anyway, winter is almost over and spring is on its way."

"All right, then. I'll read you what we've got written here, and then Yakov will take down whatever you have to add. You may stop me any time you find inaccuracies."

Rimona smiled at the picture on the calendar. For some reason I recalled that time in the dining hall when she told me I shouldn't be sad because everything was looking up.

"All right. Lifshitz, Yonatan. Father's name, Yisra'el . . . is that right? Aged twenty-six. Married. No children."

"Just Efrat."

"Who's Efrat?"

"Our daughter."

"Begging your pardon?"

I was forced to intervene at this point. "That's their baby who died a year ago."

"Our sympathy. If this isn't too difficult for you, perhaps we can proceed?"

"It isn't difficult for me. Is it for you?"

"Army rank, captain. A reservist in reconnaissance. With a medal for bravery. 'Distinguished conduct under fire,' it says here. Last worked as a mechanic. A member of this kibbutz. Five foot ten inches. Dark complexion. Longish hair. No identifying marks. Left home without notice early Wednesday morning, March 2. Destination unknown. Left behind no written message. Dressed in an army uniform and thought to be armed. Do you happen to know where he got the weapon? Did he have a license for it? What kind was it?"

"It was black, I think. From the army. It was kept in a locked chest under the bed."

"Why do you think he took it with him?"

"He always does."

"What do you mean by 'always'?"

"Whenever he's called."

"But this time I understand that he was not called."

"Oh, but he was."

"By whom?"

"He didn't say. He didn't exactly know. He just heard them calling him from far away and said that he had to go. And he really did have to."

"When exactly did he tell you all this?"

"In the middle of the night once. When it was raining very hard. He said he was being called somewhere and they wouldn't wait forever."

"When exactly did he say this?"

"I already told you. In the rain."

"Where did he say this call was coming from?"

"He didn't know. From far away. He said he had to go because it was hard for him here."

"You'll have to excuse me, ma'am, for this next question. Did the two of you ever have any problems, any family quarrels?"

Rimona smiled. "He just went away. Everyone would like to go away. He went where he wanted to go. Azariah wanted to come, and so he came. And he stayed. We can wait. We won't be sad. And don't you be sad either."

"But what was the stated purpose of his departure?"

"He said: 'I'm going to my own place.' "

"His own place?"

"I think there might be such a place."

"You think there might be what?"

"A place that's his own."

"To be sure. But where do you think this place is?"

"Wherever is right for him. There is a right place for you too. And for Srulik. You take a spear and go out and kill an antelope."

And so it went until the captain finally threw a sideways glance at the sergeant, thanked Rimona and me, extended yet more sympathy, and promised that everything would turn out all right since he knew from experience that most problems of this nature were settled in a matter of days. Rimona remained seated. In the awkward silence that followed, she suggested that she bring in her embroidery and some refreshments. I had no choice but to tell her that I wished to be left alone with the police. Once she'd left, the captain asked cautiously, "What's her problem? She must still be in shock, eh?"

I tried to explain, delicately sketching a brief portrait, but evidently without success, because the sergeant put a finger to his forehead, looked at me for confirmation, and joked, "I'd have run away from someone like that myself."

"And I most certainly would *not* have," I said, amazed at the sternness of my voice. It wiped the asinine smirk off his face immediately.

"Well, we aren't much the wiser," said the captain. "The most important thing now is to get some good photographs."

It soon turned out, however, that there were no photographs of Yonatan. Except for a few childhood snapshots and one useless picture of him standing by a jeep with Rimona on their honeymoon, an Arab *kaffiyeh* around his head, and another, blurry shot from an old issue of the army magazine.

After the police departed, the telephone rang. It was Chupka, Yonatan's commanding officer.

"Is that Srulik? Here's the latest from this end. We already have a few of our men out in the field. Our S.I.O. has been in your area for the past two days with some trackers. And we've got a stoolie on the other side of the border, right opposite you. We'll be talking to him tonight." (What was an S.I.O.? A stoolie? I was embarrassed to ask.)

"And another thing," Chupka went on, "do you have anyone there who knows anything about maps? You maybe? Or somebody younger?"

"We might," I said. "Why?"

"I want you to go to Yoni's room and look very carefully for a box of maps. Last autumn he walked off with a whole set of 1:20,000 of mine and never returned them. Check it out. Or shall I send someone to do it?"

"What exactly do you want us to check?"

"See if there's a map missing. Because he took a complete set."

"Excuse me," I said. "Do you really need the whole set right now? Is it that urgent?"

"You don't get me, my friend," drawled Chupka. "If there's a particular map missing, that means Yoni probably took it with him. That could give us a clue where to start looking for him."

"How extraordinary," I said. "But of course. We'll check right now. That's a brilliant idea."

"Come off it, man," said Chupka, clearly appalled by my praises. "Just make sure you get in touch with me tonight to let me know, okay?"

"Agreed," I said. And added, swallowing my pride, "Right. Okay."

"And don't go making any waves."

"Waves?"

"I mean the press and all that. He may still be alive, and we don't want to make him look bad."

What a strange breed these young people are. Like a foreign people almost, as if in them our race were disguising itself so that even our worst enemies will no longer be able to recognize us. What worlds apart they and I. And yet I would give everything I have right now not just to have a son of my own, but for him to be just like them. Anything! Only what do I have to give? My old flute? Six shirts? Two pairs of shoes? Or the dozens of notebooks in this journal? In short, nothing, not a thing. And this leads me to another, in a certain sense, theological observation. Does not this inner urge to give our all for what we can never have bear a mysterious resemblance to the inner workings of the universe itself, to the orbits of the stars, the procession of the seasons, the migrations of the birds that I have been reading about in Griffin? Perhaps the correct word is not *urge* but *yearning.*

Back to today's events. At ten o'clock I picked up Hava at the sewing shop and went with her to see Yolek. Rimona and Azariah were already there, he sitting at one end of the couch and she on the straw mat at his feet. In the dimly lighted room, framed by all his books, Yolek indeed looked the gray eminence, veiled as he was by clouds of cigarette smoke. Azariah was puffing away too. Had we interrupted a political argument? A discussion of Spinoza? Azariah's guitar was lying at his left, between the couch and desk. Had he been intending to play? When he saw us, Yolek's eyes shone with amusement.

"Well, you *tsaddik,* you, how are you enjoying yourself?"

"Enjoying?"

"Your new job. How is the secretary of the kibbutz feeling today? Is everything under control?"

"Srulik," interrupted Hava, "has more brains and human charity in his little finger than you do in your whole world-famous head."

"*Na.* What do you say to that? Now my own wife has fallen in love with him too. Ah, well. At least, thank God, he's taken her off my back. I promise you that he'll soon wish that he hadn't. In my own humble opinion, though, it's an excellent reason to propose a little toast. Rimon'ka, if it's not too much to ask of you, you'll find the bottle hiding down there, behind the Hebrew dictionary."

"Don't you dare!" Hava hissed at him. "Didn't you hear what the doctor said?"

And Azariah had an aside of his own. "Stepan gave Alyosha his most precious stones. Alyosha got mad and broke Stepan's bones."

I had intended to maneuver Azariah into the other room to ask him to look for Yoni's map box and bring it to the office, but just then the door opened and in walked the Prime Minister. He entered without his entourage, a bit sheepish-looking, if ponderous, his blue shirt sticking out of his trousers, his shoes spattered with mud. He gripped Hava by the shoulders and gave her a kiss on the forehead. Yolek offered him tea and, without waiting for an answer, told Rimona to bring him some. I was amazed to notice moisture, in fact an actual tear, in Yolek's hard little eyes. He, of course, was quick to blame it on his allergy. Meanwhile, Hava had dashed off to the kitchen, where she took out a fancy white tablecloth and began preparing hot and cold drinks, fruit, and cake, making use of her best china. I couldn't keep back a little smile.

It was no time before Yolek and Eshkol were joking and bantering away. From my corner I could see Azariah devouring our guest with glittering eyes. His mouth hung slightly open, as if he were an adolescent peeking beneath a woman's dress. Once more I smiled to myself. And when, presumably in jest, Eshkol challenged Yolek to a fistfight, I couldn't resist offering to move aside the furniture to provide a proper ring for them to box in. Everyone laughed except me. Incidentally, I liked the Prime Minister at first. He struck me as a compassionate man. Not that he was above taking digs at our Yolek, which digs, I'm sorry to say, I enjoyed. At one point I was tempted to interrupt with my usual sermon about the duty incumbent on us all not to cause unnecessary pain. I managed, however, to restrain myself. Which is more than can be said of Azariah Gitlin.

When the Prime Minister rose to leave, Azariah astonished us all by breaking into a long, confused tirade. In vain Hava and I tried to make him desist. Yolek and Eshkol seemed secretly united in taking a strange pleasure in it. They even, so I thought, egged the boy on, as if they wanted him to make more and more of an ass of himself. I suddenly felt as out of place as a teetotaler in a room full of drunks. Was I the only man there capable of any sympathy for Azariah? Did Azariah's contortions tickle their funny bones? I didn't understand any of it.

In any event, I lost all sympathy for Eshkol. All my life I have found those men hard to take. Their concealed hatreds, their cunning, their self-induced illnesses, their endless recourse to Yiddish and quotes from the Bible. Even though for years I've tried to become one of them myself, deep down I feel proud for never having succeeded. Azariah wasn't much better. He ran amuck with old Russian saws, insults, and prophecies. Finally, after Eshkol had promised to extend all possible help and taken his leave, Yolek plied Azariah with brandy and even praised the poor fellow for his insolence. Eventually another guest arrived, a stout, dandyish person in a light flannel suit and a smartly trimmed Vandyke beard. He had the appearance of a worldly artist and reeked as much of smug success as of expensive cologne. His toneless, slightly nasal voice had a faint American accent. He sounded as if a pipe were clenched between his teeth.

The new arrival introduced himself by brandishing a gold-rimmed calling card and announcing, "Arthur I. Seewald. United Enterprises. Which one of you gentlemen is Mr. Lifshitz?"

"Right here," said Yolek hoarsely, banging his brandy glass on the table. Arthur I. Seewald ignored this unmistakable sign of displeasure, handed Yolek his card, and sat down without being asked.

He was, he explained, the Tel Aviv representative of a number of foreign business firms and the local agent of Mr. Benjamin Bernard Trotsky of Miami, Florida. In a telex received from Mr. Trotsky last night Mr. Seewald had been instructed to visit our kibbutz as soon as possible. A transatlantic phone call from his client this morning had given additional instructions. He wished to apologize for not having called to make an appointment. It was difficult, if not impossible, to get through to the kibbutz on the telephone. Unfortunately, therefore, he had been forced to come without advance notice, though he sought to assure us that this was not his regular custom. In any case, considering the urgency of the matter at hand—

"What matter?" asked Yolek, cutting him short. His bristling unshaven cheeks, his heavy frame wrapped in a blue robe over red pajamas gave him the aspect of an Oriental despot. Indeed, such was his glowering imperiousness and contempt, he seemed about to lift a finger and order the newcomer beheaded. "Perhaps you'll be kind enough to skip the rest of your introduction and come to the point?"

The point was a message from the secretary of Kibbutz Granot that arrived on Mr. Trotsky's desk three days ago. Was the young man in question still missing?

"My son," said Yolek, choking back his anger, "would appear to have gone off to join your Mr. Trotsky. *Psia krew.* Is he there? Yes or no?"

Mr. Seewald smiled pleasantly. According to the latest information at hand, Mr. Trotsky was still expecting to hear from the young man and, indeed, was rather concerned about him. He had even planned to fly to Israel yesterday morning, but a business matter and, above all, the possible arrival of young Mr. Lifshitz had forced him to cancel the trip. The fact that he was now in the Bahamas was the reason why he had sent a telex fully authorizing Mr. Seewald to negotiate in his name. Mr. Seewald himself, by the way, was a lawyer by profession.

"Negotiate what?"

"Yoni's alive!" gasped Hava. "He's with them! I'm telling you, Yolek, he's already there. I want you to give them whatever they ask for, just as long as he comes back. Do you hear me?"

Mr. Seewald seemed momentarily at a loss. Could he possibly have a few minutes with Mr. Lifshitz in private?

"Now you listen to me, mister. This is my wife. And that's my daughter-in-law sitting opposite you. And that young man at the end of the couch is a close family friend. And the person standing at the window has just replaced me as secretary of the kibbutz. There are no secrets here. It's all in the family. You say you came to negotiate? Then let's hear what your position is. Does Trotsky have the family jewel? Yes or no?"

The visitor regarded each of us skeptically, as if still trying to make us out. His glance finally lingered on Hava.

"Mrs. Lifshitz, I presume?"

"Hava."

"*Madame.* I beg your pardon, but I have unequivocal instructions first to talk in private with your husband and then in private with you. The matter, as you all know, is a rather delicate one. I really am most sorry."

"Will you stop talking like a goddamn popinjay!" thundered Yolek, rising to his feet like a wounded old bear and drawing up his body to its full height, his head and shoulders hunched sharply forward. He slammed his fist on the table and roared, "Where is that success story of mine? Is he or is he not with that degenerate nebbish of yours?"

"I was saying that so far—"

"Eh?"

"So far, sir, I'm afraid not. But—"

"So far, eh? You're afraid not, eh? This whole business is beginning to smell to high heaven! What's going on here, a conspiracy? Blackmail? *Gesheften?* What's that rotten clown of yours up to?" With his full weight behind him, he spun around to face Hava, turning purple, a twisted vein pulsing in his forehead. "Exactly how much, Mrs. Lifshitz, do you already know about all this? What the hell have you and that redneck of yours already conspired to do with Yonatan behind my back? Rimona. Srulik. Azariah. Out. All of you. No. Wait. Srulik stays here."

I stayed.

On his way out, Azariah unsuccessfully tried to conceal a snicker. Rimona said, "Hava and Yolek, please don't fight. It makes Yoni sad."

Yolek sat down in his chair, panting and wiping the sweat from his brow with a bare hand. As soon as he'd caught his breath, he bellowed at the visitor, "Will you sit down, mister?"

Mr. Seewald, in point of fact, had never got up.

"Hava! A glass of water. And my medicine. I don't feel well. And give this lawyer fellow something to drink too. It's time he stopped making cultivated faces and talked business."

"Thank you ever so much," said Mr. Seewald, a genially puzzled look on his neat-bearded face, "but I'm not a bit thirsty. With your permission then, we'll get down to the matter at hand. This isn't a social call."

"Oh, it's not, is it?" growled Yolek. "And here I was thinking that you'd come for a dancing party! All right, sir. I'm listening. You can begin. And by the way, I've nothing against talking to you in private. Hava, to the bedroom. Srulik, you stay.

I need you as a witness. This whole thing stinks. Hava, I said out!"

"Certainly not," exploded Hava. "I don't care if you burst a gut. This is my house. It's my son he's talking about. No one is kicking me out. Here's your glass of water. And take these pills."

Yolek roughly pushed away her hand, sloshing water. He pulled out a cigarette from the pocket of his robe, fingered it, tapped it on the arm of his chair, tapped the other end, and studied it at some length in his usual fashion. Finally, his broad nostrils twitching, he decided not to light it and turned to me.

"Srulik, perhaps I can enlist your good services. Do you think your charms might prevail on this lady to kindly leave us alone for a while?"

"It will be my pleasure to talk to you in private afterwards, Mrs. Lifshitz," Mr. Seewald offered amiably.

Hava looked at me. "Shall I, Srulik?" Her tone was downright docile.

"I think you should. But stay in the next room," I said.

"*Ty zboju!*" she snarled at Yolek and slammed the door so hard the glasses tinkled on the table.

From his pocket, the visitor produced a long white envelope and a carefully folded piece of paper.

"This is the power of attorney telexed to me by Mr. Trotsky. In the envelope is an open ticket I was instructed to purchase."

"An open ticket? Who for?"

"For the lady. Tel Aviv–New York–Miami. Round trip, of course. Tomorrow she'll have her passport and visa. Mr. Trotsky's name is a great simplifier of procedures in any number of countries."

Yolek removed his glasses from his pocket, settled them on the slope of his profligate nose, gave Mr. Seewald a crafty sideways glance, and said, without looking at the papers that had been put before him, "*Na. Mazel tov.* And what has the lady done to deserve this great honor?"

"If the young man is truly on his way to America, as Mr. Trotsky sincerely hopes, it would be desirable for Mrs. Lifshitz to be present there as well. Mr. Trotsky wishes any meeting to take place in his private residence."

"Meeting, mister?"

The visitor unbuckled his leather briefcase and took out a sheet of paper, from which he asked permission to read a few sentences. In this way, he stated, any potential misunderstanding or unnecessary debate might be avoided.

I tried to make myself as inconspicuous as possible by turning my head to the window and staring out of it. A blue sky. One or two wisps of light cloud. A leafless branch. A butterfly. Spring. Where was Yonatan at this moment? What was he thinking of? I would have given almost anything to shut out that smug, nasal voice as it read from the sheet of paper:

". . . Mr. Trotsky is greatly concerned over the disappearance of young Yonatan. He hopes and believes that in the next few days, or even hours, the young man will make an appearance. For many years now he has been prepared, should the occasion arise, to acknowledge legal paternity of the boy. Indeed, he once declared as much in writing, in a registered letter to you that was unfortunately never answered. Mr. Trotsky has reason to assume that, if the matter is put to him, the young man will wish to determine, by medical tests if necessary, who his true father is. Mr. Trotsky desires to stress that he has no intention of imposing anything on his son. He does, however, insist on his right to a private meeting with the boy and his mother."

Having finished with the formal deposition, the lawyer continued on his own. "I have been authorized to negotiate the matter discreetly with you, Mr. Lifshitz, and separately with your wife, in order to reach an understanding with you both. And I have a concrete proposal to make."

"You do?" said Yolek without a trace of annoyance, extending his head forward as if fearful of failing to hear. "A proposal?

And exactly what is it that you wish to propose?"

"Mr. Lifshitz, to put your consideration of the matter into proper perspective, allow me to state on my own the following facts. Mr. Trotsky is not a young man. He has been married and divorced four times. None of these alliances has produced any offspring. Among other things, therefore, we are talking about an estate that, without attempting to describe or assess its net worth, easily has a value, I would say, that is ten or twenty times greater than that of this entire esteemed kibbutz. Apart from his son, Mr. Trotsky has only one other relation, a mentally unstable brother who disappeared long ago and has not been heard from since. The young man under discussion, in other words, will not be left empty-handed. I have been authorized to stress the following: Mr. Trotsky has decided that the young man will be looked after even if the results of a paternity test should prove to be equivocal, or, from Mr. Trotsky's point of view, negative. This is a matter in regard to which he has not chosen to share his motives or concerns with either you or me. I was asked, however, to emphasize as strongly as I can that Mr. Trotsky has no demands whatsoever to make in return. He is not asking that his son undergo a formal change of name. At the same time, he also does not as yet wish to make any binding commitments, and his sole request at this stage is to meet with his son and talk with him and Mrs. Lifshitz privately. Such is his desire, and, if I may say so, his indubitable right as well. And now, with your permission, I would like to have a few words with Mrs. Lifshitz. Afterwards, I suggest that the three of us confer together to see how matters stand. Thank you for your consideration."

Yolek kept thoughtfully silent, still gently fingering his unlighted cigarette. With due deliberation he moved the ashtray from the edge of the table to its center and asked in a barely audible voice, "Did you hear all of that, Srulik?"

"Yes," I replied.

"Srulik, do you smell what I smell?"

"It would seem to me," observed Mr. Seewald politely, "that the most important consideration for all parties concerned should be the welfare of the young man."

"Srulik, before I say or do anything, I need to have your unqualified opinion. You be the judge. Is she involved in this? Is this an intrigue?"

"Absolutely not," I said. "Hava had nothing to do with it."

"On the contrary!" said Mr. Seewald contentedly. "Although I'm sure that Mrs. Lifshitz will be, to say the least, highly pleased. If you'll permit me to speak with her now, I can't imagine it will take long."

"I'll permit you, sir," said Yolek calmly, "to get up."

"I beg your pardon?"

"Get up, mister."

Yolek took off his glasses and stuck them in his pocket. With a cumbersome movement, he reached out, gathered up the telex, the ticket, and the page that Mr. Seewald had read from, tore them into shreds, and piled them neatly at one end of the table.

"Now get out of here," he said, as if to himself.

"Mr. Lifshitz!"

"Get out of here. The door is right behind you."

Mr. Seewald turned pale and then crimson. He rose, snatched up his leather briefcase, and pressed it to his chest as if he feared it might go the way of the documents.

"Damnation," swore Yolek. "Listen here, you tell your master over there—"

Just then, however, Hava stormed out of the bedroom, flew between them, and came to a halt facing me.

"Srulik, he's slaughtering the child! For the love of God, don't let him do it. He slaughtered Yoni in cold blood so we'll never see him ever again." She clasped my hands between her palms. "You just heard, Srulik, how he cut the last thread with his own hands. Yoni's dead and he doesn't care. The beast!" Insanely she spun around toward Yolek, trembling all over. Hard as all physical contact with women is for me, I rushed to restrain her.

Too late. She had already thrown herself sobbing on the straw mat at Yolek's feet.

"Have pity on the child, you monster! On your own child! You cold-blooded murderer."

"I'll leave my calling card," said Mr. Seewald diplomatically. "You can always get in touch with me at your leisure. It's time for me to be off."

"Don't let him go! Murderers! Srulik, quick, run after him, promise him whatever they want. Eshkol will help. Give them anything, just get me my boy back. Srulik!"

"Don't you dare!" said Yolek to me in a stifled voice. "I forbid you to go after him. Can't you see she's a sick woman?"

By now Mr. Seewald had already left. I hesitated before following him out, catching up with him by his limousine. He paused and remarked coldly that he had nothing more to say and was not prepared to regard me as a party to any negotiations.

"I'm not here to negotiate, Mr. Seewald," I said. "But I do have a message to convey. Please tell Mr. Trotsky that the secretary of Kibbutz Granot has the following to say to Yonatan Lifshitz should he turn up in Miami. As far as we're concerned, he's free to do whatever he wants and go wherever he wants. We don't want him back in chains, but he must get in touch with his parents at once. And if he decides not to return, he must give his wife her freedom. You can also inform Mr. Trotsky that if he tries keeping anything back from us, or pressuring Yonatan, or any other monkey business, this kibbutz will fight him all the way. And what is more, we shall win. Please tell him exactly what I've said."

Without waiting for an answer or offering to shake hands, I hurried back to the Lifshitzes. Somehow, with a strength that one discovers only in emergencies, Hava had single-handedly dragged Yolek to the couch and then run out to get the doctor. Yolek's face had turned blue. His hands were pressed against his chest. Scraps from the papers he had torn still clung to his robe.

I brought him a drink of water. His agony had not diminished his savage will-power, however, for he warned in a whisper, "If you made some deal with him, I'll make you live to regret it."

"Calm down. I didn't make any deals. And don't try to talk now. The doctor must be on his way."

"She's a madwoman," he gasped. "It's all her fault. She made Yonatan into what he is. He's just like her."

"Shut up, Yolek!" I said, shocked to hear myself talk to him like that.

His pain evidently grew worse, for he groaned from the depths. I took his hand in my own and held it, for the first time in my life, until the doctor arrived, followed by Rachel Stutchnik and Hava.

I went back to my post at the window. It was early evening, and the sky had begun to turn blue and red in the west. In the sunset light, the bougainvillea in the garden seemed to catch fire. It had been thirty-nine years ago in Poland that Yolek Lifshitz first introduced me to his group of young Zionist pioneers who later founded this kibbutz. He called me "a cultured youth" and, on the same occasion, referred to German Jews like me as "first-rate human material." It was he who taught me how to harness a horse, who persuaded a general meeting of our commune to buy me a flute at a time when "artistic tendencies" were considered a grave bourgeois deviation, who more than once scolded me for not getting married and even tried fixing me up with a widow from a nearby kibbutz. And now here I had been holding his hand. From somewhere deep inside me came a feeling of indefinable peace. As if I were someone else. Or as if I had managed at long last to play a particularly difficult passage on my flute, one that for years I had been unable to master, and had acquired the confidence that I could effortlessly repeat it from now on without a single false note.

"We can't force you to go to the hospital," said the doctor, "but your life will be in danger, and I'll have to wash my hands of all responsibility for it."

"Forgive me for everything," implored Hava. "I swear I'll be good from now on. Just listen to the doctor, I beg you."

I turned around to take a look. Yolek was gripping the couch with his packing-crate hands as if he were really about to be dragged away by brute force, and there was a contemptuously bitter look on his ugly face. There was something quite horrid about him, yet at the same time—why deny it?—something positively majestic that I admired and envied with all my heart.

"He has to go to the hospital," said the doctor.

"Yolek is staying here," I heard myself say. "That's his wish, but there will be a driver on duty all night long."

I then set out to arrange the matter with Etan R. and astonished myself even more by issuing a second command when I reached the doorway.

"Rachel, you stay here with Yolek. Not you, Hava. You're coming with me. Yes, right now."

She followed me, all obedience. Her eyes were full of tears. Although, as I've said, touching a woman is, for personal reasons, very hard for me, I put my arm around her shoulders. From the path outside I called back to the doctor, "We'll be in the office. And afterwards at my place."

After we had found Etan and I had told him to go sit all night in the pickup truck by Yolek's apartment, Hava finally spoke up, meekly. "You're angry with me, Srulik."

"Not angry. Just concerned."

"I'll be all right."

"I want you to go to my place now and have a rest. Later I'll have the doctor give you a sedative."

"You don't have to do that. I'm all right, I told you."

"Don't argue with me."

"Srulik, where is Yoni?"

"I don't know. But he's not with Trotsky. At any rate, not yet. The whole thing strikes me as rather fanciful."

"But supposing he does end up there?"

"If he does, I'll see to it that Trotsky realizes we must be informed at once. We won't put up with any funny stuff. Leave that worry to me. And now goodbye, Hava. Go to my place. I'll drop by as soon as I get the chance."

"You haven't eaten a thing all day. And you're not well either."

"I'm fine," I said.

At the office, Udi Shneour was waiting with what seemed to be an important piece of information. Despite Azariah's protests, he had gone to Rimona's apartment as I had instructed, searched all the closets, and found Yoni's set of maps, from which, it seemed, the whole triangle of the Negev from Sodom and Rafiah down to Eilat was missing. I told him to get hold of Chupka and let him know this, even if it took all night.

Meanwhile, I used our one other phone, in the infirmary, to call the Prime Minister's personal secretary at home and give him the addresses and phone numbers on Seewald and Trotsky. I told him we had reason for suspicion and suggested that the right people keep an eye out. I also asked his secretary to follow up on the Prime Minister's promise to release the Lifshitzes' younger son Amos from the army for a few days.

Azariah was lying in wait for me in the office. He wished to ask me a question of principle. Did I or did I not approve of Udi Shneour's breaking into his, Azariah's, apartment, going through all the closets. Incidentally, he wanted to request—or rather, not request, but apply for—that is, fill out—the necessary forms for acceptance as a full member of the kibbutz. He would marry Rimona and devote himself to the common good. Both the worm and the man must do the very best they can. He was through with his wandering and intended to stay put for the rest of his life.

I told him to leave me alone.

Except for tea, crackers, and aspirin, I haven't eaten all day. But my head is clear. Between me and the pages of this journal

I might as well confess that I have increasingly been feeling an unfamiliar, almost physical joy. The very act of walking has become easier and more pleasurable. Decisions seem to make themselves. My first official day was by no means simple; yet I fail to see where I have made any mistakes. Whatever I did today I believe I did right.

Just where is Yonatan? Most likely still on the road. Nothing terrible, I'm sure, has happened. Soon we'll hear from him. At this very minute the lines I cast today all the way from the Negev to Miami are being tightened.

Hava is sleeping in my bed in the next room. Two hours ago I had the doctor give her a shot and she went out like a baby. I'll sleep on a mattress on the floor tonight. But I still don't feel the least bit tired. I've put a record on the phonograph—softly, of course, so as not to disturb Hava—and I'm listening to an Albinoni sonata. All's well with the world. The whole kibbutz is fast asleep except for the one lighted window I see from here. Whose can it be? Judging by the direction, most likely Bolognesi's. No doubt he's sitting up like me, muttering his charms and incantations.

When the Albinoni is over I'll put on my coat, hat, and scarf and make the rounds of the kibbutz. I'll look in on Yolek. I'll drop by the office. I'll even say good night to Bolognesi. The truth is, I just don't feel like sleeping. My guiding principle, which I've stated more than once in these pages, is that there is already enough pain in this world and that we mustn't do anything to add to it. Must even try, as far as such a thing is possible, to alleviate it. Stutchnik sometimes calls me the village priest. Well, the priest has been promoted to bishop. Yet he still has no intention of compromising with any of the cruelty, the insanity, the lies and suffering that people inflict on one another. Telling good from unadulterated evil is simple enough. The real difficulty, though, lies in telling the truly good from the seemingly good. Some powers appear in disguise. One must be alert.

It sometimes happens in the animal world, certain birds being an excellent example, that the migratory instinct splits off dangerously, even destructively, from the instinct of survival itself, so that the latter seemingly fragments into two elements, each threatening the very existence of the other. (Donald Griffin again.)

So be it.

Soon the watchman will wake Stutchnik for the night milking. How well I remember the gay blade of a pioneer's face he once had. Now the years have given him the look of a weary old Jewish shopkeeper sitting behind a rickety counter, studying the Talmud between his all-too-infrequent customers. For all that, he still insists on milking his cows every night and has turned down my suggestion that he replace me as bookkeeper. The man has always been stubborn, but now I see something bewildered and tragic in his eyes.

I'm off. It's early Monday morning. I'll go out to see what's new on Kibbutz Granot.

P.S. One a.m. The air outside was refreshingly brisk and heightened all my senses. The paths and benches were covered with a heavy dew, or perhaps a light rain. The whole village was asleep. I walked to the end, lighting my way with the little pocket flashlight I took this morning from Yolek's desk. What's that favorite expression of his? *Mea culpa.* I have expropriated a flashlight. No good will come of your Dostoyevskyizing, said Eshkol. Well, and what if it doesn't?

As I was walking down the path, something sprang out of the darkness behind me, giving me quite a start. Is that you, Yonatan? But the something, which proceeded to trot in front of me, was only Tia, who decided to join me on my stroll. Here and there we paused to turn off a leaking faucet, pick up a scrap of paper and put it in a basket, or turn off an electric light burning on a deserted porch. Tia cooperated by bringing me a torn shoe from a bush.

Near the club I met Udi on his way back from the office. He had finally managed to get through to Chupka with the news of the missing maps. The Negev, of course, is a very large area, but it does give us a clue. And a man out to commit suicide, as Udi argued, is not likely to take a set of 1:20,000 maps with him. I told him I hoped and believed he was right and sent him off to bed.

I found Yolek sleeping soundly on his living-room couch, though his breathing was heavy and broken intermittently by snores. Rachel Stutchnik was sitting in the armchair by his side, embroidering. Just as I had instructed. She told me that the doctor had been by twice during the night, given Yolek an injection, and found him slightly improved. In spite of this I decided then and there that I would have him sent to the hospital in the morning whether he agreed or not. I'd had enough of his whims.

On the path outside, Etan R. was sound asleep at the wheel of the pickup truck, just where I had told him to be. No, I see no mistakes in the arrangements I made today.

I did not, however, enter the last shack. Some inner discomfort held me back. Through the curtainless window, by the light of a bare yellow bulb, I did see Bolognesi, however, his head wrapped in a cloth that hid his rotten ear, a woolen blanket around him, sitting erect on his bed, his knitting needles clicking away, rocking rhythmically back and forth, his lips moving.

We stood there for a few minutes, the dog and I, sniffing the night breeze. Had not Rimona promised that winter was over and spring was on its way?

Some day, when all this is only a memory, I'll ask Hava to have Bolognesi over to my place for tea. No good can come of such total solitude. No good has come from my thousands of lonely nights of flute playing and journal keeping. Twenty-five years of them. How old would my oldest child be now if I had fought for P.? How old might my grandchildren be?

I purposely took a roundabout route to pass by her home. Darkness. The privet-and-myrtle hedge. Her underwear hanging on the laundry line. Shush, whispered the horsetail tree. Why haven't I given her so much as a single hint that I love her? Supposing I wrote her a letter? Supposing I brought her, one by one and without any warning, all forty-eight volumes of this journal? Should I? What better time than now, when Hava is installed in my apartment and I am the new secretary of the kibbutz?

Just then I saw the headlights of a car in the square in front of the dining hall. I hurried, almost ran, there, Tia loping in front of me. An army vehicle. The slam of a door. A rifle. A uniform. My heart skipped a beat. But no, it wasn't Yonatan; it was his younger brother Amos, sweaty and frazzled-looking. I sat him down on a bench beneath a light at one end of the square. Amos had been on a routine patrol along the Syrian border when a special car manned by the brigadier's driver picked him up and brought him straight home without explanation. Did I have any idea, he demanded to know, what exactly was going on and what all the fuss was about?

I explained it all to him as succinctly as I could. About his brother, his father, his mother. After asking him if he wanted anything to eat or drink, I considered for a moment bringing him back with me and waking Hava, but in the end decided against it. It could wait, and I'd already had enough melodrama for one day. If he wasn't hungry or thirsty, then, I wished him a good night's sleep.

And so I went home, giving Tia a long goodbye pat at the door and smiling at myself in sheer amazement. Since when have I become a dog-petter?

I'm writing these last lines standing up, without taking off my coat, hat, or scarf. I'm wide awake. In fact, I have an urge to go back out and stroll some more, perhaps even join Stutchnik and help him with the night milking as I used to do twenty years ago. We could harmonize our baritones again to some old poem of Bialik's or Tshernichovsky's set to music. Anything to avoid talking, because we have talked more than enough.

Yes, that's exactly what I'm going to do. I'm going to make the rounds once more. It's been a long, complicated day, and who knows what's in store for me tomorrow. Tonight's report is done. And so I'll say to myself, good night, Secretary Srulik.

17

His rifle dangled from his shoulder, his day-old beard was powdered with gray dust; his bloodshot eyes squinted in the harsh light. It took almost a quarter of an hour of wandering among the shacks and tents of Ein-Husub before Yonatan finally found the kitchen, where he wolfed down four thick slices of bread spread with jam and margarine, three hard-boiled eggs, and two cups of what passed for coffee. Surreptitiously making off with a can of sardines and half a loaf of bread for the trip ahead, he returned to Michal's room, lay down on her rumpled bed, and, drenched in sweat, slept for over an hour. In the end, the flies and the suffocating heat roused him. He got up, stepped outside, stripped to the waist, stuck his head and shoulders beneath a faucet, and let its warm, rusty water run over him. Then, his rifle and knapsack at his feet, he sat down behind an empty corrugated lean-to. He spread two maps side by side on the sand in the shade of its asbestos wall, weighted their corners with stones against the desert wind, and began to study them. He also leafed through the booklet entitled *Sites in the Arava and the Desert* that he had taken from Michal's shelf.

The route seemed simple enough. He would hitch to a spot just before Bir-Meliha. From there, in the twilight, it would be two-and-a-half kilometers by foot to the unmarked border running along the bed of Wadi Araba. He'd follow this bed in a northeasterly direction until he reached the mouth of Wadi Musa. Then a brisk walk up the wadi through the night.

Some five kilometers east of the border the Jordanian road runs south to Aqaba. I'll have to cross it carefully. Then, if I cover twenty kilometers during the night, I can reach the junction of Wadi Musa and Wadi Sil-el-Ba'a, where the ravine narrows to a deep gorge, by daybreak. I'll have to hole up there among the rocks, or in some cave if I can find one, and kill the day. Then, Friday night, I'll work my way up the gorge. After about two kilometers it swings almost ninety degrees to the south, and from there it's a pretty steep climb of some eight more kilometers to the outskirts of Petra. On Saturday morning I'll catch the sunrise there and maybe find out what this is all about. I wonder if Michal would have come with me. No. Don't kid yourself.

What's to see in Petra? According to Azariah Alon in this booklet, Petra is not, as was previously thought, the biblical Rock of Edom against which the prophets Jeremiah and Obadiah vented their wrath. I suppose Alon knows what he's talking about, but personally I don't give a damn. It could be the Rock of Chad for all I care. *Petra* means "rock" in Latin. And it happened to be the capital of the same Nabateans who lived in the Negev in the cities of Shivta and Ovda. A tribe of merchants, warriors, builders, farmers, and highwaymen. In short, a tribe just like us. Their king was called Haritat. They built Petra at the junction of the ancient road from Damascus to Arabia and the Darb-es-Sultan, the trade route from the desert to Gaza, Sinai, and Egypt. It was carved from the rock of a deep crater at the upper end of the wadi. Whole temples, palaces, royal tombs, and the great sanctuary called ed-Deir by the Arabs. All of this, it says here, has been standing *unmarked by the tooth of time for two millennia.* I like that: "the tooth of time." *Desolate and without a human presence.* Like my life. *Save for the generations of grave robbers who ransacked its red palaces.* And looted only to die. *For the past fourteen hundred years Petra has been uninhabited.* Except for the prowling fox and the night bird and the Bedouin of the Atallah tribe, who roam the area and make a living from herding and brigandage.

As he read still further, Yonatan's eye was caught by a line of English poetry that cast a strange spell over him:

A rose-red city, half as old as time.

He repeated the words over and over to himself, moving his lips silently, only to have his wife Rimona appear, lying cold and naked on the snowy sheets of their bed in the pale light of a summer moon that was turning corpse-white in the window. With a sad shake of his head, he went on reading.

At the beginning of the last century, John Lewis Burckhardt, an intrepid Swiss traveler, reached the ghost city disguised as an Arab. Looking down from a precipitous height, he caught sight all at once of the red shrines that time forgot and was staggered by their awesome majesty. For a full hour he stood there, a man turned to stone. Later he described in detail the enormous columns carved with mysterious glyphs, the stone galleries climbing one above the other in the torrid air like catwalks, the Greco-Roman auditorium built by the Emperor Hadrian, the palaces, the fortifications, the arcades, the temples, the tombs, and all of them rose-red. Oleander bushes blazed among the ruins. Whole forests of them grew in the gorge that wound up to the site. At sunrise and sunset the vaults and archways and sculpted rock flared upward in tongues of red, purple, and vermilion flame.

Half-awake, Yonatan sought to picture the magically moribund world that awaited him. The steep steps cut into the mountainside, the great staircase ascending almost two hundred meters above the city to the sanctuary of ed-Deir, its walls surmounted by Medusa heads. And still other stairs leading up to the Mount of Sacrifice, with its pool for collecting the blood of the victims, on either side of which, lifting skyward, were two colossal monoliths carved in the shape of human phalluses, the remnants of a vanished orgiastic cult. An unearthly dread, so the booklet reported, overcame all those who dared to climb the mount and look down on the nightmarish ruins below. Here and there among the mounds of debris the visitor to Petra might encounter human skulls and thighbones, even whole skeletons, bleached by the sun and preserved by the dryness and heat in a state of polished perfection. Even in the empty passageways of Petra the oleanders grow. Solitary lizards slither over the forsaken ground and jackals wail into the night.

Once upon a time myrrh and frankincense scented this valley. Its priests and priestesses lifted their voices in sacred hymns. Lewd pagan revels and human sacrifices took place side by side. Orchards, vineyards, and gardens, winepresses and threshing grounds, ringed the city. The desert gods dwelt in perfect peace with Baal, Aphrodite, and Apollo. Until all was struck down. The ancient gods perished utterly. Man turned to dry bone. An angry, wrathful Jehovah, as always, had the last laugh. *Who is it that cometh from Edom, in crimsoned garments from Bosra?* It is the God of the burning bush, of the fiery wilderness, Who has come to spread the stillness of death.

For fourteen hundred years the ghost city of Petra was not mentioned in a single known document. Only in recent times had a few moonstruck adventurers tried reaching it across the hostile border. A few had made it safely back. Nearly ten had died in the attempt. The Atallah Bedouin were a notoriously bloodthirsty lot.

He picks up and goes, said Yonatan out loud, swept by a drunken joy. He stuck the booklet in his pack, rolled up the maps, and slipped them under his shirt. It was almost noon. He badly wanted a cigarette. Oh no you don't! You're all through with that.

He stripped his rifle and cleaned it with a barrel rod and a flannel swatch, taking time to do a thorough job. Once it was reassembled, he lay down on his back, his head on his pack, his rifle resting on his chest, only to feel last night's thrill of pleasure once again in his loins. He yawned and stretched luxuriously. Scattered words and phrases from the booklet passed like clouds through his mind. Ghosts. Unearthly dread. Jackals. Human skulls. We'll go have a look-see. Once we've come back it'll be time enough for life to begin.

He dozed off. As flies paraded across his face, he envisioned his death that night from a burst of bullets in the chest or a curved dagger between the shoulder blades. There was no fear in the thought of such a death, alone in the wilderness on enemy soil, face down on the dark sand, his blood soaking into the dust like a venom purged from his body. In such a death, he might at last find perfect peace, as sometimes he had found it when, during a childhood illness, he had lain between the cool sheets of his parents' bed, in the dim light of the shuttered blinds, beneath his mother's quilt. Yonatan yearned for a death as gentle and painless as this, one that would turn him into just another rock in the stony desert, one that would leave him without a single thought or longing, cold, inanimate, and forever still.

Anyone looking at Yonatan at that moment could have easily detected beneath the mask of dust, the scraggly growth of beard, and the tangled, grimy hair the face of the delicate eight-year-old boy he had once been, the sleepy-eyed child always enveloped in a quiet sorrow, as if the grown-ups had made him a promise that he had been sure would be kept but still had not been. Even sleep, when it came to gather him up, failed to wipe away the lines of hurt from his face. So he appeared to the man leaning over him now, staring at him intently with light blue eyes, his gaze slowly shifting to take in the pile of equipment, the sleeping bag tied to the pack, and the rifle cradled on the young man's chest. A weary, compassionate smile spread over his face. With the tip of a long finger, he prodded the sleeping Yonatan.

"Hey, you *chudak,* dehydrate is what you'll do here. Come on now, let's put you to bed in style. In a fourposter, like a king. On sheets of royal purple, of byssus and lace."

Yonatan gave a start. Opening his eyes wide, he cartwheeled backwards, supple as a cat, gripping his gun with both hands, prepared to fight for his life.

"Bravo!" laughed the old man. "Bravo! What reflexes! Splendid! But have no fear. You face a friend, not a foe. A hat you have maybe? To be put on immediately. Tlallim."

"Excuse me?"

"Tlallim. Alexander. Sasha. That was one horrible dream I woke you from, eh? Come, *malenki* mine, off we go. When you fell asleep, there may have been shade here, but now it's a blazing furnace."

Yonatan glanced at his dead watch. His voice dropped to its lowest register. "Do you know what time it is?"

"The very best of times! Here, give me a hand, my love. We'll put you to bed in the royal palace until morning comes. And we'll feed you with sweetmeats and cakes. And bird's milk will be yours to drink. Come on, now. *Kushat i spat. Dayosh!*"

Yonatan vaguely remembered this tall, thin codger from last night, when, upon arriving in Ein-Husub, he had made out among the soldiers, workers, and transients a lanky, long-limbed bushranger with an unruly white beard, a naked, gray-curled chest as brown as a Bedouin's, and a pair of blue eyes peering merrily out of a copper-colored face.

"Thank you," said Yonatan. "But I've got to be on my way."

"*Nu*, hit the road, by all means." The old man grinned, his twinkling eyes sly and friendly. "Hit it as hard as you can. Only with what, eh? The only vehicle in all of Ein-Husub right now is Burlak."

"Excuse me?"

"Burlak, my beloved jeep. It was once the apple of General Allenby's eye. He used to take it for spins from Cairo to Damascus, but now it's my own pet. In a few hours Burlak and I can bring you with all honors to Bir-Meliha. You won't be slipping across the border before nightfall anyway. And what about water, *krasavits*? Do you really mean to try to get by on that one pathetic flask? Believe me, you'll die of thirst, man! I'll give you one of those plastic, *nu*, what do you call them, jerrycans. Then you'll have enough water to get you there. You call me Tlallim. Or Sasha. Or Grandpa. Whatever you call me, I'm still in charge of the desert around here. Come on, let's get moving. Just please stick a headpiece on that crazy skull of yours before I count to three. You call me Tlallim, and I'll call you *krasavits. Dayosh!*"

It took Yonatan a while to take all this in. He was dumbfounded but managed to stammer at last, "What border? What are you talking about? I was just—"

"*Nu, chudak.* It's no business of mine. You want to mislead me? So tell me lies. They say a lie has clay feet. Idiots! It has wings! And I can see, *zolotoy partsufchik*, that you had a gay old time last night, no? It's written all over your face. Never mind. You want to deny it? Deny! To lie? Lie to your heart's content! Who was it? Little Yvonne? Michal? Rafa'ella? Well, it's no business of mine. Between their legs they've all, heh, heh, got the same honeypot. Come in, please. We have tea, we have dates, and we have vodka. I'm strictly a vegetarian. A vegetarian cannibal, that is. You are my guest now. Sit! We'll talk. Eat. Drink. And then—*chort evo znayet.* God be with you! Or the Devil. Come on now. Let Burlak and me drop you off near Bir-Meliha, and from there you can go straight to hell, if that's where you're bound for."

Yonatan followed the old man into a dilapidated trailer at one end of the camp, near the perimeter fence. Its tires had gone flat long ago, leaving the rubber to fall apart and the metal hubs sunk halfway into the sand. The cool, dimly lit interior had a faintly disagreeable smell. It was furnished with two mattresses—one of them stuffed with rags, the other spilling wisps of dirty straw through a hole in its lining—and a peeling table on which stood a great many empty beer bottles, half-empty wine bottles, and a mélange of tin plates and cups, canned foods, piles of books, bread crusts, and eggs in a cardboard box. On a shelf tied by ropes to the ceiling, among numerous colorful rock samples, Yonatan made out a kerosene stove, a heater, a tin of tea, a broken accordion, an oil lamp, a blackened frying pan, a sooted-over Turkish-coffee beaker and an ancient Parabellum revolver.

"Step right in, *krasavits* of mine. My home is your home. My bed is your bed. You can throw down all your junk wherever you like. Sit, *malchik.* Make yourself comfortable. Relax. I'm not going to steal any of your treasures. You can hand me that rifle, though. There you go, we'll lay it down so it can take a rest too. Tlallim Alexander's the name. Certified surveyor, desert rat, devil of a fellow, geologist, lover, and lush. Life has he loved and its reprobates hated with the fury of a wild beast. To numerous frightful temptations has he his own soul subjected. Peace of body or of mind has he never found. Women has he worshiped above all things, and all his sufferings has he bravely endured. So much for me! And you, my boy, what are you? A desperado? A babe in arms? A poet? Here, have a shot of gin. I'm sorry, but I'm out of ice and soda. In fact, I never stock any and never will. But a warm, true heart, that I can give you. Drink up, *krasavits*, and then get it all off your chest. *Ay, mama*, just look at the tears this child is choking back. You *chudak-durak*, you! What bloody devils, I'd like to know, seduced you suddenly to go to Petra?"

The old man broke into a childish guffaw and wiped tears of laughter from his face. Just as suddenly he grew angry. Pounding so hard on the table that all the bottles jumped, he roared furiously, "Live, you bastard! Live and go on living! *Ty smarkatch!* You spoiled brat! You little snot! Have a good cry and live! Crawl on your belly and live! Suffer, you bastard, I say! Suffer!"

Yonatan winced. He hesitated, cringed, reached for the battered tin cup he had been offered, gulped some gin, felt it sear his throat, coughed, wiped his eyes with the back of his grimy hand, and decided to try to defend himself.

"Excuse me, friend."

"Friend?" roared the old man. "Have you no sense of shame? Bite your tongue! How dare you? The nerve! What friend am I of yours? The Devil is your friend! I'm Tlallim to you! Or Sasha! Not *friend*! Here, eat some figs. Eat! And some dates. And olives. There's bread too. And under those socks over there might be a tomato. You ate already? So eat again. *Paskudniak!* Eat, I said!"

All of a sudden, in a totally different tone of voice, his palms pressed against his cheeks, his head and torso swaying from side to side like a distraught mourner's, he wailed bitterly, "My child! *Zolotoy* mine! What have the bastards done to you?"

"Excuse me . . . but it's the furthest thing from my mind, what you were saying. The only reason I'm down here is because I was sent by my kibbutz to look for a fellow named Udi who disappeared a few days ago."

"Misery, *krasavits*! Misery and lies! There's no Udi and there's no Gudi. Listen. Sasha Tlallim is going to speak now about a matter of principle. If you want to, you can listen. If you don't you can go straight to the bottom pit of hell. *Dayosh!*"

"I'll have to go soon anyway."

"I said quiet! Tlallim has the floor now and *krasavits* will listen politely. What kind of education have you had? Where are your manners?"

Yonatan kept quiet.

"See here, my charmer. Let me explain a thing or two to you. Death is disgusting! Revolting! Abomination! It stinks! Not to mention that it will not run away. You're going to walk all night up that black wadi, yes, sir, and all night long you'll be pleased with yourself—ho ho ho, have I screwed them, have I given those bastards what they deserve, ho ho, they sure will cry for me when I'm dead, they'll rue the day they were so mean to me, they'll never forgive themselves for as long as they live. I'll be dead and they'll be sorry, eh? You damn fool! Next time they'll be especially nice to you, eh? Next time they'll love you properly, eh? And in the morning, you genius, in the morning you plan on hiding out there in the rocks? On going to sleep there like one big happy *durak*? You poor idiot slob, you! You'll be asleep and the Atallah will be following your fresh tracks up the wadi like the wind. No one's ever going to find better trackers than the Atallah in the whole of the desert. Though once they've got a whiff of you from afar, they won't even need tracks. And then what? You'll play at being a martyr? You'll play Custer's last stand? You'll regret that you have only one life to give for your country? Let Sasha teach you a thing or two. No life is worth giving for anything. Life is worth saving. Especially from the Atallah. If those demons get hold of a *krasavits* like you, a real peaches-and-cream kibbutz sweetheart, they'll fall on you like darkness. Before you can reach for your gun, they'll be ass-fucking away like mad. Ten, twenty, thirty Atallah, all with their pricks up your ass. And then down your throat. How does that grab you, *malchik*? And when they've fucked you fair and square, they'll kill you. But not all at once. They'll kill you piece by piece. First they'll slice off your ears. Then they'll slit open your belly. Then they'll chop off your cock. And maybe then they'll get around at last to cutting your throat. And you, O best beloved, will be screaming your guts out. Will you ever scream to high heaven. Like an animal you'll scream: Mother, Father, help! And when you can't scream any more, my dear child, you'll gurgle like a camel. Tell me, a slaughtered camel you've maybe seen once in your life? No? Khhhhhrrrr! Like that!"

The old man rose to his full height. His eyes rolled. His face was contorted. The gray curls on his naked chest bristled like porcupine quills. Unwashed, insane, berserk, his wild beard glistening like snow on a mountaintop, a hideous froth on his lips, he bent low over Yonatan, stinking of garlic, alcohol, and sweat, his face close enough to kiss him on the mouth. Then, from the depths, he gave vent to a horrible, bloodcurdling roar: "Khhhhhrrrr!"

Yonatan retreated to the end of the mattress and hid his face in his hands like a child bracing for a blow.

When he finally opened his eyes, the old man was shaking with silent mirth. His blue eyes sparkled mischievously as he poured the last of the gin into the misshapen tin cups.

"Enough of that little exercise," he said warmly. "Now have a drink with me. Get all that foolishness out of your head. Relax a little, and then, my best beloved, have a good cry. *Ay, mamushka*, you need to weep, not to die, to weep if it takes you all night. Well, what are you waiting for? Weep! *Yobtvuyumat*, I said weep!"

"Knock it off," said Yonatan lifelessly, his head thrust forward crosswise in a movement that resembled one of his father Yolek's efforts to hear. "Why don't you just drop it. I don't know what you want from me. I'm not going to any Petra. I'm not one of that crowd."

"Bravo! *Molodets! Stakhanov!* So you're just looking for Udi, eh? It's Udi who wants to go to Petra. You just happen to be down here and while away you are spending your nights shtupping Michal. Or was it Rafa'ella? Or little Yvonne? No difference there. As long as you get to the honeypot, *bozhe moy*, and have a stick to stir it with. Excellent! To live! To fuck and to live! To weep and to live! Death is filthy. Feh! Dirty! And it hurts too! Khhhhhhhrrrr!"

"Thanks. I've already got the idea. Thanks for the drink, and all the rest of it. Just let me go now," said Yonatan with as much firmness as he could muster. "I've really got to get going."

"All right, *malchik*, let's go."

"What?"

"You wanted to go, didn't you? Come on, then. We'll go harness Burlak and hit the road. Go to Petra. What do I care? Every man's his own master. When it comes to his own life, every idiot is as free as a king. Go right ahead. Die and enjoy it. Just take that, *nu*, that jerrycan over there, so we can fill it up with cold water for you. It holds a lot more than that puny flask of yours. Here, we'll tie it nice and neat to your back to make sure you don't die thirsty. What do they call you, son? By now they were walking out the door.

"I am . . . Azariah."

"Liar!"

"Sasha?"

"Go on. Lie all you want."

"You won't tell on me, will you?"

"You poor nincompoop! Shame on you! Bah! To die is a human prerogative! It's in the constitution! It's in the bill of rights! It's written in stone. Who am I, Stalin? *Ay, mama.* 'You promith not to tell on me? Naughty-naughty!' " The last in a high-pitched voice, mimicking that of a whining child. "Although if I were your father I'd beat the daylights out of you. Your behind would be as red and purple as a baboon's. Now allow me to introduce you. This beautiful devil here is Burlak. A sight for sore eyes, no?"

It was a broken-down jalopy of a jeep, one headlight discolored like a blackened eye and the other shattered. The front windshield was missing from a frame gone to rust. A woolen army blanket had been spread over the filthy stuffing that spilled from the tattered seats. In the back were some jerrycans of water and gasoline, a few red-and-white-striped surveyor's poles, a theodolite, some greasy ropes, a few rags, a box of K-rations, several samples of quartz and bitumen, and the torn remains of old newspapers. Matzos on the floorboards crunched beneath Yonatan's feet.

"My dearly beloved Burlak." The old man laughed, showing his fine white teeth. "Churchill himself once rode him into Venice, but now he's all ours."

The engine barked, yelped, hemmed and hawed, until suddenly the jeep took off, pitching Yonatan forward. The old man put it through a few twists and turns and ran over an empty oil can before reaching the main road. He drove with a Cossack spirit, pumping the gas pedal on curves and occasionally kicking the brakes, though rarely bothering with the clutch. Under his breath he hummed a broad Russian melody.

Where is he taking me? Straight to the police? Why do I keep attracting such crackpots? My father. My mother. Trotsky. Azariah. Rimona. Myself. From no more than a pace-and-a-half, what a dunce! How can you miss a bull from a pace-and-a-half? I could have killed him with my eyes closed. He must have missed on purpose because death stinks. Crawl and live! Suffer and live! But for what? At least I didn't crack. Didn't even tell him my name. Although maybe he's just mad enough to have guessed that too. In a minute he'll probably roll this jeep over and kill us both. What time is it? It's getting dark. By sunrise tomorrow I'll be dead anyway. My last night, this one. And a good thing too. Khhhhrrr! . . . Even a broken watch is right twice a day. And there I'm being waited for. Not forever, though. But I'm coming.

"Do you have the time?"

"Son," said Tlallim, "you've got plenty of time. The Atallah will be more than happy to wait. It so happens I was in Petra myself eight years ago. It's just another ruin. A pile of stones. Like all ruins. No Peterburg, Petra. Just one big hole."

"How come they didn't do you in?"

"Silly boy!" laughed the old man. "The Atallah don't take me for a Jew at all. And by now I'm really not one. I'm sort of a, *nu*, a holy man to them, a dervish, a *yurodivy*. And that's what I am around here too. You just ask about Sasha, how he rode to Petra on a camel like Father Abraham, with the Atallah wining and dining him all the way and their daughters dancing for his delight. I, O dearly beloved, am not a Jew any longer. I'm not even a man. I'm the Devil's own, a desert rat. Of life he could not get his fill. Women he adored. Vodka he did swill. The reprobates to trap him sought, the fools to lay him low. But he never said die. *Nikagda!* Come on now, *zolotoy* mine, please don't go to hell. Why don't the two of us take off and have a blast?"

"Sorry," said Yonatan, "Drop me at Bir-Meliha, and forget you ever met me, please. I don't owe anybody any explanation. My life's my own."

"A philosopher!" crowed the old man with the glee of a mind-reader who has just had an astonishing prediction come true and is taking a bow before an audience of unseen admirers. "Your life is your own! Original! Profound! Whose did you think it was, mine? The Devil's? Of course it's your own, *krasavits. Ay, mama*, it's a crime what those reprobates must have done to make you look the way you do. The bastards! Damn their souls! Well, go to hell then. Only take my advice. Don't spend the night. Come back to Sasha. Steal across the border if you must and have a peek at Transjordan. No harm is likely to come of it. Just don't go beyond their road. And then as soon as you reach it, turn around and come straight back. Lovely, eh? *Molodets!* And remember the name—Tlallim! Easy! Sasha! Come back to my royal palace tonight and stay for as long as you like, no questions asked—a day, a week, two years—whatever it takes for you to think the bastards have cried their hearts out long enough to have learned to treat you better. All the while I'll be offering you olives, figs, and dates, a bed of royal purple, and plenty of booze to keep you warm. Mind you, I'm a vegetarian by conviction. A vegetarian cannibal, that is. I'll even give you a face-lift. A brand-new kisser. You're already growing a beard. No one will know who you are. You can team up with me if you'd like and be my deputy surveyor. We'll ride the desert range, and you'll be the king's viceroy. Or if you'd rather not, no problem. You can spend all day long on your ass at my place and at night take your rod and make a beeline for the honeypot. No one in the whole world will know you're staying with me. How about it?"

"Pull over right here," said Yonatan. "This is where I get off."

"*Ay, mama!*" groaned the old man. "I've been foiled by the Foul Fiend again."

The jeep came to a stop, with an almost tender precision this time. Yonatan climbed into the back and threw his knapsack, blankets, windbreaker, jerrycan, and sleeping bag onto the sand beside the road. Then, clutching his rifle, he jumped down. The old man did not look up. He sat behind the wheel limp as an empty sack, chin down. Only when Yonatan began to disappear against a darkening embankment did he raise his magnificent head and say softly, "Take care, son." All of a sudden, from the depths of his chest to the ends of the desert, he thundered, "Wretch!"

Yonatan felt a wave of affection wash over him. Biting his bottom lip he struggled to force it all back.

The jeep drove off. The roar of its engine was gone. A breeze arose from the north. The desert darkened. At long last he was truly alone.

18

Night fell. The tepid desert breeze blew salty dust from north to south. The first stars were out, though a trace of light still lingered on the ridge line. A far-off scent of smoke tickled his nostrils and was gone. Yonatan stood on the embankment bent beneath his burden, as if waiting for someone to join him. He had a long pee, filled his lungs with air, and noted with satisfaction that he had not had a cigarette in nearly forty hours. He loaded his rifle with one of his three ammunition clips and slipped the other two into his trousers. It pleased him to think that never before had he been so utterly alone, so far from another living soul. Even Ein-Husub suddenly seemed a wearisome, noisy place of onerous chores. But that was all over with. The loudmouthed old man as well. It's all over with, he kept repeating to himself as if it were a password. Far ahead, in the mountains that rimmed the sky to the east, a weak light flickered. A Jordanian outpost? A Bedouin encampment? There lay the Land of Edom. The Kingdom of

Transjordan. The city half as old as time. The enemy's home.

Not a sound to be heard. Trying the depth of silence, Yonatan said, "Silence."

A milky vapor swirled at his feet. The breeze died down. A car sped by on the road behind. The noise of its engine roused him to action.

"Let's go. Now."

At the sound of the words his legs began to move. So light were his strides that he could barely sense them. Despite his load, his movements were silken. The soles of his paratrooper boots were Mercury's sandals. A slow, caressing relief spread through his limbs. Even the sweat on his brow felt pleasant, like a cool touch. The very ground he was treading seemed no harder than a carpet of ash left from a whirlwind of fire. Almost magically he was swept eastward, emptied of thought, emptied of longing, in the thrall of ecstasy. His potent muscles sang as they bore him along, wafting him on air.

Who's calling me? I'm coming. Didn't I always say I would? To another country? To a huge, mysterious city? And study and work and meet enchanting women and sit behind blinking panels? But who needs the women and the panels. I have my freedom. I have what I want and I don't give a damn. Let those Bedouin jump me right now. Who cares? I'll put my rifle on automatic and mow them all down. Tak-tak-tak-tak.

Azariah's story about the teacher who had his brains blown out by a bullet wasn't really true. And Azariah himself wasn't real. And neither were all those years. Or home. And neither are Michal and that old madman. What's real is my life that's beginning now. That's my justice, to be by myself in the night, to belong to the silence, to go at my own pace, heading eastward, taking a bearing on the highest peak.

A patriotic song kept running through his head. "What more, O what more do you want, our land, that we haven't given you yet?" A question for which he had no answer, but he couldn't stop humming the melody. "Full are our granaries, teeming are our homes." That's all over with. I have no more home. Up in that wadi in the mountains of Edom the nomads are on the move. And I'm a nomad now myself. I'm as good as dead to them all, but I've never been more alive to myself. No one will ever tell me what to do any more. Just let them try and I'll plug them full of holes. I was born dead. Like Rimona's baby last year. I never even asked what that Syrian gynecologist in Haifa did with her body. What do they do with the stillborn? Store them in some ghost town in the mountains? In special hideaways cut out of stone? Deep in the valley of the shadow of death?

Rimona's Efrat must be there. My daughter? Am I her father? How scary, that word "father." Me? And how could I recognize a child I've never seen? Among so many children? If I called her name out loud—Efrat!—would she come to me and give me a hug?

He wiped his brow with the back of his hand and slightly loosened his shoulder straps.

She used to put my hand on her belly to feel the baby move, and peer at me as if I really cared. Me? A father? Efrat's? The other baby's too? When she had that abortion? Madness!

Mysteriously, Yonatan had the sensation of the baby moving in his own belly. Just then, the soles of his boots made a crunching sound. Clearly, he was now walking over gravel. Am I in the bed of a wadi? It wasn't long before his feet could once again feel the silent sand beneath them.

Soon the moon will rise. That wadi I crossed a few minutes ago must have been Wadi Araba. That means I'm over the border. Out of Israel. In the Kingdom of Jordan, home of the cut-throat nomads. I'd better be alert.

How come I never cried over her? How come, whenever Rimona wanted to talk about her, I told her to cut it out? She was my child. How could I have forgotten that Rimona was pregnant two years before Efrat? Come on, I yelled at her, it's too soon for us to have children. The two of us are fine by ourselves. It's not my job to sire a dynasty for my father. I don't want my parents getting into bed with us. And so one morning she went to Haifa and came back empty. I bought her a record for a present and for five days she did nothing but listen to that record over and over. It was because of that abortion that Efrat was born dead. That's what the Syrian doctor said when he told us not to try again for a while, because Rimona was lucky to have pulled through. I killed my own two children. And I drove my wife mad. That was how the magic of Chad started.

What was that? A jackal? A fox? Nothing. Just stars and silence.

At this time of night we would have been putting Efrat to bed. Putting her into pajamas. Singing her a lullaby. Telling her stories and making animal sounds. I'm good at that. This is how the fox goes. And this, the hyena. We would have been giving her a warm bottle with some sugar or a little honey. Putting a teddy bear or a toy giraffe into bed with her. Don't be afraid, Efrat, Papa will lie on the floor beside your crib and hold your hand until you fall asleep. And Mama will cover you.

And then Rimona and I could have sat quietly in the next room, I with my evening paper and she with her embroidery or a book. Maybe she would have sung something. Before Efrat died she used to sing. Zaro and I could have played chess. And drunk coffee together. And Rimona could have ironed Efrat's blue dress instead of all her magic of Chad. One peep from her and the three of us would have run to change her diaper, to cover her, to give her a fresh bottle.

Why did I kill them all? Why am I killing them now? What did they do to me? What did I ever want that I didn't get? Who am I looking for out here in the wild? I must be stark raving mad. That old man in Ein-Husub called me a wretch. My mother is a wretch. And my father. For I killed Efrat, and that other baby before her, and turned Rimona into a corpse. And now I'm killing their son. And Zaro's a wretch too. It's only me who isn't, because here I am, as happy as a lark, going straight to hell. Let Zaro give her a baby? Let my father die? What was I thinking of all those rainy nights when I wanted to pick up and go? Warmth? Life? Love? Pain and anger mixed? Is that what I was missing? To kill? To be killed? To destroy? No, he isn't a wretch any more. In fact he's on top of the world. He's going to get Efrat.

Yonatan halted, wiped his face, and scratched his stubbly beard. He swallowed nearly half a canteen of water and strained to catch the slightest sound. There was none. But in the silent sky, a lightning-quick movement took place. A star bolted loose, traced a fiery arc across the firmament, and disappeared near the southern horizon. Its companion stars went on twinkling coldly, undismayed.

Yonatan adjusted his pack on his shoulders and shifted his rifle from his right hand to his left. He sniffed the air, then made up his mind to cut a little more to the north. Was that nearest hill on his right Jabel Butayir or Jabel-et-Teybe? Soon the moon would be up. But what was that rustling? A black shadow flitted past. A night bird? Am I the only thing breathing here? Or are they lying in wait for me, watching me this very moment? Quickly, with a light click, he cocked his rifle and stood stock-still. His heart beat wildly. He slipped shut the safety catch and forced himself to resume walking. Nothing to worry about. I'm heading straight for Wadi Musa. I'm not afraid because I don't care. Not tired, not hungry, not thirsty. Efrat has a brave papa. And the night has just begun.

What's out there? Who's shining that light on me? Is that an enemy outpost? A Bedouin torch?

It was a softly muted, otherworldly light. A slight shudder ran along the ridge line, and then, red, enflamed, huge, the moon emerged from behind the Edomite range. In an instant the world was transformed. Bright swaths of moonlight streaked the swarthy mountainsides. Ripples of the pale light eddied in the plain. Lifeless silver flowed silently over the lifeless earth. Here and there, a rock loomed. Fast as he walked, Yonatan could not escape the shadowy specters that split off from his body, dancing in ghastly shapes.

They are the ghosts. The Syrians we've killed. The Arabs my brother bayoneted. And Rimona naked on a white sheet, a frozen smile on her marble face. My parents in the valley of the dead, her head wrenched back, his sunk on his chest, amidst the ruins of Sheikh Dahr, soaked in the dead pale silver. They are dead. I am alive. I've murdered them all.

He fell face down on the parched, salty ground. What have you done, you madman, what have you done, it's your death. He grabbed his rifle, released the safety catch, and squeezed the trigger as hard as he could, whimpering like a dog. The butt kicked back against him. The smell of the gunpowder turned his stomach. The long volley merged with the pounding of his heart.

The desert and the wadi walls returned the fire with high, whining echoes, bullet for bullet, each reverberation more distant and muffled, yet proliferating, as if all the mountains around had taken up the challenge and were zeroing in on one another. The silence returned, and Yonatan knew there was no going back. He loaded a second clip and fired it off in one burst, raising his rifle, catching the moon in his sights, and blasting away at it to the last bullet.

He undid the buttons of his pants. He urinated in fits and starts, pissing and puking, puking and gagging out loud, his knees knocking, his stomach churning, his pants wet with his pee and his boots spattered with his vomit. A perfect target in the light of a full moon.

Panic-stricken, he spun around and took off on the run. He ran as he had never run in his life, stumbling without falling, lurching blindly down inclines, gasping for breath, sobbing aloud, a vicious stitch in his rib, his rifle held before him with both hands as if he were leading an assault, and he did not stop running even when his feet encountered the gravel bed of Wadi Araba again, he did not stop running until, ringed round by cobwebs of moonlight, he fell to the ground, face down in the silvery sand.

It was nearly three in the morning when he reached the trailer at the far end of the camp at Ein-Husub. The old man wiped his face with a filthy, tattered towel soaked in gin and icewater. It was half-past-three when Yonatan began to cry.

He slept all of the next day. In the evening the old man made him a salad and served it with dark bread and jam. Within a day or two Yonatan was doing the cooking. Before the week was out he was accompanying Tlallim on expeditions to survey sites and on forays to collect rock and mineral samples from all over the desert. He cleaned up the trailer. He scrubbed the theodolites. The old man called him *malchik.* He brayed with laughter every time he remarked, *Pshol von, ty chudak*, and Yonatan would respond with a faint, bewildered smile. One day, Yonatan happened to see that smile reflected in a broken mirror in a corner of the trailer, and he was struck dumb. It was an exact replica of Rimona's, the woman who had been his wife.

"Listen. Once I had a little friend who taught me a Russian proverb—'He who helps a friend in woe is like a fur coat in the snow.' "

"A lie!" roared the old man. "No such proverb in the whole Russian language! Never was! Never will be! A bald-faced lie!"

But nothing else is. I'm rid of my allergy. I've stopped smoking. And I've grown a beard. I'm beginning to understand. And my heart is getting true because everything is looking up. Maybe I should go see Michal tonight? Why not?

19

At last the winter came to an end. The rains had stopped. The clouds were gone. Punishing winds gave way to soft sea breezes. By the last week of March Srulik could sit every evening on his little porch and watch the flocks of migrating birds cross the reddening heavens on a northwesterly course.

Despite the winter floods the crops did well. By April the barley and wheat fields had spread ripples of green all the way to the hills in the east. Only now did the apple orchards burst into full bloom. The pears put on their nuptial raiment of trembling white blossoms, and westerly winds carried their carnal scent. The mud roads had dried up. The fig, the almond, and the walnut put forth their rejoicing leaves. Dormant grape arbors reawakened to their entwined green lives. The rose bushes, pruned during the winter, were again in bud. Early each morning, long before sunrise, the whole kibbutz echoed with the outcry of sparrows in treetops. The hoopoe tirelessly repeated its daily matins and doves cooed insistently under the eaves.

One Saturday, while walking in the ruins of Sheikh Dahr, Anat suddenly noticed, and quickly pointed out, five gazelles outlined against the sky. No sooner had Rimona, Zaro, and Udi seen them too than they were gone. In the courtyards of the Arab village the bougainvillea blazed through the stones, wild grape vines inched their tendrils up the smashed archways, acacia trees spread a fragrance thick as thieves. In a wagon hitched to a tractor, Udi hauled away from the ruins a large grindstone, a stone lintel, and a blackened threshing sled, all of which he displayed prominently in his garden. Forgotten, perhaps, was his plan to dig up a skeleton from the Arab graveyard and turn it into a scarecrow to shock the old-timers. Perhaps he had only been joking. Azariah brought back for Rimona a large, cracked pottery jar. He planted a red geranium in it and placed it in front of their home. "Yoni will like that a lot," she said. In her voice he heard neither joy nor sadness.

Every morning at four Little Shimon took the sheep out to pasture on the hills to the east. And once a day Etan R. cut a wagonload of alfalfa to scatter among the feedstalls in the cowshed. In the afternoon, their communal chores finished, the members of the kibbutz once again began to tend their little gardens, hoeing, pruning, and mowing. The news on the radio continued to report tension on the northern border, infiltrators, the imminent danger of war, the vigorous protests and warnings lodged by Prime Minister Eshkol with the ambassadors of the Four Powers. Sometimes, between one news bulletin and the next, an old Hebrew song tugged at the heartstrings.

Life went on. Except that in mid-April Stutchnik suddenly died.

One morning, on his way back from the night milking, he had entered Srulik's office in his boots, trailing a barnyard smell, and shyly asked for permission to send a telegram. To his only daughter in Kiryat Gat to come at once and to bring her husband

and children with her. When asked what the happy occasion was, Stutchnik turned pale and leaned on Srulik's desk. No more could be got out of him than a vague reference to something personal. Srulik wondered at the meekness in Stutchnik's voice. Gone were the days when he quickly lost his temper, argued with anyone in sight, attacked everything under the sun by dismissing it as a *muktse*, forever righteous and angry.

Once, he refused to speak to Srulik for six months because Srulik had proved to him that Denmark was not, after all, a Benelux country. Eventually he forgave, but not without insisting that Srulik's source was "badly out-of-date."

He declined a glass of tea, then extended his hand, which Srulik shook, not without surprise. Stutchnik turned around and trudged out of the office.

Srulik decided not to send the telegram before speaking with Stutchnik's wife Rachel.

But this time he was too late.

Stutchnik had gone home, removed his boots by the door, stripped off his work clothes, and stepped into the shower. Hours later Rachel found him, seated on the floor of the shower stall, his back against the tiled wall. His eyes were open. His sinewy body had turned blue from the torrents of water that had poured on it since early morning. His face bore a look of peaceful repose, the look of someone who has wept at great length and now feels better at last.

Srulik delivered the eulogy at the graveside. The deceased, he said, was a humble man and a good friend, though never one to compromise his beliefs. He valued comradeship, yet never backed down on a matter of principle. To his last day, Srulik said, indeed, to his last hour, he remained at his post. He died as he had lived, in humility and purity of heart. All of us would always remember his gentle soul until our day came to join him. Rachel Stutchnik and her daughter cried. Etan, Udi, and a few other young men spaded earth into the open grave. Azariah, too, grabbed a spade and tried to help. Once the grave had been filled, the mourners continued to stand around it as if waiting for something else to be said. But no one spoke after Srulik. The only sound was the murmur of the cemetery pines, answering the sea breeze in the sea's own language.

All day long, since his return from the hospital, Yolek sat in a deck chair under the fig tree near his porch. For hours on end, his arms resting limply on the sides of the chair, he would watch the magic of spring, as if for the first time in his life. On a small stool beside him lay a pile of newspapers and magazines, an open book, face down, a closed book, and his reading glasses. None of these seemed to hold any interest. Only the sights and the scents of springtime appeared to touch him. If a small boy in pursuit of a ball approached, Yolek would nod once or twice as if trying to puzzle out a difficult problem, only to pronounce, "A boy." If Hava came bearing his medicine and a glass of water, he submitted. *"Shoyn.* Everything is fine now," he would say. If the kibbutz secretary came to sit with him at dusk, to tell him of problems and solutions, Yolek would remark, "Really, Srulik, it's simple." Or, *"Vus brennt?"*

No more thunder and lightning, no more *mea culpa*s, no more biblical rage. The doctor found his condition stable. He had become an obedient, tractable patient. When Rimona came to see him, always bearing a myrtle branch or oleander blossom, he would lay a broad, ugly hand on her head and say, "Thank you. Nice. You're a saint." More often than not, the flowers would remain in his lap until evening.

His hearing had grown worse, almost to the point of deafness. Even low-flying jet planes savagely crisscrossing the sky failed to make him look up. After consulting Hava, the doctor, and the nurse, Srulik ordered the latest-model hearing aid. Meanwhile he rested with Tia drowsing at his feet, no longer bothering to chase away flies.

Every weekend Amos came home on leave. One Saturday he turned up with a ladder, a can of paint, and a brush to paint his parents' kitchenette. Hava presented him with a small transistor radio. Azariah brought a wheelbarrow full of concrete and patched all the cracks in the pavement and stairs so that Yolek wouldn't stumble. On Saturday nights they all drank coffee together and listened to the sports roundup. Once, to the amazement of all, Amos picked up Azariah's guitar and managed to play three simple tunes. Where could he have learned to do that?

And yet another little wonder: Bolognesi appeared one day with a blue woolen wrap that he had knit to protect Yolek's knees from the evening chill. Hava gave him the two bottles of brandy that were left in the house, one full and one half empty. Since his return from the hospital, Yolek no longer drank. "Bless'a God Who wipe'a away the tears of the poor," remarked Bolognesi.

Srulik, the secretary, had meanwhile been busily planning some innovations. After a number of feelers that amounted to a careful canvassing of the whole kibbutz, he succeeded in convincing the general meeting to approve funds for vacations abroad. Over the next fifteen years, it was calculated, each member would be awarded three weeks to see the world. Srulik also revived the youth committee, commissioned preliminary plans for adding a room to each of the family units, reactivated the singles committee. He also appointed a team to study the possibility of introducing a light industry. Young people, he felt, needed a challenge.

He still found time for his quintet. Having agreed to the group's public debut in the dining hall of a neighboring kibbutz, he had begun to put it through a weekly rehearsal. Late at night, framed by the square of light in his window, he could be seen at his desk, writing. Some said he was working on an article. Others that he was composing a symphony. Still others speculated that he was writing a novel.

Udi's Anat was pregnant. So was Rimona. Her Haifa gynecologist, Dr. Schillinger, said that anything could happen. The conception, to be sure, was against his better judgment, but statistics, if you asked him, was still a primitive science. However, he did not wish to take any responsibility for deciding whether the pregnancy should be continued. Perhaps it would turn out well after all. Srulik heard of all this from Hava, who had insisted that it was her right and duty to go with Rimona to the doctor and hear what he had to say, Rimona herself being so hopelessly distracted.

Each day, when she came back from her work in the laundry, Rimona found on the marble counter in her kitchen oranges, grapefruit, jars of honey, dates, or fresh cream that Hava had smuggled into the house. Once, finding a record of Mississippi blues instead, she recalled that it was Yonatan's birthday.

Every Thursday, Rimona baked Hava and Yolek a cake for Amos's weekend visit. Sometimes, on a Saturday night, Major Chupka dropped by. He would sit for a while with the family, Yolek, Hava, Rimona, Azariah, and Amos, drink a cup of coffee, put away a few sandwiches, and say little. Yonatan was seldom mentioned. Each in his own way had concluded that nothing terrible had happened. But Yolek, once, waking from his lethargy, snapped, "What's going on? That rascal is still busy? Not coming today either? About time he grew up!"

One Saturday night Chupka maneuvered Srulik outside to talk with him in private. He had some news, or rather, a rumor, that he preferred to share with Srulik alone. "It's like this: One of our boys, Yotam from Kfar Bilu, was down in the Negev this week with two other fellows to check out a new back road that the Bedouin have run from Bagpipe to Donkeyfoal Mountain. Where you cross Scorpion Gulch, there's a track that's never used any more. What we call the Nowhere Trail. They came upon a civilian jeep and a half-naked character with a Father Time beard sweating away trying to change a tire. He wouldn't let them help out. In fact, he began to swear at them. So they said we'll be seeing you and drove on."

"So?"

"Wait a second. Listen to this. Yotam swore to me that he

saw someone off in the distance who looked a little like Lifshitz, only with longer hair and a black beard. When they got near the jeep, only the old man was around. This other guy had scuttled off into the rocks like a lizard."

"And then what?"

"Nothing. The old man called them psychopaths and said that no one was with him. That they must have been seeing things. He even waved a pistol at them and swore at their mothers."

"And then?"

"Nothing. They just drove off."

"And your man? He's sure it was Yonatan?"

"No. He just thinks it might well have been."

"What do you intend to do about it?"

"Nothing now except poke around a little more down there. If he's alive and in the country, you can count on us to get him. Just give us time."

"And the old man?"

"Forget it, Srulik. I tell you, that whole desert down there is swarming with freaks. This whole country, in fact. How the hell would anyone know? This Yotam is slightly spaced-out himself. A year ago he told me he'd seen a lion in Gravel Gulch. And he's into ghosts and Ouija boards too. For my money, Srulik, we've got the highest percentage of nuts of any country on earth. Take care. And not a word to his parents about this."

After Chupka had departed, Srulik went to sit alone for a while in his office. It was hot and the mosquitoes were out in full force. If there really is a Higher Being, he mused, whether God or Whatever, I personally beg to differ with Him, or that Being, on several issues, some of them quite fundamental. He could have done everything in a far better way. But what I most dislike about Him, if I may say so, is His cheap, vulgar sense of humor. What He finds amusing is unbearably painful to us. If He gets such pleasure from our suffering, then He and I are in deep disagreement. It's almost eight o'clock and the general meeting's at nine. I'd better start going over the agenda right now.

On the fourth of May, at two in the morning, in the ruins of Sheikh Dahr, Chupka's men caught the murderer who had broken out of the prison not far from Kibbutz Granot some four months before. They found him sleeping like a baby in the sheikh's abandoned house, tied his hands behind his back with his shirt, and marched him off to the Afula police station. There, after vigorous questioning, Captain Bechor was finally satisfied that this client had never encountered Yonatan Lifshitz. All this time he had been living off the land, poaching chickens, stealing oranges from the citrus groves, drinking water from irrigation pipes. From time to time, too, he confessed, he was supplied with fresh clothes, matches, and even a bottle of arak by Bolognesi, who had come to know him in prison many years before. If you'd like, said Bechor, we can give that crackpot the third degree as well. No, thank you, said Srulik. Don't bother. Bolognesi is harmless. Leave him alone.

The tractor shed was now being run by Azariah Gitlin. He had a hired hand to help him. It had taken all of Srulik's influence to get the young mechanic's candidacy for membership approved at a general meeting, and since that time, Azariah's garrulousness had somewhat diminished. Only rarely would he inform Yashek and Little Shimon over breakfast that there is no embarrassment like a bad comparison or remind Etan R. of what Spinoza already knew hundreds of years ago, namely, that we must accept all things with serenity because fate in all its manifestations is as much the product of Eternal Decree as the sum total of the angles of a triangle must always be one-hundred-and-eighty degrees.

If someone prodded Azariah these days to hurry up and finish working on the combines before the barley harvest began, he would stick his hands in his pockets and drawl in the lazy voice he had picked up from Udi Shneour, "Haste killed the bear, my friend. Why don't you just leave it to me."

Yet he started the day before any of the others, rising at four with the first chill light, and put on the beat-up brown jacket Rimona had fixed for Yonatan. Now and then the two of them spent their evenings at Udi and Anat's or with Etan R. and his girlfriends in their room by the swimming pool. At such times Azariah not only played his guitar but felt free to air his political views. He also found time to turn the earth behind the house with a pitchfork and plant it with sweet peas, and to look after Yolek and Hava's garden as well. There he cheerfully hoed, raked, pruned, and mowed, fertilized chemically and organically, planted everything from cactuses to carnations, and decorated the fences with various gears, pistons, and other pieces of junk taken from the discard pile in the tractor shed.

Every day after breakfast, before returning to work, Azariah would sit for about ten minutes with Yolek under his fig tree, reading aloud from the headline news of the morning paper. Yolek didn't hear a word, since he loathed his new hearing aid and refused to wear it. Laying a large, leathery hand on the back of Azariah's, he might ask, with a trace of wonder, "Eh? What was that? What's new?" Or declare sadly, "Berl was an old fox himself." Or else, "No question about it, Stalin never liked us."

Azariah would straighten Yolek's knit woolen knee wrap before returning to the tractor shed. He saw to it that the vet who visited the kibbutz every two weeks gave Tia her annual injection, reconditioned and painted an old wheelchair in case Yolek should need it, and accompanied Rimona to Haifa to buy her maternity clothes. On that occasion he bought her a little English book from India on reincarnation and the way to inner peace.

He worked hard in the tractor shed and ran it well. By the time the barley harvest was at hand, the combines were not only ready but freshly cleaned and painted till they gleamed. During the first week of May Azariah sent a brief letter to the Prime Minister, assuring Comrade Eshkol that, despite the ridicule and ugly jokes at his expense, many of the common people loved him. Eshkol responded immediately in his own hand on an ordinary postcard. "Thank you, young man," it said. "You have bolstered my spirits greatly. Do not forget to pay my respects to Yolek and Hava. All the best."

Srulik continued to play his flute whenever he had the time, which was only at night. Hava had long since moved out of his rooms and ceased being a burden, but all day long he was being buttonholed on the paths of the kibbutz, or dropped in on at his office, by people with problems or requests. Would he please use his influence to help get them into or out of this or that job? Would he please be so good as to take this or that stand on this or that economic or educational issue? He made himself a little notebook in which to jot down each petition, crossing them out one by one as they were dealt with. Not until night came was there ever any time for writing or music. Yet wonders did not cease. It was said that Paula Levin, one of the original founding members of the kibbutz and a kindergarten teacher of long standing who headed the tots committee, had received an album of Dürer reproductions from Srulik out of the blue. What could such a gift mean?

What a pity Yolek's new hearing aid was gathering dust in a drawer along with his glasses. The man simply did not want to hear. Or to see. What a wreck his face had become. And the splendid spring had only made his hay fever worse. His breathing was loud and labored, and though he had stopped smoking altogether, his allergy often brought tears to his eyes. Few things could arouse in him anything more than a blank stare. Even when his young son Amos informed him that he planned to marry his girlfriend in the fall and had made up his mind to leave the kibbutz and join the professional army, Yolek's only response was "*Shoyn.* Fine. Never mind."

A letter from Trotsky arrived one day. It was not addressed to Yolek this time, but to the new secretary. He was sorry to say that he had still not heard from his son. In vain he had waited, but still refused to give up hope. And never would. Why should he? His only brother had vanished twenty years ago, yet he had not despaired of him either. All things were possible. Would Srulik agree on behalf of the kibbutz to accept a donation for the construction of a music room? Or perhaps a library or lecture hall? He beseeched the secretary not to turn him down. He was a lonely man, and no longer young. God only knew how many years he had left. And it was on Kibbutz Granot, in spite of everything, that he had spent the best days of his life and fathered his only child.

Srulik wrote back without delay: "Thank you for your offer. In two or three weeks I will bring it before our steering committee. I myself am in favor."

Azariah had put away the kerosene heater in the storage space above the shower and taken down the electric fan, for spring had already given way to summer. On the top shelf of the bookcase he had neatly arranged all of Yonatan's chess books. On the bottom shelf, in alphabetical order, he had arranged Rimona's books on Africa.

At ten-thirty the double bed was turned down for sleep, Rimona sat in her easy chair, in a sleeveless blue summer house frock that revealed her pregnant state. Her hands lay in her lap. A subdued light in her eyes. What might she see among the folds of the brown curtain? Perhaps the forms of the music that issued from the record spinning on the turntable—not *The Magic of Chad*, not the Mississippi blues given her by Hava, but a Bach violin concerto. Azariah could scarcely take his eyes off her, the stomach swelling beneath her small breasts, the thin knees parted slightly under her blue frock, the blond hair falling on her shoulders, on the left one a bit more than the right. The radiance of her face enveloped her like a fragrance.

She no longer copied out African charms on little index cards. She no longer shaved the light fuzz under her arms either. What was she waiting for? For the cake that was baking in the kitchen? For Azariah perhaps? Almost manly-looking now, not so homely as before, he sat quietly pondering some chess problem on the little board Yonatan had carved out of olive wood. The board was set with only a few pieces: the black king and queen, a black rook and black knight, two black pawns, the white king and queen, two white rooks, and one white pawn. He was taking his time. All was still in the house except for the sound of the turtle scratching away at his cardboard box on the porch. Once Azariah had a secret name for him, Little John. Now he simply called him The Turtle. Once he had played chess intuitively, gambling on wild inspirations. Now he studied it systematically from the books and journals Yonatan had left behind. Once he had relied in the tractor shed on his knowledge of mechanics acquired in army workshops. Now he pored over the maintenance manuals of Ferguson, John Deere, and Massey-Harris. Once he had chain-smoked at this very table across from Yonatan. Now he had cut down, having read in the newspaper that smoke was harmful to pregnant women and could even endanger a baby in the womb.

Rimona suddenly got up from her chair and smiled at Azariah like a child whose naughtiness has been forgiven. She went to the kitchen to test the cake with a match to see if it was done. It was not. As she passed him on her way back, her fragrance of lemon shampoo and bitter almond soap wafted over him. She laid a hand on his forehead, and he responded by touching her on the shoulder.

"Rimona, do sit down."

"Next to you, so you can explain something in chess to me? Or where I was before?"

"Next to me."

"You're so good."

"What have I done?"

"You took him some lettuce."

"I did? Who? What lettuce?"

"The turtle. And you fixed our faucet."

"Because that drip was getting on my nerves. I put a new washer in."

"I'll bring you some tea now and soon there'll be cake. I'll have tea too. Not hot tea, though. Cold."

"Incidentally, I just happen to have had something to drink. With Etan and his volunteers. Did you know he's got a new one? Brigitte, you remember her, has gone. Now there's Diana. But Smadar is still there."

"That's not true," said Rimona cautiously.

"What isn't?"

"Incidentally. Once you explained to me that nothing was incidental. You said that Spinoza discovered that. And you told us about your teacher, Yehoshafat. I believed you, but it made Yoni sad."

Azariah removed a white rook from the board, replaced it with a knight, and shook his head. "You remember everything, don't you? You never forget a thing."

They lapsed into silence. The violin concerto concluded in diminuendos of resignation. The cake was done. Rimona sliced and served it, then poured them both cold tea. "I dreamed about Yoni last night," she said. "That he was in some army barracks playing your guitar. You could see in the dream that he liked it, and that all the soldiers who were there did too. You were also there, knitting him a sweater."

Although the cold weather was long gone, and Rimona no longer pulled her hands back into her sleeves, she still gripped her glass of cold tea with both hands as if trying to warm herself.

The floor gave off a subtly clean smell. Azariah absentmindedly shifted his gaze to the bookcase on the other side of the room. The framed gray snapshot of Rimona and Yoni on their honeymoon in the Judean Desert caught his eyes, a squashed jerrycan in the sand before them, behind them the back of a jeep. It's an odd thing, he thought, but I never noticed that there's someone else in that photograph, a hairy leg in shorts and paratrooper boots.

"He had ten or twenty children, and he was a poor man. He played the organ in church and he did not earn much. Mrs. Bach had no time for him with all her children. Surely he had to help her with washing and cooking, he had to borrow money to buy coal, since it's always winter in Germany. It was very hard for him, yet sometimes he exudes joy."

"I've had no one since I was a child," said Azariah.

Rimona asked whether she should turn on the radio for the eleven o'clock news.

"Forget it," said Azariah. "They talk endlessly, not realizing that we are on the verge of war. Everything points to it: the Russians, the arms race, their impression that Eshkol is weak and sheepish and that we are all tired."

"He is good," said Rimona.

"Eshkol? Yes, he is, though even someone like me reads the situation better than he does. Only I've decided to keep my mouth shut. What I have to say always makes them laugh."

"Wait," said Rimona, "wait, Zaro, time will pass, you will grow and they will start listening. Don't be sad."

"Who's sad?" Azariah asked. "I am not. Just a little tired and have to be up at four. Let's go to sleep."

In bed, by the glow of the radio, which was playing late-night music, he kissed her tenderly a few times. The doctor in Haifa had advised that since her pregnancy was not a routine one, she must refrain from completed sex. She moistened her palms with saliva and began stroking Azariah's penis between them. Almost at once his sperm jetted upon her fingers, and he buried a high, sharp cry in her hair. Once at peace, he kissed her in the corners of her eyes.

By the time she returned from the bathroom, he was already

sleeping like a child. She turned off the radio and lay down wide awake beside him, listening as peacefully as the earth itself to Efrat breathing in the dark. As soon as Efrat had fallen asleep, she did too.

Much later, near midnight, Srulik passed by on his nocturnal stroll. He turned off the sprinkler that Azariah had forgotten to tend to on the lawn.

20

By four, Azariah was out of bed and off to work in the tractor shed. After changing the radiator in a D-6 and fixing an oil leak in one of the combines, it occurred to him to remove the picture of the Minister of Welfare that he had clipped from an illustrated magazine during the winter. In place of Dr. Burg, he put up a colorful picture of the sea, which had been much on his mind as the summer heat grew more intense.

Rimona was off to work in the laundry room two hours later.

"So how's everything?" asked Hava. "Are you sure you're all right? Nothing hurts? Just remember you're not to carry anything."

"I made you a pot of orange marmalade yesterday," said Rimona. "Please don't forget to look for it. I left it on the marble counter in your kitchen."

In the metal shop a barefoot Bolognesi donned his welder's mask and set to work repairing chicken cages. Sparks flew in all directions. "By day'a drought consume'a me an' frost by night," he mumbled.

Etan R. had made some far-reaching changes in the cowshed. Now that stubborn Stutchnik was gone at last and there was no one to stand in the way of progress, he lost no time in streamlining the operation. Both his girlfriends worked alongside him, and the lunacy of the late-night milking had been relegated to the dustbin of history. The three of them now began the milking at the eminently civilized hour of nine p.m. On finishing around twelve, they would go for a starlit dip in the pool, open a bottle of wine, and let nature take its course.

Finally yielding to suasion, Yashek had agreed to take over Srulik's old job as bookkeeper. Since it was off-season in the citrus groves, Udi Shneour was once again working in the grain fields, swearing he would straighten out the mess come hell or high water. His wife Anat was due in December.

From time to time the two of them would have Azariah and Rimona, who also expected to give birth in early winter, over for Turkish coffee with cardamom. Udi still enjoyed talking about past and future wars. Azariah had a penchant for politics—Nasser's trouble in Yemen, the dilemmas facing King Hussein, the blindness of Eshkol and his cabinet—and for the dark labyrinths of the Russian soul. Azariah was no longer the object of snickers behind his back. He had learned the art of pausing for effect between one sentence and the next and of making people laugh when he wanted them to. He had also mastered the trick of interrupting himself with an unexpected rhetorical question, the unconventionality of which tended to make his audience feel it was considering the subject without prejudice for the first time.

Azariah had long since given up strutting about in cuffed gabardine slacks, haunting the high-school girls' dorm, boasting of telepathic and telekinetic powers, and exasperating Srulik with his feverish confessions of undying love. Upon leaving the dining hall after supper he would put an arm around Rimona's waist, his green eyes glinting with the unspoken arrogance of a male who has taken another male's female and might do it again any time he wants. At last all could see who he really was. And they had seen nothing yet. The day would come when only historians would recall Yolek Lifshitz, but every child in the land would know that Kibbutz Granot was the home of Azariah Gitlin. Gitlin? Shouldn't he perhaps adopt a more Hebrew-sounding name, like Gat or Geytal?

These days he was in consistently high spirits. After putting in fourteen hours in the tractor shed, he still managed to find time to be with Rimona, to socialize, to help out Hava, tc play the guitar, to chat with Srulik, to bone up on professional literature, to improve his chess, to keep up with world and national affairs, to crack a book of poetry, and even, now and then, to take yet another peek at Spinoza.

Azariah had grown tan. The summer sun had singed his light head of hair, which had grown longer since his arrival last winter, when it was short as a hedgehog's. A scar on his chin courtesy of some red-hot engine oil had given him a no-nonsense look. Come August, he promised himself, he would learn to swim and take driving lessons.

He had even become a source of comfort to others. One day, with tears in her eyes, Anat accosted him in the tractor shed and begged for a private talk. Azariah took her aside to the very spot behind the hayloft where, many years previously, a maniac had fired his revolver at everything in sight. She could not go on living like this any longer, she said. Udi had become an animal.

Now that she was pregnant he was spending every night with Etan and his two whores in the swimming pool and not coming home until three in the morning.

Azariah recalled how this same tearful young woman had once taken cold-blooded pleasure in teasing him, in making him play peekaboo with the hem of her dress and her neckline, in driving him half out of his mind with the foul torments of lust.

He put his hand gently on the nape of her neck, overcame a momentary hesitation, and reminded her of all this. Not letting himself be flustered by her blushes, he proceeded to speak about the recalcitrance of the flesh, how it was different with men, far removed at times from any emotion, piercing, almost like pain. He tried to explain to her that Udi was still partly a child and that all his boastful war stories, his bravado about killing and death, and his deliberate coarseness came from the same inner fear of being tender or soft. When Anat's eyes overflowed and she begged him to tell her what to do—look the other way? quarrel? move out?—Azariah only said, Anat, you know he is frightened, try to help him not to be, only don't ask me how, because you are the one who knows him. She went on crying for at least ten minutes while Azariah stood there, holding her by the arm until she felt better.

Now and then he would have a chat with Hava too, often talking about his childhood. For some reason he felt the need to tell her things he had never been able, or wanted, to disclose to Yoni, Yolek, Srulik, or even Rimona. About the hungry years on the run in the forests, villages, and snows of Russia, about the freight trains all the way across the Urals, about the filthy cities of Asia and their sweltering steppes. About having no parents. About the horrid old aunt who tyrannized him until she went out of her mind in an immigrants' camp in Israel. About his years in the army that failed to break him, though he had been humiliated and picked on, because from the time he was little he had believed he had a mission. And about how the winter night he had arrived, Yolek had been so caring toward him, and you, Hava, took me for the first time to the dining hall, and then Yoni came to take me to work the next morning. It made Yoni angry to be told that there was no choice, and angry too that nothing ever happened here, so that one day was just like the next. He used to talk to me about setting out for Bangkok or Karachi, places like that, and couldn't believe that I was happy to stay put and live in one place. He even laughed at me for being that way and once he almost hit me, but we are brothers all the same. Whenever she asked him where he thought Yonatan was, Azariah could only tell her that Yoni had been unhappy and had gone away to be by himself and perhaps to punish everybody else.

"Oh, you can talk, all right," Hava would say, with more wistfulness than malice, and pour him a cold soda to drink.

One evening she asked him to play something on his guitar for them, because it would make Yolek happy. Azariah complied with the haunting melody to Tshernichovsky's "Play, Play Upon My Dreams," but Yolek gave no sign of hearing a note. Later, Srulik dropped by to say good evening, and when the two men left together, he asked Azariah to serve as an instructor in the summer work camp for city youth. Although Azariah was thrilled, he protested that he had too much work to do already and forced Srulik to take a good five minutes to convince him. That same evening, having found a broken old fan in Etan R.'s room, he took it apart, repaired and reassembled it, and, before going to bed, carried it over to Bolognesi, whose low-ceilinged room was stifling on these hot nights.

Summarizing the day's events, Srulik wrote in his journal:

There is apparently no social or political remedy for the simplest, most common suffering. One can try to do away with the master-slave relationship in the outward, material realms. One can put an end to hunger, bloodshed, and the grosser forms of cruelty. I am proud of the fact that we have fought to accomplish these things and have proved that the battle is not hopeless. So far, so good. But that's where the trouble begins.

I say "the battle"—yet as soon as I say it, I sense, staring down at me through the thin curtain of ideology, the savage peaks of a suffering far more primeval. The very suffering that drives all of us to look constantly for battlefields, for "challenges," to fight, to defeat, to win. How shall we tame the ancient instinct to seize, in Rimona's words, a spear or a sword and run after an antelope and stalk it, hunt it, kill it, and then celebrate the killing? What can we do against the weariness of heart, the subtle, cunning cruelty which is not openly sadistic and can even masquerade as the most reasonable and "constructive" of behaviors? What shall we say in the face of the secret brutishness lurking within each of us, what our forefathers called the uncircumcised heart and what even a logical-minded, self-disciplined, monkish, musical village priest like myself sometimes discovers in his own soul? With what weapon can we repel this interior wilderness? How can we overcome our dark desires to dominate others, to humiliate them, to subjugate them, to make them dependent on us, to chain and enslave them with the gossamer threads of guilt, shame, and even gratitude?

I have just reread my last few lines. "With what weapon can we repel?" "How can we overcome?" Even as I seek to avoid the horror, the horror is infecting my own way of speaking. To repel. To overcome.

I am seized by fear and trembling.

The mountains and the desert say nothing. The very earth is dumb. The sea booms, but it booms indistinctly. The sky burns by day and freezes by night. Winter follows summer and summer succeeds winter. People are born and die, and slowly all things disintegrate. Our surroundings. Our thoughts. My hand that writes. This pen, this paper, this desk. All our beliefs and convictions. Families. Everything is consumed by the cancer of time. Decomposed like the notes of my flute in this lonely room at night—sounding forth, dispersing, then gone. All things entropize. Everything unravels. Even as they persist they are on their way to nonbeing. The strongest emotions. Words. Stone buildings. Fortified cities. Whole nations. Perhaps the stars above as well. Time devours all. And yet all the while human wisdom goes on trying to distinguish the good from the bad, the true from the false, though it too must crumble before the onslaught, which grinds to smithereens the good, bad, right, wrong, beautiful, ugly labels that we seek to pin on things.

When I keel over one morning and die alone like a bug on the floor of this room, the slate will be wiped clean. A note was heard but it is heard no more. To quote Bolognesi, Bless'a the name of the Lord Who grant'a a perfect peace. But there is no perfect peace. Time that takes us apart will take away all traces of us. As the waters cover the sea. Would it have been any different had I been loved by a woman? Had I had children and grandchildren? The waters would have covered the sea just the same. I am seized by fear and trembling.

What exactly is it, then, that has been happening to me? All of a sudden, on the brink of old age, I have begun to crave a smidgeon of power and honor. Not only to crave them, but to get them, absurd as that may sound. Why, what better example could there be than Yolek, a man sated with honor and power. How I have envied him all my life, how I have longed to be a witness to his downfall, suffering, anguish, even death, so I could take his place. Why, though? To be loved? But Yolek was not loved. Eshkol is not loved. Who is? And Bialik, in one of his poems, asks what love is. Well, just for the record let me answer.

My dear poet, you'll have to forgive me, but I don't know either. It's a rumor. A fleeting shadow. A will-o'-the-wisp. Is this what Yoni went to look for God-knows-where? What Azariah came here to seek? Is there such a thing at all? I can't help smiling as I write this—a man of my age and position mewling like a schoolboy about whether love exists. And yet I insist on asking, does it or does it not? And if it does, how can it possibly when all other things contradict it?

I could take, for example, any father and son. Or any two brothers. Or any husband and wife. All of them, like carriers of the same mysterious virus, harboring their own particular loneliness, their own particular estrangement, their own particular pain, and their own dark desires to inflict such pain on others. Or if not to inflict pain, to use others. To change them. To mold them. To dominate them. To reshape whomever they most love like a lump of putty in their hands. As the waters cover the sea. If I had a son or daughter of my own—a Rimona, say, or a Yoni or Azariah—then would not the cruel inner tyrant in me be brought out too, like a monstrous shadow emerging from the darkness to knead, crush, and reform that child in its own image or that of its most secret desires? Had I dared when I was young to tell P. I loved her, and had she agreed to be mine, wouldn't a Fifty Years' War have broken out on the spot? The Gorgon and the Basilisk? Who will subdue whom? Who will bend whom to his will? And even assuming that such a hideous struggle had taken on the subtlest, most genteel form possible, without claws, without blows, without even a raised voice, would that have been any comfort? How would that have helped to rid us of the pain? For that matter, what can a man of modest ambition do by himself to mitigate the pain, even in his own immediate circle?

Having spent my whole life in sterile observation of what goes on outside my window, I know that in the end there's no way, that pain inheres too deeply in the nature of things, that we are attracted to it like moths to a flame in whatever good or bad we do, and that implicit in all our carnal appetites, in our most private sexual fantasies, in our philosophies, in our parental roles, in our friendships, in our creativity, even in our declared intention of ministering to the suffering around us, is the secret wish to inflict yet more pain as well as to suffer it. What an infernal verse in Genesis: "Sin lieth at the door, and unto thee shall be his desire, and thou shalt rule over him." Perhaps it means:

To take pain.
To inflict it.
To pity.
To inflict yet more to pity more.
To do so to another and to self.
Unto pain shall be thy desire, and thou shalt rule over it.

Rule over? Horribly enough, the monstrous shadow is already ensconced in the very heart of this nobly sensible commandment, tainted as it is by the exhortation to *rule.* What does that mean, to rule? What, if not to suppress? To put down. To crush. And then to pity and set free, as it were, so as to crush again more subtly. *To rule?* Over pain? While pain itself is the rule?

What a farce it all is. What a crude joke is being played on us. So banal and vulgar, so repetitious.

What is that saying Azariah is so fond of? "Only the man who has gone down to defeat knows that the taste of triumph is sweet." Defeat? Triumph? No, thank you. All I ask is to know how the pain can be lessened, even if slightly, even if for a time. Through solitude? Asceticism? Language? Or, on the contrary, through mindless ecstasy, sensual riot, turning a deaf ear to everything but the clamor of the blood? How dearly I would like to know the answer.

> Matthews calls this "purposeless navigation," not because, in his opinion, it has no biological value, but because its function is simply not known to us.

And Yolek was also right. As always. This impossibly self-indulgent man saw right away that the bizarre, suspicious-looking, hysterically garrulous boy who turned up here one winter night had something special about him that needed to be cultivated, that he might accomplish great things one day and even prove a blessing to us all. Only how did Yolek detect it? Honesty compels me to admit that had it been up to me, and had I been secretary at the time, I would probably have sent Azariah right back out into the night, whether out of caution, narrow-mindedness, the inner equivalent of a shrug, or just a simple disinclination to stick my neck out.

What magical power made Yolek, in his way, and Rimona, perhaps in a totally different way, adopt Azariah? I wish I knew. But I don't. I am sorry. I'll stop here because it's late.

21

The agricultural season was at its height. The days were long and hot and the nights were short. No breeze. Harvesting was done in three shifts, at night too, by the floodlights. Soon fruit picking would begin, followed by the grape and cotton harvests. On the northern border hardly a day went by without firing. One night the kibbutz was hit by border raiders, who sabotaged the water pumps, blew up the empty tin shack in the citrus groves, and crossed back into Jordan before dawn. Nearly everyone—men, women, and children—spent an hour or two weeding and thinning the cotton plants before the regular work day began.

Azariah put in a fourteen-hour day to keep the farm machinery running. Even so, he managed to find time every evening to sit with the campers, discuss and defend kibbutz life, and sometimes lead them in song on moonlit nights.

On the fourteenth of May, our watchman shot and killed an infiltrator by the perimeter fence. On the seventeenth the barley harvest ended and the wheat harvest began. The following day the chamber quintet gave a recital in the dining hall of the neighboring kibbutz. Two days later, as evening began to fall, Yonatan Lifshitz returned. The next day he was back in the tractor shed in his work clothes as if he had never been away. He had grown a black beard, turned brown and lean as a Bedouin, and had as little to say as ever.

Chupka in person, so it was said, had collared him by a kiosk in Yerucham. "Let's go home, pal. You've caused enough trouble already," he said. "Now get into the command car." "Okay," said Yonatan, "just let me get my things." It was evening when he finally arrived at the kibbutz, reluctantly kissed his parents, reached out to touch his brother, and lugged his knapsack, rifle, windbreaker, greasy blankets, and dirty sleeping bag back to his place. While in the shower, he asked Azariah to throw his things into the overhead closet and put his rifle in the chest under the bed. When he emerged, he asked what was new. And said no more. Until Rimona arrived, when he stated, "Okay. I'm back."

"You look nice with that beard," she said. "And with that tan. And you must be hungry."

The two of them, Azariah and Yoni, slept in the living room that night, leaving the bedroom to Rimona. They continued to do so on the following nights too, Yoni on the couch and Azariah on a mattress on the floor. They moved the radio to their room so they could listen to the news.

"Tia looks fine," said Yoni one night just before falling asleep. "And you took good care of the garden too."

"I promised I would," said Azariah.

Every morning they rose early to go to the tractor shed, returning only at nightfall because there was plenty of work. Then they would shower, drink cold tea or coffee, and sometimes play a game of chess. Azariah won as a rule, though sometimes they adjourned midway. Seated at the chess table pondering a move, Yonatan, with his black beard, slightly sunken eyes, and a cast of new-found seriousness about the mouth, resembled a young scholar of proud old rabbinical stock who was studying to become a rabbi. Yolek, however, in one of his rare moments of lucidity, made a face and muttered, "*Yoh. Azoy vi a vilde chayeh.*" "Yes, like a wild animal." Yolek's hearing aid was gathering dust. Most of the day he would sit in the garden and at dusk they would push him in the wheelchair back into the house.

For a day or two, it seemed, he had a new pastime: Bolognesi gave him knitting lessons. Yet after completing ten or twenty rows of stitches he had had enough. Most of the time he slept. He would doze sitting up and even at bedtime he would refuse to lie down. With a throw over his knees, a drop hanging from the tip of his nose, and spittle drying in the corners of his mouth, Yolek could sit sleeping for nearly twenty-four hours a day.

On summer nights Prime Minister Eshkol would sit up long after midnight in his Jerusalem office, his secretaries gone home, the night operator dozing off by the telephone, his bodyguard on the couch by the entrance, city lights shimmering in the windows, heavy trucks growling outside. Leaning his elbows on his desk piled high with documents and letters, the Prime Minister would bury his face in his hands. At last his chauffeur would appear and politely suggest, "Excuse me, sir, perhaps we'd better go home."

"Right you are, *yunger mann*," Eshkol would reply. "*Geendikt.* Let's go home. What more is there to do here?"

At the end of that summer Azariah and Yoni decided to make their own wine for the winter to come. Yoni hauled ten crates of muscatel grapes from the vineyard. Azariah rolled home an old barrel he found behind Bolognesi's metal shop. The two of them pressed the fruit, strained the juice, and added just the right amount of sugar. The must was left to ferment. When the time came, they siphoned the cloudy liquid from the barrel tap into empty soda bottles.

Rimona had grown heavy. Sometimes she would bump her shoulder against a door or run into a table. Frequently, when she started to ask for something, she would immediately forget what it was. Twice a week Hava would come to clean up the apartment. She did all the baking and took care of the laundry. Occasionally she would sit with them for a while after her chores were done, though she never seemed to know what to say.

In December, Anat had a firstborn son, Nimrod. Two weeks later Rimona gave birth to a daughter. Although the baby was slightly underweight, the birth itself went off without a hitch. When Azariah suggested that they call the child Na'ama, Yonatan's only response was "Why not." The baby's crib was placed in the bedroom with Rimona, and the two men continued sleeping in the living room.

The rainy season returned. It poured all day long. Since there was little to do in the tractor shed, Azariah and Yoni would rise late in the morning and stay up until late at night. They drank the wine they had made in the summer.

And so 1966 came to an end and 1967 began. Once again Rachel Stutchnik was asked to look after Yolek to give Hava more time for the children. After putting a bib over his nightgown, Rachel spoon-fed him a soft-boiled egg every morning and made sure he had some tomato juice or lukewarm tea. She helped him get to the bathroom and cleaned, washed, and shaved him every day. Yolek was near-comatose. When Hava drew up a chair to sit by him and hold his hand in hers, he probably did not even notice. A dozen times a day she would look in on her grandchild in the nursery, where she never failed to scold the housemothers and give lessons on how to do things properly. Between rains, she proudly wheeled the baby around the kibbutz.

"Just look at her, Srulik!" she would say to the kibbutz secretary. He would bend over the carriage sheepishly and say, "Yes, yes indeed. A little charmer." Hava's face would light up and continue to glow for a long time even while she sterilized bottles, boiled sheets and diapers, scrubbed floors with a mixture of soap and chlorine, and annihilated every single germ that dared make an appearance in the toilet bowl.

Oblivious to her two men, unmindful of the winter storms, Rimona would sit and nurse Na'ama. Her breasts had grown heavy, her thighs had thickened, and her eyes seemed always half-shut. Seated in the armchair she would take out her breasts, squeeze one of the nipples until it spurted, and give it to the baby to grasp. When that nipple was finished, she would give it the other. Her face, now grown rounder, shone with a soft radiance like a nimbus around a full moon. Now and then she would lift the infant to burp it. In her absorption, she often followed suit without bothering to cover her mouth.

She no longer washed all day long with her bitter almond soap. Her body had its own special smell now, the smell of ripe pears. She no longer watched the chess games. Or made tea for her men. Or told them not to be sad. Sometimes she would spread a clean diaper on one of their shoulders and give them the baby to walk around. She herself would lie down on the couch with her knees up, indifferent to the plunging slip that bared her thighs, looking at whoever happened to be holding her baby as one might look at a seascape or distant mountains. Perhaps as inanimate nature looks at us.

Yonatan and Azariah built a dog house for Tia in the garden, her home for as long as Na'ama was small. Inside, Hava had become undisputed boss of the household. Whenever she told Rimona what she must and mustn't do, Rimona would solemnly reply, "Fine. Thank you. That's fine."

Hava could not do enough to make life easier for all of them. She was full of wild energy. Once she went off to Haifa for two days to furnish a new apartment for Amos and his young wife. Amos was rarely home on leave from the army because the situation on the borders had worsened and crack units were almost continually in a state of full alert. As soon as she got back from

Haifa, Hava sewed four nightdresses for her granddaughter and knit her a pair of woolen booties and a sweater. When Azariah grew delirious with fever from a throat infection, she took him to Srulik's bedroom without even asking the secretary's permission and nursed him like a baby. When Yonatan broke a finger in the tractor shed, she took him to the hospital and never left his side until it was set in a cast. Once, when Rimona suggested that she ease up on herself, Hava broke into uproarious laughter and proceeded to take down all the window screens and scrub them one by one. In late May, both Yoni and Azariah were mobilized. Soon after, the war predicted by Azariah broke out. Israel won and pushed forward its front lines. Etan R. was killed on the Golan Heights. His two girlfriends went on living in his room by the swimming pool. Yonatan's reconnaissance unit fought in the Sinai. On the sixth and last day of combat, he took over its command from Chupka, who had been torn to shreds by a direct artillery hit. Azariah, serving in a front-line grease pit, worked around the clock. Major Zlotkin called him a miracle and promoted him to sergeant as soon as the war was over. On their discharge, Hava baked them a cake. Srulik threw a small welcome-home party for the sons who returned from the battlefield. Yonatan and Azariah discovered when they came back that the baby had learned how to turn over. Soon she would be crawling on the straw mat. "Look at her. She's laughing," said Rimona. "It's because she understands," said Hava.

If anyone dared say a slighting word about her happy trio, Hava would bare her fangs like an old she-wolf.

"You, Paula, are in no position to talk. Not with a daughter like yours, a nebbish who's been through two divorces in two years."

The next day, however, she would apologize. "Please forgive me. I lost my temper yesterday. I went too far. I'm terribly sorry."

In his journal, late one night, Srulik wrote:

The earth is indifferent. The sky is mysterious. The sea is a lasting menace. And the plants and the migrating birds. The stone is as silent as death which has dominion over all. Cruelty is in each of us. Each of us is a bit of a murderer, if not of others, of himself. Love is beyond me still, perhaps it has always been. Pain is a fact. But a thing or two we can do, and since we can, we must. As for the rest, who knows? Let's wait and see. Instead of continuing this entry, I think I'll play my flute tonight.

1970
1976–1981